D1742512

The Queen's Tragedy

By

Robert Hugh Benson

Wildhern Press 2007

Published by

Wildhern Press
131 High St.
Teddington
Middlesex TW11 8HH

Editorial and layout copyright Wildhern Press 2007

ISBN 978-1-84830-043-9

POPULAR UNIFORM EDITION
2/6 of the famous novels by 2/6
ROBERT HUGH BENSON

The King's Achievement
30th thousand

By What Authority?
30th thousand

The Queen's Tragedy
30th thousand

Richard Raynal, Solitary
30th thousand

The Light Invisible
30th thousand

The Sentimentalists
30th thousand

The Necromancers
16th thousand

Come Rack! Come Rope!
20th thousand

The Conventionalists
44th thousand

Oddsfish
54th thousand

THE QUEEN'S TRAGEDY

By

Robert Hugh Benson

LONDON:
BURNS, OATES AND WASHBOURNE
Publishers to the Holy See
1927

Principis est virtus maxima nosse suos
Mart. Epigr.

TO BETH.

Upon the publication of former books of mine several kindly critics remarked that the reign of Mary Tudor told a very different story with regard to the Catholic character. It is that story which I am now attempting to set forth as honestly as I can.

I must express my gratitude to my sister, who has kindly read this book in proof, and made many valuable suggestions; to R. B. Fellows, Esq., and to all others who have allowed themselves to be consulted.

ROBERT HUGH BENSON.

Cambridge,
May 1st, 1906.

CONTENTS

BOOK I

Paratus omne Caesaris periculum
Subire.   HOR. Epod.

The Queen's Tragedy

CHAPTER 1

MASTON MANTON COMES TO COURT

1

THE little square court of Gonville College lay in shadow beneath a rosy evening sky as the door from the hall opened, and a young man in a master's gown and cap ran out and across the cobbles, followed by half a dozen others. He waved his hand hurriedly as they called after him, shouted something back, and disappeared into a staircase-door in the chapel corner

Supper had been done ten minutes before; and the half-dozen sizars had been eyeing the cooling dishes regretfully as the old Master, standing up in his place, had told to the company the news for which they had almost forgotten to look.

It was now nearly a year since the fierce domgs of the previous summer, when Cambridge had been full of Northumberland's soldiers, and the Duke himself had been taken in King's College, and sent with the Vice-Chancellor and others up to London for trial; and the whole place had hummed with gossip, and reverberated with the tramp of armed men.

Their own College, too, had distinguished itself. Master Guy Manton, one of their Fellows, had ridden out to Sawston through the gloom of the July night, to take news to Mary Tudor that an assault on her lodging was imminent. He had come back with one of Huddleston's men on the following morning, with an arrow-wound in his arm, and reported that he had seen the smoke rising from the burning house whence the new Queen had just made her escape.

Little by little more had come out. Master Manton had not said much himself, but Tom Bradshawe, his boy, had whispered that the Queen had made great promises, although his master had not been the first to bring her the news; that she had thanked him, for what he had done and suffered, and asked him for his name. The arrow that pierced his arm had been shot by one of Northumberland's men in a drunken fit, who had staggered out beside the watch-fire at the noise of the galloping hoofs

But the months went by, and the rebels had paid the forfeit for their fierce game, and the Queen had been crowned, and the arrow-wound long healed; Mary had slept at Cambridge on her return-journey, had sent for Master Manton and talked with him and then had gone her way, to meet the smouldering sedition in London. This had burst into flame in Wyatt's rebellion, had been quenched by a strong hand and died down again. Yet no word had come for Master Manton.

And now it had come; and he was to go next day.

Some of those who heard the news in the College hall from Master Bacon's lips were not altogether displeased. It was pleasant to think that the little community had a finger in public affairs—the last connection of the kind had consisted in the removal from their jurisdiction of Physwick hostel, at the hands of King Henry—and it was not wholly unpleasant to one or two of the company to think that they had seen the last of Master Manton. He was a strange creature; they could understand neither his tendernesses nor his spasms of rage. He had made himself ridiculous more than once in his friendships, showing a compassion for queer persons that they could not comprehend; and he had made himself a little terrible, too, half a dozen times in his furies against disloyalty, and his contempt of what they considered academical finesse. "*Pecca fortiter!*" he had cried indignantly at a College meeting, gathered to consider what form of religion should be observed in chapel. Unconventionality was hard to bear from a young man who had shared in collegiate advantages for little more than ten years, six as a fellow-commoner, and four as a Fellow.

Guy's whole air and appearance, too, these gentlemen told one another, were scarcely academic, and they wondered that his tastes had once seemed to be so. His square-built six feet of body, his square jaw and thin, resolute lips, his bright kindly brown eyes, his abrupt judgments, his generosities, his unconcealed impatience, even his very scruples—all these would have been seemly enough for a gentleman of the country or Court, but they were hardly suitable under a Master's cap and gown.

Guy's gesture, as he disappeared, was so decisive that his friends hung back. He had still plenty to do though he had half-packed his couple of trunks in the afternoon as soon as the messenger had come; and the silversmith would be waiting upstairs with the piece of plate that he proposed to present to the College. There was another interview, too, that lay before him, which he did not wholly welcome.

His brain whirled with excitement as he groped his way up the dark stairs. His universe had shrunk to pigmy proportions, and a crowd of giant faces looked down, kings, prelates and statesmen, whose names he knew, and who waited now for him to take his place at their feet. He must leave the nursery for the limitless world. The master's ten minutes' speech had brought that fact home to him as he listened with grave downcast eyes and a beating heart. This had been the last supper that he would eat in the dark hall to the accompaniment of the Vulgate droned from the little wooden pulpit at the lower end. To-morrow he would eat in kings' palaces.

He must be strong now—he told himself—he must be strong. There must be no more sentiment.

He was unusually brusque with the silversmith who saluted him deferentially in the entry upstairs, and called to him to come after as he went in through the outer door into his own room.

It was a wide low chamber, strewn with ill-smelling rushes on which lay his two leather trunks, and a couple of beds stood side by side at the further end between the windows that looked out on to the eastern end of the chapel and the old priory buildings. The room was in confusion. A pile of books lay on the table, ready for packing, and three or four chairs with tumbled clothes upon them were pushed back against the tattered hangings of the outer wall. Two more windows opposite gave on to the court of the College.

He took the silver salt-cellar from the man, and turned it over. It appeared satisfactory. It was octagonal with an oval depression, and on the side he saw the arms of the College, the inscription in usum Coll Gonv., and his own name. It was curious to think that he would never put knife to it himself.

"Twelve ounces?" he said sharply.

"Twelve ounces, sir," said the man.

"Very good I will send the money in the morning."

Guy set the silver down when the man was gone; looked round the room, drew a long breath, and went across to his trunks.

But he was not long left to himself; there were footsteps and talking on the stairs; a couple of the young Fellows came in, and were presently leaning against the wall, striding about, examining the salt-cellar, criticising his packing, asking a hundred questions; while a group of pensioners gathered continually at the door, eyeing awfully this man on whom had fallen the shadow of Royalty.

Guy glanced up at them once or twice, but did not see the man he wanted, and went on answering questions as he packed.

Yes; he would be off by nine o'clock, he said, and in London by the evening. He was to go straight to Whitehall. He would ride with the Queen's messenger, and Tom, too, was to go…. He did not know whether he could keep the boy, but he hoped so; for he was to have half a dozen servants of his own. If not, Tom should be sent straight back at the first opportunity…. Yes; he was at the tailor s now being fitted for a suit.

Master Sweetnam's face fell.

"We shall miss him in chapel," he said.

"We shall be the gainers at Court," observed Guy over his shoulder as he knelt at his trunk "He sings better every day. He must enter her Grace's choir Master Denison says that his voice will last a long while yet."

He was very cheerful and good-humoured this evening; and answered all their questions politely as he went to and fro in his shirt and hose, and struggled with his packing. He mourned over the quarto Terence that he could not get in, and presented it elaborately to Master Sweetnam with his loving regard; he did not brag once of the life that lay before him, or sneer at that which he left behind. Yet he sighed with contentment when the chapel-bell began to ring, and his friends trooped out.

Master Sweetnam, burdened by the Terence, turned to his friend as they came into the court.

"As satisfied as ever' he said.

"Pah! He is mad with pride. But he will find out." The two nodded their heads sagaciously as they went into chapel.

Guy was serenely unconscious and careless of their opinion. Of course he was satisfied! Why should he not be?

He drew back a curtain presently in a pause of his packing, and looked out on to the east window of the chapel, and the glimmer of light within and Blessed Mary with her Child in her arms in red and blue on the centre pane. The sight gave him a further thrill of freedom There they all were, that little set of folks with whom he had lived so long, repeating together the old acts that they had repeated for twenty years past, some of them, though in varying phrase and language, and would repeat for twenty years more, with their heads down on their books, and one of the priests leading them from his stall; and then they would come out and go to bed soon; and come out again in the morning, and re-enact the uneventful day, toiling over their microscopic crumbs of Greek, laying down the law to gaping boys, and quarrelling among themselves as to the law they laid down; and all was to do again, over and over again.

And here was he with his face towards a new and vivid mystery and excitement and self-reliance in his heart.

He turned back again exulting as the door opened and a boy came in.

"Well?" he said.

"The suit will be here by six o'clock, Master Manton."

Tom Bradshawe was flushed and excited too. He was a dark well-grown child of twelve years old, pale-faced and black-eyed; and had been a sizar in the College for nearly a year. Guy had taken pity on him, soon after his coming. He had found him tied under the pump one cold morning, and, in a kind of fury, had released him and taken him upstairs to his own room Guy's wrath on that occasion had caused laughter in the College; but he had spoken his mind and gone his way. He had presently attached the boy to himself, had become his tutor by backstairs influence, and taken him to sleep in his room. Then he had discovered that Tom possessed an extraordinary contralto voice, and the boy had been set to sing in chapel—the fame of his voice had spread; but he had declined all offers, and refused to leave his master. Now Tom's reward had come, and he was to seek his fortune in London under the patronage of her Grace's new gentleman.

Guy made an enquiry or two about the horses, deputed him to go with the silversmith's money next morning, and finally asked him whether he had seen Master Stephen Brownrigg.

"I saw him coming out of chapel just now," said the boy.

Guy pondered.

"Well, go to bed," he said, "and go to sleep. I shall not be coming yet."

Ten minutes later Guy slipped on his doublet, and went out.

As he walked across the court in the summer darkness to Stephen's room he was wondering what he would say. He knew he would meet with reproaches and sullenness, and he was doubtful how to deal with them. He was tired of patience.

Stephen had come up to Gonville College as a sizar six years before, a clumsy, high-shouldered lad of eighteen, and Guy, as usual, had been sorry for him. He had watched him, at first with amusement and then with pity, carrying four tankards at once and dropping two of them, and shedding salad along the rushes of the hall. Then he had begun to patronise him a little, though he was only Stephen's senior by four years; he had allowed him to bring his lexicon and his grammar up to the comparative quiet of his own study; and little by little had begun to get at his heart. He had found there a very fierce and uncontrolled fire that burned as hotly for disorder as Guy's for authority. Guy did not care very much for what was taught or done, or as to who sat on the throne of England; but he did desire that all should be in order; and it seemed that on the other hand Stephen Brownrigg's soul was one of those doomed from infancy to be opposed to government. As a boy he had headed an ink-pot rebellion at Norwich grammar-school, and had made passionate speeches on the inherent freedom of manhood; then he had quieted a little on coming to College, till again his ardour had broken out in a wider field. On Edward's accession he had presided at indignation meetings in the sizar's room in favour of the Lady Elizabeth; then he had become reconciled when he understood that the new government did not make for peace, but again had flared out at the prince's death; and Guy had observed him with mingled irritation and amusement, marching beside Northumberland's men across the market-place, and bellowing once more for the Lady Jane Grey. Now there was an end of all that; the Lady Jane had suffered for the sins of her father-in-law and her own acquiescence in treason; Mary ruled at Westminster, and there was nothing left for Stephen but the luxury of a desperate cause.

And what was Guy to say to him now? Stephen had said violent things last year when his patron had done what he could for the Queen. What would he say now, and how should it be met?

Guy had tried patience, and it had been met by insolence. So at last he was beginning to be a little tired of his friend; and as he climbed the stairs, he did not find it very difficult to resolve that sternness was best Sentiment was out of place m one who was to take part in public affairs; a career could not be carved out except by strength; tenderness was very well in college life; it did not hinder academical advancement; but a Court was a different matter; and it would not be amiss either for Stephen's sake or his own to practise a little severity and self-control.

2

But his heart relented again as he pushed the door wide after tapping, and remembered all that had happened here.

It was a depressing little room, under the roof, low, and with sloping sides; a great table in the centre, on which burned a single candle, was piled with confusion; books, papers, a gown, a heap of dirty linen, a couple of plates and a jug lay together there, with the tail of a quill cocked arrogantly from an ink-horn in the middle. The scanty rushes on the floor resembled ancient hay; the hangings, of an incredible age and filth, showed patches of discoloured wall through their rents; and in the midst of the debris, between the table and the tumbled bed, stood Stephen, pale and high-shouldered, with long light hair, in his old green clothes, with a prayer-book in his hand, and an expression in which resenment, dramatic pride, reproach and dignity strove with piety. He had apparently been saying his prayers, and had stood up at the sound of the footstep.

Guy shut the door and came across to the table.

"Do not be a damned fool," he said quietly.

Stephen put his hands together on the table, with the book in them and faced him.

"So this is what you came to say, Master Manton?"

Guy sat down on the table sideways, pushing aside the dirty linen, as he had pushed it twenty times before. His appearance was a very strong contrast to Stephen's. He looked a capable, reasonable person, who had both a heart and a will of his own. At present, however, as he addressed himself to speak to this tiresome lad, his will was more evident than his heart, both in his bearing and his sharp resolute voice. He knew this man's temper, and was not discouraged by the acrid fierceness of his voice.

"I came to say good-bye, Stephen," he said, looking at him, "because you did not come to me. I expected you. Tom and I are off by nine o'clock."

Stephen stood as rigid as a statue.

"See here," went on the other quietly, still watching that thin sharp-cut face. "I am not come to weep, or to ask your pardon for following my conscience. I have told you a hundred times what I think; and I have as much right to a conscience as you. Mine tells me that Mary is Queen, and that the old Religion is the better; so I propose to serve them both by going to London. I do not wish to talk about my plans. I wish to talk about yours, and to say good-bye."

Still Stephen glared at him without moving.

Guy's impatience surged up.

"You might be civil," he said. "I think I have not been unkind to you."

Stephen caught his breath sharply; but there was nothing but cold anger in his answer.

"I do not wish to be uncivil, sir, so I cannot say what I think."

"My good fellow, I have told you that I do not want you to say what you think about me. I am quite aware that you think me a knave for serving my Queen. I wish to talk about you."

"Then I will not," barked the other suddenly. "I have my own plans, Master Manton. They do not concern you."

Guy slipped off the table and stood up.

"That is uncivil and churlish," he said sternly. "I came here to ask if I could serve you. I am not going to whine and coax any more; but I will say my say and begone. It is this: you will find yourself in trouble soon. I sheltered you last time when you were playing the madman in February. Your name was before the master for damning Queen Mary on the marketplace, and I quieted him. You know that! And now I am going, and there will be none to shelter you."

"I do not want to be sheltered."

"Very well, then. I hope you will remember—"

"See here, Master Manton; we are on opposite sides now, you have told me so yourself. Well, I do not take counsel from my enemies."

Guy looked at him; at his sharp, out-thrust chin, his excited eyes and his pale writhing lips. For a moment he thought of keeping his resolution, and stamping out without another word. Then he relented again; this impotent rage was so piteous in this frail unbalanced creature. Besides, they had been friends for a year.

"My dear lad, you do not know what you are saying Cannot you be civil? You will be sorry to-morrow."

"I shall not," cried the other. "I have borne with your patronage too long."

"You will be sorry to-morrow," said Guy imperturbably, "and you will be in some trouble the day after; and I shall not be here as I was last time Be reasonable and civil"

Stephen slammed the prayer-book on to the table. "Master Manton, will you do me the honour to take my word? We are enemies, not friends. You are going to serve this—this——"

"Ah! be carefull" cried Guy.

"——this—this Mary Tudor," hissed Stephen, "who has slain hundreds of God's people already"

"Rebels," put in Guy's voice.

"——who has slam her own cousin."

"A rebel again," said Guy.

"——who is to make a Spanish marriage, and set about burning Christians."

"——heretics," slipped in the other voice.

Stephen slammed his hands down, too, and leaned across the table, like a mad cat on the point of springing.

"Well, sir! Go you to serve that side, and I go to serve the other"

The moment he had said it he seemed to recover himself. He stood back and took up his prayer-book. But Guy was startled.

"What is that?" he asked.

"That is my affair," said Stephen sullenly.

"You go to serve the other?"

The other was silent.

"Listen to me, Master Brownrigg. I do not know what you mean by that; but I will tell you something. If I hear a word of any plotting or such folly, I shall not shelter you again. I shall work against you with all my power; I shall not scruple to give you up. Remember that."

Stephen was looking at him steadily now, and smiling bitterly.

"That is better, Master Manton. Now we understand one another. I will wish you good-night now with all my heart, on those terms."

For a moment Guy thought of making one more appeal. This mad fool seemed in earnest as never before. It was a man, no longer a boy, who had said that; and it was evident that he meant it. He would surely find himself in prison soon; and Guy hated the thought of it. But he remembered his resolution; he had tried tenderness, and it had failed; he would try it no longer, and his decision was almost a relief.

"I do not wish good-night to my enemies, sir," he said coolly. "I wish them a better mind first. If you wish to ask my pardon for this insolence before nine o'clock to-morrow, I shall be ready to hear you. And be good enough to remember what I have said"

He wheeled about and left the untidy room, and the venomous figure standing there.

He was still angry as he came up to his own room. Stephen had never been so outrageously offensive before; and the ingratitude of the whole affair stung him bitterly.

He went straight across the darkness of his room to the boy's bed.

"Tom, are you awake?"

"Yes, sir"

"Tom, I have quarrelled with Stephen. He is mad, I think. Have you heard anything?"

"He is going to London, Master Manton. I thought you knew that," came the voice from the bed.

"To London? When did you hear that?"

"To-night, sir. The sizars were talking of it."

"Why is he going?"

"I do not know, sir."

There was silence for a moment. Then Guy turned away.

"Very well, boy. Speak of it to no one, and keep your eyes open in London. Now go to sleep." "Yes, sir."

Guy lay long awake that night in the warm summer darkness, staring out over the College roofs at the unfathomable depth of stars, with no sound in his ears but the steady breathing from the truckle bed at his side, and the occasional scamper of a rat across the rushes.

It was all very strange and bewildering; the quarrel he had had with Stephen, and the news he had heard of him, no less than the prospect of the next day.

He set his teeth at last, and fell asleep.

3

Whitehall stood up blue and splendid against the flushed southern sky as Guy and Tom, with a couple of the Queen's men, rode up to it from Charing Cross at sunset.

They had ridden all day through the hot summer scents and sights, now on the wide road, now in short cuts under leafy roofs where the gnats sang loud in the green gloom, and rustlings and cries in the undergrowth had told of the life of the woods; they had halted for three hours in the middle of the day, ridden on towards London in the afternoon, and caught sight of the palace soon after passing the City, a huddle of roofs and towers set in greenery, the shining river on the left, and faintly seen, far behind, the long white line of the Abbey.

Tom's tired horse felt himself pressed very close to his companion, as the four passed in at last through the gate from St. James' Park; and Guy, looking at the boy, saw that his black eyes were wide and anxious and his lips parted

He himself forgot the dust and the weariness; but it was in expectancy rather than anxiety. Cambridge seemed smaller than ever now; it had receded more quickly than they had ridden, the fractious College meetings, the tiny stir of academic politics, even his quarrel with Stephen—all seemed very little and unreal now that he had come to the heart of affairs. Yet half a dozen times he had turned, thinking that Stephen was by his side. He had talked a good deal to Tom as they rode—of pageants, of floating towers on the Thames, from which men shot with culverins, of the lord of misrule with his heralds and trumpets, even of matters of State, and the Queen's enemies, of loyalty and treason He had told him of Wyatt's rebellion, and had pointed up at Ludgate where the traitor had demanded entrance, and Temple Bar where he had been taken. Above all, remembering his own resolutions, he had hammered into his mind that they would both have to stand alone now; Tom must not expect to be cossetted and protected any more.

But under all ran a current of other thoughts, that merged now and then in long silences. He was come up by special favour of the Queen; his opportunity was held out to him, and he did not doubt his capacity to grasp it. Only, he reminded himself for the hundredth time, he must be hard and resolute.

The palace wore something of a collegiate air to their eyes as they rode across the great court and dismounted; all about them lay long walls pierced with windows, with here and there a gateway, and on the further side the hall itself; but the figures that moved there were in green and white instead of black, and the brazen cry of a trumpet sounded in place of the mellow bell of Great Saint Mary's.

Their horses were led away, when the luggage had been unstrapped, and a blue-livened fellow with a silver badge on cap and sleeve bearing the impaled rose and arrows of Mary, took them through the little vestibule and up a flight of stairs. The passages were not yet lighted, and Guy felt the boy again press close to him as they passed on in the gloom, up the stairs, along a passage or two, down a few steps, and on again till all sense of direction was lost. The house was very still, as most of the inmates were at supper, but once or twice they passed a motionless figure, armed and silent, standing before a closed door.

At last the servant threw a door on the left open, and waved them in.

It was a pleasant enough room, with green saye hangings, a great bed on the right hand side, a settle before the cold hearth on the left, and a round table with two or three chairs in the centre. A couple of other doors opened again to right and left, and a long window, through which showed the river, faced the door by which they had entered.

"You will sup here, sir," said the man, setting down the trunk he carried. "And the Queen's Grace will see you at eight 0,'clock."

When the man was gone, Guy went across to the window and opened it. The sun had dipped below the palace roofs, but the sky was still glorious, and the ruddy splendour blazed below on the broad out-flowing tide. Across the water showed the green banks of Southwark, with the houses to the left; and on the right among the trees the red and white towers of Lambeth. The river itself was all astir with swans and shipping; a couple of barges were making their way upstream with laughter and music, trailing rich tapestries, and streaming their standards behind; and between and about them whisked the wherries, like swift water beetles intent on busy idleness. The air was full of joyous sound, the cries of voices across the water, the chirp of birds overhead, and the mellow fairy-thunder of the bells of the City tolling out the Angelus.

When he had fastened the latch again and turned round with an almost uncontrollable excitement and pleasure beating at his heart, Tom was still standing by the table, staring about him, at the rushes underfoot, the barred ceiling overhead, the dim design of wreath and blossom on the walls, the sepulchral bed.

Guy gave a snort of laughter.

"Dear boy," he said, "do not look like that. It is no prison we are in, after all."

They supped presently, when the candles were lighted and the windows shuttered, from two or three dishes and a jug of ale that the servant brought and set down on the table, and then fell to unpacking. Guy had a very tolerable russet suit that he had got during Northumberland's stay in Cambridge, as it was necessary then for even Masters of Arts to be decently dressed: and with Tom's help he put it on, combed out his hair and adjusted his lace

Then the two sat down on the settle side by side.

Tom began to ask questions again, and Guy had to break his pleasant tram of thought to answer him. He wished to know what was the position of the gentleman in blue and silver; whether the Queen's Grace would come herself to the room or not; what had happened to the horses; whether he would have to wear his sizar's gown at dinner; where he would sleep.

Guy satisfied him, assured him that the horses were well cared for, and showed him the little truckle-bed, pushed under the great four-poster.

Meanwhile his own mind worked and postured. He would know in an hour now what his work would be; what would be the personality of his mistress, better than he could gauge it during the terrible minutes at Sawston or the few words in Trinity—in less than an hour, in fact, for a bell somewhere in the crowded palace beat out the half-hour. He would hear her gratitude, and deprecate it, and use It—the gratitude of a Tudor, of a daughter of that fierce king who had wielded the powers of Church and State at his will; of a woman who had suffered cruelly, and persevered and won her crown.

And meanwhile Tom questioned, and mused in silence over the answers, till his eyes rolled in his head with the weariness of long, hot hours in the open air.

The servant came in again presently to take away the supper things, and Guy's heart leapt at the hand on the latch; but the man said nothing and went out.

Guy turned to the boy. He felt strung up now and strong; and he thought it a good opportunity to drive the lesson home he had begun to teach him during the ride.

"See here, Tom," he said; and at the tone in his voice the boy was awake and alert, watching him nervously.

"See here, Tom. You remember what I said to-day? You cannot be tied to my side always we must each fight for our own hand. I cannot run after you here, as at Cambridge—you understand?"

Tom nodded.

"You will have to do the best you can; and you must not run to me m every trouble. There is sure to be trouble. You are certain you can put up with it? If not, you had best pack again to Cambridge to-morrow."

The boy nodded again.

Guy had a sharp prick of tenderness at the mute anxiety in the black eyes. For a moment he wished to reassure him—to tell him that he did not mean what he said; and that this strange world should not come between them.

Then he fought down his tenderness.

"Very well," he said abruptly, "I think you will do well now. Only you will remember. And meantime, my dear boy, we are both going to be very happy indeed."

Once more, ten minutes later, Guy rose, smoothed down his silk, flapped the lace clear of his sleeves, and pressed his straight brown hair: and as he did so there came a knock at the door.

"The Queen's Grace will see you, sir," said the servant, with the faintest addition of deference in his manner.

Guy licked his lips, glanced at Tom who was upright and awake enough now, and walked out.

They went along a passage or two, up and down stairs; and as they went the appearance of the walls and floor changed a little. Here and there was matting instead of rushes, the hangings were more sombre and splendid, the lamps at the corners more frequent and better trimmed, and the few silent figures by the doors more formal in their attitudes.

A door closed the end of the passage, and at this the man stopped and tapped. There was a footstep within, and the door opened. A page stood there, a lad of sixteen, with an air of astonishing arrogance that modified itself a little as he understood Guy's errand.

He said nothing, but motioned him in with a smooth and lazy inclination. Guy found himself in a small room, evidently an antechamber, with a table along one wall and chairs beside it, a hearth decked with flowers, and a tall crucifix above the mantel-shelf. There was a double door at the further end.

Towards this the boy went, and threw both leaves open.

"If you please, sir," he said; and Guy went through.

He found himself, as the door closed behind him, alone at the lower end of a long room, plainly some kind of presence-chamber. There was little furniture in it; a chair with arms stood on a low dais at the further end beneath a canopy on which was emblazoned the rose and arrows of Mary Tudor. The walls were hung from roof to floor with tapestries, the ceiling was painted with wreaths, a table ran the length of the room with chairs pushed against it; one more chair stood by the hearth on the right; a door with a curtain half hiding it was at the further end of the left-hand wall, and the recess of a deep window faced it from the other side.

He stood there, excited and apprehensive, glancing this way and that to take in the details; and then suddenly remembered that he did not know the etiquette. He half turned to the door through which he had come, but wheeled back again; he must not be found whispering and questioning. He reminded himself of his resolutions to be natural; that at least could not displease the Queen; and he could not be far wrong if he knelt and kissed her hand, supposing that she extended it.

Then as he argued with himself, the floor vibrated, there-was the sound of an opening latch, he saw an arm shoot out through the further door as if to push back the curtain; and a woman came swiftly through.

Guy dropped on his knees.

4

She stood there a moment, hesitating, a splendid little figure in the light of the candles that burned round the room.

Guy was aware in a moment of the purple velvet, the deep hanging sleeves and train, the cloth-of-gold under-skirt, the voluminous lace, and the startling blaze of jewels on stomacher and head-dress. Then she spoke, and his heart leapt at the deep virile voice.

"Master Guy Manton?"

He understood that he was to advance, and he rose from his knees.

The Queen passed the chair-of-state and the table, going towards the hearth, and even in that moment Guy perceived that extraordinary dignity of gait that he remembered at Cambridge.

Then he, too, went across the room towards the hearth.

The Queen stood for a moment by the chair, extending her hand, and he knelt again and kissed it as he came up.

Then she sat down, drawing her skirts aside, and motioned him to stand.

"You are Master Guy Manton from Cambridge?" she said glancing again at his very unacademic figure. "I sent for you"

Guy bowed. In spite of his resolutions his tongue was as dry as a stick.

"You came to-day?"

"Yes, madam."

"I must thank you again, sir, for your courtesy to me at Sawston, and your courage: your arm is healed well?"

Guy bowed again; and made an effort to speak; but she cut him short.

"I wish to do something for you; but I have so few places left."

"I wish for no place, madam, beyond "

Again she cut him short with a glance, and Guy was thankful he had not finished his fatuous deprecation.

"If you would wish to be one of my gentlemen, I shall be happy to have you near me. And you are a scholar, sir? '

"I was Fellow of my College, your Grace."

The reference refreshed him, and he straightened his back a little and began to observe her face. It was bent down as she talked, but he saw in the candlelight, the prim, sad lips, the paleness of the forehead, chin and throat, and the slight flush on the cheeks It was the face of one who had found the world hard. When he met her eyes for a moment at her next sentence, he noticed that even more; they had the same air of aloof suspicion that he had seen in Tom's eyes during the first day of his acquaintance with him Her deep voice, too, had in it a kind of pathetic steadiness.

"I should wish to read Greek a little, sir; not very much; I am no scholar; and the breviary perhaps. If you take the place, will you be content to be my instructor in that? I should relieve you of many other of your duties."

"I will take very willingly whatever your Grace is pleased to give me."

Again she looked up at him steadily a moment; and he dropped his eyes.

"That is very well, sir. You are a good Catholic, you told me?"

"I have always observed my religious duties, madam"

The Queen was silent.

Guy felt he had turned that comer well. It was an answer he had rehearsed, knowing that it would be needed. And he was not fervently religious.

"There are other matters, too," went on the Queen presently, "but I need not speak of them, beyond saying that I value fidelity in my servants more than all else in the world"

Guy prepared himself for the obvious smooth answer; but he had no time.

"But I do not value assurances," she ended, "so I will not ask for yours."

Guy's ideas of courtliness received a check at this. He did not quite know what to say. This woman was in earnest.

Her next remark was on a simpler plane.

"Your rooms satisfy you, sir?"

"Yes, indeed, madam."

"You shall keep them then. They will be near enough to me. Your duties will be very light. You shall hear of them from Sir Robert Rochester to-morrow."

"I thank your Grace."

"I shall ask for no lessons for the present. That shall be later. Have you any books?"

Guy described his small library.

"The Iliad then, first. I have not read it since I was a child."

Her lips tightened slightly as Guy watched. Some memory, he thought, had pricked her

They talked for a few moments on Homer; and the Queen asked a question or two about Cambridge.

"The studies have been greatly disturbed," said Guy.

"Like all the kingdom," said Mary; "Please God we will quiet it now."

She looked up at him again a moment; and he felt that there was something more in the air.

Then she began, hesitatingly, but with a certain deliberation, too.

"You will meet many strange folk here," she said. "Do not trust all who talk smoothly. Listen much and speak little. That is a lesson I have learned."

Again that cold sorrow sounded in her voice.

"Do not expect too much, Master Manton."

There was a rustle by the door, and the Queen rose. Guy stood hesitating a moment, and as she held out her hand, he dropped on his knees and kissed it. Beneath the mass of rings were lean fingers, well shaped and white, and a thin arm disappearing above into the deep sleeve.

"Good-night, sir."

As she went out by the door through which she had come still with that stately gait, he saw that two ladies had been standing there, one old and little with grey hair, the other very young and very tall. The younger now held back the curtain for the Queen to pass.

Then the door closed softly.

Guy told Tom briefly that all was well; that he had not been able to speak of the boy's wish to serve him, but that he did not doubt that it could be arranged, as well as the matter of the choir. He told him also of the room and the hangings and the chair-of-state, and the page; and how the Queen had worn no crown but only a jewelled head-dress.

"And you are pleased, sir?" asked the boy.

"Oh, yes," said Guy shortly; and sent him to bed.

But he was not pleased; and after Tom was asleep sat down to review the situation.

First he was not pleased with the position offered him. A few Homer-lessons and a place in processions were not what he had been led to expect. And the Queen's personality did not compensate for his disappointment.

He had somehow expected more Joyousness—an air more in accord with the gaiety and splendour of the humming palace and the exhilarating view from his windows. After all, he told himself, here she was, safe at home, and secure at last. She had put down a serious revolt in the spring, men said, with both courage and mercy; she had re-established her Religion at a very small cost; she was to be married in a couple of months to the man whom she had chosen from the whole world.

Why was she so cold and peevish?

He supposed, however, that memories were still too strong for her. That chilliness must be the result of her years of watchfulness and terror when she had trembled for her life; her very eyes had screens of reserve drawn behind them that told of a soul that had learnt discretion in a hard school; the prim, sorrowful lips tightened now from a long habit of self-repression. Her ideal virtue for her servants—fidelity—rose from a thirty years' experience of treachery. She "trusted he was a good Catholic"—she who had seen her church profaned and robbed by her own father, and on a black day of terror had herself yielded. She "hoped to read the Iliad and the breviary"—she who had sought to distract her thoughts so often with such books from prospects of disgrace and death. She "trusted her servant's rooms satisfied him"—she who had been servant herself to the daughter of her father's concubine, and had known what it was to have no house that she could call home.

In fact, Guy told himself, as he stood up and stretched, this was not the kind of mistress for which he had looked; nor was his position the one he had had before his eyes. He wondered whether it would have been better to have been more outright.

She had asked him for fidelity. Well, he would give her that, but no more, so long as he thought it worth while to remain in her household.

It would be amusing for a little perhaps; and after that, if matters did not mend, Cambridge was always open.

He was conscious of a considerable disappointment as he climbed into bed.

Semper ne causae eventorum magis movent, quam ipsa eventa, Cic. *ad Attic.*

CHAPTER II

MASTER MANTON LEARNS HIS TRADE

1

GUY felt very strange, and not a little exhilarated, two mornings later as he stood in the gallery of the hall with Master Norris, one of the gentlemen-pensioners, to watch the ceremonial observed at the queen's dinner and to learn his own duties at that function.

He had been told on the previous day that by her Grace's wish many of the customary duties of his post would be cancelled, and that he would only have to take his turn each day at waiting at either dinner or supper, at officiating at public audiences and the occasional progresses-in-State Besides this he would be expected to be present at one mass each day behind the Queen's chair; and to occupy his spare time, the accounts of the game department of the kitchen were to pass through his hands before going on to the steward. Sir Robert Rochester had warned him to keep a sharp eye on those, as her Grace was determined to cut down the vast extravagances of the previous reigns. He was provided also with two horses of his own kept in the royal stables, and three servants, and he found no difficulty in including Tom Bradshawe in his tiny staff. He was allowed to take his meals alone or in company as he wished, except on certain occasions when the whole household dined together. The title he bore was that of Gentleman-Usher.

It was a very splendid sight that he looked down on now, as he stood leaning with his hands on the carved railing with Master Norris beside him. Overhead the roof rose up into dusty sunlight, from which stood out a profusion of decorated work, and between the bright windows hung tapestries of green and gold. The Queen's table at the further end shone with silver and linen, and behind the chair rose up the splendid cloth of-estate before which stood a row of silent figures waiting for the Queen's coming. At the door on the right stood a double line of ushers, and it was to these that Mr. Norris directed his attention in a whisper.

"You will have to stand there, Master Manton, five minutes before the Queen arrives. You observe the dress——" he pointed out one or two details—" and then——"

Through the door came the sound of trumpets, and Guy's heart quickened at it. They sounded again nearer; and a moment later the procession began to come in. He turned quickly to the other.

"Who are they all, sir?"

The first few were ushers, it seemed; and after that came a few personages.

"There is Sir Robert Rochester—the Comptroller—" whispered Mr. Norris "You know him—you see where he stands. And that is Master Gage, in the velvet, with the grey hair. He is Chamberlain of the Household—he ran away in

Wyatt's rebellion—and the Vice-Chamberlam beside him, Sir Henry Jermngham. He is Captain of the Guard, too…."

There was another burst of music, and a small stately figure came in with shining head-dress and dark shimmering robes over cloth of gold, and Guy gripped the rail and watched, as she passed up to her solitary place and stood there a moment while a priest, stepping forward from behind, blessed the table with the sign of the Cross. Then she sat down, and an ordered bustle began.

Guy hardly noticed what was happening. Figures moved below with dishes and napkins, coming swiftly from beneath the gallery where he stood, handing their burdens on to others who passed them on in turn, and returning silently again across the sunlit rushes. Mr. Norris gabbled in a quick whisper at his side, pointing out the duties of this man and that, and the precise etiquette of each action, but he heard very little of it all. His eyes were on that lonely figure in the centre of the shining table, with the arms of England burning in tapestry behind her high chair—the white, refracted light on her face, the deliberate movement of her head, her downcast eyes, the slow gestures of her jewelled hands. It was very strange to think that he was in real relations with this woman now; that it would be his duty to move about there below, day by day, watching and ministering to her on whom all eyes were set; that she would no longer be merely a person in tales to him, a pivot on whom government turned, a stiff figure head of pageants and processions, but a living creature who ate and drank before his eyes, into whose private life he would at least in a measure be admitted. He wished, however, that that private life were more interesting.

He turned to Mr. Norris again.

"Thank you, sir. I fear I cannot remember it all yet. Tell me some more of the great folks, if you please. Which of them were with her in the old days?"

"Well, sir, there are two you should know quickly. Master Englefield and Master Waldegrave. They are standing together there, behind her Grace's chair"—he pointed them out—" they were in her household in the old days, and fell into trouble with the Council because they would have nought to do with putting down the mass there. That tall girl is the Lady Magdalene Dacre, lately come to Court. She is a friend of mine already. And beside her is Mistress Jane Dormer, who sleeps in her Grace's room sometimes. But observe, Master Manton—you see what is to be done when her Grace drinks…."

He was off again with explanations of the ceremonial.

It was over presently, and the two descended and went out into the court.

Guy had more leisure now to observe his companion, whom he had met for the first time in the gallery that morning He was a well made man of about thirty years old, remarkably handsome, with yellow curls and blue eyes, and looked very well in his cloak and green and white livery, plumed cap, and sword, and seemed very perfect in his knowledge of the court.

Guy was pleased when he proposed that they should walk in the garden for a little, for he had a friendly air and would no doubt be very useful as an instructor.

A minute later they were going up and down together on the broad walk in the shadow of the ivy-covered wall of the privy-garden on one side, and with the glowing lawn and flower beds on the other. There was a fresh breeze blowing off the river, and Guy, in his gay suit and satin shoes for the first time, with his sword at his side, felt his spirits rise.

"Tell me everything. Master Norris," he said." I know nothing."

The other smiled at him pleasantly.

"Well, sir," he said, "you will find it happy enough, if you know how to please yourself. The ladies are very kind There is plenty of sport, tilting, riding, singing—what you will and the duties are not severe. It is better than in King Edward's time—we all pulled long faces then. God rest his soul!"

Master Norris signed himself devoutly.

"Well sir? And what else?"

"There are some knaves," he said, "of whom you will dc well to keep clear. We learnt that in the spring."

"And their names, Master Norris?"

The young man pursed his lips humorously.

"Their names are best left alone," he said, "but I will tell you one. Master Edward Underhill, whom I have the honour to command."

"He is in the Court then?" asked Guy astonished.

"Why, yes; and there are others, in high places too; but it is best not to speak of them"

And what of the gentlemen

"Well, sir, there is old Dick Kearsley whom you have not seer yet. A good fellow enough, but as sour as a berry. You had best not cross him. He is away on an errand; but you will see him in the parlour some day I dare say. We three are to share the little room by the lodge."

"And the ladies?"

"Aha!" said Jack," You will not see much of them, unless you be one of the fortunate ones. They keep very close to her Grace. You will see them in the barge sometimes, maybe, or in the gardens."

Guy began to have a better idea of this gentleman presently, and to understand that he would be a useful gossip; but for a while he could not turn him from the ladies.

"Mistress Jane Dormer is old beyond her years," he proceeded. "She is hardly twenty yet; but as discreet as forty. She is always with her Grace. She will make a great match some day. She has refused my lord of Norfolk already. She is very intimate with her Grace. She had an uncle who suffered under Henry for the Faith, you know, and that makes her dear. Then there is old Mrs. Clarentia, a stiff old thing, but very much attached; and there are others—Mrs. Rise and Mrs. Young; and best of all there is my Lady Magdalene Dacre."

Jack looked so significant that Guy put in a word here.

"You must not ask too much," cried Jack archly;" it will be enough for you to see her at a distance."—God bless her bright eyes!"

Before the two gentlemen went in to their own dinner, Guy put his last question.

"And what of her Grace, Master Norris?"

Jack took him by the arm confidentially.

"See here, sir, you must not put a question like that to all you meet. They would take it amiss; they would tell you she was royal and holy; or they would tell you she was a bastard and a brute. But I will tell you what I think."

He looked so profound that Guy expected a revelation.

"Well, sir?"

"Well, sir," said Jack, pressing his arm, "this is what I think. God alone knows!"

He released his arm dramatically, and stared him in the face. Then he burst out laughing.

Guy was a little aggrieved and showed it by his silence.

"There, there, Master Manton, you must not take it amiss," whispered Jack, grasping his arm again. "It is God's truth I think no one knows but He. She is pious; she is zealous; she has a will of her own; she is cold; she is hot; she is miserly; she is liberal; she has a sad soul and a merry dress; she is silent; she can speak like an orator, for I heard her at the Guildhall in February, and she set my heart a-fire; then she put it out again next day by her coldness. She cut off the head of her cousin, and half a score more; and she let four hundred rebels go free. There, Master Manton; and if you can make a woman out of that, you are wiser than I."

The bell began to ring for the pensioners' dinner; and the two went in without another word.

2

A week or two later Guy had made progress in more ways than one.

First, he had learnt his very simple duties, and took his place at dinner and in processions with scarcely more than a tremor. He had been sent for once by the Queen, and had sat by her in her own room, listening to her rendering of the Matins lessons for the day; and had gone again more perplexed than ever by her character, and still less attracted towards it. She was terribly self-controlled; she had reproved him passionlessly because he did not correct her more, and received his spasmodic attempts afterwards with silence.

Jack had been perfectly right about her. There was no inspiration to be found there, there was scarcely even interest. He had been right, too, about her miserliness; the accounts were checked with a disagreeable accuracy; and a rebuke had actually come down to Guy from Lord Winchester himself, who superintended her Grace's finances, for some small oversight.

In larger affairs, too, Guy had learnt more in a few days than he would have thought possible, under Jack's tuition.

He understood that there were three parties, each striving to influence the Queen; Bishop Gardiner's, which represented the loyal insularity of England,

and the Spanish and French factions under Renard and De Noailles. The former of these two, who had triumphed at last in the matter of the Spanish marriage, was supported by such persons as Sir William Petre of Ingatestone and other members of the Council. De Noailles, on the other hand, still struggled to overthrow it as involving a continental coalition antagonistic to French interests. In this the Frenchman was supported by a large English party, whose leader, some said, and whose dupe, others said, was no less a person than the Lady Elizabeth herself.

It was wonderful, observed Jack, to see these two ambassadors, with their courtly friendliness in public, and to remember their fierce antagonism behind the scenes. It seemed to Guy, as he lounged and listened in the parlour, that they resembled two ringed and scented hands, stretched across the Channel, alert and strong to grasp or stab or salute as occasion served, capable, remorseless and gentle all at once.

He learnt gradually, too, day by day, to know the other great folks by sight; and to discern their significance in the bewildering warp of royal and political life—the small black-haired Duke of Norfolk, the ruddy Bishop of London, loud-voiced and hearty, and above all Stephen Gardiner, the strong and genial Bishop of Winchester and Lord Chancellor of the realm, on whom Mary relied so much in her schemes for Catholicising the country.

He saw, too, that times were strange—there were few about the Queen who had not changed their creed or their politics at least once to save their position; and he began to understand, as never at Cambridge, the conditions of the intricate game that lay under Mary's hand. For those who served her there were two roads to success, the one pliability and the other rigidity; and he determined that the latter should be his own.

Meanwhile, until something should open out, he gave himself up to observing the life round him, and joining in it so far as he could.

He was not greatly taken with Master Kearsley.

He was sitting in the parlour with Tom one evening after supper, when the door was thrust open, and a stranger walked in, covered with dust.

"I beg your pardon, sir," said Guy stiffly, "but this is the private parlour."

The stranger looked at him from under bushy eye-brows, and his mouth twitched in his lean face; but he said nothing, went across the rushes and sat down in the window-seat.

Guy stood up indignant.

"I tell you this is the privy parlour of her Grace's gentlemen."

"Then what does that lad do here?" snarled the stranger.

"He is my servant, sir."

"Her Grace's gentlemen's servants are not allowed in her Grace's gentlemen's privy parlour," remarked the other caustically.

"Who are you, sir? By what right do you speak to me like that?"

Guy was aware that the stranger's eyebrows twitched at him fiercely; but he came a step towards him, hitching forward his sword, and trembling like a terrier-dog.

"I tell you sir——" he began; but turned round at the sound of the latch to see Jack Morris come in

"Ah! Master Norris——"

"Why, Dick," said Jack, paying no attention, "when did you come back?"

Guy stepped aside feeling a fool.

"But five minutes ago," said Master Kearsley drily, "and am met by a fellow who would have me out of my own room."

"I beg you pardon, Master Kearsley," put in Guy confusedly.

"I did not know——"

Dick sniffed and stood up.

"I suppose you are Master Guy Manton," he said.

"Yes; this is Master Manton," put in Jack, looking from one to the other

"Then Master Manton had best bid his lad begone," went on Kearsley, "I have had the honour to inform the gentleman already of the regulations."

"Go, Tom," said Guy, abashed.

Jack gave a squirt of laughter.

"Already, Dick?" he said.

"If Master Manton considers himself aggrieved," went on

Dick coolly; "he has only to ask——"

"I am very willing to do what is proper," said Guy, deliberately hitching forward his sword again, "but I will say for the last time that I regret I did not know, Master Kearsley."

Dick sat down again.

"Very well," he said brusquely, "that is enough."

The three sat together amicably for a few minutes; but Guy was not greatly pleased with his new fellow. Master Kearsley was sour both in appearance and speech, and said very little, except to complain of the bad roads and the heat, and the stupidity he had found in the small household at Richmond whither he had been sent to prepare for the Queen's coming.

"The landing-stage was all to pieces," he said, "and not one had had the sense to repair it."

"Her Grace will have no unnecessary expense," began Jack,

"It is not her Grace," cried Dick angrily, "it is those idle folk of hers."

He snarled so fiercely that Guy was glad when he got up presently, and said that he must be off to supper. When the door closed behind him Guy looked at the other questioningly.

Jack's face broke into lines of mirth.

"To think that you should have met him so," he said, "and bidden him begone from his own parlour!"

"He did not explain," began Guy with some irritation

"Why, of course, he did not. Dick loves a sour jest like that."

"He is a sour fellow, I think."

"Why, yes; you have hit him there. And see, Master Manton, that you do not slight her Grace before him. He will have none of that."

"Does he love her then, so much?"

Jack lifted his eyebrows.

"Why, we all love her," he sneered, "and Dick is one of us."

When Guy had gone presently to look after Tom, Jack sat still in the window-seat for a few moments, looking out on to the cobbled court and the pleasant activity of the green-and-white figures that went to and fro. He was wondering what this new pensioner would make of the life at Court. He did not think he would be altogether happy there.

From a word or two that Guy had let slip, Jack understood that he took his position very seriously and looked forward to some sort of a career; and that, Jack knew very well, was not an easy ambition for a gentleman-usher. There were no great openings for distinction except for persons of an extraordinary ability. Besides, Guy did not seem to him to have the brutality necessary for a career. Only that afternoon the two had ridden together past Cheapside pillory at the moment that a woman had fainted during her flogging for harlotry, and Jack had been astomshed at his companion's white face. Guy had recovered himself the next moment, and rapped out a harsh word or two, but it did not quite compensate for his appearance the instant before.

On the other hand he had taken to his new duties with sufficient address; he knew how to behave and to carry himself, and even Mrs. Clarentia had remarked on it that morning as she and Jack waited for the Queen in the antechamber.

The old lady had confided to him that she had had a terrible time with young Magdalene Dacre, her Grace's new lady; she had found the girl in hysterics with home-sickness m her own room, and had been forced to correct her sharply, telling her that the Queen's Majesty did not want pining misses about her.

"The poor child!" said Jack sympathetically. "Let me talk to her, mistress."

Mrs. Clarentia eyed him severely.

"I felt that myself," she said, "but I did not tell her so."

"She should take example by Master Manton," observed Jack sententiously.

The old lady threw up her hands.

"Eh! That young man! And you should see how he bears himself with her Grace. He might have been born at Court."

That was all well enough, Jack told himself now, as he sat in the window-seat and played with the shutter. If Master Manton would be content with the small affairs of life, and would develop his courtierly graces, and learn perhaps to play on the virginal and accompany that divine boy of his, and talk to the ladies properly in the barge—all might go very smoothly; but it was a pity for him to attempt higher flights, unless he was able and prepared to develop the sterner virtues.

He determined to talk to him paternally.

3

Jack Norris found the text and the occasion for his fatherly discourse a week later.

The Court moved to Richmond at the end of June; and the gentlemen had a very merry journey by water, preceding the Queen's barge by an hour or two, in order to have all things ready for her arrival. Masters Norris and Manton escorted four of the Queen's ladies, among whom was the Lady Magdalene Dacre herself; and there was a good deal of pleasant talking under the canopy between the tall, innocent-eyed girl, who seemed to have recovered her spirits, and the kind gentleman who wished to help her to it, as the painted barge swept up the river, driven by the twelve oars in the hands of the silver and blue-liveried watermen.

It was a glorious summer day; and after they had dined under the trees on the Brentford shore, and thrown pebbles at an overbold water hen, Jack got out his lute and sang a love-song or two, sitting apart in his comely dress, with his sword unbuckled and his jewelled cap on the ground beside him; he had drunk a trifle too much of the spiced wine——; rolling shallow, passion ate eyes between the verses at the pale downcast face of the splendid girl, who sat in her place with her buckled shoes crossed before her, her gemmed hands in her lap, with the flecked sunlight on her white head-dress and great coils of black hair.

He was thankful that Mistress Jane Dormer was not there: she would have checked the singing in five minutes; but the other women were quacking among themselves on the bank, and the girl sat still and listened, and made no attempt to call them back.

Jack strutted like a peacock beside Guy on the way up from the landing-stage to the palace. He was delighted with his success, and his pleasure presently overflowed in admonition.

"That is the way to get on, Master Manton," he said. 'You must not be glum, as you have been all day. Is she not glorious?"

Guy roused himself from abstraction.

"The Lady Magdalene? Indeed, she is. What were you saying?"

"I was saying you must not be glum, sir. That is no way for her Grace's gentlemen to carry themselves."

"How should I carry myself?"

Jack showed his white teeth, he felt extraordinarily gay.

"Why," he said, "Though I say it with shame, you should take example by me."

"But Master Norris," said Guy gravely, "I do not wish to be like you. I am come here to make a way for myself."

Jack gave a shout of laughter.

"Then you must carry yourself differently again you are too kindly, sir, to make such a way."

"Too kindly? Too soft, do you mean?"

"Well, it is your word not mine."

Guy set his teeth.

"Thank you, sir. You are perfectly right. It is what I have told myself."

Jack looked at him queerly: this fellow was really too solemn, he thought.

"You shall not see it again, Master Norris; I promise you that. I shall correct it."

This was serious talking, but Jack did not see his way to pursue it.

"I saw that damned heretic Underhill in the City yesterday with two fellows," he went on as they neared the entrance. "One of them, I think, was Master Ashton."

He was astonished by his companion's start. Guy was looking at him.

"When you were with my boy Tom?" he said.

Jack nodded.

"I thought your boy Tom knew one of them," he said, "but he swore he did not."

Guy laid a hand on his arm to stop him,

"Who is Master Underhill?" he asked.

"Why, he is a pestilent fellow in the Court. I sent him packing from my company in Wyatt's revolt; but he is back again now?"

"He is a heretic?"

"He is a heretic and a bloody traitor; and I am a devout Churchman, as you have no doubt observed. Let me pass, Master Manton."

"And the other?" insisted Guy, still detaining him.

"Master Ashton? I do not know—I have seen him at Court. But I cannot prove what I said just now about Master Underhill. I would to God I could. Let me go, sir."

There was a great deal to be done that evening before the Queen arrived, although they were to stay at Richmond only a few days, and it was not until nine o'clock when supper had been despatched, and her Grace gone to her rooms with trumpets before her, that Guy had an opportunity of speaking to his boy Tom.

Tom was in a whirl of excitement. It was his first journey by water; and he had been made much of all the way by the household servants in the red barge that came last after the Queen. He had sung song after song, and had been kissed and petted by the women, and smiled upon by the men, and all that, with the splendid exhilaration of the summer day, the crash of music, the flocks of swans, his own gorgeous dress, the swift clean water in which he trailed his hands, the sight of the wooded banks and the deer and the birds streaming past; and finally the arrival at the tall towered palace, and a piece of news he had heard there—all combined to make him jubilant and noisy.

He burst into his master's room to tell him that he had heard he was to be appointed to her Grace's choir—that Master Norris had told him so and clapped him on the back; but he stopped short and stared as he saw his master's expression.

Guy was sitting in the window-seat, his arm flung across the sill, and he turned a heavy face as the boy came in. He nodded to him to shut the door.

"Tell me, Tom. No, I am not angry. Tell me again where you saw Master Brownrigg, and what he was doing."

Tom put his hands behind his back and looked at him nervously.

"It was on the steps of Paul's, sir, as I said. He was with two gentlemen He turned away when we came by."

"How was he dressed?"

"He was dressed in a dark suit—like—like a clerk."

"Did Master Norris say aught?"

"He asked if I knew any of them; I suppose I said something, sir."

"What did you tell him?"

"I told him 'No,' sir. I remembered what you said about Master Brownrigg."

"What was that?"

"You told me to keep my eyes open, sir; and say nothing but to you."

Guy looked at him intently a moment.

"That is very good, Tom. I am pleased with you."

The boy flushed with pleasure.

"Listen, Tom. I am going to tell you a secret. Understand, you must tell no one. I fear that Master Stephen will be in trouble soon. He was with a plotter yesterday, against her Grace. It was about that that we quarrelled."

Tom's face fell; then it brightened again with excitement.

"And what will you do, Master Manton?"

Guy looked at him, and went on, as if talking to himself.

"I shall do nothing," he said. "I shall not inform I shall do nothing. He must see to himself. But I cannot act against him this time."

He stood up suddenly.

"By God, I cannot, this first time. But, by God, the next time——"

He broke off, wheeled round and stood staring out of the window.

Presently he turned round again, and his face was steady.

"You understand me, do you not? You are not to speak of this again. Master Brownrigg must do as he will."

"And what may I do, sir?"

"Do? You may keep your eyes open, as I told you, and your tongue silent."

Donec ens felix, multos numerabis amicos; Tempora si fuerint nubila, solus ens. Ov. Trist.

CHAPTER III

MARY THE QUEEN TAKES A HUSBAND

1

ON an evening in the middle of July, Mistress Jane Dormer was sitting alone after supper in a little dressing-room at Waltham Cross.

They had arrived a couple of hours earlier, riding over the rough, dusty roads from Norton; and the streets of the market-town were still noisy with the footsteps of men and horses seeking lodging, for the abbey would not hold them all.

A pleasant murmur came up, mixed with the pealing of bells, to this little shadowy room, for the window was flung wide to let in the soft summer air, cooling now after a hot day, and the western sunlight streamed in down from the hills a mile away, across the smoky roofs of the town, and fell on the new-hung walls within, the embroidered fountains and wreaths, and upon the girl herself in her chair among the trunks.

She was tired out, and her fair-skinned face and clear grave eyes showed it. There had been the ride, then the stress of unpacking and of dressing the Queen for supper, for Mary abated none of her magnificence even when she supped alone. Then Jane had supped herself, and gone out for a stroll with Lady Magdalene and a gentleman to attend them, but had found herself back again at the abbey ten minutes before the time fixed by her mistress.

She was anxious, too, about her mistress It had been one of Mary's silent days; she had scarcely spoken all day or at supper, except to bid her lady come in an hour's time; and Jane knew perfectly well what was troubling her mistress. It was one of those days on which the whole burden rested heavily; and from hints the night before Jane had recognised that it was imminent.

The girl leaned back sighing, and passed her hands behind her head and began to review the details.

First of all, the marriage, only a week or so away now. Opposition was not dead yet. Parliament had yielded, and the Spanish prince was on his way with his splendid escort across the long rollers of the West; but was not England silenced rather than persuaded?

Then there were fifty other signs of hostility. Jane had a sight now and again of the papers that poured in morning by morning, denouncing Mary, crying for her death, telling of the whisperers that gabbled and the fanatics that raved against the blood, the faith and the politics of their Queen.

She had seen Mary, too, again and again receive the news month by month, of the Protestant outbreaks. There had been the menace at Colchester which Mary had treated with a strong hand; there had been the horrible outrage on Easter Day—the theft of the Sacred Host from the Sepulchre, and the sneers that followed it. *"Surrexit! Non Hic!"* the priest had sung as he drew back the door. Folks had laughed and whispered as they repeated the tale. God was not there, they had sniggered. He was lost; but the priest could soon make Him again.

There had been the horror in April, when a cat had been hung on the Cheapside gallows, in mass-vestments and with a white disc elevated between the dead paws. At Corpus Christi a danger had been drawn on the priest who bore the Sacrament in Smithfield; later, a shot had been fired at the preacher at Paul's Cross; and last, there was the feigned miracle in Alders-gate—the affair of the girl who hid herself in the wall and cried out in a ghostly voice against the mass and the Queen, and the Spanish marriage and the increasing of idolatry.

Jane knew what these insults meant to Mary; she had heard her sobbing softly one night; she had seen her set face in the morning.

Yet that was not all There was the misery of treason from Mary's own blood relations and friends. The Lady Elizabeth had not wanted for tenderness and love, she had been loaded with toys as a child, by Mary, and with jewels as a woman; and she repaid it—this thin tight-lipped pale creature—by treating her sister as a tyrant, by allowing herself to be used as a claimant to the throne, by denying the traitorous interviews with De Noailles' agents and the messages to Courtenay, by flinging herself down, all in white as a virgin-martyr, crying to God to strike her dead if she were untrue, and to Mary to forgive and trust her—Mary who knew her as false

It was a miserable affair, thought Jane. The Princess had been sent to the Tower at last; and there, too, she had posed and ranted, crying out at the Traitor's Gate, and passing through to her lodgings in a dramatic, agonised silence. All that had proved useless too; Mary had tried tenderness again, had told her of her refusal to listen to Renard's demand for her life, and had sent her home to Richmond. There, too, there had been treachery; clear proofs of collusion between the Princess and De Noailles; and now Elizabeth was once more at Woodstock, a piteous martyr in public, and a discreet schemer in private. Was loyalty an impossible lesson for Anne Boleyn's daughter to learn?

Mistress Dormer sighed and sat up It was nearly time to go to the Queen.

She knew well that in Mary's opinion there was but one hope, and that the Spanish marriage

Jane had listened to a passion of enthusiasm a week before, as to what the marriage would do Philip would be with her then, the Queen had cried, and all Spain behind him; a flood of Catholic life would pour again through the heresy-shrivelled veins of the country, brace its sinews and inspire its heart; the old way should come back, the old loyalty to God and the Prince; these new fashions would melt before the fire of the Holy Sacrifice streaming out from every town and hamlet; the Precious Blood would flow again and make all clean—the sombre face had brightened at the thought and the shallow eyes lost their screens. She cried out that she knew as few else what was the power of that faith, for she had tested it herself through years of misery and weakness.

When the bells were set ringing again, and the processions went about the streets, and the Religious Houses throbbed again like great workshops of prayer and grace, and the children were taught the Faith that Christ brought on earth, and the priests went about loved and honoured as they had been thirty years back, and every church was instinct with the Divine Presence, and the altars were up again, and the carved and painted tale of God's mysteries on wall and window and loft; then these new mean ways of isolation and craft and men's doctrines, and sedition and schism and the brood of evil things that loved the darkness—all would go; and the country should be happy and clean once more.

But there had been a reaction a minute later. The Queen had flung herself down in a chair and lain there silent and piteous once more.

"And what of me?" she had cried. "What will my prince say?':

She had said no more than that; but Jane had known what was in her mind.

She rose now and went to the window, thinking of it again, standing there with her peculiar air of grave steadiness.

The sun had dipped below the hill, and the country beyond the houses was dark and colourless; only overhead beyond the haze of smoke the sky was luminous and tender. The cool evening air, fragrant with earth and flowers rose to her nostrils and a blackbird on the grass outside hopped and eyed her, and flew away chattering an alarm.

But the girl scarcely saw what her eyes rested upon. She was thinking of the Queen—of that rigid personality that could not express itself and, most piteous of all, that knew it could not, of the lack of wit and gaiety and the consciousness of that lack and above all, of those cold black eyes, the mouth that found it hard to smile and easy to contract, the pale cheeks, the tiny wrinkles. . She contrasted it with the gay portrait of the Prince that hung at Richmond, the red painted lips to which she had seen Mary press her own…

But it was not wholly for herself that the Queen was marrying, the girl had heard her once speak of a boy that should be her' and Philip's and England's; a straight-limbed gallant prince with fearless eyes and true heart, who should rule the country in the Faith of God—who—who would perhaps remember some day the soured mother who bore him, and sacrificed herself for his love—herself who had so few to love her.

The girl turned away from the window, with her quiet eyes full of tears, and went across to the Queen's door.

It was a pleasant panelled room, new-carved with three rows of medallions bearing the Tudor rose and portcullis with other emblems and faces, but it was too dark now to see clearly.

A great wave of rose-fragrance met her as she came in, pouring from the window and the heaped bowls set here and there.

"Will not your Grace have lights and go to bed? Or the priest is ready for prayers."

A figure turned away from the window and sat down.

"No, sweetheart," came the deep voice.

"Sit down and talk to me, Jane."

The girl could not see much, for the Queen was in her tall chair now, with her back to the square-framed pale green sky that darkened every moment There was a star out now, like a radiant jewel; and from jewels on her mistress' head-dress ran out swift sparkles. But the face was in deep shadow, a patch of paleness resting on a pale arm, that ran up slender and weak into the deep brocaded sleeve.

Jane talked of a hundred things in her slow soothing voice with her bright eyes downcast; of Sir Philip's stables, of a brawl between an archer and a rustic, of the kitchens she had been to visit, and the new-fashioned spits that they used there—all trifles such as the Queen liked to hear; and went on taking silence for words and words for speeches, for nearly half-an-hour. She perceived that the heaviness lay on her mistress still.

She ran dry at last, and sat waiting.

The Queen lifted her head a little.

"Yes," she said, "and we have not said our Lady's office. I cannot to-night. Compline will have to serve. The priest is ready."

"He has been ready an hour past, your Grace."

Still Mary did not move. She dropped her cheek on her hand again and was silent.

Mistress Dormer began to tell her of the abbey-church which she had been to see, of the goodly carving in it, and the monks' stalls, and the remnants of Harold's tomb by the high Altar, destroyed fourteen years ago.

Again there fell a silence, and again Mary broke it.

"There is no courier from the coast?" she asked.

"No, madam."

"Nor from town"

"Not since the one that came at supper-time, madam."

Still the Queen sat on, as silent and cold to her friend as to others. In a minute or two Mistress Dormer made a little movement in despair, half-afraid that the other had fallen asleep; but she saw the dark eyes rise for a moment and look at her, and then drop again into paleness.

Mistress Dormer was longing for bed, but she did not dare to move again. She could see that it was one of Mary's obstinate fits in which it was useless to make a proposal. She must just wait.

The room was as dark as a July night could make it before the Queen spoke again

"Jane," she said softly, "what gentlemen are with us? I mean of the ushers."

Mistress Dormer mentioned a dozen names.

"Not Master Manton?"

"Your Grace sent him to Southampton a week ago."

Again there was a pause.

"Jane."

"Yes, madam."

"Is that gentleman happy at court?"

"Surely, madam."

"Ah! We have not done our Homer yet. Remind me when we are back in town."

"Yes, madam."

Again there was a silence. Then Jane lost her patience.

Madam, will you not go to bed?"

"And what of prayers?"

"Well, prayers then, madam."

Mary rose abruptly.

"Prayers then, Jane. Do you lead the way—I cannot see in the dark."

2

It was late on the Saturday evening, ten days later, when the procession crossed the steep high-street of Winchester, and turned towards Southgate.

It was a bewildering sight to Magdalene Dacre's eyes, as she sat between old Mrs. Clarentia and Mrs. Jane Dormer in the back seat of the great red carriage that followed just behind the Queen's.

The street was as bright as day, though the sky had faded to a kind of storm-lit glory. In every window blazed lights, from the twinkle of rush-lights high overhead in the jutting attics to the flaming street below where torches, blown about by the furious storm of wind, moved along in endless profusion, marking a road of splendour down to where the two lines curved out of sight under the archway Between these lines went the long rows of heads, in feather and steel, four abreast, guarded on either side by the ripple of pike-points From every window hung tapestries and arras and cloth-of-gold, so that the street seemed like a vast and richly-furnished corridor. A roar moved with the carnages as they went, tempestuous and overpowering; and Magdalene turned her eyes now and again from that stiffly bowing head before her in the Queen's carnage, to the banks of open mouths and crimson faces contorted with effort and the swaying lights, to the open mouths of alleys and streets on either side that disgorged fresh bellows of loyalty as her Grace's figure came in sight The girl was almost deafened by the roar of voices, by the brazen music of the church-bells overhead and the long shattering cries of the trumpets, punctuated and steadied by the deep boom of the great bass-bell of the Cathedral far away to the left.

Old Mistress Clarentia came to her in her room in Wolvesey Palace half an hour later, as the girl sat pale and tired in her satin and jewels, waiting for her summons to attend her Grace to supper.

"Will you not go to bed, my dear?" she said. "You are wearied out. I will explain to her Highness."

Magdalene shook her head.

"I would not lose it for the world," she said, "now that I am here Oh, Mistress, what does her Grace think of it all?"

The old woman's face wrinkled up with emotion.

"I am just come from her," she said. "I have never seen her so happy. God bless my lamb!"

Magdalene looked at her anxiously. Was this emotion sincere? Was it possible for any emotions, but those of excitement and ambition and disgust, to be sincere in this gaudy false atmosphere? Since her recent arrival at Court she had done little but long for her home, and the wind-swept heather and the clean breezes, and the wholesome rain and cold.

"She is happy, Mistress?" she asked slowly.

The old woman's eyes looked at her suspiciously, but there was the glimmer of tears in them.

"Why, surely" she began.

Then the page came in to tell them that her Grace was ready to go down.

Magdalene watched the Queen eagerly that night; but there was little to support Mistress Clarentia's opinion.

She supped in state in the great hall, and on either cheek burned a spot of crimson.

Stephen Gardiner saw it; and Magdalene heard him congratulate the Queen softly on her health as he stood afterwards by her chair under the canopy which he had caused to be set for her two days before in the Presence-Chamber.

"I thank you, my lord," said Mary, stiffly; and Magdalene saw her neck flush as she answered. Was that delight or weariness or shame?

He added a word or two about his poor house that she was honouring, and then apologised for the adjective, reminding her that it had been built by Royal hands: described the preparations made in the Deanery a hundred yards away for the coming of the Prince, and the traverses set up in the Cathedral choir; and at last kissed her hand and stepped aside

Throughout the hour and a half of that audience the Queen seemed as stiff and passionless as ever, bowing her rigid head, giving her white jewelled hand, uttering to each who came up a word or two in her deep man's voice.

"I thank you for your hospitality, sir," she said to the Dean who had left his house for Philip's convenience.

"I am grateful for your good wishes, my lord," she said to the Lord Treasurer who, Magdalene knew, had opposed the marriage from the beginning.

She bowed her head and said nothing at all to the quiet little Duke of Norfolk who was supposed to understand her as did none else.

"I thank you, sir You did not think so once," she said shrewdly to her Secretary of State, who had become her partisan from policy, and who now, kneeling in his new Order of the Garter, strove to forget that he had ever come to her to forbid her mass in the days of her humiliation.

"You must pray for me, my lords," she said to a couple of bishops who came up together: "Without God's grace all is useless."

It was over at last.

Mary turned to the girl as they passed into the bed-chamber, and caught her suddenly by the arm. Magdalene, startled altogether out of her complacent interest, saw that the Queen's cheeks were burning and her eyes alight with some emotion.

"Thank God I" she cried. "Now I have time to be merry alone. Kiss me, sweetheart. Nay, you must not hate me!"

Magdalene went away that night more puzzled than ever. The Queen had said no more; but had withdrawn once more into self-repression. She had slowly kissed the girl good-night, but without a word; and Magdalene's last sight of her had been as she sat half undressed in her deep chair, her hair on her shoulders, and old Mrs. Clarentia's arms round her rocking her gently to and fro. There had been a look of content in the old woman's face, and in Jane Dormer's too, that had puzzled this new lady-in-waiting. Were these two consummate hypocrites, or did they indeed find something in that unloveable woman that no others could find?

As Magdalene brushed out her hair that night opposite the silver-framed mirror she did not notice her own pretty face. She was thinking of the Queen's shadowed eyes, her repellent dignity, and wondered, as many others were wondering, at the shrewishness she had shown that night And why had her Grace said that about hatred? She shivered and shook her head.

The groups dispersing through the still lighted Close also discussed her Grace's bearing and her future A couple of furred and cloaked canons walking together commented frankly on her chance of bearing a child.

"There will be no prince," concluded one, as they came to the Slype passage; "believe me, sir, that Philip will be off to Spain again in a fortnight. We must look to the Lady Elizabeth to give us a king."

"Did you see her coldness to my lord Bishop?" said the other. "I think she has no friends."

"There is yet my lord Cardinal. How of him for a husband if Philip will not have her? He is no priest yet. And he is her cousin."

The two came through the Slype and reached the west door of the Cathedral as they talked; and one of them pushed upon it gently. It yielded; he pushed yet harder and it opened, and the two looked in.

The great place was full of sound and darkness only broken by the glimmer of lights m two or three places where the workmen were still busy upon the preparations for the wedding. From somewhere in the roof clear through the soft riot of the wind came the echoing blows of a hammer that drove the pegs from which the arras was to hang, but it ceased as the two watched Huge shadows barring the light of the lantern carried along the clerestory, wheeled out like spokes to mix with the deeper gloom of the roof. There was another light burning within Wykeham's chantry on the right, and it threw bars of darkness and patches of brightness on a great shimmering sheet of cloth-of-gold already in its place on one of the vast pillars on the opposite side of the nave. The choir was in shadow, except for the glimmer of the upper lines of the reredos and the carved roof above it on which shone and faded the flickering light of the lamp before the most Holy Sacrament Up the paleness of the floor ran a long wooden platform to the entrance beneath the screen above which rose the three huge figures of the Passion, and shapeless heaps of rugs and furniture and timbers lay piled on either side. There were lonely voices calling out of the darkness one to another; a figure crossed the nave noiselessly over the carpets fifty yards away, bearing a beam across his shoulders; it seemed like one carrying a cross.

The whole vast place was like a pillared hall, where the dead moved and cried to one another, and went about strange ceremonies; its shadows and paleness seemed wholly apart from the glare of life and movement whence the two priests had come—from the buzz of the Court, the flare and shouting of the streets, the steel-clad knights and tabarded heralds. It found there its only echo in the central figure herself, with her silence and self-repression and with it all her significance and secret life.

The two closed the door again as noiselessly as they had opened it, and went on their way.

Dick Kearsley and Jack Norris were still lounging in the hall half an hour after the Queen had retired and the company gone. It was their duty to wait there until the signal was given that the Court was clear of strangers.

Kearsley was leaning against the scaffold at the upper end; and Norris was astride of a bench beside him. They, too, were gossiping.

"Her Grace was in a panic on Thursday," remarked Jack, "when the wind blew. She feared for Philip. Mistress Dormer was saying that she neither ate nor drank till after three o'clock. To-day she cares nothing for the storm. Her lord is landed."

Dick grunted sourly.

"And the Frenchmen are a trouble to her,' went on the other." I saw her eyeing De Noailles at Richmond, as if she sorely wished to ask him how his master did."

"There is more reason in the Frenchmen," snarled Kearsley, "and that damned Eliza."

But in spite of his bitterness he was triumphing in his heart. It seemed as if other schemes had come to nothing, and that Mary was conqueror.

"You saw the jewels he sent last month," went on Norris presently. "I was at Guildford when they came, and saw her go white and red as the Don brought them up. She has them here too, and will wear them at the wedding."

Dick nodded abruptly. He was biting his nails as if ill at ease.

"He has reached Southampton at least," proceeded Jack, "in spite of the seamen. You heard of their matter?"

"Yes, the dogs!" snapped Kedrsley.

They talked for a minute or two of the report of Lord Effingham that he could not trust his men to guard the Prince of Spain on his voyage; and of the Queen's instant action in ordering their dismissal.

"There will be more trouble yet," observed Jack Norris finally. "I heard a fellow say that Philip drew his sword as he came to land. Pray God we may come peaceably out of it here. Master Manton will be here when the Prince comes. He is gone to Southampton with Sir Anthony Browne. That is a good fellow, Dick; but harder than I thought him at first."

"He is well enough. But he is too much of a scholar for the Court. We do not want Terence here."

"He will not be here long, I think," went on the other. "He said as much to me one day. He is no lover of her Grace. But I would sooner have him a thousand times than that damned hot-gospeller Underhill."

Dick grunted again.

Three or four servants came in, and began to clear up the hall and the two could talk no more. Through the open door that gave on to the Court Jack could see a link or two still moving about The rush and bustle were over; but from the direction of College Street still came the cries of the servants and the sound of wheel; and horses' hoofs Through the high windows of the hall then still shone fitfully from outside the dying illuminations kindled to welcome the Queen. The house itself was quiet

Jack wondered what the Queen was doing Perhaps she was at her prayers; perhaps gone to bed; perhaps looking our over the glare of the town.

He loved her no more than did the rest of her servants. He would have preferred a sprightlier Queen, less icy, more genial but it seemed to him now that this marriage of hers was more human than almost any of her acts. The romance with which she regarded it was evident even to him. He had seen it in her flushed cheeks to-night, and had recognised it from the tales that ran about the Court of her passionate suspense when a storm blew from the south-west, or a veiled threat from France came to her through the hands of a courier.

What nonsense it was, Jack said to himself—this love for a man whom she had never seen! He had laughed over it in private frequently, during this last three months—over her folly about Philip's picture, her anxiety for a letter of his that never came her poses and her smiles before the painter who had made her portrait for the Prince. It was surely a ludicrous affair enough this coquetry of a haggard woman of thirty-seven towards a young man, who, if tales were true, had other loves to occupy him.

He would not have laughed if she had been as sedate in this affair as in others; if she had passionlessly accepted any husband whom her Council advised, and had prepared to do her duty and bear a prince with as little emotion as that with which she ate her dinner. But those raptures and love-sicknesses were absurd They should be left to younger folks.

But Jack had not laughed with Dick Kearsley. Once when he had attempted it, a year ago, he had received such a scornful glare that the mirth had died on his lips, and he did not think it wise to attempt it with Guy Manton.

But there were other good fellows besides these, who better understood the cynicism of thirty years, and the ripe experience of one who had lived in three Courts and knew the follies and weaknesses of men and women. And they could always be silent and laugh in secret when persons who still kept their youthful illusions or had not sufficient good-humour came into the parlour.

So Jack sat now, swinging his white silk legs, his cap on his head, and a flush of excitement in his cheeks comparing Magdalene and Mary, while Dick bit his nails beside him.

3

The Queen sat in her private parlour opening out of the Presence-Chamber in my lord's palace, waiting for news.

She had scarcely shown herself in public since the Saturday night, and it was now forty-eight hours after Three of her ladies were with her; Mistress Jane Dormer as always, irresistibly soothing and friendly, stood leaning at the back of the Queen's chair, Margaret Clifford waited by the half-open door, glancing now at the Queen, now into the room beyond as if expectant; another, Mistress Susan Young, stood patiently by the bedroom door on another side, waiting and watching

Mary herself sat upright, gripping the bosses of her chair-arm, tense and tight-lipped Her head trembled a little. Once Jane leaned forward and stroked the Queen's arm gently, but the coifed head jerked abruptly, and Jane sighed and drew softly back.

Half-an-hour before they had heard the crash of artillery, and then the bells, the trumpets and the cheering that told them of the Prince's arrival at the Cathedral; and Mary had started up with clenched hands and taken a swift step towards the window; but Jane had caught her and drawn her back softly; since then she had sat silent.

Outside the evening was closing in; there were heavy clouds scudding swiftly in a grey sky angry with sunset light; and from time to time a gust of rain-laden wind shrilled from the southwest, shaking the latches of the windows, lifting the arras curtains that hung beside them, and blurring the panes with the flying water. It had rained heavily all day, and night was coming on dark and comfortless.

There sounded once more a crash of bells, windy and mellow, and a torrent of sound followed it.

Again Mary sprang to her feet and stood swaying there, listening to the gusts of cheering, the shrill distant trumpets and the brazen thunder from the tower. But Jane was behind her with a caressing murmur which did not cease m spite of the Queen's sharp gesture or silence, and presently Mary was down again in her chair, with parted lips and white face, listening and waiting once more.

Then Margaret nodded to her, and threw the door wide; there was a sound of footsteps in the Presence-Chamber; and Magdalene came swiftly through, panting a little, with her splendid head upraised, and her skirts rustling behind her.

She came straight across the room, dropped on her knees, and lifted one of the cold hands to her lips. Mary had not stirred again at her coming. Jane nodded impatiently from behind the chair.

"He is come, madam," stammered Magdalene, glancing anxiously at Mistress Dormer.

Margaret closed the door, and came across to where Jane stood behind the chair Susan had vanished into the bedroom beyond; and the four were alone.

The Queen drew a slow breath, and sat a little forward.

"Tell me all," she said.

Magdalene Dacre lifted her eyes waveringly, dropped them again; drew a long breath, and began, tremulously as if repeating a lesson.

"I was within the Cathedral as your Grace bade me; just within the west door with Mrs. Rise below the scaffold. The bishops stood outside on the edge of the scaffold with their backs to me in copes and mitres—my lords of Winchester, Durham, London and the rest. I could see the space cleared before the door for His Highness to dismount, and the guards keeping it, with my Lord Pembroke on a horse at one side—and the torches burning.

"Then the Prince came——"

Mary made an impatient movement of her head. Magdalene understood, and went on hastily.

"I could not see him clearly at first, your Grace. I could not tell which was he, there were so many with him—they filled all the space so far as I could see. Then he dismounted, and came up the steps on to the scaffold, and he knelt down before my lord of Winchester. I could not see what he. did; but one told me afterwards that he took the crucifix and kissed it The organs were playing all the while, and the trumpets blowing outside…

"Then they came along the scaffold, and I saw His Highness."

She looked swiftly up at the strained face watching her, and went on more quickly than ever, as if m desperation.

"Your Grace, he bore himself very gallantly, walking behind my lord, with his cap on his head. There was a white feather in it, but draggled somewhat with the ram, and he had on a rich purple coat with gold and lace. He—he is as the picture shows him, but more gallant."

The Queen drew a swift breath, but said nothing.

"They went away, your Grace, with the clerks and priests and boys before, singing *"Laus honor et virtus"* as they went, as your Grace directed, and the organs playing The tapers were alight upon the high altar, and all the altars and on the roodbeam.…

"His Highness took off his cap as he entered the choir, and made obeisance to the most holy sacrament. Then he turned off to his traverse on the left, and went up into it and kneeled down, but I could not see him there.

"The organs played for a while softly till he had done his prayer, and then struck the tone of *Te Deum*. My lord began it, and it was sung by the clerks…

"When it was doing I came out, and passed through the cloister on my way and saw the guards on the way to the deanery. They were in their rich coats, and everyone bore a torch, as your Grace said was to be As I came through the garden, I heard the bells again to show that His Highness was come out."

Magdalene Dacre hesitated, leaned forward, lifted the passive hand to her lips and kissed it once more, as Jane nodded and smiled encouragingly.

The Queen sat rigid a moment longer, and then spoke in her hard voice.
"And the other matter?"

"It is arranged, your Grace My Lord Arundel will bring His Highness here to-night at ten o'clock."

There was a profound silence for a moment or two, only broken by the stir of the wind and the scuds of rain against the window-panes. Then Mary rose abruptly, pushing back her chair, Jane Dormer took two swift steps round and caught her by the waist.

"Ah! you do not understand—you do not understand 'not one of you!" sobbed the Queen

Three hours later they were standing again behind the Queen's chair. Her mood had changed again, and she was radiant, Again she was flushed, and in the soft light of the candles round the walls looked ten years younger. She was in a magnificent costume of white and silver, sewn with pearls in every seam on her head was her white coif, alight with diamonds, and another great stone burned on her breast below the collar of pearls that lay on her pale bare neck

There was another tall chair beside hers, empty, and a footstool stood before it, embroidered with the loves of Apollo. She had chosen it herself three days before. A little wood-fire burned on the wide hearth.

The door into the Presence-Chamber was open, and Master Norris stood there in rigid profile, bare-headed and in his white suit.

Magdalene Dacre looked gloriously young and splendid behind the chair, half a head taller than the others; but she was not thinking about herself. She was doing her utmost to realise the mind that was so alert in the figure beneath. From where did this passion come, the hysterical screaming of three hours ago? They had carried Mary into her bedroom and laid her on the bed, and she had lain there sobbing half an hour, reproaching them for lack of sympathy, crying out that no one loved her or understood her; but that her Prince would come soon to comfort her. Magdalene thought of the face she had seen that afternoon going up the long raised walk from the west end to the choir of the great church, and wondered whether there was a power to comfort in the soul behind. She had been more interested than she had thought possible.

How strange was this mistress of hers! She had dressed with enthusiasm, when the fit of crying was over. She seemed more like a girl than a woman of thirty-seven; both her coldness and her weakness had gone together. Was there anything but love to explain it, and what was there to explain the love?

Mary turned and smiled into her face, as she pondered.

"You are too grave, sweetheart," she whispered, and the girl smiled back with troubled eyes.

Jack Norris made a slight movement at the door, and a stir ran through the four ladies as they heard footsteps in the outer room.

But Mary was on her feet, too, now, slender and perfectly upright, her hands folded before her, as the gentlemen bowed low at the door, and a figure came through alone.

Magdalene swept down to the ground in a great courtesy with the three beside her, and the Queen in front, and then lifted her eyes and looked.

There were two or three gentlemen at the door, in its shadow, and bright against that dark background was a splendid creature, gemmed from head to foot, with a short crimson cloak thrown back from his white costume; the diamonded Garter blazed below his left knee; his plumed cap was in his hand as he recovered from his deep bow; and his pear-shaped head, crowned above by flaxen hair and ending below in a short fair pointed beard, was thrownback on his shoulders From beneath his white forehead his large blue-grey eyes ran swiftly up and down the Queen's figure, and dropped again. He looked his full ten years younger than Mary.

The Queen's deep voice said something in Spanish that Magdalene could not catch, and Philip answered with a low dehberate word or two, bowing again as he did so.

Then they advanced to one another, the Prince holding out his jewelled hands. Mary laid her own in them, and he kissed her delicately on the cheek.

Then they turned and came hand in hand towards the two chairs, and as the Queen made a sign to her ladies, Magdalene saw that her face was flushed from forehead to chin.

The girl made her courtesy with the others, and the three ladies went out from the parlour.

There were a dozen gentlemen in the Presence-Chamber; Lord Arundel with a small group of English and Spanish nobles, stood in the centre of the room; two ushers were by the further door leading into the great hall, and Mr. Norris, who had closed the parlour-door, stood now like a statue a yard from it. A long cushioned settle was placed beneath the high scaffold between the windows on the left, and on this the three ladies sat down in silence.

Magdalene Dacre looked round the room with a strange sense of excitement. The whole matter seemed unreal—this great silent room, blazing with lights from its tapestried walls, the group in the centre talking with almost soundless voices, the stiff ushers by the doors, the absence of the clamour and movement that had filled men's ears and eyes during these past days, and yet she knew very well that the heart of this quiet event was more momentous than any of the rest. It was fitting, she vaguely felt, that the trumpets and bells and shouting should be silent at this crisis, as the music of organs and choirs, the movements of the sacred ministers and the rustle of the people is suddenly hushed before the supreme climax of the Sacrifice.

She longed for an instant to whisper to Jane Dormer, whom she could feel slightly shivering beside her; but the desire passed; she dropped her eyes again, folded her hands and gave herself up to astonished reflection.

Jane, too, was meditating on what she had seen.

In that swift glance from behind the Queen's chair she had seen the first meeting of man and a woman who were to be husband and wife in two days—a meeting which was the result of a long and slow approach; she had watched for months past, though she had scarcely realised it at the time, the gathering into the woman's hands of the threads, strung with jewels and gifts that were drawing the man slowly across land and sea into an intimate relation that should endure till death. The threads had been coiled in richer day by day in the loads that hung on them and in their promise of the final prize. Then the end grew more imminent; the woman had advanced southwards to meet her husband, and had paused at last in that little room next door; the last moments had passed; the door had opened, and in silence for the first time the jewelled prize had shown itself. "What of it?"

Now they were together, each eyeing the other.

But Jane had watched more than that. She had watched from her side a passion that grew day by day hotter and more fierce, as imagination and hope and religious fervour and desire for love wrought their effect on a lonely soul She had seen a woman, cut off from the world by ramparts first of suffering, then of high rank, and lastly of unloveability, stretching out thin hands more passionately every day as the hot fire raged within her, crying out to the fancy that her own mind had wrought on the clouds to come down and be incarnate and take her to himself, and compensate her for the long years of isolation. And a figure had answered the call, and stepped to her side—a figure with blue eyes and yellow hair as of the Prince she had dreamed of—gallant and upright and of flesh and blood like her own.

And now they were together, each eyeing the other with clasped hands.

But there was one more point in the drama These two persons next door were not as others, for neither approached the other apart from the world. Behind them stood the nations, two temperaments, two ambitions, almost two faiths. Behind the woman lay a sea of pale and ruddy English faces, watching jealously her every movement, alert to perceive the smallest falter, quick to detect mistakes, eager to punish, sullen and remorseless to resent them—an army of persons who had scarcely yet accepted her as their champion, who doubted her ability, distrusted her sincerity, and repudiated her aims. And behind the man stood a dark mighty nation, hot-blooded, proud with the conquests of centuries, rich beyond belief, contemptuous of rivalry, watching their lord too, jealous lest he should even for a moment betray their interests to this new little northern power whose insolence almost equalled their own pride.

Behind that door there was a great mystery beginning; of which no man could see the consummation, it was well that the trumpets and bells should be silent, that the door should be closed and the curtain against it; the bellowing uncouth crowds, who understood nothing but their own mean passions, excluded; and that only a few who knew, not all indeed, but more than the rest, should wait silent on the threshold during those first pregnant rites

Then back on the girl's mind rushed the amazing human interest of it all once more. She forgot the vast issues, or what men count vast, the destinies of the nations; she forgot even her own homesickness in the drama before her—a man and woman side by side, each utterly ignorant of the other, but already bound each to the other as firmly as ever marriage vows could make them. Ah! how horrible that was, but how fascinating!

Of the character on the one side she knew what few others knew—its needs, its aspirations, and its weaknesses; of the other side she knew nothing except what tales and a moment's look could give her.

It was said that the Prince's life was impure. If that were true, would it be likely that Mary would win him to chastity? Mary demanded faithfulness above all else, it was the lack of it that had soured her. Was it probable that she would find it in the person from whom she needed it most, and had the most right to demand it?

Was it prejudice only, the girl asked herself, that made her think that the Prince's face justified the tales? Or had there been something in his quick look as he entered, in his scarlet broad lips and gay eyes that lent colour to what she had heard?

Ah! Well—it was horrible—horrible and inevitable!

She looked up sharply at a movement.

Master Norris had turned his head slightly by the door; and at the same instant the gentlemen in the middle of the room ceased their low talking.

She saw two ushers by the further door straighten themselves, and then on the silence rasped the hiss of curtain strings, as Master Norris tore back the hanging arras and laid his hand on the latch.

A moment later he had flung the door wide, and Jane rose to her feet with the others.

She did not see Philip's face, for she was only rising from her courtesy as he turned; but she watched him go briskly down the room, putting his cap on his head as he did so. She saw him turn, however, for a moment at the further door, and saw again his yellow beard, his white forehead and blue eyes as he spoke with the smallest inclination to the Englishmen who bowed behind his own Spaniards.

"Good-neight, my lards all."

Then he was gone, and Jane, after another glance at Jack's disappearing green back, led the other ladies into the Queen's parlour.

Mary was standing there with the gleeful flushed face of a happy child. For a moment the shadows on her face were gone; her stiff lips were smiling, and her shallow eyes shone like stars.

"Did you hear my Prince?" she cried to Jane, holding her by the shoulders. "I taught him that!—'Good-night, my lords all.'"

4

Mistress Jane Dormer was early in the Queen's bedroom next morning. The extraordinary reaction of gaiety had not passed with the night, and as she helped

Mary to dress, the Queen talked incessantly, when the maids were out of the room, of the Prince's gallant bearing, his beauty, and his nobleness.

The mood lasted all day till evening.

After mass and breakfast till dinner Mistress Dormer was busy with the dresses and jewels, and Mary was continually in and out of the room where she sat, directing and counter-ordering, there were some new jewels that Philip had given her that she must wear next day; she would have two rows of diamonds on her coif, not three.

Mistress Dormer did not dine in hall that day, nor attend the public reception of which the affair of last night had been but a private rehearsal; but she was busy all the afternoon with the final preparations upstairs, looking out only once on to the court, as the crash of horns and the shrilling of strings and voices told her that Philip was come to make love before the crowd.

There they went; the train of dark nobles before and behind between the lines of the guards, and in the midst came Philip, stepping deliberately with downcast eyes, in his black and silver cloak and white hose, with the insignia of the Garter. De Feria was behind him.

Then they went in, and Mistress Dormer knew what was happening, for the Queen had told her what she would do She would be on the scaffold as he entered, and come down from it to welcome him. She would kiss him then, and lead him up into the Presence-Chamber, where they would sit together beneath the cloth-of-estate that blazed with the English and Spanish arms behind them, and would talk there in Spanish as they had talked last night

She went in again from the gallery and listened a moment. From beneath still rang up the instruments and the noise of cheering from the hall Then she passed on into the Queen's room where the women sat and stitched, to give final directions and examine their work. She took up the coif which had just been laid aside, and looked at it.

"This will not serve," she said, "the jewels are too close. Give me the scissors."

She went through into her own room, next door and as she sat down by the window, the door opened and tall young Magdalene Dacre rustled in Her red lips were tightly closed and her head was thrown back almost defiantly.

"Her Grace sent me to you," she said, "to see how all went. Let me help you"

The two took each one end of the coif, opposite to one another in the window-seat, and began to unpick the upper row of diamonds. Neither spoke for a while, but worked in silence; and one by one the shining stones, each in its tiny ring of silver, dropped into their hands and were laid aside.

As Jane reached across for the silver thread to begin the restitching, the two girls' eyes met.

Jane sighed softly.

"Well?" she asked.

Magdalene's lips twitched a moment

"Well, all has been as was arranged," she said. "Her Grace came down from the scaffold and kissed him, and led him through to the Presence-Chamber, and there they sit now, smiling and talking, with all eyes on them"

She spoke with a touch of bitterness, and Jane glanced at her again—at her flushed cheeks and bright eyes

"It must be so, sweetheart," she said, "you and I cannot wed like that, but she must"

"And the end of it?" asked the other sharply, intent on her stitching again; but the needle paused as she put the question.

Jane sighed again.

"If he is good to her" she began.

Magdalene lowered her hands for a moment and looked across indignantly.

"Are any good to her?" she said, "or has she ever asked it?"

"She has asked it in her own way a thousand times," said Jane quietly, "but it seems that none has the heart to understand. But this time surely all but the blind must see. Are you blind, my child?"

"I have seen a woman in love with a picture."

"Not a picture," said Jane, "that is nothing, it is a" heart that she wants, and she cannot find one. God grant that she may!"

Magdalene dropped the diamond she was holding, and stooped for it.

"I do not believe it," she said steadily, as she sat upright again; "she has no heart herself And she is playing to herself now. And if not, can this Prince give her one?"

Mistress Dormer was silent a moment.

"Dear child," she said, "you do not know her. She has not shown her heart to you. You did not know her when her mother was taken from her. I saw her then"

Magdalene bent her head lower still and gave no answer.

Jane drove the lesson home.

"It is not that she has no heart, but that it has been broken too often, and she fears to show it now."

Magdalene drew a swift breath that was almost a sob.

Jane glanced at her.

"Sweetheart," she said softly, "you hate her Grace, do you not?"

"God help me! I don't know…I hate it all. I am afraid, Jane…And what if the Prince breaks her heart once more—as he will?"

"Then our Lord must comfort her," said Jane.

It was late that night before Mistress Dormer was alone with the Queen. Mary was in the Presence-Chamber doing business till ten o'clock, and Jane was occupied in the bedroom laying out the splendid things that would be used next day.

A broad low wardrobe with a table on either side of it stood at the foot of the Queen's bed, and on these were ranged the shining masses of silk and brocade and jewels, down to the cloth of silver shoes and the pins for the hair.

In the centre lay the great outer robe of French brocade—Tudor roses, sheafs of arrows, dragons and wreaths, raised on a gold ground. There were great *rebras* sleeves attached to this that would sweep the ground when the robe was put on; but turned up within the elbow, so as to show the gold lining, with clusters of gold and jewels. Beside it lay the train of the same material, blazing with diamonds, and with every design outlined by countless pearls; and on the right hand table the white satin kirtle, embroidered all over with silver, and stiffened within by whale-bone and netting. The coif, finished at last, rested on the second table, and about it, laid out on shimmering silk, flashed the jewels—an endless profusion of ropes of pearls to be worn about the neck, diamonds, rubies and emeralds; and, above all, laid by itself, winked the huge stone that Philip had sent.

Jane lighted two pairs of candles and set them here and there among the clothes, and as she stepped back the Queen came in with her ladies

Mary stood in silence before the long array of glory, and Mistress Dormer, also in silence, turned a candle this way and that, lifted the chinking train that hung down upon the floor and let it drop again, smoothed out the folds of the outer robe to show the pattern.

Still the Queen said nothing, and Jane glanced at her. Mary was flushed again as she had been last night, and her eyes were bright, but her lips were closed with a kind of seventy. The girl's heart sank at the sight

Then the Queen turned to her ladies.

"Good-night," she said "I shall need none but Mistress Dormer to-night."

When they were gone out she turned once more to Jane, and looked her in the eyes.

"Prayers," she said steadily, "I had no time for the priest."

Jane lifted two of the candles and carried them across to the prie-dieu beside the bed, and set them down there on the upper ledge, on either side of the Spanish crucifix that stretched lean silver arms against an ebony cross. Behind it hung a picture of Mary, the crowned Mother of God, with the Divine Prince in her silver arms smiled and lifted two fingers as a pontiff wherewith to bless the world.

The Queen went across the room, pushed aside the book that lay on the sloping desk, and knelt down. The girl knelt down behind her.

The palace was silent now. The wind had dropped; the guards had been changed ten minutes before in the court out-side, and the tramp and challenges were over. The last page had left the Presence-chamber two doors away, and there was not a sound from within, or from the sleeping city without, to break the stillness.

As Jane, despairing of prayer after one passionate effort, looked round the tall dark room, all was motionless there; there was no wind to-night to stir the hangings on the walls, or the tapestries of the great bed; there was not even the quick flicker of a flame on the hearth to break the dead peace. The Queen was motionless in front, her hands clasped on the desk, and her steady head raised towards the royal Mother and Child, across which, as if to bar the road to joy, agonised the silver crucifix. The candle flames on either side were yellow spear-points against the dark arras. It appeared that inanimate things had a consciousness of crisis.

The minutes passed, and Jane wondered that the Queen did not open her book. It seemed to her, who knew Mary so well, that another subtle element had been woven into her mood. Her voice as she told her ladies to go had had the old touch of coldness; and her eyes had been reserved and controlled.

And then before Mistress Dormer had come to any conclusion the climax came swift and dramatic.

Mary threw herself suddenly forward on to the desk, her face on her arms, with such passion that a candle reeled and fell and went out as it crashed on to the floor. Jane was at her side, her arm about her, and her voice whispering she knew not what, as the long, half-audible wailing began.

"Oh! my God, what have I done?...What is this that is come to me?...Oh! my God, am I not punished enough for my sins?...I dare not; I dare not.... I am Thy maiden...I know I have sinned...I have denied Thee so often; and I confess it again and again...When...when I denied Thy Vicar to save my life...Oh! my God...have mercy on me.... I dare not even for Thy sake...but I have kept myself pure for Thee, my pure Saviour...and now I dare not...*Ave Maria, gratia plena, Dommus tecum*.... Oh! Mary, maiden and mother...for thy dear Child's sake...help me. But there is none to love me but thou...they are all against me.... Am I not punished enough,...but that this must come to me.... Oh! pure Virgin have pity on a virgin.... Oh! Jesu, sweet Saviour, the maiden's Child..."

The wailing died away into silence, and the Queen's body sank lower still.

Jane held her tightly, feeling the labouring heart under her hand, and the noiseless sobs that shook it. Then she began, piteously in a quiet voice, scarcely knowing what she said:

"Pater noster qui es in caelis..." and the Queen answered her at the end:

"*...Sed liber a nos a malo.*"

Then again after a long silence, the two rose together.

Mary was quiet enough after that, as her lady helped her to undress, laying the clothes aside one by one in the press beyond the bed, for they would not be needed on the morrow.

The Queen washed her face, slipped into bed, and lay there silent with closed eyes.

Jane looked at her once or twice as she went about the room with an agony of pity in her heart—at that ageing face, white and framed in her dark hair against the white pillow; at those thin down-turned sullen lips, those shadowed eyelids with the tiny lines at the angles, that sharp chin that had lost its softness, the cheeks that had lost their colour; and at the outline of the hands clasped on the breast beneath the rich lion-embroidered coverlet.

As she turned from the press at last after latching the doors, she saw that Mary's eyes were open and fixed on her.

"Sleep with me to-night," said the rough, piteous voice, "it will be the last time"

Jane went across to the bed and knelt down by it, laying her hands across the Queen's.

"Dear mistress!" she said, "you know I would die for you. But what can I do? Leave all to God. He knows all."

Mary turned her head away. Jane could only see the smooth neck beneath the heavy coiled hair.

"Madam," she said again, pressing the hidden hands tightly, "is there aught that I can do? You love him now, do you not?"

The Queen's face turned sharply back again, and it was alight with emotion.

"Love him?" she cried. "Who could but love him? And for all that he brings? Is he not a gallant Prince? But what of myself?"

"Madam—" began Jane again, but the Queen tore herself
free and sat up

"What of myself?" she cried again. "Oh! Jane will you lie to me like the rest? Am I not old and withered?"

"Ah! but your Grace is comely," said Jane in an agony. "Has he not told you that?"

Mary stared at her a moment; and then dropped back on the pillow.

"Well, well," she said, "I do not know—" her voice broke.

"Make haste and come to bed."

When the girl came back in her night-clothes a few minutes later she found the Queen lying on her side with closed eyes once more; her lips were parted and she seemed asleep.

Jane drew the curtains softly, and blew out all the candles but one tall one, that would burn till morning, which she set on the Queen's side of the bed, and then going round the tables where the wedding-clothes lay ready, she slipped softly between the sheets, unlooping the heavy tapestry so that it fell forward on her side too.

In the dark twilight of the shrouded bed she could make out the Queen's face lying towards her as she herself lay down.

Then she heard her name whispered, slipped towards her mistress, and took her in her arms without a word, and so they lay.

The deep silence settled down again; there was no sound in Jane's ears but the soft breathing on the pillow beside her, the tiny rustle of the sheet as it rose and fell with each breath, and the sensation rather than the sound of the beating heart against her own.

It was two hours later when she woke, for she heard a bell beat one o'clock, but a sound close beside her reminded her where she was before she moved.

The Queen was whispering in her sleep, but so low that the words were scarcely audible—only the whistle of breath and the movements of lips; but Jane thought she spoke Spanish.

Then she suddenly stirred and sighed and spoke aloud,

"Is he not gallant—my Prince?"

5

Master John Norris, gentleman-usher, was becoming a little tired with his long station in the cathedral.

He had stood there, on the south of the high altar for over an hour, and had looked at every detail fifty times over—at the huge stone canopied reredos overhead, with its central crucifix above and the glory of plate and tapers below, at the two tapestried traverses for the King and Queen, one beside him and one opposite, at the mortuary chests hung between earth and heaven in the screen on the other side with the striped arras behind it; at the northern row of the stalls disappearing westwards; at the high blazoned roof overhead, and the glimpse of the transept. Then he had brought out his beads and said them twice, then he had fallen to looking about him again. There was no one to whom he could talk; his friends were elsewhere, with the exception of Guy Manton, who faced him from the other side of the choir resplendent in his green and white and gold—he seemed sullen again, thought Jack, and stood staring moodily about him. Dick Kearsley and the other gentlemen were to come in her Grace's procession, and near himself there were only a couple of Hampshire squires in tight, ill-fitting clothing, who had somehow obtained places here, and were glaring solemnly at him and one another and their unfamiliar surroundings.

Jack became desperate. He could see so little from where he stood; the side of the Queen's traverse blocked out his view down into the nave, whence came a steady murmur of voices from the hundreds of folk gathered there.

He hesitated what to do; and as he hesitated, there came a sudden burst of sound, the murmur waxed to a roar, the pealing bells overhead clashed all together, the organs sounded out, and trumpets tore the air with a shattering cry.

Jack stepped softly forward from his place and looked out from behind the traverse.

Westwards stretched the choir, carpeted throughout its length, with a blaze of colour on either side, where the copes of the singing men and clerks, and the surplices of the boys—Tom Bradshawe among them—led by two lines down to the rood-screen where the mitred prelates stood raised high on the scaffold on which the wedding would take place Beyond, there was little to be seen, but the hangings of the nave with the sunlight on them, the vast white pillars and clerestory above now reverberating with sound, and between the rows of splendid figures beneath the rood screen a glimpse of the packed heads of the crowd.

The murmur of bells and music and talk grew louder yet as he stared; an instant later the prelates moved in their places, and Jack could see that a procession had come up and halted outside the choir. No doubt it was the King and his sixty Spanish nobles.

Then again the minutes began to pass slowly; the organs sank to a lower strain, the bells resolved into their measured peal again, and the murmur of the crowd died almost to a whisper.

Jack sighed, took out his beads once more, and began to tell them; and as his lips moved, his mind worked elsewhere.

He was sincerely pleased at the success of the whole affair, though he was amused at the emotions that were carrying it through. Her Grace's love-sickness was absurd enough; but her obstinacy was respectable, and would bear good fruit. There would be a prince no doubt in nine months; Philip would be little more than a King-Consort in the government of England; and would carry on his Spanish life of love and hot wine behind closed doors, though he might drink beer in public and say, "Good-night, my lords all," every night of his reign. But England would be pacified by an English prince; the wretched insular mingle-mangle of politics and faith would be done away with for ever, and the old ways would come back with the Cardinal next winter.

He looked round him again presently, as he thought of it, at the glory round him that told of the old worship for which this splendid place had been built, the curtained pyx above the altar, the rich credence-table, the canopy and the care-cloth laid ready, and all the rest, and as a devout Catholic he thanked Mary Queen of Heaven for Mary Queen of England, and began to attend to his Aves

Ten minutes later the exultant tumult of sound broke out again, and he knew that Mary was come.

Of the wedding itself he could see nothing and hear little. There was only the shining group dimly seen beyond the rood-screen raised high on the scaffold; and in the silence the murmur of voices, now one, now another. It was Bishop Gardiner's first—his, who had opposed the marriage, but would reap its harvest—Jack could hear little of what was said, and he had no book.

There was a question asked at last, and a silence; then a murmur, then a stupendous roar of applause Jack craned his head this way and that but could see nothing; no doubt it was the giving away of the bride by the four English peers, he told himself The applause sank to silence, a voice rose and fell murmurous and inaudible, and finally was drowned once more in cheering, the sudden clash of bells, and the cry of trumpets. Then as the organs began to make themselves heard, and the group outside the screen shifted and broke, Jack leapt back to his place.

They were coming up to the altar.

As the Latin psalm rolled out from the doubled choir, he was standing again erect at his station on the first step, with his back against the south screen, a yard from the two squires on either side, and to all appearances no more than a stiff

Court figure emotionless and correct. But his eyes moved from left to right steadily, as the stream came up and broke into glittering backwaters and eddies; he saw the scarlet and white and gold surge to the steps, then the five Bishops with their crosses—London, Durham, Lincoln, Ely, Chichester—and lingered on Winchester a moment as he came past and up to the altar, on his long, dark-round, chinned face, his full lower lip, his pleasant eyes, his curved black brows, his gorgeous mitre, his stiff jewelled vestments, his pontifical shoes

Then Jack's eyes turned suddenly back to the left, for here came the two for whom he looked

A great tasselled canopy moved along on four gilded staves with silver bells along its fringes, swaying and tinkling as it went, borne by four knights, and surrounded by others, up to the lower step of the altar, and there it stopped. Lord Derby stepped aside, bearing the sword of state, came towards Jack, wheeled and stood still; on the further side Lord Pembroke imitated him; the group dispersed, breaking the line of vision for a moment; the canopy moved off; and Jack could see clearly.

Two figures kneeled there on the step, gorgeous even to the courtier's eyes. Nearest him was the woman whose heart he thought he knew, in her brocade robe and satin kirtle, alight with diamonds on head and breast, her long train streaming from her shoulders three yards behind, a scarlet shoe just visible beneath it. She bore a taper in her hand, and her face was downcast. Jack could see her lips moving gently as she prayed Beyond her knelt her husband, bare-headed in the presence of the Most Holy Sacrament, he, too, in jewels and brocade and white satin, and with a taper in his hand; but his head was thrown back. Jack could see his yellow hair falling to his gold collar that bore the Order of the Fleece Behind the Queen stood Lord Winchester and Master Gage, who had borne her train, and behind them again the shining troop of ladies—the peeresses, Lady Margaret Clifford, Lady Magdalene Dacre, on whom his eyes rested a moment, Mistress Shirley and the rest. Beyond those the company of the Spanish nobles—the Duke of Alva, Don Cesar de Gonzaga, the Marquis de las Navas, and others, whom he already knew by sight, a squadron of gorgeous splendour behind the Prince.

The *Gloria Patrin*, sung by the full choirs of the Cathedral and the Queen's Chapel began to a bowing of heads; and the two kneeling figures rose together, adored, bowed one to the other, and separated each to a traverse Mary turned slowly to her right, and for a moment faced Jack Norris; then she passed on and disappeared round the corner of the traverse near which he stood, to go up to her seat.

But what he had seen held him so much astonished that he forgot to bow. He had expected dignity, magnificence and a rigid face, above all at this moment; but he had seen instead a passionate lover. Her face was flushed beneath her white coif, her lips parted and trembling, her dark eyes incredibly soft and ardent with love and tears. He had seen the great diamond on her breast rise and fall with her sobbing breath, and the swift look that she gave, as she turned, to her clasped hands on one of which, Jack knew, lay among her jewels the gold ring that made her wife.

The nuptial mass began; but he saw little of it. That radiant face was before him still; those eyes shallow and reserved no longer; those stiff sullen lips broken into curves of tenderness.

Did she then feel all that, for that gay spark opposite? Jack stared across at him; the Prince was kneeling in his seat; and over the screen of gold arras looked out that pear-shaped face, broad at the brows, narrow at the bearded chin, but his eyes were downcast in solemn devotion, and the cloth-of-silver edge of his great missal peeped over the line of the book-board Beneath and on either side stood the stately Spanish nobles, scarcely less gorgeous than their master, in white satin trunks, gold-clasped cloaks and great ruffs that seemed to support their dark faces as in plates of gauze and pearls.

Once more Jack remembered the Prince's reputation, and for an instant pity touched him for that woman, past her youth, but not past passion If it had been Magdalene Dacre now!

He saw her again presently as she moved out after the gospel to meet her husband and kneel once more side by side with him on the step; but this time he could see no more than her profile; and as she knelt all view was shut out by the nobles who held the care-cloth over the heads of the two.

At the altar the splendid movement went on; the Passion of Christ re-enacted itself in glorious drama, staged on the high carpeted footpace and interpreted by the gemmed figures of the three bishops who came and went and moved their hands and bowed their heads to tell the ineffable mystery; but the usher's eyes turned again and again to the curving line of the care-cloth between which Mary knelt beside her Prince.

A profound silence fell as the celebrant leaned forward with elbows on the altar and the white disc between his fingers; and when the few words were said, and the bell told to the crowds within and without that the Saviour of the world was come again to His own, from end to end the Cathedral murmured with sound as the worshippers relaxed their attitudes and kneeled back once more.

There was a soft chord on the organ presently; silence; a chord again, and with it a boy's voice began in deep contralto, inexpressibly moving

"*Agnus Dei*," pealed the sexless voice—" O Lamb of God, that takest away the sins of the world."

Jack craned his head in desperate desire to see Tom Ah! what a voice that was! He had only heard it in boarded rooms hitherto. Then he forgot; and abruptly turned his eyes back to the little human and divine drama of the kiss of peace. The Prince went up the steps and received it from Stephen Gardiner, returning again with stately and deliberate gait to where his wife waited to receive the kiss from him

Jack was kneeling, but he saw the care-cloth rise for a moment as Mary stood up, and then sink again a few inches as the kiss was given, and the two went on to their knees once more.

Ten minutes; later all was done, the celebrant had given the final benediction; the last gospel was read, and the hallowed sops and wine had been administered from a gold plate and cup to the two beneath the care-cloth.

Then as the canopy moved forward from the north to receive them, borne now by seven knights, the herald stepped forward m his tabard to announce the titles of the royal pair.

His voice pealed out the sonorous words, and the murmuring crowds hushed to hear the glorious arrogance:

Philippus et Maria, Dei gratia Rex et Regina Angliae, Franciae Neapolis, Hierusalem...Fider defensores.... Principes Hispaniarum et Srcihae.... Flandriae et Tyrohs...."

Then once more in English, that all might understand what had been done that day; how protesting kingdoms and states were claimed now under a single sceptre, and that the sceptre they would see presently pass down the nave on its red cushion; how the two mightiest powers of the world had clasped hands and kissed each other and would go out presently beneath one canopy to begin their journey of love and conquest side by side.

"Philip and Mary," cried the herald, "by the Grace of God King and Queen of England, France, Naples, Jerusalem and Ireland; Defenders of the Faith, King and Queen of Spam, Sicily, Leon and Arragon, Archdukes of Austria, Dukes of Milan, Burgundy and Brabant, Counts of Hasborough, Flanders and Tyrol, Lords of the islands of Sardinia, Majorca, Minorca, of the Firmland and the great ocean Sea; Palatines of Hamault and the Holy Empire, Lords of Friesland and Ireland, Governors of all Asia and Africa."

Jack's heart quickened as he heard it, and he felt really serious for the first time. This then was the beginning of peace, England and Spam were one, and the Vicar of Christ had sanctioned the union. In a few months his Legate would be here, and the reconciliation sealed. It was not possible that such a triumphant beginning could have any but a happy ending, if not for the Queen, at least for her kingdom.

Jack stepped from his place as the tinkling canopy moved off, and Guy Manton came forward to meet him; and, after a pause while those nearest the royal couple took their positions and wheeled westwards, the two ushers met, adored together and turned too.

It was an amazing procession.

Far m front moved the canopy with its tassels and bells swinging and the long lines of heads following; and as it came out under the rood screen from the shadowy choir into the white nave a tumult of cheering rose to met it, drowning the cry of the trumpets that went before, the melodious thunder overhead and the pealing organs.

The great west doors were open wide, and the daylight poured in through them and the huge coloured window upon the crowned heads on either side of the raised way along which the pageant went; and from among these rose a forest of waving hands and tossed caps to acclaim what had been done that day. There was little doubt what Hampshire folk thought, in the visible presence of splendour and strength; and they expressed it by roaring.

It was not until they had passed through the cloisters between the lines of guards, leaving the surging mob behind them at the west end of the Cathedral, had crossed the little stream between the planes, and come through the court of the Palace into the hall already hung and decked for the afternoon banquet, that Jack spoke to the man who had walked beside him in silence.

"Well?" he said; and then, "Tom sang Agnus Dei well."

"Yes, "said Guy.

Ille pustllus ac degener, qui…emendare mavult deos quam se
Sen *Epist.*

CHAPTER IV

MARY THE QUEEN HAS HER HEART'S DESIRE

1

FOUR months later on a November afternoon Mary stood alone in her room in Westminster well pleased. She was just come from Parliament; Philip had come with her and had left her not five minutes ago, after saying a word or two of congratulation, then he had smiled at her, kissed her hand, and gone out to his gentlemen

It was done at last; her third victory had been won First there had been the matter of her own coronation (she had fallen on her knees to win that), then there had been her marriage; and now there was the reversal of Cardinal Pole's attainder

Those three victories fulfilled her desire to reign as a Catholic Queen; there was but one more boon that she asked, and that God, not Parliament, could give her

She was very happy as she stood now in her rich riding dress and ruff with folded hands m the middle of her room, looking out with unseeing eyes at the roofs beyond her window. God was surely good to her! He had given her struggles enough and tears enough; but joy was come now She could surely trust Him for the rest—for the little anxieties that gnawed sometimes, the suspicions and the fears She would put them away and trust utterly.

She had held little Lord Darnley on her knees that afternoon, His mother had brought him up, and stood smiling down on the two, as the boy played with the jewels in Mary's hair

The Queen had asked him what he would do when he was a man; and he had said he would fight for his princess

"But your princess will be dead and gone," sighed Mary.

Then the boy had dropped the jewels, put up his face and kissed her, and she had seen his eyes grow bright with tears

"No, no," he had said.

As the Queen had set him down at last, she felt his warm lips on her hand, and watched him going to the door, she had been comforted. How gladly would she die, if she could leave a prince behind her as sturdy as this little Scottish noble!

As she stood there now with the happy thrill running through her and her eyes still bright with excitement and pleasure, there was a tap at the door, and Mistress Dormer came through with candles, for the evening was closing in.

"It is done, sweetheart," said the Queen gently, smiling at her.

Jane smiled back, and set the candles down.

"My lord Cardinal will come across in a few days," went on the Queen. "Kiss me, Jane, and say Laus Deo!"

Mistress Dormer came up to her, took the smiling face in her two hands, and kissed it softly over the eyes.

"Thank God," she said, "and your Grace's courage. My lord is here."

"My lord?" asked Mary puzzled.

"My lord of Winchester Your Grace said——"

Mary threw back her head "Why, yes—I had forgotten. Tell him, in five minutes "

Five minutes later the Queen passed out alone, and turned down towards the little chapel where the Bishop was awaiting her.

It was the little room where she had taken her vow to marry Philip, before her two or three witnesses—where she had knelt before the Sacrament and sung Vent Creator to guide her to a decision.

It was the same now, with its temporary altar, and new-fashioned standing-tabernacle, its gold candlesticks, its single lamp, its carved rail before the footpace.

The Bishop was sitting there now on a chair within the rail dimly seen in the half-light, and he did not rise as she came in; for he was judge and priest now, not courtier; and she no more than a penitent.

She went up the open space with clasped hands, adoed, knelt down and made the sign of the cross.

My lord's hand rose, and moved in the air to a murmur of Latin.

Then she sighed, for she had a great deal to say, and began.

There were a few external sins, first'—she had shown sullen-ness half a dozen times, had cried "By God!" once, had been guilty of venial gluttony at breakfast thrice, had yielded to irregular movements—she asked a question or two about these and was reassured—she had been guilty of wilful distractions at mass; and of pride three or four times in public.

Then she paused.

"There is more, father. May I speak at length? '

"If it is necessary, my daughter."

"It is necessary—I cannot say it otherwise…. It is this; I wish you to receive and bless a resolution that I will trust God. I have been distrustful; I have wondered whether He loved me—whether I were not deceiving myself…. It is this, father…. There is one whom I love…who…who is always courteous to me…. I—I—have listened to tales about this person…. I reproved them at the time…but I thought of them afterwards…. I—I wept one whole night alone, and reproached God…. I know now that I should not have thought of them again…. It was not loyal, and I am always asking for loyalty myself…I—told him once that he was unkind to me…and—and he never is, and he was not so then. He listened patiently, and told me it was not so. I wish to resolve that I will trust him, that I will not believe tales of him; or—or ask too much of him. ."

Her voice faltered a moment. No sound came from the Bishop.

Then she went on.

"Then there is another matter, father…I desire to have a son…. I have not trusted God in that…I have thought I knew better than He…Now He has…has shown me I shall have one; and I am very sorry I did not trust Him more. I am very happy and very sorry. I wish to resolve now that I will trust Him in any event...whether or no..."

"I understand, my daughter," said the voice over her head gently.

Mary writhed her fingers together on the altar-rail.

"I must say it, father; it will help me.... Whether it be only a daughter...or...or even if the child be not born alive."

She gave a great sob, and bit her quivering lips

"I understand, my daughter, "said the Bishop again. "You wish to trust God whatever may befall. That is a good resolution, it is the way to win His blessing "

Mary drew a long breath, and went on.

"There is another matter, too, different from the rest. It is this. God has sent me here to do my duty; to punish ill-doers as well as to cherish the well-doers.... You have told me so, father, when I asked you once before. And...and I do not know how to hold back my passion.... I hate heresy so much; I know that they are the enemies of God's Church..."

"Their heresy, my daughter," corrected the Bishop.

"Yes...their heresy.... I must punish soon...they cannot go on...they insult God more every day; and...and I fear to punish too hotly. How can I tell, father, whether it is my passion or not?"

"You cannot tell," said the voice decisively. "You can but control your action in this. You must punish indeed, but you need not seek out yet You can be merciful in that."

Mary nodded; it was what she had intended.

"Is that all?" asked the voice.

Mary hesitated.

"Yes; that is all, father; except..."

"Well, my daughter."

"Tell me how to trust God and—and him."

The Bishop was silent a moment.

"They are one and the same resolution. If you trust God you will trust the other as well. To trust a friend is not to believe that he can do no wrong; we must trust no man like that; for all fall at times. You, especially, must trust no man like that. You must commit yourself wholly to none other than God. Therefore we do not trust God in the same manner in which we trust man. We trust Him, and Him alone."

The voice hesitated

Mary looked up swiftly for a moment and saw the profile of the prelate's face, with long shadows drooping across it from the lamp overhead. It seemed troubled.

"I do not understand, father"

The voice went on with an effort.

"I mean, my daughter, that we must not set men on the throne of God."

Again there was silence.

"Is that plain?" asked the voice again.

"It is plain, and it is what I have done," said Mary.

"Grief and disappointment lie that way," said the Bishop softly. "No man may do that, least of all a prince. Permereges regnant, et legum conditores"

Mary bowed her head on her hands. She was disappointed and perplexed. It had seemed so easy just now to resolve to trust God and Philip; but this was a hard doctrine Yet she knew it for true

"This then should be your resolution," went on Gardiner, "to trust God, and to believe no evil lightly."

"There was no answer

"Do you accept that, my daughter"

"I accept it."

"And is there aught more"

"There is no more."

When penance and absolution had been given, the Bishop rose.

The Queen looked up for a moment

"I wish to see you, my lord. Will you wait for me?"

"I will wait, your Grace."

When he was gone out, matters seemed to clear a little. What he had said was perfectly true; and she recognised it. She had put Philip at least too near God's throne, and had then reproached him that he was not wholly worthy of it. But even now she did not dare to think of him as anything but a faithful lover. He might be a little cold; that was but natural for a foreigner in a strange country; it was his character, too; she must not ask that he should be exactly as she was What love or confidence could there be under such a demand? But the stories that were whispered were false, she assured herself once more; black lies intended to poison this spring of joy that she had found. No, no Philip was true and loving and courteous, and she was a wicked woman to have dreamed he could be otherwise. What could be more courteous than his manner towards her; or—or more ardent?...

Then she bowed her head again and prayed that she might be worthy of his love; she thanked God for having had pity on her at last in sending love into her life; she entreated him again to crown his gifts and fulfil His hinted promise; but she renewed her resolution to trust Him utterly Then she thanked Him for absolution, said her penance, and went to find Gardiner.

He was in her private room where the candles were now burning, and came across in his rochet and cap to kiss her hand.

Then she told him of the Cardinal, and he congratulated her on her victory.

"My lord will be here in a week, I hope," said the Queen. "He has been knocking long at the door of England."

"As Peter at Rhoda's wicket," said the Bishop smiling.

"Yes, as he said; it is Peter who comes, not Pole. My lord Montague will meet him and bring him to town."

"Your Grace has done a great work."

"We hope that God will do so," said Mary shortly.

There was silence a moment. Then the Bishop went on.

"It is true, your Grace, that the Lady Elizabeth perseveres? '

"It is true," said Mary a little coldly "Her Highness hears two masses each day, and frequents the Sacraments.

"That is good news, madam!"

Mary lifted her chin a little

"I wish you to go to Lambeth, my lord, and see that all is m readiness My lord Cardinal will go there at once as you know. My lord of Canterbury—" she stopped.

Gardiner glanced at her under his black eyebrows.

"We will deal with him," she said. "He is still Archbishop."

She asked a question or two presently about the effect of the Articles that the Bishop of London had put out during his visitation two months before.

"There are some malcontents," said the other. "How should there not be, your Grace?"

"I fear that Parliament will be too urgent," said Mary; "there is talk of the bill against heresy I know not how that will be. I would my lord Norfolk had not left us for Paradise."

"We must wait for my lord Cardinal to bring us Paradise instead," said the Bishop smiling.

"All waits for him. To me he comes as an angel of God. Then you will go to Lambeth, my lord, and come and tell me again to-morrow."

But the Bishop's face lost its smooth gaiety as he went across the court to his carriage. There was another side to the tale of which the two had not spoken, though they both knew it to be true.

2

On the Saturday of the following week the Court was awaiting the arrival of Reginald Pole

Couriers had come in day by day to Westminster announcing his movements since he had landed at Dover on the evening of the twentieth; his welcome by the escort on the following day, his torchlight reception at Canterbury and Sittingbourne, his progress northwards. Early on the Saturday a messenger had arrived in haste to say that the Cardinal would enter the Queen's barge at Gravesend, as had been arranged, and come up with the tide to Westminster a little after midday; and that he desired now to be received with legatine honours.

The last preparations had been hurried through Lambeth had been made ready, for he would go on there to dine immediately after paying his respects at Westminster. Whitehall stairs, where he would land, and the rooms through which he would pass, had been hung with scarier to do honour to his dignity; and a cloth-of-estate erected in the Great Hall.

The Queen had given all directions herself, and had visited the hall and the stairs before going in to dinner, and now was seated at table in her own chamber opening out of the King's Hall, silent and exultant, with Philip at her side.

The two hardly spoke to one another, except a short sentence now and again in Spanish, and the attendants went about their business swift and alert. Special sentries were set at the water-gate outside with instructions to send news in immediately at the first sign of the Cardinal's approach.

It seemed to Mary that she was in a dream too good to be true. With a strange exultation she had thanked God that morning at mass for the hundredth time that it was she who had been raised up by Him to undo the work of her father and brother. This poor country of hers, like a lopped limb, had been shedding blood and life for the last twenty years, separated from the Heart of Christendom that alone could nourish it; but God had not forgotten. He had been preparing a heavenly physician—a man who had suffered bitterly for the Faith, who had lived in exile on its behalf, who had unflinchingly received the news of his own mother's death in the same cause, and whose love had never been soured by resentment or despair. She, too, had suffered; and it was she whom God's Providence had guarded so long and through so sore perils, to be the means of bringing God's chirur-geon home again to do his healing work "0 Lamb of God," her heart, still responsive to the memory of Winchester, had cried with the priest at mass, "O Lamb of God that takest away the sins of the world, take away England's sin; have mercy upon us, and give us peace!"

She was in a mystical mood this morning at dinner. It appeared to her that all things bore a sacramental aspect. The scarlet cloth was to her stained by the Precious Blood through which redemption should come again, Christ's Blood and Roman scarlet were one thing; the beams across the lower end of the chamber were the Rood of Salvation; the very hypocras as she circled it in her deep golden cup was mingled red and white as the stream that flowed from the Saviour's side; the cold winter sunlight that poured in through the high windows sprang from the dawn of Righteousness.

There was a long silence as the capons were removed; Philip turned to her and said something; she scarcely heard what, as she answered it mechanically, for she was looking down the hall to the door by which the messenger would come. And as she answered, he came.

There was a quick movement of heads, a whisper, and then a profound stillness, as an officer of the guard hurried through, and after a swift salutation to the dais, came up with a page leading him to where they sat.

She saw him kneel again as he reached the opposite side of the table, rise, and then his lips move. Without hearing the words she knew what they meant, and rose swiftly. Philip rose a moment later, turned to her with a word, bowed ceremoniously, and passed out of his place, and she saw him go down the room with his deliberate dignified gait, and his gentlemen close in behind him Then she sat down and waited, irresolute.

The omen seemed so good! He had come an hour before he was expected!

Surely the tide had borne him gladly, knowing what it was he brought, and how the dying land desired him. The flood of England's filth and refuse was checked by the ardour of the inflowing sea, for the silver cross of God's legate had moved upon it and turned it back.

Then again she rose; she could not wait there

There was a movement as she came forward down the hall; a couple of ushers ran out and went before her; and half a dozen ladies came behind; but she was scarcely aware of them as she passed down the rushes and out on to the head of the staircase.

There she stopped, an upright stiff figure, with her hands folded decorously before her, and an impassive face.

She had had his letters so often; he had been described to her; his tenderness, his discretion, his simplicity were all known to her, but not his face. She would see that, too, in a moment now.

There was the crash of music below, but she stood rigid with cold eyes cast down the slope of the stairs. Then she saw figures advancing; and her heart leapt and sent a flood of crimson through her cheeks; it paled again and left her white.

In front up the stairs came her husband looking strangely small and tawdry in his jewels beside the solemn splendour of the figure which walked with him. This man was in plain scarlet and white from head to foot. A scarlet cap lay on his brown hair and on scarlet again beneath the veil of his long beard shone a single gleam of jewels.

From above looked up at her large soft brown eyes, and they were fixed on hers that shook to meet them.

She was hardly aware of the crowd of faces that followed, of Stephen Gardiner in the immediate rear, Lords Montague and Arundel behind, and others, of the silver light of the legatine cross in the shadow of the archway.

What was that movement within her? Was it only the leaping of her heart?...

He was close to her now, his eyes on a level with hers before he bowed, and then as if to interpret her question he spoke.

"Ave Maria—gratia plena—Dominus tecum; benedicta tu in mulienbus——"

He paused for one intense instant.

"Et benedictus fructus ventris tut."

Ah! she knew now; God's legate had spoken and confirmed it.

Then she took his hands and kissed him on both cheeks.

Half an hour later she took his hands again, as he turned to go from beneath the cloth-of-estate in the Great Hall where the three had stood and talked with all eyes upon them

He had given her news of the Holy Father, of his desires and prayers for England, of his joy in his faithful daughter, of his promises of grace for the prodigal country returning at last to the Father's house. She had questioned him about his journey and his health, had asked him of his reception at Dover and

Canterbury, and had listened to his soft voice as he told her how suffering had made him old before his time, but that the joy of the present had given him back his youth He had described his journey, his joy at Calais, the watch-word of the garrison there, "Godlong-lost is found," his swift crossing to Dover and the fall of the wind.

He had been so courteous, so strong and tender, as he looked at her and told her of his hopes.

Philip's tact, too, had not deserted him. He had smiled at her, taken her hand and kissed it, as she looked at him a moment, hesitating to tell him that the babe had leapt in her womb at the coming of the Lord's Anointed

"There shall be a Te Deum on Monday," she cried incoherently—and then broke off, checked by the shame and wonder of it. *"Facti sumus sicut consolati"*

The Cardinal finished the quotation.

"Dicent inter gentes, magnificavit Dommus facere nobiscum."

Then he smiled again as he took her hands to say good-bye.

But she still held him a moment.

"Then on Monday, my lord, we shall see you again"

"On Monday, madam"

"And you will tell us all that you wish?"

He bowed to her deprecatingly.

"My lord of Winchester will go with you now," went on Mary. "I trust that all is ready We have so looked for you, cousin."

His eyes moved from hers to Philip's and back again; and the King added another word or two in broken English.

"His heart is sounder than his tongue," said Mary smiling.

She touched Philip's sleeve softly with her fingers, and let them rest there a moment.

"Now you must not lose the tide," she added.

"It brought me swiftly enough——" began Pole.

Mary turned on him with her eyes alight "Ah you thought so, too, my lord, as I thought it. But the tide was not so strong as my desire."

She saw the axemen and pillar-bearers detach themselves from the crowd about the door as the Cardinal turned round; and the gleam of the silver emblems that had not been seen in England since Wolsey's fall a quarter of a century ago. She drew her breath swiftly at the sight

"Ah!" she exclaimed, and stopped as Pole faced her again.

"The pillars and the axes!" she cried, like a child at a new toy

"Christ's strength and justice," said the Cardinal smiling

She had more leisure to observe the other faces now, as the group reformed before passing out to the stairs where the royal barge still waited She saw Gardiner's kindly eyes without the shadow of resentment in them at the coming of an ecclesiastic greater than himself, he was smiling and bowing as he took his place beside the ruddy stalwart Bishop of London Dr. Bonner seemed glad enough, too. Perhaps, she thought, he was not unwilling to have the heavy burden lightened to his shoulders. She looked at her husband again, and what she saw beneath that courtly foreign mask satisfied her. He was acting no part in his welcome of the legate Renard was there, happy and ardent. De Noailles' face showed nothing, as usual.

There was not one scowling or uninterested look that she could see. All were content, it seemed to be, and Mary herself stood joyous and exultant as she watched the stately procession go down the Great Hall.

As it came beneath the lantern she glanced round again with a kind of pride at the rows of faces on either side immediately below the dais—at Mr. Norris' excited eyes as he craned forward to look from the row of ushers, at Mr. Kearsley's lean twitching mouth, then she caught sight of Mr. Manton's, and it was not like the others. He was staring straight at her gloomily with pursed lips. He dropped his eyes as she looked

She felt a rush of resentment at the tiny dark detail; but it was swept away again a moment later as a ripple of movement broke out.

A cap went up and a shout, and in an instant the roof rang with cheering

"Philip and Mary," "Philip and Mary," "Philip and Mary and Reginald Pole"—these were the shouts, as the pageant went down; and the trumpets took up the jubilee outside the wide-flung doors. The gentlemen had forgotten to kneel and the ladies to curtsey as the two heads went past, one shining with jewels and a great feather, the other crowned with the little scarlet cap of a Prince of the Blood Royal of Jesus

She saw the bright spot of clean colour turn this way and that as its wearer acknowledged the storm of greetings; it reached the open door, and the sunlight in a moment struck a vivid vermilion from it, and a blaze from the diamonds at its side.

Then it disappeared, and that strange sensation tore again through Mary's body.

"Magnificat..." she whispered, as she swayed and reeled a moment, and her ladies leapt forward. *"Magnificat anima mea Dominutn."*

3

The Queen did not forget the glimpse she had had of Guy Manton's face in the Great Hall as the Cardinal went out. It provoked her in the acute manner in which only a small discomfort in the midst of prosperity can provoke. It was like the toothache during a triumph.

She found herself dwelling upon the minute detail in a manner utterly disproportioned to its insignificance Her superstitious conscientiousness picked it out from the vast affairs which surrounded her, and demanded that it should be dealt with at once.

First she thought of dismissing him, for she had noticed his sullenness before now, then of ignoring him; and finally she made time for two conversations, one about him and one with him.

She sent for Master Norris after High Mass next day

He came to her in the parlour where she was waiting before going to dinner: and she began by speaking about the events of the day before, and her anxiety for the Cardinal's comfort.

"It was a glorious day, madam," he burst out, "thanks to your Grace's courage."

Mary put on her stiffest expression.

"Thanks to God's mercy," she said.

"And to your Grace's correspondence with it," persisted the theologian.

"It was not to receive compliments that I sent for you," went on Mary, drumming her rings impatiently, "but to send you on an errand. Master Englefield is to go across to Lambeth this afternoon about to-morrow's affair; and I wish two of my gentlemen to go with him besides his own."

"Yes, madam," said Jack delightedly.

"Whom will you take with you, sir?"

Jack Norris, as lieutenant of the gentlemen pensioners, had such matters more or less under his control, and he mentioned two or three names. Guy Manton's was not among them.

Mary considered a moment.

"Yes," she said, "I should wish for more discreet persons. What of Master Manton?"

Jack was silent.

"Have you anything against him, sir?"

Her voice rang hard, and the young man looked up astonished.

"Nothing, madam, except   "

"Well, sir? Is he not discreet?"

"Oh! he is discreet, your Grace——"

Mary lowered her eyelids a little at his tone.

"Well?" she said.

"He is not very well affected madam," burst out Jack at last. "He has spoken of asking your Grace's leave to go back to Cambridge."

The Queen was silent.

"I do not mean that he is anything bat loyal, your Grace, or other than a good Catholic"

"Well, sir, what is his complaint?"

"He thinks that your Grace does not use him enough," explained Jack anxiously. "He says that there is nothing to do."

"Ah!" said Mary, and sat drumming her fingers again.

Jack was afraid that he had said too much. He had no wish that Guy should get into trouble, and he began to explain again, but the Queen cut him short with a gesture

"That will do, Mr. Norris"

Then she sat silent again

Jack looked at her once or twice, but could make nothing of that discreet tight-lipped face. It did not appear pleased and yet he did not see what else he could have answered.

Finally Mary spoke again

"Very well, sir, I will speak to Master Manton myself and release him if he wishes it, but you must not tell him so. Will you send him to me after dinner, and m the meantime do not tell any of the other gentlemen that you will want them Perhaps Master Manton will go with you himself. He shall take you a message when he leaves me this afternoon."

The Queen was very thoughtful during dinner. She was astonished herself at the interest she took in this young man from Cambridge, and at the lack of it which she had shown. She felt the justice of his complaint, it was true enough that she had sent for him to Court intending to reward him and to give him suitable employment, and it was equally true that she had not done so She was not altogether displeased at the knowledge that he resented this treatment, and was ill-content with mere idleness and fine clothes and servants and horses. This then was the secret of those gloomy looks that she had noticed from time to time, and especially yesterday; he felt that he was no more than a spectator when he had hoped to be an actor. She would remedy it now, and make a beginning by sending him to Lambeth and arranging that he should have a personal introduction to the Cardinal But was that the only secret of his depression?

She said a private word to Sir Francis Englefield as she went out from dinner, and then passed on to her parlour to await Guy.

He had a restrained air as he came in, made his salutation, and stood upright again opposite her chair She noticed his capable square hand holding his cap, and his straight passionless lips, as she began to speak

"I wish you to go to Lambeth with Master Englefield," she said, "Master Norris is to go also, and some others. It is on the matter of to-morrow"

Guy bowed stiffly.

"I told Master Norris that I needed discreet persons to go with him, though it is no matter of great importance, and spoke your name to him"

Guy bowed again, but said nothing.

The Queen felt annoyed; it was no more easy to her to pay veiled compliments than to receive them, but she determined to be patient.

"I hope to employ you more, sir, in the future than I have done in the past. You understand of course that it is necessary for my servants to learn my purposes—and—and circumstances before they can do my business.... You do not say anything, Master Manton"

"I have had few opportunities, your Grace," began Guy coldly

"It is half-a-year now," went on Mary, disregarding him, for she did not mean to allow him to complain: "it is half-a-year now since you entered my service You will have learnt much in that time. I shall hope to employ you now in many matters, and if you acquit yourself well, I shall commit important things to your hand. But you must be patient, Master Manton, and you must be ready to find employment for yourself I need eyes about me at all times, and you must be very shrewd and silent, and prepared to wait."

She looked at him again, and met the look from his brown eyes. It was an interested one and that touch of sullenness was almost gone from it. But it was not altogether friendly.

"I cannot find employment myself for all my servants," she went on. "I can only give them opportunities for finding it. But there is enough for all, God knows!" she ended with energy.

"Yes, madam," said Guy.

"I have told Master Englefield to make you known to my lord Cardinal. It is round Lambeth now that the wheel will turn. But you must watch on all sides."

"Yes, madam"

"Next year there will be the affair at Oxford. I do not know how soon we may set our hands to that I shall hope to send you there You understand a University, and may be able to do some work there."

His face brightened visibly as she talked, and she understood more clearly than ever that it was her apparent neglect of him that had given him his sour looks Yet she was conscious that the barrier was not wholly gone; there was a hardness in the young man's air that she had not noticed before. Was this just one more case of alienation from her own unloveable personality? She determined to step on to yet more intimate ground.

"It is a happy time for us all now that my lord Cardinal is here You were in the Hall, yesterday, Master Manton?"

"Yes, madam."

"And you will be present, too, on Saint Andrew's Day. We must pray that all will go well."

She waited for an answer but none came. She perceived that she must give him time, and that sullenness is not dispelled by a single friendly conversation.

She rose and gave him her hand again

"The King's Majesty is gone to the tournament, is he not?"

"Yes, madam I saw his Highness ride out as I came in"

"Then I must begone after him," said Mary smiling.

But she stood a moment or two, when he had gone, with her lips sucked in, mechanically stroking the two carved rampant beasts on the mantel-piece, that guarded her lilies and leopards with one claw and menaced the crown with the other

What was wrong, she asked herself, that she could not win love from her people?

Surely she had been kind enough to this young man—perhaps too kind! Yet there was no doubt that she had not his sympathy. And there were many like him.

Well, well, she must leave all to God. He was doing miracles for England

4

She awoke early on the morning of Saint Andrew's Day, signed herself with the cross, murmured a Latin word or two and turned softly over onto the other side.

She was alone in bed; but she could hear the steady breathing of one of her ladies who slept beside the door. She drew back the heavy edge of the curtain, and peered out. The tall candle lit last night was burning to its death, but there was no glimmer of dawn yet from the window across the room, and the palace was still silent.

Mary reached out a hand to the prie-dieu, took from it a prayer-book, opened it and read softly the prayer for the Unity of the Catholic Church that she had used for twenty years; then turned the pages, and found that which she had only used for a fortnight—the prayer for the delivery of a woman in child-birth; read that too, smiling; closed the book, repeated a Paternoster and a couple of Aves, and lay still.

Picture after picture began to form in her mind of the events of the last few days. She saw again the high staircase, and the two caps ascending it; the gleam of the silver emblems; and heard the roaring of the crowd Then she saw the Cardinal again as he was on Monday when he came for the audience; he looked less tired after a day's rest, and had spoken with more animation. She saw, too, the tanned face of the courier in the back-ground—he had ridden hard from Rome and had arrived a few hours before with the final dispensations. She remembered how he had spoken, giving glory to God for the speed with which he had been able to come.

On the Tuesday there had been more business—the inspection of documents. She thought of the paper which the Lord Chancellor had laid before her, the smooth-written lines containing in black ink the short speech he proposed to make to Parliament. She had suggested a word or two of alteration, and he had made the corrections then and there; she saw again his brown hand with the great amethyst upon it, and the white-plumed quill above.

On the Wednesday there had been the meeting in the Great Hall She 'had been carried to it in her chair, and had sat side by side with Philip beneath the canopy, with the Cardinal on her right. She saw once more the Lord Chancellor Gardiner in his robes, and the intent faces turned up to him, and heard his strong voice rehearsing the little speech he had prepared. Then the legate had answered, she had leaned forward to listen to his smooth-flowing English and his queer mystical similes of clocks and lamps and the temple at Jerusalem He had traced in his soft virile voice the religious history of England, too, from its conversion to its apostacy under the man by whom his own death had been sought. There had been curious movements among the audience; she had seen a Bishop's lips twitching; Master Walde-grave, her old friend, had clasped his hands suddenly; my lord of Winchester had cast a swift glance at her and down again; someone had cried out in applause near the door

Then she and her husband and the legate had gone out together through the bowing crowd, after a few more words from Gardiner, and had left the Lords and Commons to consider the matter.

On the Thursday she had received the news of their final debate; first officially, and then she and Philip together had heard the story from the Lord Chancellor. There had been no dissentients among the Lords, and only two among the Commons: Master Bagenall had made a little speech saying that he still held with King Henry against the Pope She had watched Gardiner's face as he talked; and it came before her again now as she lay in bed with closed eyes— its kindliness, its solemn exultation. He had kissed her hand fervently before he went out

The faces came and went; she heard the rustle of skirts, the cry of trumpets, a murmur of applause. Then a figure came vivid and distinct; it was her husband; his back was turned to her, and she saw his gold collar and his yellow hair, and the swaying of his shoulders as he went Where was he going? Why would he not turn round as she called?...

Then there was a voice speaking, a flood of light poured into her eyes, and she awoke with her woman's face bending over her.

She did not go to the High Mass at the Abbey that morning; her doctors had told her to spare all exertion She had been reconciled to that when she heard that the Cardinal would not go either; and that he was reserving himself for the fierce emotion of the afternoon

She had kissed Philip before he went, laying her hands on the collar of the Golden Fleece that crossed his shoulders, and had watched him down the gallery with his gentlemen behind him, as he went to meet the six hundred nobles who waited in the court below

Then she passed back, said her prayers, heard a low mass in her little chapel, and went to dinner

It was after four o'clock, and candles were alight, when she came down to the chamber opening out of the Great Hall.

She sat down there on a chair set for her, feeling horribly ill, and waited a few minutes Mistress Dormer brought her a cup, and she drank mechanically, giving it back half-drained.

Then the silent group by the door stirred and rustled, and the King and the Cardinal came in together.

She stood up to receive them, but they looked strange to her eyes. The vermilion of her cousin's dress bewildered her, it all seemed like some unfamiliar play, and she did not know her part. Her hands were icy-cold and wet, as she clasped them and stood staring and silent She made an effort presently and said a word or two, as she listened to the stir and hum from the Great Hall outside. They were all there then, all ready to receive pardon and the kiss of the Catholic Church

Then she found herself walking by her husband, the heads bobbed and swayed before her. She became aware of a tumult in her ears, of tiers of faces on either side, colours and jewels, the white of a row of rochets on her left, a great gold canopy over head.

There were steps to be ascended, and she went up them falteringly; she felt Philip's hand for a moment beneath her arm, and she closed her fingers on it

Then she was seated, and the hall lay before her

The Commons were immediately in front, facing her, a bank of white faces m the gathering gloom, on the right were the bishops, on the left the temporal peers, at the further end a crowd of other blurred faces. Overhead the roof was darkening every moment as the evening drew in, and along the walls a few lights threw patches of brightness on to the heads below....

The Lord Chancellor was speaking now, but she scarcely heard what was said. She looked at him raised on a stage, and strove to understand

The voice murmured on, and she forgot to realise it Then it paused, and a thunderclap of assent rose from four hunded voices

"We do"

And with that she understood.

Here then they were, the representatives of the nation given her by God to rule to His glory and to bring back to His fold. All England was here, of which she was Queen and Mother, once more at the feet of Christ's Vicar, the wild beasts with whom she had fought, who had snarled so fiercely and sought to tear her down as they had torn down God's Body from their churches, the tender lambs who had cried so piteously from hamlet and back street and country-lanes, wandering without a shepherd, starving for lack of wholesome food; the wise leaders of the flock who had hesitated, turned and run for lack of knowledge—all those were here in the darkening hall, tamed and comforted and guided at last

And were there not others here, too—presences at the high luminous windows, eyes looking down from the shadow of the roof, wings and forms crowding the air, figures of those who had suffered and died, bodyless creatures of God who had prayed and striven and sought to protect those others in the days of trouble. It was here that Master More had walked and read his doom in the face of his judge, it was here that her father—

She closed her eyes a moment, bewildered and overwhelmed. These were here, and more besides. For an instant there seemed silence in heaven, a silence of wonder before a shout of praise and a silence in which God smiles as He opens His hands that flow with grace and gifts

Then the physical emotion gripped her throat; she began to sob quietly.

A paper was put before her; and she saw, through tears, Gardiner on his knees She looked through the paper, understanding not one word that was written on it, and handed it silently to Philip

Then the Lord Chancellor was reading it from the steps of the throne She watched his profile and the movements of his lips as he held the writing near his eyes, and now and again heard what he was reading.

It was Latin, but she understood here and there

"——the Most Reverend Father in God the Lord Cardinal Pole, Legate. our Most Holy Father Pope Julius the Third and the A postolic See of Rome…the abrogation and repeal of the said laws and ordinances…From the Apostolic See by the said Most Reverend Father…absolution, release and discharge from…such censures and sentences…Repentant children . . the bosom and unity of Christ's Church…serve God and your Majesties…."

He was on his knees again now, and a voice whispered to her to take the paper and stand up

This was a different paper, and she held it for a moment, not understanding what was required.

Then she began to read, hearing her own deep voice with astonishment. It was some kind of request for reconciliation. So much she gathered, but not more; though she had pored over the paper with delight two days before

She was back again in her seat now, sitting tense and upright while a murmur of applause rose and sank. Other voices were reading, she heard a Southern accent from her side; it was Philip who was reading; then another, and then silence and the darkness thickened.

Then a breeze seemed to pass and sweep the clouds once more from her throbbing brain. It was Reginald Pole who was talking, and the associations of strength and healing that were for her already connected with his voice, refreshed and uplifted her.

He was telling the silent slopes of faces before him how much they must thank God for His mercies, who was calling again the people who lived in darkness to see a great light. As they had been the first of the Northern nations to turn to Christ from idols, so they were first again to return from schism. Again his thought rose and embraced her own

"How much would the angels," he said in his quiet voice, as he sat in his chair, the legate of the Ruler of Kings, "how much would the angels who rejoice over one sinner that repenteth, lift up their voices in thanks giving over the return of so noble a people."

There fell again a deep heart-shaking silence, and Pole stood up.

For a moment Mary looked at him, at the red glow of robes that burned in the gloom like flowers at sunset, at his clean-cut profile above his soft beard, and the little scarlet cap that crowned him.

As his hand rose, she understood that the moment was come. She too rose, grasping her chair, and sank on to her knees.

There was a rustle through the hall, the groan and rattle of benches, the surge up and down of faces as the whole assembly rose and fell forward on to their knees.

Silence fell again, a silence that blended strangely with the darkness, a pause in which it seemed that the whole kingdom, come to its senses at last, waited with passionate patience for the descent of peace.

Then the voice began, very slow and tender and deliberate.

"Domtnus noster Jesus Chrislus...."

The clouds were gone now from the Queen's brain; it seemed to her that she was resting "in some mellow landscape, content and tranquil and desirous all at once Across it lay a light that was brightening with every word, from some source that she could not understand, a healing flood of grace that warmed and lightened as it fell. There was but one distraction, and that the tumult of her own body, she strove to arrest the trembling, to force back the sobs that tore her, to silence the hammering in heart and throat and brain—yet above the struggle her spirit lay as in a deep lawn of peace, with the summer sky above it, the bubble of bird-song in her ears, the sound of running water, and a vast content enfolding her. She felt she would like to die so

Her brain too was alert and illuminated, and she understood every word

"Our Lord Jesus Christ, who with His most precious blood hath redeemed and washed us from all our sms and iniquities, that he might purchase us unto Himself a glorious spouse without spot or wrinkle, Whom the Father hath appointed Head over all His Church He by His mercy absolves you. And we, by the Apostolic Authority committed unto us by the Most Holy Lord, Pope Julius the Third, His Vice-gerent on earth, do absolve and deliver you, all and single, together with this whole realm and its dominions, from all heresy and schism, and from all and every judgment, pain and censure from that cause incurred.

"And we do restore you once more into the unity of our Holy Mother Church

"In the Name of the Father, of the Son, and of the Holy Ghost"

An indescribable tumult of weeping and laughter and assent surged up from the hall.

BOOK II

Facile est miserum inridere.
Plaut. *Curcul*

CHAPTER I

MASTER MANTON KNOWS THE QUEEN BETTER

I

GUY MANTON was lounging in the parlour after dinner on a warm April day, six months later, wondering what he could do with himself.

Hampton Court was terribly dull. The household had moved down there before Easter, for the Queen's confinement, public prayers and processions had been ordered for her safe delivery, doctors were in attendance to help her, and couriers to bear the joyful news to town; and yet she delayed to fulfil her part. And meanwhile her household had to wait.

Guy was becoming very much bored by the whole affair of the Court. He had nothing to do of any importance; his interview with the Cardinal had ended in words, though he had been a little interested by the personality of Monsignor Priuli, the prelate's friend and chaplain; and the events of the winter, the concerts and masques at Christmas, the visits of Elizabeth and Courtenay, and the coming of the foreign princes, had not served to compensate him for his sense of uselessness

As regarded his attitude to the Queen, he knew very well how he stood She was a tiresome, shrewish, self-centred, disappointing woman, with neither wit nor tenderness There was a certain pathos about her, but of the contemptible sort; she had the smallness that one desires to trample, not to help Intellectually, he knew her to be pitiable; her circumstances seemed harder than flesh and blood could bear; but, emotionally he was only affected by her with a kind of resentment. He knew himself disillusioned of his dreams, and with disillusionment had come hardness; he did not care greatly whether he went or stayed

For the present, however, he was holding on to his position; there was no knowing what might not happen if a child were born to Mary; and his fellowship had been filled up at Gonville College He yearned for brisk movement.

He felt half inclined now to fetch a Greek author and read in him for a little; but he had given up his classics for eight months, and had lost his taste for them. Besides, it was not reading but action that he wanted So he sat m the window-seat with his legs spread abroad, and yawned out at the empty sunlit-court and the rows of solemn windows opposite

He saw Jack coming across presently and called to him. Jack nodded abruptly, and presently strode in with a very dark look on his face He banged the door and took up his position on the hearth

"That damned monkey of a misbegotten Spaniard had been at his tricks again Have you heard the tale"

"Which?" said Guy

"Of my lady Magdalene."

"I have not"

"Well, listen to this then," growled Jack with a very sour look in his eyes "You know her room with the window opening on to the gallery"

"Well?"

"My lady was dressing there this morning, and the foolish child had the window open His Highness comes along to mass, and spies her He scarce knows enough English to make love in it—her Grace has not taught him yet, but there is one tongue that all understand So his highness pushes the window wider, and puts in his black hand to take my lady's bare arm."

"Well?"

"Well" cried Jack "And is not that enough? So my lady answers him in the same tongue, turns scarlet, and cracks him across the fingers with her staff She has spirit, thank God"

"It is only one more of them," drawled Guy, hoping to make him angry "Her Grace is generous"

Jack growled and held his tongue

"And how have you prospered with my lady?"

Jack sighed

"She listens to my singing and my talk and goes her way heart-whole."

Guy yawned and stood up.

"Ride with me, Jack," he said. "I shall go mad if this goes on."

"It is her Grace's fault," observed the other. "It is she and her blessed child who hold us here Delivery or death is our only hope."

"And you think she does not know about His Highness and his loves?" asked Guy curiously

"She wills not to know," said Jack decisively, "she dares not ask, and none dare tell her"

A little snort of contempt broke from Guy.

"Was there ever such a woman?" he cried "She lies here a-burning heretics—not that I blame her for that——"

"Ah! do her justice," said Jack, "it is not she but this damned Don who has revived the statutes, all the world know s that."

"I do not care who has done it I tell you I approve."

Jack looked at him narrowly

"You have changed, sir," he said, "as you promised you would. Do you remember the woman at Cheapside?"

Guy sniffed contemptuously

"I was a poor fool then," he said, "but I have learnt some thing. Oh! Jack, will any work come my way? It is not amusing to watch this cold woman upstairs waiting for her baby, and her hot husband down below doing his best "

"Exactly," said Jack. "Well, I do not know. Let us ride. You may have a chance at Oxford, if you wish to go a-burning"

There was plenty to talk about as the two rode under the green trees of Richmond Park over last year's leaves, scattering the deer that fled before the jingle of the bridle-chains or at the vision of the two green and gold figures coming noiselessly round the corner of a ride.

Jack, drumming his heels as he rode, on his side bewailed more than once his ill-success with Magdalene, he had never been in such hot love, he said; and the girl treated him like a Court-fool, listening, laughing and going her way, with her head as high above other women's, as was her beauty above theirs The Court was prudish beyond belief, he declared, it had not been so in jolly Henry's days, but all the ladies seemed infected with the revolting coldness of their mistress. He had never been so treate before.

Guy listened with the same tolerant contempt as that with which he had watched the affair. Only yesterday he had ob served the two through a hedge. Jack had come upon the girl in the privy-garden, and had attitudinised, made speeches and rolled his eyes as usual Magdalene had been very proper and upright. Jack had declaimed; she had dissented. Jack had prepared to drop on his knees, and she had gone away. Bah What nonsense, Guy had murmured to himself. He could not understand such folly For himself he asked nothing more than occupation in some business that was worth doing He vowed he would rebel, if he thought there were any interest in that but there was not; there was no interest anywhere. He had been better off over his books at Cambridge.

"But it is of no use," he burst out finally, as they turned at last homewards from under the trees, and came in sight of the London road, "it is of no use, I am here and must make the best of it, but, by the mass, if I have a chance——"

Jack was not attending He had halted his horse and was looking out under an arched hand at something which was approaching them at an angle

A patch of brambles rose in front of them, and writhed up a thorn-tree on the right; beyond this the bracken pushed up its delicious green to meet the low hanging boughs of the beeches, and beyond Jay the blue distance seen through a vista of straight tree-trunks

There was a sound of hoofs from the direction of Kingston Bridge far away on the right, and it was towards the direction of the sound that Jack was staring

"What is it?" asked Guy peevishly

Jack gave him no answer; the thud on the turf was coming nearer every moment The next instant Jack flapped his reins and cried out; and the two beasts plunged forward, snorting over the tangled ground. But they were too late, and while they were yet forty yards from the road, a courier in blue and silver had passed at a gallop, his head low and his knees high, paying no attention to the shouting gentlemen, and had vanished in a fountain of flying turfs round the corner of the tall fern.

Jack was cursing softly to himself as he stared after the man.

"What is it?" said Guy again.

"How should I know?" snapped Jack, and put his horse to the test towards Kingston Bridge

They rode home in almost complete silence, but each knew what was in the heart of the other It might be on life or death that the fellow rode to town——

with the news that England had gained a prince or had lost a queen Mary had not been seen in public since St. George's day.

There was a delay at the bridge owing to a breakdown there of a Royal waggon, and it was more than half an hour before they dismounted at the stables. Jack flung himself out of the saddle and disappeared Guy asked a question or two, but the grooms had heard nothing, and he was a little reassured. Probably the message had been of a private nature.

He went upstairs to dress for supper, Jack was nowhere to be seen, and Guy came down to the parlour a little later, supposing that he had been alarmed without cause The parlour was empty and he sat down to wait

It was a dark little room looking out on to the inner court, and communicated by two staircases in the lobby outside with the gallery where his own rooms were situated, and that which led to the Queen's chambers.

He heard someone presently outside on the stairs, but did not trouble to turn his head even when the latch was suddenly lifted. He supposed it was Jack or possibly Tom come to tell him that supper was ready.

Then he heard a stifled exclamation and sprang up.

Old Mistress Clarentia stood there in her white cap and dark dress, looking at him with such an expression that for a moment he feared that the Queen was indeed dead Her face was convulsed by some excitement, and her old hands were clasped desperately before her.

"Master Manton!" she said "Is it true? Is he gone?"

"I do not know what you mean, Mistress. What is the matter?"

She pushed the door to behind her, and came forward a step.

"The courier, sir. Is he gone? And with false news! Where are all the gentlemen? "

"We saw a man in her Grace's livery in Richmond Park"

began Guy, bewildered.

"And you did not stop him, sir 'You must send after him, Master Manton. You must not wait till the morning. It is false!" she cried

"You must explain, Mistress. What is all this?"

She threw out her hands desperately.

"Why, sir, he is gone to take the news that a prince is born. It is false"

Guy sprang forward

"It is false, you say! Is her Grace dead then?"

"Dead! No, sir, God forbid. But it is false There is no prince, nor ever will be"

She gave a great sob, and stood looking at him with her eyes full of tears

"And there will be bell-ringing to-morrow. And my poor lamb!"

She turned swiftly towards the door.

"Shall I send, mistress?"

She turned again.

"Yes, Master Manton. Send at once; I can find none of the gentlemen"

Then she was gone again, and Guy stood for a moment dazed with the shock. Then he dashed out of the room towards the stables, nearly upsetting Jack who stood rocking with laughter in the lobby.

2

A fortnight later Guy had his first private sight of the Queen since her interview with him in the previous November.

It was now half-way through May, and all hopes of a child, except within the Queen's own bed-chamber, had long ceased. Mrs. Clarentia's courier had not arrived in time in London to prevent the tragic bell-ringing that she feared Te Deums had been sung, there had been wild scenes in the streets, brawls and shoutings, and all had given way to the laughter of the many, and the sorrow of the few when the tidings were contradicted.

It seemed to Guy abominable that no one had the courage to tell the truth to the Queen All except herself knew now that it was a shocking disease that had deluded her, and that she could bear no child He swore to Jack Norris that her women ought to be ashamed of themselves, and that if an opportunity was given to him he at least would not fail to be brave

Then his opportunity came

He was in the very act of bragging about it in the parlour an hour before dinner-time one morning

He and Jack Norris had been talking about the wretched young man who had claimed to be no less a person than Edward the Sixth, supposed to be deceased; and who had attempted to raise followers against the Queen. He had been brought to Hampton Court three or four days before for examination, and had been sent off again to prison.

"I wonder there are not a hundred such," said Guy bitterly. "Any stick will serve against the Queen"

"Now a prince—" began Jack.

"A prince! there will never be a prince, Elizabeth will be queen, and you and I will be sent a-packing or a-hanging It is a foul shame that not a woman will tell the Queen"

"Now if you were one of her women——" sneered the other

Guy faced him smartly

"If I were one of her women, or even could see her for a minute, I swear by God she should know the truth"

"I hear that she has made baby-clothes," chuckled Jack

There was a tap, and a page looked in

"Mistress Dormer wishes to see you, sir, immediately, in the Queen's gallery And will you bring Master Homer's 'Iliad? 'Is that right, sir?"

Jack gave a sudden bark of laughter

"There, sir," he said "Now we shall see"

Guy looked from one to the other with a fallen jaw Then his lips snapped together

"I shall do it," he said "Tell Mistress Dormer I will be with her in five minutes."

Jack threw himself into a chair as the page went out "Now, Master Manton," he said. "Prospere procede! Thank God I know no Greek!"

Guy's mouth worked a little, as he stood irresolute Then he turned and left the room

In less than five minutes he came out into the Queen's gallery with his brown hair newly combed, his short white silk cloak buckled with silver at the throat, and Master Homer's "Iliad" under his arm Mistress Dormer faced about as he came in, and then walked towards him with rather a perturbed air

Her fair cheeks looked pale and a little fallen, and her eyes had dark rings round them as if with long watching.

"Her Grace wishes to read with you, sir," she began. "She stirred an hour ago, and asked if you were in the palace"

Guy bowed, but he did not feel so easy as he looked.

"You understand, Master Manton," went on the other. "He Grace must not be excited or troubled You will speak low will you not?"

She glanced at his embroidered shoes

"Those are noiseless, are they not?" she said.

"Yes, Mistress Dormer. Will her Grace talk to me?"

"Oh! she can talk a little, but not too much. She has hardly spoken for a week till to-day."

The girl turned to go, but Guy was at her side, and touched her on the arm

"Mistress," he said, "Mistress You must tell me. Doe: her Grace know that she will bear no child?"

Jane's eyes filled with tears, and her lips began to tremble She shook her head Then something in the young man's fact startled her.

"I think she may guess it," she said hurriedly, "but she may not be told. Do not speak of it at all, Master Manton."

She hesitated yet a moment, looking at him; and then lifted the latch of the door.

The two went softly across the ante-chamber; and the page that stood by it laid his hand on the curtain over the further door

"She is here," whispered Jane. "Walk softly, sir."

Guy felt a qualm of physical sickness seize him, as Jane's hands were laid on the latch with infinite precaution He knew he was as white as paper, and bit his lower lip furiously to bring back sensation. Then he followed the girl through the doorway

For a moment he saw little, as the low square room was partly darkened; but between the shutters of one of the windows on his left came a glare of refracted sunshine and the song of birds from the privy-garden beneath A great bed stood opposite him, with tumbled sheets and pillows seen between the half drawn curtains; and for a moment he stared at this, thinking that the Queen was there.

As he stood hesitating whether to kneel, the door closed almost noiselessly behind him, and Jane came swiftly past and across the floor towards the dark corner between the closed window and the bed

Then he saw the girl drop on her knees beside a shapeless thing that crouched in the corner on a pile of pillows For an instant he could not make out what this was, then he understood, and fell on his knees

As he looked, and Jane whispered, a white face lifted itself from the dark heap and stared across at him Then he saw Jane beckon; and rose and came across the floor, horribly frightened and bewildered.

He stood hesitatingly, looking down at the heap on the floor, and as his eyes became accustomed to the twilight his horror deepened Mary had her eyes downcast now, her chin rested on her knees as she sat crouched among the pillows, and her hands seemed clasped round them with a rug thrown over all. But her face was a terrible sight It was enormously swollen, her eyelids were sunken in dark pools of skin, her lips had vanished, pinched and bitten together, and showed only a thin downturned line for her mouth She wore some kind of kerchief tied beneath her chin so as to hide her hair, and her forehead showed beneath it wrinkled and creased with pain. It was the more repulsive in the half-light of the room.

Jane who was still whispering, now looked up and spoke in a thin sibilant voice.

"Bring up the table and chair, Master Manton, and read aloud softly. Her Grace wishes you to read a little of the third book in Greek, and then to English it"

He went on tip-toe to the end of the bed, brought across the table and chair and set them a couple of yards away from the Queen Then he sat down and turned the pages of his heavy book till he found the place But his hands trembled so much that he fumbled as he turned, and he looked up desperately once or twice at the sharp crackle

Then he began to read.

He could not imagine why the Queen had chosen this It was a description of the Trojans going to battle like a flock of screaming birds. And surely this pitiable bedchamber——Then as he reached the fifteenth line he remembered, and understood; then again he wondered whether he were not mistaken in his interpretation. It was the story of Paris, with his leopard-skin and bow over his divine form, lording it in the front rank of the Trojans, till he saw the man whom he had wronged. Was it conceivable that the sick brain saw some fantastic type here of her own prince and her own sorrows?

He read on fifty lines or so, his voice becoming steadier as the sounding Greek inspired it; then he turned back once more and began to read fluently in English.

It was a relief to him when he reached the end, and began again in Greek. He could think better when the exercise was more mechanical As he read, he began better to take in the situation

The Queen's face had dropped again upon her knees, and there was only a huddled figure to be seen. Close beside knelt Mistress Dormer, sitting back on her heels, motionless except for her eyes that rose now to the reader, and sank again to her mistress There was a sensation of pain in the air; the room was soaked in it, the tumbled bed-clothes behind him, the faint smell of drugs, the darkness of the room, mocked by the vivid dusty bar of light between the shutters, and the summer song of birds—all suggested to this healthy sturdy man some impression of what the past weeks must have been within here, while without Philip hunted and swore and drank and made love to other women; and the pensioners laughed in their parlour over the fantastic fond creature upstairs

A kind of angry pity touched his heart for the first time now for many months, but he still resented while he perceived the pathos of it all What folly it all was—and yet how piteous! Then he remembered his determination to tell the truth to this poor Queen, and with the memory came the knowledge of its impossibility Strong out-of-doors resolutions became hopelessly coarse and futile in this soft thin atmosphere of a woman's pain. He saw now why she had not been told before; it was infinitely better that she should have one solace however false, and gradually, as she grew stronger, correct her own ignorance

He was so much absorbed in the tragedy that he read aloud far beyond what he had intended.

Then came a violent shock. A man's voice, that cracked into falsetto like a growing boy's, came from the heap on the floor.

"English it, Master Manton"

The white swollen face looked up for an instant and down again, as he stopped in the middle of a word, and snatched at the pages.

Then again with a shaking voice he began to translate

He reached the end and paused, and again the Queen spoke.

"I thank you, Master Manton"

Guy did not like to move without further instructions, but he closed the book softly on his finger "I cannot bear more to-day, sir," went on Mary very slowly, "but it has done me good. My needle-work, sweetheart"

Jane fumbled in the heap of stuffs beside her and drew out a piece, and as Guy stood up he saw that it was embroidered all over with golden pomegranates, then he recognised the design, it was the symbol of the Queen who had been Mary's mother. No doubt she was finishing her mother's work But how terrible! And where were the baby-clothes?

"Wait, Master Manton," said the voice again. "The needle, my love."

She took a painful stitch or two, and Guy, as he stood with that same physical repulsion creeping over him again, saw her shrunken ringless hand and the bones that stood out in clear white lines on the back

Then she paused

"I can do nothing, Master Manton, while I am like this . . But you saw my lord Cardinal . . and I shall send you to Oxford in the autumn…"

Again she took a stitch or two. Guy watched the thin gold thread curve and tighten suddenly, and heard the rasp of it through the heavy brocade

"I cannot do it to-day, Jane," she said wearily; dropped the stuff and leaned back again Guy saw the girl throw one arm round her, and pass a handkerchief softly three or four times over that white wrinkled forehead and the closed eyes. Then the Queen motioned her aside with her head, leaned forward again and clasped her hands tightly round her knees

"Yes, Master Manton . to Oxford in the autumn…. We shall deal with the heretics then, and I wish you to be there"

"Yes, madam," said Guy with a great effort He felt his knees begin to tremble as he watched

"That is all then. . Another day perhaps ."

Guy came forward a step and knelt, then he half-rose as Mistress Dormer beckoned him sharply away But Mary unclasped one of her hands and held it out hanging, with the faintest possible suppressed moan.

As he took it on his own hand and, with a great effort, kissed it, he felt that it was icy cold and wet.

Then he rose, knelt again, rose once more and went noiselessly across the room, taking up his book as he passed the table.

He was scarcely conscious of anything except a kind of anger as he passed through the sunlit court on his way to the hall. The bright light round him, the chirping of the birds under the leaves, the radiant sky overhead, the hot stones underfoot—all seemed external and unreal He still walked softly, and he still carried his great book beneath his arm He had left reality upstairs behind him, in the darkened room, in the scent of drugs and flowers, the presence of the kneeling maid in the corner and the heap of agony on the floor

He felt a clap on his shoulder as he went up the steps, and turned round viciously.

"Well, sir," cried Jack, "and did you do as you said?"

Guy snarled silently and fiercely, and the other fell back astonished at the fury in his face.

Imquum est collapsis manum non porrigere
Sen. *Contr.*

CHAPTER II

MASTER MANTON GOES TO OXFORD

I

THE summer crept on to August.

There were some more burnings. Flower, the monk who had taken a wife and preached heresy, was burned in Westminster for stabbing the priest as he gave Holy Communion on Easter Day in St. Margaret's; the ciborium had caught the blood Cardmaker, the married friar, after the withdrawal of his recantation, suffered at Smithfield with Master Warne, the upholsterer But the trial of the bishops at Oxford still lingered.

On the twenty-third of the month the Court returned to town. Mary showed herself to her subjects, and went down to Greenwich with her husband, visiting the Friary where her mother had so often prayed, and passing on into the Palace by torchlight. Three days later Philip took his leave and went. The Queen's health gave way once more, and she disappeared from public life.

On the day after Philip's departure Jack Norris came up to Guy's room and announced to him that he was to leave for Oxford in a fortnight's time, with Master Kearsley.

"Master Rochester told me to tell you," he said. "He had it from her Grace this morning"

Guy asked for details.

"You are to go in the train of my lord of Lincoln, who is to despatch the business."

"Despatch it?"

"Why, yes, there has been enough delay surely?"

"It is high time," observed Guy coolly, lounging at the window

He had made himself decide the question of burning long since, when he had had occasion to take a side in the discussion that followed the Spanish friar's denunciation of execution for heresy, in the presence of the Court in February

An old priest from Cardinal Pole's household who was being entertained by the gentlemen in the parlour while his master was upstairs, had supported the friar, he had declared that it was contrary to the spirit of Christ; and had instanced his patron's own words on the subject, and the action of Bishop Gardiner in helping suspects out of England.

But Guy had supported Jack Norris in his answer.

"I cannot understand that," Jack had said "You would surely execute for treason and murder, and how much more then, for treason to God and the slaying of souls?"

Guy burst in furiously on the mild old priest.

"Surely, father, you would not allow them to breathe God's air another moment. They infect it for all Christian souls. And what of the insult to our Lord?"

The priest had no formal answer to that For him as for others the Catholic Faith was as obvious a truism as the constitution of the State and the Prince's inviolability. Only madmen questioned either.

"Master Cranmer is to have a further respite," explained Jack. "They say he will yield But the others are sturdier knaves. Master Latimer has a coarse wit. I would I were going"

Guy remembered a tale or two he had heard at Cambridge, and mentioned some sermons preached there by Master Latimer on a pack of cards

"He will not have to preach, but to play them now," observed Master Wentworth, the cofferer, caustically. "And he will lose the game too, in spite of his tricks. The times have changed since clubs were trumps."

Master Wentworth had a ready, but an elaborate wit, and was forced to explain his jest at length to the old priest

Now that the news had come, Guy was more satisfied. He was ready to grasp at any distraction that offered itself, and die not fear that his resolution would fail. But he could have wished that his own share in the work had been important He said so to Jack.

"Well, I would I were in your place," said Jack; "this Court is as dull as hell—duller, if we may trust the theologians."

Dick Kearsley came in presently, as peevish as ever; and, under pressure, added some more details. It seemed that they were to go down to Oxford on the fourteenth, and there make things ready for the bishop. Gloucester and Bristol were to send their prelates to sit with Lincoln upon the Commission. The gentlemen's own parts were to help to swell the train of the bishops, as her Grace desired the affair to be as solemn as possible. Guy enquired about servants

"We are each to take two," said the other, "and a couple of horses."

There seemed to be something on Dick's mind He gnawed his nails as he talked, and glanced so often at Master Norris that at last the other understood. Jack rose from his chair

"I must be off," he said genially, "there be mysteries abroad."

When he was gone Kearsley turned to Guy

"He is right," he said tersely, "there is disaffection at Oxford; though nothing is known. But Monsieur Renard has been closeted with her Grace this past two days, and she sent for me an hour ago, when he went."

Guy was interested, and asked what the Queen had said

"Why, nothing," growled the other, viciously "She will not. But there is something forward We are not to go as her gentlemen at all."

"But" began Guy, sitting up in astonishment.

"Yes, sir. I lied just now. All here are to think that we go as her gentlemen; but we are not to wear her livery And she said enough to show me——"

He stopped and bit his nails again, staring moodily out of the window.

"We are to wear my lord's livery, then?" questioned Guy.

Dick turned on him sharply.

"Why, no, sir," he snapped, "why should we do that? That would ruin all. We are just intended to mix with the folk, and pick up what we can. We shall be given nought to do there. See if I am not right!"

Guy was still more astonished three days later, when his preparations were nearly complete He was sent for by Sir Robert Rochester himself, and given further instructions.

"You will travel as her Grace's men the first day," said the old man. "At Beaconsfield where you will sleep, you will change into common clothes, and leave your others there. You will not be in my lord of Lincoln's train at all, but you must not speak of that here. You and Mr. Kearsley will take lodgings at her Grace's expense I have told Mr. Kearsley all the rest."

Guy looked at him.

"Can you tell me any more, sir? I would sooner have it from your lips"

The old man looked at him suspiciously

"Well, Master Manton, I will tell you this. I think there is nothing in the matter. But her Grace—Monsieur Renard thinks there is trouble at Oxford He has had a letter; but he knows nothing."

"And why are we sent, sir? What are we to do?"

"I have told Mr. Kearsley, sir. That is enough"

Guy saw he would get no more out of him, and took his leave.

His preparations were not elaborate, he took a couple of suits for change, arranged about his horses, curtly informed Tom that he was to be his body-servant, and that the other man he was to take would have charge of the beasts He chose his arms also: a pair of swords, a dagger, a light brigandine and a steel cap, and ordered Tom to furnish himself with the same articles.

Tom was enormously pleased. He had been left much alone by his master during the continual moving of the Court here and there, and the journey would be exciting Still more exciting would be the trial and death of the great heretics at the further end

Guy gave him a few facts about them on the night before they left.

"We shall not see much of my lord of Canterbury," he said; "his affair will not be settled yet But remember, Tom, that he took a wife in spite of his vows, that he brought her to Lambeth where my lord Cardinal now reigns, in a packing-case, for fear that folks should know of it He has broken his oaths to the Holy Father over and over again; feigned to marry the Lady Anne to King Henry when Queen Katharine was yet alive, and then he divorced her at his Grace's word. He has taught now one thing and now another, as the wind blew He has burned half a dozen men who were no greater heretics than himself He has plotted against her present Grace till he was laid by the heels, and now he has to answer for it all."

Guy thought it good for the boy to know the truth before he came on to the stage, and his tales about the Archbishop lost nothing in the telling.

"And Master Latimer?" asked Tom with sparkling eyes.

"Ah! Master Latimer! Well, he has sworn one thing and done another, like them all. He has mocked from his pulpit at all holy things, and among them at good Friar Forest, who was Queen Katharine's confessor, as he hung a-burning over a slow fire He entreated the King's Grace to give him leave to do it. He has called the Holy Father Anti-Christ and the Catholic Church Babylon. He has sharpened his wit against the sacrament of the altar"

About Dr Ridley Guy found it hard to say much except that he too had been blown about like a weather-cock, and believed and preached as the King told him But there seemed no need to reassure Tom; the boy was content to know that these divines were on the other side to his master and the Queen's Grace. Since that was so, they must be reprobate, and no punishment could be too severe.

"But they will have their chance," added Guy, yielding in spite of himself to an unwilling qualm at the boy's vindictiveness. "If they will submit themselves they will find pardon. And it is not the Church that will burn them, it is the Parliament that will do that."

He took Tom down to the parlour presently, as a treat, for half an hour; and Jack Norris insisted as usual that he should sing a song or two before going up to bed again.

Guy sat in the window-seat, looking out on to the lawn that ran up on the south of the house into the rough grass of the park, all transfigured now in radiant evening sunlight, and listened to the extraordinary sweet voice and the ripple of the wires touched skilfully by Master Norris in the background; and as he listened he thought of the journey next day, of the pleasant ride between the fields along the Oxford road, and of the tragedy that awaited them at the end.

Somewhere overhead too in the huge palace of Placentia lay the woman in bed, whose hands held the strings that made the puppets dance. Or was it wholly her hands? At any rate she permitted it all, and with that hateful coldness that he knew so well and loathed, and admired in spite of himself. She had suffered certainly, but suffering should make a woman soft, not hard! It was different for a man.

He looked across at the two who played and sang in the mellow twilight of the room; and there was no bewilderment there. Jack's comely face was bent down over his instrument, and he plucked the strings softly as if he loved them. His lips were parted, and his cheeks flushed with pleasure. And Tom was singing with all his heart, his hands holding the music, his head thrown back framed in his long black hair, and his pale face alight with a pair of black eyes.

There were no problems for those two.

2

It was very pleasant to Guy to find himself again in an University atmosphere, and he passed some delightful days in Merton College, where rooms had been assigned to him and Master Kearsley in the front quadrangle next the gateway.

It was pleasant to awake in the quiet academic room, to hear the sounds of the College servants about their business in the court, and the chiming of the grave bells that called the students once more to mass; to see the familiar dress in the quadrangle and streets, to dine with classic ceremonial in halls that somehow retained an air which the Court had lost, to watch the sizars, the Fellows, the pensioners, each .with his assigned part—all this pleased him, in spite of his emancipation from it.

Merton College, under Dr. Thomas Raynolds, was strongly Catholic in its sympathies, and there were many victories over the heretics won night after night in the hall. Guy found himself among experts here; Dr. Martiall, once deputy commissary to the Warden, and now himself Vice-Chancellor of the University and Dean of Christchurch, dined there two or three times; Dr. Robert Ward, one of the Fellows, had been appointed to sit on the Commission; and the Regius Professor of Divinity, Dr. Richard Smyth, also one of the Fellows, and thebes schoolman of his time, had already received a hint that if an execution-sermon were required he would be called upon for it.

Guy learnt a good deal during the week or two before the Commissioners arrived of the condition of the prisoners, and the effect of their presence upon the University. It seemed that they passed their time contentedly enough, but in private, and separated from one another, Master Cranmer in Bocardo, Master Ridley in the Mayor's house, and Master Latimer in other lodgings. They had been examined more than once since their arrival together eighteen months before, and the Archbishop again only a few days previously; but their residence for so long did not conduce altogether to the peace of the University and the country round.

"They are obstinate fellows," explained Dr Ward one evening as they sat at supper in the dark old hall, "and have the trick of speaking coram populo. If theology were not a science it would be easy enough to convince all men of their heresy; but now that every Jack thinks himself a doctor it is hard to show the common folk the subtleties of the New Law."

Then he went off into a learned discussion, his finger-tips together; and Guy left off attending.

It seemed from what he heard on that and subsequent evenings that the state of public feeling was only as vaguely known as Master Rochester had hinted. There were malcontents certainly, as there were everywhere; but it appeared from the pamphlets and papers that were found here and there that the punishment of heresy was an occasion rather than the cause of the disaffection. It was Mary's Spanish marriage rather than religion that distressed the common people; but the imprisonment of the divines here served as a useful goad to drive them towards revolt. Of any positive intention of rebellion there was no more evidence than that offered by the anonymous lampoons and the occasional brawls. Still, he understood that he was here to keep his ears open, and determined to fulfil his mission.

On the twenty-eight of September the Commissioners arrived and Guy went out to meet them. There seemed sufficient enthusiasm as the procession came into the City along the London road, with the three bishops in their purple and insignia, riding together in the midst with their chaplains and gentlemen behind them; and there were no unfortunate incidents to mar the general impression.

The following day was full of suppressed excitement; great numbers of people came in from the country round, and Guy and Tom amused themselves by visiting the Divinity School and St. Mary's church where the workmen were busy with the preparations for the trial

On the last day of September the examinations began.

Guy and Tom breakfasted early, and set out immediately after mass in the College chapel But they were too late to get inside. The schools were already full to overflowing, and a mob surged and clamoured on the steps and in the street The two managed to force their way almost to the door, and there stood gripping the stonework and watching the faces below

There seemed every kind of character there; and Guy, remembering for what reason he had been sent to Oxford, kept his eyes and ears wide open

There were students of the University, Masters of Arts, Doctors in their scarlet, country gentlemen booted and spurred who had ridden in that morning, townsfolk, priests—all jostled and swayed and talked, half-across the roadway, waiting for an opportunity to get inside It seemed that all were either loyal or cautious; there was not a word spoken, that Guy heard, that could be construed into infidelity or treason. The chief talk was about the chances of the prisoners, the tales told about them, the supposed proceedings inside It appeared that Dr Ridley was being examined first, and that there might be an opportunity of getting in when he was removed and Master Latimer took his place.

For a couple of hours it went on; the crowd in despair began to melt a little; and it was not until nearly eleven o'clock that a sudden din rose from inside, and people began to force their way out. Guy seized Tom by the arm, and began his struggle.

He found himself at last with Tom beside him in the front rank of the enclosure thrown open to the public, Before him stretched the heads of officials, a row of billmen, a square of scarlet and black-gowned figures to right and left, an empty space with a table in the midst for the notaries, whose heads were bent over it writing busily and above rose up the high tribune, trimmed with cloth of tissue. Over this looked the faces of the three Commissioners in rochets and caps, leaning together upon the velvet cushions and talking. Above their heads beneath the window hung a crucifix on the wall, and high over all rose the dark open roof. The sunlight poured in a long dusty ray from a side-window.

Guy had hardly time to take in a general impression, before a sudden buzz broke out in the court, and all heads turned to a side-entrance near the tribune.

Three or four figures were advancing from it; and in a moment Guy detected Master Latimer in the midst.

He presented an extrardinary appearance.

He was dressed in an old frieze-gown, green with age, strapped round him tightly by a leather belt from which hung a book on a string; on his breast was a pair of spectacles fastened from his neck; and his head seemed smothered in caps, all held in their place by another broad cap with flaps buttoned under his chin. He carried his hat in his hand, and blinked at the sunshine that streamed straight upon him Guy only had time for one glance at his face, which was ruddy and strong and fringed with grey hair, before the prisoner turned in his place and presented his back between his warders.

The buzz died to silence as a strong rough voice broke out—

"My lords, if I appear again, I pray you not to send for me until you be ready; I am an old man, and it is great hurt to me to tarry so long gazing upon the cold walls."

There was a faint murmur of laughter at his harsh complaint, the Bishop of Lincoln glanced about him from his high seat, and then answered courteously:

"Master Latimer, I am sorry that you are brought so soon, although it is the bailiff's fault and not mine. It shall be amended."

Then the examination began.

Guy listened for a minute or two to the bishop's charge, which was quietly and persuasively delivered. He began at once by entreating the prisoner to consider the unity of the Catholic Church; it was true that many had fallen from it in recent times; that now all the kingdom had returned, led by the Queen's Majesty, and there could be no shame in returning with it. That Church was built upon Peter, as the Scriptures of God plainly proved.

As the Bishop went on to enlarge upon this, Master Latimer lifted his head from his hand, and began to unbutton his flapped cap. Guy watched him with a kind of angry fascination; it was terrible to see those old hands fumbling, and to think what lay before them Yet—Guy reminded himself fiercely—had not this sturdy old man himself delivered like charges to culprits in even more shocking circumstances?

The Bishop was just ending when he attended to him again.

"For the love of God consider your state! Remember you are a learned man; you have borne the office of a bishop; remember you are an old man, and specially remember your soul's health and the quiet of your conscience. It is the cause that maketh the martyr, not the death Let not vainglory have the upper hand, humiliate yourself, subdue your reasoning, submit yourself to the determination of the Church. Do not force us to do all that we may do. Let us rest in that part which we most heartily desire, and to that, I for my part——" the Bishop raised his cap to the prisoner courteously—" I for my part again with all my heart exhort you."

Master Latimer lifted his head again from his hand, and again the rough voice spoke.

"Will your lordship give me leave to speak a word to two?"

"Yes, Master Latimer, so that you use a modest kind of talk, without railing or taunts "

"I beseech your lordship, license me to sit down."

The Bishop bowed

"At your pleasure, Master Latimer, take as much ease as you will."

The prisoner sat down, settled himself and began.

Guy soon lost his thread, for he was no theologian; and the prisoner so tossed about his words and his argument, crying out the differences between ruling the Church of God *secundutn Verbum Dei* and *secundum voluntatem suam,* that it was hard to follow him. At one shrewd taunt the audience laughed.

He ended

"Now, I trust, my lord, I do not rail yet"

"No, Master Latimer," came the answer from the high seat, "your talk is more like taunts than railing"

The people laughed again once or twice at the old man's fire. Latimer turned fiercely round.

"My masters, this is no laughing-matter," he cried. "I answer upon life and death. *Vae vobis qui ridetis nunc, quoniam flebitis*"

The Bishop of Lincoln looked round severely and called for silence. Then he added.

"Master Latimer, if you had kept yourself within your bounds—if you had not used such scoffs and taunts this had not been done."

Guy was greatly bored before the end came.

He had been present once before at a heresy-trial in Bishop Bonner's court, and had seen that stalwart prelate lose his temper and beat upon the desk with impatience at a prisoner who would not take his point. That had been more interesting; the Bishop had been so very human in his anger, and the argument on the impossibility of a final appeal to Scripture had been easy to follow, but here it was otherwise.

One by one certain Articles were put to the prisoner, to see if he were of the same mind as in his previous examination; and at the end of his short answers the notaries wrote busily at their table. The questions chiefly concerned the doctrines of the mass and of the Real Presence, and Master Latimer spoke a word or two to each

About one o'clock came the end for that day. The prisoner entreated that he might not have to appear again

"I pray you not to let me be troubled to-morrow again."

"Master Latimer," said the Bishop shortly, "you must needs appear again to-morrow at eight o'clock in St. Mary's Church."

Then the mayor came forward from his place by the door, and the curious stalwart old figure disappeared

There was a hot discussion again at supper that night, and the prisoners came in for some severe criticism for their behaviour.

"These men have no courtesy," snapped the Warden, "or rather they mock while they use it There was a deal of playacting to-day over cap-raising by Dr Ridley. He would not salute the name of His Holiness nor of his legate."

"They are hair-splitters, sir," put in another Fellow. "He removed his cap at the mention of my lord Cardinal's Royal descent, and put it on again at his legateship. That is blowing hot and cold."

"They will make an end to-morrow," observed the warden, fingering his silver cup, "and they will not need their caps much longer then. And it will be cold blowing that they will need on that day," he added, lifting his drink to his lips

Guy obtained an order that evening as a Master of Arts; and next morning presented himself with it at St Mary's It was impossible to take Tom in with him, so the boy was left to do the best he could in the crowd; and Guy was passed up through a side-door to a seat in the last row to the south of the tribune where the Commissioners were to sit. In front of him and opposite sat the Heads of Colleges in scarlet; and in the middle below the throne stood a silk-covered table with an empty chair at its west side. From where he sat he could not see the high-altar, but the other altars were in their places at the ends of the aisles. The stately church was already thronged from end to end, and a steady murmur of talk rose on all sides.

He had not very long to wait. A little procession appeared presently, led by javelin-men and proctors; the vice-chancellor came behind, and the three commissioners in their rochets and caps followed after, adored the Sacrament, and went up to their seats. In another moment there fell a sudden silence, and Dr. Ridley was in his chair with his hands folded before him, and a couple of beadles on either side

It was the first time that Guy had seen him, and he had a good view of him in three-quarter profile across the intervening heads He seemed younger than Master Latimer, and of a finer presence. His lips and chin were covered with a beard beginning to turn grey; his eyes were steady enough as he looked up at his judges His dress, too, was better than Latimer's; he wore a black furred gown and tippet, and a velvet corner-cap upon his head.

He sat now quite silent, waiting, with his eyes cast down.

The cap dispute of yesterday was resumed at once—The Bishop of Lincoln asked him again whether he would be content to do as others, and salute the name of the Pope's holiness—and at the words all hands but the prisoner's went up. If not, the beadle must take it from him, unless he pleaded sickness.

Dr. Ridley looked up

"I pretend none other cause," he said quietly "than I did yesterday; that it may appear that not only in word, but also by all my behaviour, in no point do I agree or admit any authority that comes from the Pope. As for taking my cap away, your lordship may do as it shall please you."

A hand from behind removed the cap, and the Bishop got to work

Guy soon wearied of it again, and leaned back. The whole matter was a foregone conclusion On the one side was the prisoner asserting that there was no sacrifice or altar in the Christian community, and alleging the Fathers and Scripture in his support On the other side the Commissioner declared that the Catholic Church was the interpreter of the Gospel, and that that Church believed in the sacrifice of the altar. Where was the ground for argument?

Why would not the authorities make an end? demanded Guy

The Bishop lost his temper once.

"A goodly receiving, I promise you," he cried, wrathful at the memory of the past twenty years, "to set an oyster-board instead of an altar and to come from puddings at Westminster to receive! And yet you could never be content in placing the table now east, now north, now one way, now another, until it pleased God of His Goodness to place it clean out of the church."

Ridley retorted instantly, silencing Guy's merriment.

"Your lordship's unreverent terms do not elevate the thing. Perhaps some men came more devoutly from puddings, that other men now do from other things."

The Articles were presently put to the prisoner and he answered them partly by word and partly by referring to a paper of his that the Bishops held There was another dispute as to how much Master Ridley should be allowed to answer, and then the Bishop held up his hand.

Guy listened eagerly, watching the prelate's steady face as he began in a deep silence:

"In nomine Patris, et Fili, et Spiritus Sancti. Amen...."

He was not able to hear it all; it was read so quickly; but the tenor was plain enough. Nicolas Ridley was found guilty in three points, first m obstinately denying the presence of Christ's Body and Blood in the Eucharist, secondly in affirming the presence of the substance of bread and wine after consecration, thirdly in denying the mass to be a lively sacrifice for the quick and the dead For these heresies the prisoner was commanded to be degraded from his office of bishop and priest and from all ecclesisatical order; he was no longer a member of the Catholic Church; he was excommunicated in the greater degree; and was hereby delivered to the secular power to receive the punishment prescribed by the temporal laws.

Then without a word the prisoner rose and disappeared with the mayor leading him, in a profound stillness, a beadle stepped forward and drew off the cloth from the table, for Master Latimer who was to come next was no Doctor of Divinity like the other; the notaries laid down their pens, and the three Commissioners sat back in their thrones

Guy drew a long breath as the murmur of talk broke out again in the church, licked his lips, and leaned back, a little annoyed at his own trembling.

As he did so, he felt a touch on his shoulder, and a piece of folded paper was passed across into his hand. He glanced behind him and saw a beadle standing there

He opened the note and read it

"Master Manton, Master Brownrigg is here. He has not seen me yet He is just within the great door Shall I speak to him?—T. B."

Guy rose quickly and made his way out

3

Tom was standing in the outer fringe of people who were gathered about the great south door. He was looking out eagerly for Guy, and slipped towards him as he came up.

"I saw him just now," he whispered, "as he turned his head. Have I done right, Master Manton?"

"Who is with him?" asked Guy breathlessly.

"Nay, but how can I know?" said Tom.

Guy looked at him, considering.

His suspicions were all alert now. The talk he had heard in London and Oxford had affected him more deeply than he had guessed. On the one side there was a rumour of conspiracy; on the other side there was Stephen. Was there any connection between them?

He took Tom by his frill.

"See here," he said, "you love her Grace, do you not? Well I think there may be a plot here. Master Brownrigg must not see you or me; but we must learn what he is doing here"

He drew him along the street twenty yards away and placed him with his back to the paling that ran up the south side of the church

"Stand here," he said, "and watch the folk come out. If Master Brownrigg comes this way, cross you over and come behind him; if he goes the other way follow him. In any case follow him to the house where he goes; and find out who is living there. Mark the fellows that go with him, that you may remember them again. Do your best, Tom. Do you understand?"

Tom looked at him mutely, with dancing eyes.

Guy shook him irritably

"Do not play the fool," he said "You understand?"

"I understand, Master Manton"

"I shall stand on the other side of the way, and watch too."

He left the boy standing there, and crossed over to the other side There was an inn there, and a group of idlers hung about the door Guy went through them, faced about and leaned against the wall...

It was an hour before anything happened.

His eyes moved rhythmically from point to point; now on Tom leaning back against the railings opposite with his arms curled over the cross-bar behind him;

now at the porch where the backs of men still shewed listening to the voices within the church where Master Latimer was on his defence, now up to the roof, the spire and the clear October sky over it. The pause seemed interminable, as more and more he began to understand what he was doing.

The half-dozen men in front of him talked m low voices and in a dialect that he found it hard to understand. They were plainly countrymen come up to see the show, and were ill at ease in the busy town; but they had determined if they could not get inside the church, at least to see the folks who came out. Guy began at last to study their clothes, the heavy leather boots, the stained hose, the flat weather-beaten caps. One held a crook in his hands.

Then there was a movement and an exclamation, and Guy's look sped across the street again. The people were beginning to come out.

Half a dozen students came first and stood talking on the pavement immediately in front of the porch. Guy frowned, moving his head this way and that, for they interrupted his view, and he glanced quickly at Tom The boy was on the alert, too, and was strolling quietly out into the roadway looking over his shoulder at the porch.

Then he looked back again; and Stephen was coming out with a companion whom Guy did not recognise, a middle-aged man in the dress of a gentleman. Stephen was in a dark suit and cap, and a sword trailed from his belt.

The two turned immediately to the right, and Guy saw Tom quicken his pace a little towards the other side. Then the boy wheeled round and came behind them, and a minute later, first the two figures, and then the one thirty yards behind them, turned the corner and disappeared

Guy still hesitated, but he dared not follow for fear that he should be recognised; and, after all, Tom was shrewd enough. So he turned and went back to Merton College.

He found it very difficult to attend during dinner to the conversation of the Fellows, who were fighting the theological battle over again; and he was clapped softly on the back by the young man who sat next him.

"Were you not there, sir? Have you nothing to say?"

Guy smiled with an effort.

"I am no schoolman," he said. "My business has been the classics and medicine.'

"It had been best for Master Latimer if his had been so too," observed the other, "but they know no theology at Cambridge—eh, sir?"

Guy was on good terms with one or two of the younger Fellows, who were proud of having the company of two gentlemen from Court, and found his conversation a relief from the sour silences of Master Kearsley, who sat alone at the end of the high table. But Guy thought their friendliness a little trying just now; he would have preferred silence.

But there was no help for it, and he was listening presently to a full and rhetorical history of the morning's disputation, and how Master Latimer had begun as usual by complaint, this time against the crush of the crowd through which he had been brought to the church. He had then answered plainly enough to the questions; and it had ended with his condemnation. He had been kept back by the Bishop of Lincoln's express orders until the crowd had dispersed, that he might not again be subjected to inconvenience.

"And the fellow had the impudence," added the storyteller, "to appeal to the next General Council. I wonder he did not appeal to God's Judgment Day."

"He did so," said Guy, "yesterday, at least."

"Well, one is as good as the other as regards his damnation. But of course the fellow will attend no General Council except where he is pope."

Guy excused himself so soon as dinner was over; and hurried back to his rooms; only to find them empty. Five minutes later there was a quick step in the paved court, and Tom ran in, flushed and out of breath

"I have found it all out, Master Manton," he cried

"Shut the door first," snarled his master.

Tom obeyed, and came back a little more subdued

"Well?" said Guy, sitting astride of a chair, and putting his arms on the back.

"They are in an inn, sir; the 'Blue Boar 'in St. John's Lane. They have taken the rooms till the heretics are despatched They have been here since last week."

"And the name, boy!"

"Mr. Christopher Ashton, sir He has a house at Abingdon, and Master Brownrigg is his secretary."

Guy remembered the name. Jack Norris had mentioned it to him more than a year ago

"How did you find it all out, sir?"

Tom began to smile, showing his white teeth, and wrinkling his eyes.

"Well, sir," barked his master again. "I—I made love to a maid, sir"

Guy frowned mechanically. He was thinking very hard. "Go to your dinner," he said at last, "and come back when you have done."

In less than half an hour Tom was back again with a streak of grease lying down his chin, and found his master in precisely the same position in which he had left him.

"Sit down, sir," said Guy, "wipe your mouth, and attend to me."

The instructions he gave were simple enough. Tom was to cultivate his female friend at the "Blue Boar," and if asked questions, was to say simply that he was a gentleman's servant, and had come with his master from London to see the trial of the heretics. He was to fish for every detail of information about the two men at the house, and to report it all immediately to his master. He was not to think that any fact or even gossip was immaterial; all was to be reported alike—the number of suits that they had, their horses, their business, what was thought of them, their visitors.

"Do you understand?" asked Guy sharply.

"Yes, sir," said Tom solemnly, while his eyes twinkled in his head.

"Very well, then. And you must not let them see you. Remember, this is serious work, and may lead to great things—or it may not."

"Yes, sir."

Dick Kearsley looked in presently, and sat down stiffly by the fire, hugging his hands between his two knees.

"It is useless," he said grumblingly. "We should not have come to the College We should have mixed with the common folk. They do nought but talk theology here"

He looked at Guy complainingly. He would infinitely have preferred that the Warden and Fellows should have talked treason.

"You have heard nothing then?" put in Guy absently.

Master Kearsley paid him no attention, and went on.

"I do not know why we have been sent here at all. It is a wild goose chase."

"And there are not even wild geese," observed Guy, looking at the fire

"No, sir," said Kearsley, with a kind of peevish grin, "but there is a plenty of tame ones"

He began to give his friend more gossip about the prisoners. There had been a great crowd to see them go back to prison for the last time; but it had been a silent one; and there were no cries to catch hold of. The executions would probably take place in about a fortnight, or as soon as the Queen had been communicated with and allowed a decent space for consideration. The Regius Professor of Divinity had been sent for by the Bishop of Lincoln, and it was supposed that he was being told to hold himself in readiness for the sermon at the stake

Guy nodded from time to time, and put in suitable remarks and questions, but he was only half-attending

"They will be degraded from ecclesiastical orders in a few days," said the other finally. "I shall go and see that."

He left Guy still sitting astride of the chair.

4

A fortnight later the executions took place.

Guy had not learned anything of importance of the two travellers at the "Blue Boar" in the meantime. Tom had come to him every two or three days with a nearly blank report; sometimes they went out together, sometimes separately. Master Ashton had been once or twice to Balliol College—Tom had followed him—and half a dozen times had ridden out with Stephen along the Abngdon road, presumably to his house there. They saw few visitors, but there were one or two who came several times—a Master Kingston, and a swaggering gentleman of the name of Horsey. Of Christopher Ashton Guy knew nothing, except that Stephen had been in his company eighteen months before.

That was really all the evidence that Guy had to think over as he sat on his horse on the edge of the town-ditch in the fringe of the crowd that were gathered below him round the stake; and that soon moved into the background of his mind as he watched the preparations and the gathering mob.

Overhead was a clear October sky, with a woolly cloud or two passing across it. Behind, him not five yards away, stood the wall of Balliol College, and opposite him the city wall, now crowned by a fringe of spectators Beneath him the ground fell away swiftly into the broad ditch that ran to the edge of the wall, and along the side of it as far as he could see to his left. On the right rose up the fortifications of the city and the battlemented roof of Bocardo prison where the Archbishop lay.

The ground about and beneath him was a dense pack of heads, all facing inwards to the open space in the centre where the stake stood, a beam of strong oak clamped with iron, some eight feet high rising out of a low platform of stones and faggots. This space, that contained also a movable wooden pulpit placed some ten yards to the west of the stake, was kept clear by a double line of bill-men and guards, whose weapons showed like a steel fence above the heads of the crowd. There was a deep murmur of talking on all sides, and from Christchurch came the sound of the huge Mary-bell, slow and solemn.

It was the first execution of the kind that Guy had ever seen, and he was aware that a certain fear had to be combated. He had seen death often enough, and it was not that that frightened him It was the dignity of the prisoners, the history of honour that was leading to such an end, and the cause for which they suffered; mingled with this was the thought of the peculiar agony that he would witness. He had been a little reassured however by the news given him by Kearsley that morning that, as usual, gunpowder would be allowed to the prisoners to shorten their pain. Yet, fire was fire! Yes! he said to himself fiercely, and fire was their due!

He was conscious, too, though in a confused manner, that, this scene would be a kind of test of his firmness, or rather an opportunity of increasing it A work lay before him which, in all probability, would require that virtue in an extreme degree—a work which, it seemed to him, there was no evading. He determined, therefore, to be rigid, and, for the twentieth time, in order to crush down the last lingering touch of sympathy in himself, he recalled the conditions under which these seditious heretics suffered. They had known the penalty of the game when they embarked upon it; they had approved of that same penalty when in past days they had the upper hand. It was with the sanction of those and others like them that the religious of King Henry's days had agonised under the knife, and poor crack-brained fanatics had been burned by the Defender of the Faith and his son for heresy on the doctrine of baptism. The Carthusians and the Franciscans too, the great abbots, whose names were now and again honoured, had suffered for allegiance to the Faith in which they had been brought up, and than which none other had been previously known in England; while these who were to die this morning were to suffer for new doctrines that they had voluntarily embraced in place of the Old Religion. It might be bad policy to burn them, it might even be, as Father Alphonso di Castro had proclaimed before the Court, contrary to Christ's Gospel, but Guy did not care greatly for either of those considerations

The crowd was very quiet, except for the steady murmur of talk; Guy passed the time by listening to the scraps of conversation he could catch from those who stood by him. There were a couple of students on his left, in gay clothes, who seemed absorbed in the physical details of death by burning, and exchanged statistics of the time that various persons had taken in dying; Master Robert Glover only had a minute or two of it, said one who seemed to come from Lichfield; old Master Rawlins, however, had had more of it at Cardiff. On the other side stood an old man in a Master's gown, who talked, to himself in his beard—scraps of theological controversy, staring all the while with bleared eyes at the stake and the heap of faggots and straw beside it and the pulpit From a window behind Guy's station came other fragments of talk, and on turning in his saddle he saw faces at every opening, and even high above looking over the parapet.

The murmur suddenly grew louder, a rustle of expectation sounded on all sides, and bills were seen advancing slowly through the crowd from the direction of Bocardo.

Master Ridley came first with Mr. Irish in his mayor's robe walking on one side of him, an alderman on the other, and a little group behind.

As he came out into the open space by the stake, Guy could see him plainly. He was in his black furred gown and tippet, with his velvet cap on his head, and walked steadily enough with upraised hands, turning his bearded face neither to right nor left He went forward to the stake and stood a moment alone, looking at it. Then he turned round and his face changed.

An extraordinary figure had just entered the arena behind him, with an old buttoned cap upon the head, holding in its place a white handkerchief with its ends hanging down, a frieze gown covering the knees and a kind of white underskirt falling to the feet below

Dr. Ridley came briskly forward, took the old man by the shoulders and kissed him

Then the two turned together towards the stake.

The arena was filling fast now, and as Guy ran his eyes over it he recognised many whom he knew. Standing by a long settle placed near the pulpit were Lord Williams of Thane, Lord Chamberlain to the Prince of Spam, talking with the vice-chancellor and one or two others; and Dr Richard Smyth in surplice and scarlet hood was just going up the steps of the tribune. On this side was another group, with their backs turned to Guy, talking eagerly together.

When he looked back again at the prisoners the two were kneeling one behind the other at the stake, engaged in their prayers.

A minute later the magnates were seated; Masters Ridley and Latimer had risen and were standing with their friends and Dr. Smyth, aloft in the pulpit, raised his hand for silence.

"Si corpus meum tradam igni, chantatem autem non kabeam, nihil inde utilitatis capio"

Then he gave it out in English, turning his head from side to side, and his voice sounded clear and distinct across the silent crowd.

"If I yield my body to the fire, and have not charity, I gain nothing thereby."

He made the sign of the cross and began to preach.

It was a very short sermon, not more than a quarter of an hour; and was interrupted more than once by gestures of dissent from the two prisoners, who watched him closely.

The preacher warned his congregation against the doctrines of these men, showing how to leave the unity of the Catholic Church led infallibly to interminable disputes and contradictions. Already were the Protestants divided into half a dozen sects, with promise of more to follow. Neither were the people to think that death made the martyr, but rather the opinions and good will of those that died. The woman that had died by her own hand in Oxford a week before was no martyr. Finally he urged the prisoners to recant before it was too late. Let them have pity on themselves and turn and ask pardon!

"The Queen's clemency will yet give you your lives," he cried. "And God's mercy your salvation."

Again he made the sign of the cross, and turned to leave the pulpit.

A murmur of talk had broken out again, and Guy could not catch what Ridley was saying. He seemed to be speaking across to the officials who sat still on their bench. He was kneeling now with his hands outstretched, with Latimer on his left.

The Vice-chancellor rose and came towards them, with a couple of bailiffs beside him, and together they lifted the prisoners to their feet. There was a short colloquy, and Ridley turned round.

"I commit our cause," he cried, "to Almighty God, which shall indifferently judge all."

Then he walked towards the stake, and Master Latimer followed.

In five minutes all was ready, and the two climbed up on to the low platform of stones put about the stake.

Guy strained his eyes to see them. There seemed a faint red mist between him and them, in which the figures danced and wavered as if seen through water He was furious with himself, with the fierce loathing against the miserable Queen that surged up within him as he watched the scene, with his own beating heart; with his clenched hands that shook on the pommel of his saddle; he knew that he could only keep his pity down by a sheer constrained effort of the will. For a moment it mastered him, he stood where they stood with a certainty of a blessed eternity in their hearts, and rank after rank of hostile faces without Then again he controlled it, and saw two pestilent heretics, enemies to God and man, foresworn and mad with pride, ringed by temporal and eternal fire.

There they were!

Master Latimer faced him, standing with his back to the post in a long white shroud falling to his feet, and the handkerchief on his head. He seemed taller and more upright than in his old cap and gown, and his ruddy bearded face looked out steadily at the crowd that surged to get a sight. On the other side Master Ridley was standing, his white shirt showing on one side of the post against which he leaned. Then Guy saw his hand go up; but he could not hear what was said He made another fierce internal act of hatred and contempt.

A smith was by them now with a long chain in his hand. Master Latimer lifted his arms to allow it to pass beneath them; and presently it was fastened about the bodies of both, and the man was driving a staple to secure it to the post itself

There was someone talking to Master Ridley now, as the men began to bring up the faggots, he had something in his hand, but Guy could not see what it was Presently, however, the gentleman came round to Master Latimer, and began to fumble with his shroud, passing strings over his shoulders and round his waist.

Then Guy understood, and torn by passion, he cried out:

"No powder!" he shouted, and then stopped, abashed by his own fury and the ripple of faces turned for an instant towards his own.

The crowd was very quiet now, the murmur of talk had died away, but the heads were shifting this way and that as the people struggled for a better view.

Guy was watching every detail so closely that he was scarcely conscious of his own beating heart, or of his horse who tossed his head and stamped with the long wait. Once he looked up towards the tower of Bocardo, a stone's throw away to his right, and saw that three heads were there watching the tragedy.

There was a crackle from the arena, and a man ran forward with a faggot from which a little smoke was curling up and laid it at Dr. Ridley's feet. Simultaneously another did the same for Master Latimer, and a murmur rose and fell from the straining crowd. Guy moaned once in the stress of the conflict that was wrenching him

A voice cried something from the stake, as man after man ran up with faggots and straw, gradually raising a wall of them round the two white figures at the stake Smoke began to pour out, and a vivid tongue of flame shot up once or twice in the midst of it.

There was a loud cry:

"In manus tuas, Domine, commendo spiritum meum!"

Then another from this side, hoarse and choked with smoke.

"O Father of Heaven, receive my soul!"

There was a loud report; and through the heavy drifting smoke that poured up thicker and thicker, Guy saw something fall forward. When he could see the post again for a moment, the upper part of it on this side was clear

But there was still movement on the other side Once he saw arms shoot out of the smoke, and twice heard a scream of pain, that tore his own heart, as he murdered the pity that it inspired.

"I cannot burn. For Christ's sake   "

The bill-men were busy now about his feet; a flaming mass of gorse rolled out and lay smoking; and up to heaven, blotting out the clear sky over the city wall rose a cloud of black vapour.

Again there was the cry from the stake, and a faggot fell out of the heap. A man with a bill-hook was tugging and pushing this way and that to allow the flames to rise. One long tongue shot up; then another; there were a couple of quick reports; something wheeled in the smoke and fell sideways; and then there was silence except for the roar of the fire, the rising murmur from the crowd, and the solemn shock of the Mary-bell overhead in the smoky air

Guy turned his horse homewards half an hour later, noticing nothing of the crowds that clamoured and jostled along the street towards Merton.

He was quieter now; the conflict was over, and pity lay dead—pity for those who were dead, and, as he thought, for the Queen who yet lived He knew now that he could do anything that would be asked, there was no sacrifice that he could not offer if his intellect approved and his will dictated it. He dimly recognised that the last hour had been decisive in his own soul, that a battle had been fought there between his emotions and his intentions, and that the latter had gained the victory. He had seen a pitiable sight, a mistake, a martyrdom, though for an unworthy cause; he had seen two obstinate old men who believed they were serving God, suffering acute mental and physical agony; and his will had driven down and beaten the response that his heart had made.

He was clear-headed now about Stephen, there should be no thought of relenting, but it should not be for the Queen's sake but his own.

As he came within sight of Merton, Dick Kearsley trotted up beside him; his face was flushed and animated.

"Well, that is over," he said.

Guy said nothing, and the other looked at him curiously.

"Why, you are white," he said.

Guy smiled, but said nothing.

"Master Cranmer was on the top of Bocardo," went on Kearsley, "with Friar Soto. I trust it has been a lesson to him. I saw Master Kingston in the crowd"

Guy turned to him sharply.

"Who is that?" he said.

"Why, Master Kingston, lately from the Tower."

"The Tower?"

"Yes, sir; he was put there for seditious language Do you know aught of him?"

Guy shook his head.

"Nothing but what you tell me," he said.

When Dick left him a moment later to take his horse to the stables, Guy was even paler than he had been just now; his lips were sucked in, and his eyes bright and hard It was Master Kingston's name that Tom had mentioned to him as being one of the visitors at the "Blue Boar." Was it not one more indication then that Stephen was in bad company?

There was a figure waiting at Merton gateway that ran forward as he drew up.

It was Tom, and his face was lit by excitement

"Master Manton," he whispered, holding the stirrup for his master to dismount

"Master Manton; they have left this morning."

Guy paused, with his right foot dangling.

"How do you know?"

"I was there before the burning. Jane told me that the luggage was sent on to London; and that they were to ride there when all was over."

Guy, in the saddle, was motionless so long that the boy released the leather and looked up at him astonished.

"Will you not dismount——" he began, and then stopped, half-frightened at his master's face.

Still Guy waited, staring down at the boy with steady calculating eyes, and twisting a wisp of mane between his fingers.

Then he drew a long breath, and fumbled for the off-stirrup with his boot.

"You must come with me, Tom," he said briskly, "and show me the way to the inn."

Plus amici nocuimus quam inimici
Quint *Decl.*

CHAPTER III

MASTER MANTON SERVES THE QUEEN

I

JACK NORRIS could make nothing of Master Manton's behaviour when the latter came back from Oxford There was a mystery even connected with his return. He had left six hours before Dick Kearsley, and yet did not appear at Greenwich until twelve hours after the other's arrival, and he gave no account of himself when he came.

Master Norris had tried to pump Tom Bradshawe; but that too had failed. The boy looked at him, shook his head, and referred him to his master

Guy's behaviour for the next month or two was equally strange. He scarcely appeared in the pensioners' parlour at all, either at Greenwich or at Westminster, when the Court moved there for Parliament; he went long rides alone or with Tom, and evaded all enquiries.

Even when he talked, Jack was aware that there was an odd reserve in all that he said; he appeared preoccupied, he continually checked himself, and he asked curiously irrelevant questions.

On one evening he discussed the names of inns, the origins of them, and their situations; at another time he appeared to listen very eagerly to some idle gossip that Jack was pouring out about people of no importance.

There was one other characteristic that Jack had noticed before, but never in such intensity as now; and that was his extraordinary hardness. One or two incidents took place that especially drove this home.

The two gentlemen were riding back together from St. Maxy Overy, where they had been present at the dirge sung over the body of Stephen Gardiner, who had died that day.

Jack was talking, as were most others, of the bishop's life and policy, of his successor in the Lord Chancellorship, of Mary's despair at his loss

"He was penitent enough at his fall from the Faith," said Jack, "in King Henry his time Did you hear what he said this morning as the priest read the Passion to him *Negavi cum Petro, exivi cum Petro; sed nondutn flevi cum Petro.*"

Guy grunted.

"And no man can say he was not merciful to others," went on Jack. "He would have no more to do with the burnings at the end They were forced to send the heretics out of his diocese to be tried."

"And is he the better for that?" observed Guy coldly.

"You would have said so a year ago," remarked Jack.

"Yes, a year ago"

Jack paused, and looked at him.

"You are a hard devil," he said. "God knows I am no favourer—"

Then he stopped He had caught such a look from the other's eyes that he was afraid to go on

"Then you think it is not to his credit, before God?"

Guy flapped his reins impatiently

"Leave him alone!" he said "What do we know? *Mortuus et sepultus est. Descendit ad inferos.* There is the last word."

Again, a week or two later, there had been a question as to the flogging of a kitchen-boy. His fate had hung in the balance till Guy threw himself passionately against mercy.

"God help us!" he cried. "What is all this pother? Flog the knave He deserves it, I make no doubt; if not for this, for something else"

It had turned the balance, and the boy had been whipped

This development in Guy was very puzzling to Jack whenever he gave it a thought. It was strangely unlike what he had diagnosed of the other on his arrival, and what he had heard from Tom as to his master's kindness.

He remarked on it one day to Kearsley when they were alone together

"What has happened to the fellow?" he said. "Did aught happen at Oxford?"

Dick stopped gnawing his nails and glanced at him.

"Happened?" he snarled. "I do not know, and I do not wish to know."

"Do you understand it?"

"No, I do not. Let it alone What of his Highness? Will Parliament crown him, think you?"

Then the two went off on to politics; and Dick prophesied dark results from Gardiner's death and Paget's succession to him, from Philip's insistence and arrogance, and English stubbornness; he spoke too of more evidence of sedition; and Guy sank into the background.

It was not until towards the end of February that Jack Norris was admitted into one of the secrets that were working in Guy's soul; and even then much remained unexplained

Guy had not been seen at Court for two days; there was little to be done, as the Queen lived now so much in retirement; and Jack had learned from the Comptroller that Master Manton had been given leave of absence for forty-eight hours. Then he suddenly returned.

Jack was in his own room, preparing for bed. His doublet was off, and his shoes, and he was warming himself before the fire, for the last time before plunging into the chill bedroom next door His mind was far away from Guy; it was running indeed as usual, in melancholy fashion, on Magdalene Dacre, with whom he had had a word or two that evening in the long gallery. She had settled down well to Court life now; she took things more lightly, made less fuss about matters which she could not mend, Jack told himself; she would make a fine lady, and a good wife for some lucky devil. He sighed a little, stretching himself before the fire. He had never been so long in love before

There was a sudden knock at the door Jack cried out to enter, and the next instant Guy was in the room, and the door shut behind him.

He was in a suit that Jack never remembered having seen before, a gay doublet slashed with crimson silk at the shoulders, a crimson cloak, a great broken feather in his hat and rather tawdry riding-boots of yellow leather He looked like a gentleman of fortune. He carried a little riding-whip in his hand, and a long sword in a tarnished scabbard trailed from his belt.

Even his brown, pale face bore out the impression; his eyes were extraordinarily bright and hard, his mouth was set tight in a kind of desperate recklessness, and he looked as if he had been drinking There was an air of shabbiness and smartness about him that would have made it very difficult to identify him as an officer of the Queen's household; and still less as a scholar and a Master of Arts.

Jack stared.

"Christ!" he said.

Guy came swiftly across the room, his eyes fixed hard upon the other's

"Can you keep a secret, Jack?"

"I suppose so," said Norris, starig back. "Are you drunk, Guy?"

"Yes, so drunk that I am going to tell you a secret. Will you swear?"

He spoke in a sharp, harsh undertone, still looking steadily into Jack's eyes.

"I swear it by the mass," said Jack deliberately.

Guy kicked aside his sword, took off his cap, and dropped into a chair beside the hearth.

"Very well, sir, then you may listen."

Jack held up his hand for silence a moment, took up his doublet again and slipped it on, pushed his feet into his soft shoes, and sat down too, his chin on his hand, watching across the red glow of the fire the clear-cut profile of the other, the movements of his lips, and the little pulse that beat in his cheek.

"Now listen.

"When I was in Oxford for the burnings, I kept my eyes wide open. It was why we were sent there. There was a man there, Master Kingston—you know him, do you not? He was lately in the Tower. There was another fellow there, Master Christopher Ashton. These too were in company there, with a third—Master Ashton has a house at Abingdon.

"Well, this third—oh! you may have his name, it is Brownrigg—Stephen Brownrigg. He is a pestilent, seditious knave, and has always been so. He is a friend of Master Edward Underhill too——"

He paused a moment, as Jack sat up suddenly

"Yes, sir, Master Edward Underhill," continued Guy, "and there is a pretty nest for you——"

"Master Underhill was not there," put in Jack.

"No, but there were these other three, and others I will give you the names presently Well, these three were much together; Ashton and Brownrigg lay at the 'Blue Boar ', and the others I know not where—perhaps at Abingdon

"When I knew they were together, and heard the talk of the place, I thought I had found my birds, and laid my dog Tom on to them. He has a nose like a hound, that lad——"

"And the voice of an angel," put in Jack nervously.

Guy paid no attention, and went on

"As I came back from the burnings, my lad told me that the birds were flown I went to see the inn, went back, changed my clothes, told Dick that I was off, and rode away to Abingdon. There was a couple of fellows in the garden; one of them was named Horsey, I learned afterwards; I saw him over the wall; but there was nought to be done, I dared not stay; and I went back to Oxford, to the 'Blue Boar 'I had sent my baggage to London with my man, all except a little bag that Tom carried for me.

"Well, I gave a name, I said that I had come to find Master Ashton and Master Brownrigg who were my friends; but the landlord was mum He said he knew nothing of where they were gone. Then I knew better than ever that they were there for some private business I stayed there that night, keeping within doors for fear that folks should know me and speak to me; and to make the landlord think I was hiding I dropped a word or two about Abingdon, and Master Ashton's house there; and Master Horsey who I knew had been to the inn, but the fellow shook his head and eyed me like a rat.

"There was no more to be done; so I packed my bag next day and ordered my horses Then I went to the fellow's room to pay my score; and I said a word or two about life and death; and the sore inconvenience it was to me to have missed my friends. Still he said nothing, and I went down the steps, thinking I had lost them. As I put my heel to my horse, he ran down from the house, and came up beside me.

"'You are a true man? 'he said.

"I laughed and said nothing

"'Well, you will hear of them at the old place,' he said For a moment I thought all was up. Then I remembered that these dogs have scores of dens, and I tried my luck "'That is easy saying,' I said, 'but which of them?'" He looked at me again at that; then he put his hand on my knee.

"'Well, the "Queen's Arms,"' he said.

"That was a pretty tale, when she hath a thousand, I thought; but I thanked him, and went off. Then I came to town."

Guy stopped and looked questioningly at Jack.

"So far, so good," said Jack

He was extraordinarily interested in the story. Guy's manner was utterly uncharacteristic; he had lost his slow speech, his changes of expression, his air of boredom. His eyes as he turned were intent and bright, his sentences rapped out with a tinge of slang in them, and under every tone and word and look some clear purpose was evident.

He laid his fingers together and went on.

"Well, Tom and I went, one or both of us, to every 'Queen's Arms 'in the City, and asked for Mr. Ashton. And we could hear nothing of him. At one place we thought we had; but 'twas another Mr. Ashton from Yorkshire. At another place a Mr. Ashton had drunk a pot and gone again. I went to see the man at that, but could get nothing from him; he had never seen the gentleman before, he said; and I could see he spoken truth; but it was our man, for he described him when I said he was my friend.

"Well, then I near gave it up, for how was I to know that the fellow at the 'Blue Boar 'had not fooled me, or that it was not in some other town?

"Then a week ago Tom came to me I had sent him out to hunt and to see that we had missed nothing; and he told me there was one more 'Queen's Arms 'that had been so till lately at least; and that it was by the water at Lambeth. The name had been painted out, he said, and another over it.

"Well, I rode up the bank next day, and round through the marshes; and came to the inn, as if from the country; and went in to have a pot."

"And if they had been there and seen you?" put in Jack swiftly.

"Why, none of them know me, but one—no, two, with Master Underhill; but Master Underhill, I knew very well Was at Court."

"Which was the one then?"

"Why, Brownrigg Brownrigg knows me, and I him."

Jack was astonished at the vehemence of the last words; but thought it better not to enquire further.

"Well, sir '"he said

Guy went on again quietly.

"I went in to have a pot. There was no one there but a couple of watermen. I took the landlord aside into his own parlour, and shut the door. Tom was outside with the horses.

"What of Master Ashton?" I said

"He shook his head and looked at me

"'I know nothing of him,' he said

"'Bah! I come from Abmgdon,' I said.

"'Well, sir, and what of that? 'he said, and put his hands on his hips.

"'And there is nothing for me? 'I asked.

"He told me 'No 'but I thought I knew better. It was just such a place where the dogs would meet; there is just a stable opposite; and no houses for a hundred yards, there is a landing where the wherries put in beside the garden wall, and a little water-gate in the garden itself, so that they can come by water; and there is the way through the marshes behind, so that they can come by land And then the fellow too—I could see he knew something.

"Well, I saw I could get no more, and of course I might be in the wrong; so I clapped him on the back, and drank my pot. I could see him looking at me; and then presently he said a word.

"'And if your friends from Abmgdon should come for you, sir, and ask for you, what shall I tell them? '

"'You may tell them I come from Abingdon,' I said.

"'And your name and lodging, sir.'

"'My name is No man,' I said, 'and I live at the sign of Nothing.'

"And with that I left him."

Guy paused again; he was breathing a little quickly now, Jack could see, and his nostrils opened and closed Jack was amazed, and almost shocked too, at the fierceness of that face. It was keener than ever. What a mistake he had made about this man in the first days of their acquaintance '

"I was back there again on Monday," went on Guy, "and it was the same tale.

"The fellow had not heard of Mr. Ashton yet, and there was no news from Abingdon, or for me to take there

"I went again to-day; to the City yesterday, and slept there, but heard nothing, and went on to Lambeth this afternoon; but it was to be the last time, I thought I must be in the wrong of it, and that I had lost my birds And to-day I had news of them."

Guy sprang up so suddenly that Jack leapt in his chair; but he only strode across the hearth with his hands clasped behind him, and went on in a lower voice than ever, with his face in shadow, staring fiercely down at the other, as he talked.

"To-day, there was a message.

"The fellow came into the parlour, and this time it was he that shut the door, not I

"He came close up to me.

"'You are from Abmgdon, Mr. No man,' he said, grinning at me

"I told him, Yes.

"'Then there is one who looks for you,' he said, 'who is in town now.'

"'Not Mr. Ashton? 'I said.

"'No, not Master Ashton,' he told me. 'Did you not know that? 'he said.

"Well, I saw there was something there I should have known. So I put a cool face on it.

"'I knew it very well, you fool,' I said," but I did not know that you did!

"He seemed comforted at that; so I made a shot at a venture.

"'And it was not Master Brownrigg either, I suppose,' I asked him.

"He went white at that; and though he told me it was not Master Brownrigg either, I knew very well that it was. You see they were the only two that I knew had come to town; though indeed that was three months ago.

"Well, then, this was the message. If I came from Abingdon

I was to be at the inn alone to-morrow night at ten o 'clock The gentleman who wished to see me, I was told, would not be there then But the landlord would send to fetch him as soon as I came, if I came alone There, sir"

Guy ended with a snap, and stood silent

Jack was bewildered The tale had come out so concisely; Guy's sentences and manner had been so curiously abrupt, that he scarcely yet took in what was asked of him He could see that matters looked black enough, that at any rate the mysterious company who came and went from inn to inn and took landlords at least partly into their confidence, had, considering their secrecy and their past record, a sufficient weight of evidence against them, but he did not yet understand what his part was to be. Surely the precautions already taken by the opposite side put action out of the question

"But what can we do?" he asked

Guy snorted with contempt

"Do!" he said "Why what is simpler? I shall go there alone at ten o'clock—"

"Yes," put in Jack quickly, "and half a dozen of them come, armed——"

"Wait," barked Guy. "I go there at ten o'clock, alone, and armed. There was nothing said about that. You bring half a dozen fellows across the river to the landing stage, five minutes later. You must come in a barge, and you must come up slowly, singing as you come They will think nothing of that. It will be a parcel of drunken fellows and no more. There will be half a dozen more across the marshes, I will send Tom with you to the place to-morrow. You will come up with no lights, and keep about till you see the inn door open; I will be there when I hear them coming, they will certainly come a-horseback, if not by water; and you will see the light from the door. Then you come to shore, and we have them."

"And you will be stabbed meanwhile"

"Bah! If the fellows do not know me, I can hold them in parley, and make mysteries, and if they know me—Lord! I can fight, can I not, for three minutes?"

"And there may be only one of them," mused Jack.

Guy nodded.

"And what will you get out of them, if you take them?"

"The plot," said Guy.

"By the torture?"

"If they will not speak."

Then Jack put a question that had been on his tongue for some minutes.

"And this Master Brownrigg," he said, "what do you know of him?"

"That is my affair," said Guy very quietly.

There was silence a moment. Jack looked up at the other and saw his face, set like iron, and his hard bright eyes bent on to the floor.

Then he rose.

"Guy!" he said suddenly, "Why are you doing this?"

The eyes of the other shot a look at him.

"What do you think yourself?" he asked.

"For the sake of her Grace?" murmured Jack uneasily.

Guy laughed suddenly and harshly

"For whom else?" he cried. "God save her Grace!"

There was silence a moment between the two. Then Jack broke it.

"Well, I will think," he said. "We will talk again tomorrow."

"And I have your word," put in Guy swiftly, looking at him. "Remember this is all my affair. All is under my command?"

He held out a scrap of paper.

"You have my word," said Jack; and took the paper.

When Guy was gone, Jack stood still staring down at the dying fire, stretching his fingers to it mechanically. The plot whirled through his head in a bewildering maze

Then he spoke aloud, softly; twisting the list of names still in his hand.

"And what the devil is the matter with Manton?"

2

It seemed to Jack as he sat in the stern of the barge on the following night, that it was the most curious adventure in which he had ever been engaged; and the most curious element in it was the spirit of the author. He was utterly at fault as regarded Guy's motives; he knew it was not simple zeal, he was loath to believe it simple cruelty; and yet besides these there seemed no other adequate inspiration for his energy and skill. The two had had a conference that morning, and a little excursion on the river to identify the inn and the stations to be taken up, and the details had been arranged on the lines suggested on the previous night. Jack had undertaken to gather a dozen men partly from those under his own command, and a few who were off duty and ready for anything where a reward was in question. Half of these had been sent off under Tom as their guide a little after eight o'clock to take up their post in the shelter of a barn a few hundred yards from the inn, and Guy and Jack had gone down with the rest to the stairs There Guy had engaged a wherry to carry him up to Lambeth, and after seeing his light fade into the black river haze ahead, Jack had embarked with his men

They had come now, after a long row, past the lights of the City, up to Lambeth, now and again catching sight of Guy's light ahead; and as the men roared their songs according to orders, Jack was sitting in the stern and looking eagerly out for the landmarks that told him when he would be in view of the inn door. He calculated that Guy would be within by now, and the landlord gone to fetch the stranger, and it was entirely a matter of conjecture as to how long that would take Guy had argued in the morning that this stranger would be neither too far nor too near, probably he would wait in one of the houses near the parish church, perhaps three hundred yards away. He would certainly be prepared either to come or to fly; and from ten minutes to a quarter of an hour might be allowed for the time in which the landlord might go and return again with him But this again was doubtful

"Cease rowing," said Jack in a low voice, "let her drift." He had found his station.

On the left, slightly behind him showed the three towers against the night sky—the two of Morton's gateway, and that of the parish church—looking at equal distances from one another, and as if they formed part of one building. A hundred yards ahead, and fifty to the left, so at least it had seemed in the morning, lay the inn, he knew; and this was indicated now by a tiny patch of light from some window on the ground floor. The door, he knew, was beside it

"Silence a moment!" said Jack again, straining his eyes this way and that, to see how far the tide had carried them down again.

In the pause of the singing the night was very quiet. Folks were in bed by now for the most part; from across the water behind them came the distant noises of a city turning towards sleep; and beneath the boards of the broad boat came the rush and suck of the out flowing tide. Below, above, and round about lay the vast darkness

"Sing again," said Jack, "one by one—now all together. Row six strokes."

There was no light in the boat, and he could not see the faces turned to him. He was only half aware of the heads against the glimmering sky, the gleam of the brigandines, and the pale patch of the man's face who sat on the stroke thwart, as he strained his eyes forward to the lighted window on the left shore, back to the three towers behind him, and once again to the lighted window

He had no idea how long he had waited; it might be five minutes or twenty; and yet there was no signal ahead. He wondered what was happening; was the whole affair a hoax, or a trap? He did not know. Guy Manton might be waiting in the inn-parlour still, or his body might be lying with the throat cut under a dust-heap in the yard

What did it all mean? and what gave him his fierce courage—his zeal to take such a mad risk?

Once or twice again, Jack gave a low order for silence; and during it heard again the suck of the water, the creak of the boards, and the breathing of the man near him The third time there was another sound—the stumbling walk of a horse over gravel.

Jack rose swiftly, and sat down again, and gave two or three sharp undertone orders.

"All ready," he said, "row steadily with little noise; keep up the song. Give a curse or two, Ned—keep her head just off the window. Keep it up.... Now all together!" he roared suddenly.

He had seen a tall patch of light suddenly appear and vanish beside the window

He should not have thought it possible that he could be so much excited, as the boat began to groan and splash on its way to shore. The men were silent now as they tugged the six oars through the water, and the window grew larger every moment; and now the chimneys of the little inn, and the garden wall that ran down to the river began to raise themselves against the low-hung stars. Jack's sword was out now; he gripped the hilt with one hand, with the point resting on the bottom of the boat, and with the other hand held the wooden edge that laboured under it as the men tore at the oars.

He kept his eyes fixed steadily on the darkness where the light had shown and vanished again; but there was no sign there of any confusion, he was so intent that he was thrown violently forward in his seat, as the prow crashed into the gravelly soil of the landing place

Then he was out, shouting, dashing up the little dark slope, while his men clamoured and tumbled behind him.

It was a curious and very unexpected sight that he saw when he had run past the tethered horse, banged the house-door open, and the second door on the left, and stood blinking in the entrance.

There were three men only in the little parlour

Close beside him, stood Guy Manton, with a long sword in his right hand and a dagger in his left He had turned at the sudden noise, and stood snarling and smiling, with his cap pushed back and his legs apart It was plain he had been keeping the door

With his back to the window, pressed against it as if in terror stood a stout little man in an apron, his hands flung out as if in expostulation, and with a face of ludicrous alarm and distress.

Halfway across the room, holding along dagger, and crouched as if to spring, stood the third man, as lean as a starved cat, with a white furious face, pale hair falling to his shoulders, and his cloak flung back This man rose upright, and laughed aloud as Jack appeared with his men behind him He was a little high-shouldered, Jack noticed

"By God!" he said. "Here be enough true men!"

He threw his dagger down on the table, and folded his arms dramatically.

Guy looked at Jack, still grinning, and lowered his own sword.

"And all to take one poor fool," he said

"And this is all" exclaimed Jack

"This is all; but an all that is all damned traitor Master Brownrigg, I make Master John Norris known to you—another of her Grace's gentlemen "

He gave an ironical bow from one to the other. Master Brownrigg answered instantly.

"I make Master Manton known to you, Master Norris We were friends at College."

This was very pretty behaviour, thought Jack, and the way in which things should be done Yet he did not entirely understand it. But he took up the same strain

"And this is Master Landlord, I suppose We had best all have a pot, and be marching."

"We will have a look through this gentleman's pockets first," drawled Guy, turning to sheathe his sword. "Will you take Master Landlord out, Jack, and leave me a couple of fellows?"

Stephen leapt to his dagger and seized it.

"Now, by God I will not have your dog's hands on me," he screamed

"Disarm him," said Guy, without turning his head.

The piteous work was done in half a minute A couple of the men came forward with cudgels, caught him, knocked the dagger out of his hand, and stood holding him.

"Very good," said Guy. "Now Jack, if you please We will not put him to too much shame."

When Jack got outside again he found that the mounted party had arrived, they had heard the shouts and had ridden up at once. He explained the situation, took them through into the common parlour, received instructions from the landlord as to how liquor could be obtained, and in five minutes had dismissed them all, with the exception of Tom, who begged to be allowed to see the end, and a couple of his own men.

As they waited Tom said something confusedly, and then stopped.

"Master Brownrigg! Do you know him too, then?" asked Jack

"I—I have seen him," stammered the boy. "Ask Master Manton, sir."

"Was he truly at College with you?" persisted the other.

Tom looked piteous

"Ask Master Manton, sir," he knows

Jack did not understand it at all Was it credible that the three had been friends at College? And if not, why was this boy so plainly troubled?

A minute later he heard Guy calling to him, and went in at once, leaving the landlord under the care of the other three.

The prisoner was seated at the table, with his cap beside him, staring defiantly out at them all, with a man guarding him.

"Have you found aught?" said Jack

"Half a broken groat, and three papers," said Guy deliberately, holding out the little bundle.

"There are but two here," said Jack

Guy nodded

"The third I keep to myself for the present Now we should be marching"

It was a very silent voyage through the dark on the slack of the tide to Greenwich Jack sat forward with the landlord; Master Brownrigg was set in the middle thwart with his arms bound, among the four rowers. Guy and Tom sat together in the stern.

Once as they came out from under London Bridge Jack could have sworn there was the sound of sobbing from the further end of the boat, and then low talking, but he could see nothing, it was too dark.

As they disembarked, and stood for a moment by the link to help the prisoners out, Jack caught sight of the boy's face. His eyes were oddly bright, and his lips twitched a little.

Then they all went forward together in silence towards the guard-room.

An nescis longas regibus esse manus?
Ov. Her

CHAPTER IV

MARY THE QUEEN DECIDES A FEW MATTERS

I

LADY MAGDALENE DACRE sat over her needlework in the little room opening out of the Queen's chamber at Greenwich, with her serious beautiful face bent low over the wooden frame from which a lily looked out, half filled in with yellow silk, and half an outline of red cotton The cold spring sunshine poured in from the south-east, and threw lozenges of colour and pale light on to the flattened rushes by her chair

She worked with great deliberateness drawing the thread tightly through, and patting it down with her white fingers, but she was thinking of other things She had sat here for over an hour, ever since the messenger had come from Oxford, and the Queen had passed through alone with the papers in her hands, saying that she must not be disturbed till she gave the signal.

Since then there had been no sound from the inner room except once the opening and closing of a further door, and half an hour later the same sound again. Magdalene knew what that meant, it was the Queen going to her private prayers in the little chapel down the passage, and returning from them.

She knew too what it was that waited for the Queen's decision. Mistress Dormer had looked in once to tell her in a whisper what was said downstairs It was Master Cranmer's fate that was to be decided He had been degraded a little more than a month before, one by one his powers had been taken from him under the symbols of the canvas vestments stripped from his shoulders. Since that he had broken down utterly; he had signed half a dozen recantations, each more abject than the last; he had confessed his heresy; he had compared himself to the penitent thief; he had submitted himself wholly and without reserve to the judgment of the Holy Roman Church in all matters of faith and morals; and had entreated mercy from the woman in whose hands lay life and death, and whom he had wronged again and again from her childhood to her coronation by every means in his power. In former years he had declared her mother a concubine and herself a bastard; he had insulted her faith as well as her birth, had taken an oath to support the Religion which at the very moment of swearing he intended to subvert, he had plotted against his Queen's succession; he had repudiated the Sacrifice for the offering of which he had been ordained and which she regarded as the most sacred act done on earth; he had betrayed the vast trust committed to him on the most solemn pledges at his consecration—and now, after all this he lay in prison, a broken-down old man, in agony at the prospect of the death that he had inflicted on others for crimes almost identical with his own, signing everything that was put before him, recanting all the opinions which had brought him prosperity, and crying out for pity from the woman whom he loathed and distrusted, and had declared no Queen.

Magdalene could not doubt what the decision would be; she knew too well what was the mind of the Councillors who had come and gone during the last month, even if the Queen had wished to show mercy, it was impossible for her to withstand such a weight of opinion.

Yet her mind shrank from the thought in horror. It was such a piteous picture of humiliation and misery; no submission could be more abject; and, she thought, no lesson more salutary than the sight of Master Cranmer going softly through the few years that remained to him on earth, alive because he was not worth the killing, and free because he was not worth his prison fare—an object lesson of the futility of ambition and heresy and of the mercy of God's ministers. This would be surely better than the fiery halo that the stake would give him. Then he had always been gentle and kindly himself, except when it had been necessary for him to show his zeal for his new-fangled religion; he had had all the domestic virtues—he had been twice married, and had been a good husband, rumour said, to the woman whom he called his wife; he had, in fact, been a timid, quiet, scholarly man all his days, entirely incapable of coping with his public duties or of withstanding the fierce master whom he served. The same feebleness of character that now allowed him to sign his numerous recantations had brought him to the situation where signing was a necessity.

So Magdalene sat and embroidered, and pitied and loathed him in her heart.

Behind that curtained door she knew the final decision was being made. A sickly withered woman was biting her pen as she looked at the papers spread before her, and the tall trembling letters "Thomas Cranmer" at the foot of each. Was it possible, Magdalene wondered, that she should disentangle what he deserved for his heresy from what he had merited from herself, for his treason towards her? Perhaps it was to help her in that unravelling that she had gone out half an hour ago to where the Crucified King of Kings, shrouded in silk, hung over His altar.

There were other matters, too, that helped to complicate the issues

Scarcely three days before the Queen had told her of another of the new threads that had come into her hands of a plot so mysterious and far-reaching that none knew how far it extended. She had broken out in passion in her bed-chamber, binding them first to secrecy, and had hinted of an assault upon the Tower; of a scheme to sweep the Channel and secure the great forts on the south-coast. Henry of France was in it; members of her own Court against whom she had refused to believe evil had joined her enemies, the Catholic Religion, her own claim to the throne, the Spanish marriage, the peace and unity of England were the objects of attack. The following night Manton had brought in a prisoner secretly, and had given in a list of names of those concerned. Was it possible then to expect the Queen to deal lightly with this old ringleader of former conspiracies against her throne, who added to that crime the sin of heresy?

Magdalene sighed, laid down her embroidery and listened.

As she did so the door from the corridor opened noiselessly and old Mrs. Clarentia looked in.

Magdalene shook her head, and the old lady came through and sat down beside her opposite the hearth.

"Eh!" she said, "it is past dinner-time"

"I dare not disturb her," whispered Magdalene. "She bade me not"

"The gentlemen are all waiting," went on Mistress Clarentia; "they would have me come in to see how long her Grace would be"

The girl shook her head, and took up her embroidery once more

"My lord Cardinal will see her this afternoon, I hear," said the other, watching the growing lily approvingly, with her hands folded together

"He was here last night, too," said the girl. "I suppose it is all the same business"

"But her Grace will make up her mind without him," said the old lady decisively "None can do it but she"

"Did you ever see him?" asked Magdalene, suddenly, looking up at her

"My Lord   ?"

"Master Cranmer, I mean"

"Yes, many a time I saw him in his barge once coming from Lambeth to see his Grace; he passed close beside me."

"What is he like?"

"Nay; I could see nothing of him but his purple and his cross He has a beard now, they tell me"

Magdalene was silent again for a minute or two Then the old lady went on

"He will be burned, I am sure of it They all say so."

"My lord of Ely did not think so," said the girl

Mistress Clarentia said nothing She was plainly thinking more of the Queen than of the Archbishop, and was distressed that dinner was kept waiting

They could hear low talking from the gallery outside where the ushers were waiting to form the procession to the little room where the Queen dined during these days, for her table in the great hall had not been used for months She was not well enough to bear publicity.

From her own room came still no sound. That heavy flowered curtain veiled all mysteries.

Mistress Clarentia could bear it no longer.

Magdalene watched her rise uneasily and go towards the door, and presently saw her old white head bent down to catch the faintest sound from within, with her wrinkled hand, dripping with lace, raised for silence,

The girl sighed once or twice, laid down her embroidery once more, and stood up, stretching herself

Then the old woman suddenly turned and made a swift tremulous gesture, and the next moment drew back the curtain. There was the click of an opening latch, and the Queen came silently through and stood for an instant in the doorway

Magdalene looked eagerly at her face, and thought she had never seen it look so worn

It was terribly old and drawn now. Her beauty had faded with extraordinary swiftness during her short reign Beneath those hard, tired eyes lay dark pouches, her nose stood out sharp beneath white tight-drawn skin, the corners of her mouth were lined with months of pain and sorrow, and her throat above her square-cut dress was thin and shrivelled

So much Magdalene saw now, as the Queen stood in her rich robes framed in the dark oak, alight with jewels from neck to waist, but she could read no more from that stiff, wrinkled mask of what the decision had been It might be life and death, she bore either with equal sorrow for herself and others,—a queen of desolation.

The girl recovered herself, and went swiftly across to the gallery door and threw it open There was a stir of footsteps and then a sudden silence at the sound, and she saw the half-dozen gentlemen spring quickly into position

The Queen was close behind her as she turned; and Mistress Clarentia followed Magdalene looked at her questioningly as she fell into her place beside her in the gallery, and the old lady turned and nodded twice with solemn eyes

Then Magdalene followed on down the corridor with beating heart.

From behind the Queen's chair at dinner Magdalene, trained now in the instincts of the Court, could see that there was a suppressed excitement in the solemn faces that went about the ritual of the table She could hardly have said what it was that told her that; it was partly the alert silence, partly the quick slight glances at the Queen. Master Manton was there to-day, she saw, he seemed less aware than any, and stood in his place, or went this way and that, with a heavy sullen face. It seemed to her that he was suffering, it was scarcely possible otherwise that a man could look so; and yet so far as she knew he should have been all the other way. It was said that his prisoner had been an important one, at any rate he had been sent to the Tower, and Master Norris had been loud in the praise of Master Manton's skill and patience. It was certain that the Queen could not allow her zealous servant to go unrewarded Yet his face showed no excitement or pleasure

Magdalene ran her eyes along the other gentlemen, Master Kearsley as always, with a peevish air, was taking the rose-water from another. Master Norris, who was standing unoccupied, lifted his eyes to hers, with a question in them. She looked down; she dared not nod; she knew nothing for certain

As the Queen turned away from table when grace had been said, she paused a moment, and put her hand on Magdalene's arm.

"Tell Master Manton I will see him," she said, "when my lord Cardinal is gone again "

Then she was gone through the doorway, and the girl called up a page and gave her message As she sped along the gallery after the Queen she met the gentlemen coming back, and was surrounded in a moment.

"I know nothing," she said, "nothing Her Grace has been alone and has told me nothing"

"What think you yourself, my lady?" said a voice.

"I think he will burn; but I know nothing. We shall not know till my lord Cardinal has been"

The ante-chamber was empty when she reached it, and the Queen's door closed. Magdalene sat down by the window to wait

What a life this was! How strange and difficult! Here she was, set close to tragedy after tragedy, yet untouched by them all. The great personages who swept by her and disappeared through closed doors, had nothing but smiling courtesy for the beautiful maid-of-honour, even the chief of them all, the odious little Spanish Prince whose courtesy had once over-balanced itself—he, too, had been tame and respectful enough when she had last seen him. And yet while their faces smiled, their minds were on other things—on plots and counter-plots and policy. Even the mistress of the great company, whom she had seen at her weakest moments, was fire and steel in affairs of State, unapproachable, consuming, adamant.

Magdalene had longed once, when she had conquered her timidity, to be admitted to those secrets, now she feared it. It had given her nothing but distress to receive the Queen's confidence three days before. She knew she was not suited to this life She was more at her ease in it now, she had no fits of shyness or home-sickness; but she desired simplicity with all her heart; a house in some pleasant country place with tall grey walls, a timbered park, a towered gateway—she could rule such a place as this, she thought; she could say her prayers in peace, govern her servants, please her husband—for she would surely marry some day, though certainly not gay Mr. Norris; and develop her own serene nature without the warp that the close presence of a hard complex personality such as the Queen's could not but cause She trembled at her still, shrank from her caresses, did not wish even to search for the heart that inspired her.

The bell rang out suddenly for the ladies' dinner, and, as she rose to go, the door from the Queen's chamber opened and Mistress Clarentia came out with a packet of papers in her hands.

Magdalene stared at them brought down to earth in a moment, and terrified at the thought of what they contained.

"Nay, child," said the old lady, coming up to her, "my lord Cardinal is to see them all before the messenger leaves again."

"Has she decided "asked the girl, trembling a little.

"I think so, my dear."

2

The Queen came slowly back from the Presence-Chamber an hour later; passed through the ante-room without acknowledging the courtesies of her ladies, shut the door behind her, and sat down in the wide arm-chair before the hearth.

She was miserably tired, and for a few minutes was scarcely conscious of anything but the pleasant warmth of the fire, the comfort of the deep chair and the restful silence and peace of the room She felt she could not bear to see anyone just now; Master Manton must wait a little; she knew she would not be disturbed till she gave the signal.

She lay perfectly passive, her buckled shoes stretched towards the burning logs; her chin on her breast, her hands listless in her lap, and her whole body from head to feet one mass of sick weariness.

She felt terribly alone Philip was abroad and would not answer her letters, Gardiner was dead, the Duke of Norfolk was dead, and even the Cardinal this afternoon had been of no help to her; and, worst of all, she did not know how far his deficiencies had arisen from her own fault

Perhaps she had been too decisive, she thought, too clearly resolved on Master Cranmer's death; but she had not meant that; she had only wished to show that for her part she was ready to take the consequences of his death. On the other hand she had been perfectly prepared to listen to persuasion. Yet the Cardinal had said very little; he had looked at her out of his deep eyes and told her that she was Queen; he had not offered in the least to shift the responsibility from her weary shoulders She had told him shortly of all the advice she had received, of the will of the Council, she had reminded him of the laws of three of her predecessors, of the Pope's instructions, and of the Archbishop's crimes; then she had shown him the recantations and looked again at copies of the letters that the Legate had written to the prisoner. Then she had waited for help, for a strong approval or of a dignified entreaty; and there had been silence instead.

They had gone on to speak of other matters then, of the diocese of Canterbury which would presently be vacant, of the arrangements for the Cardinal's consecration and appointment. He had asked again after her health; spoken a word or two on other things, and that had been all And here she sat now, worn out and distracted, and the messenger was on his way to Oxford with instructions for the case to go forward according to law.

It seemed to her now as if some irresistible force had closed round that compelled her to act in a certain way She had done the utmost of which her broken-down body and mind were capable, to dissociate herself from her own passions on the one side and from external influences on the other; she seldom saw her Councillors, she tried to be human and natural; she struggled to pray, to follow internal guidance; but, in spite of all, circumstances would not let her alone. On the one side her people were still busy against her, with plot after plot, on the other side there was the machinery of the law brought into being by the votes of her Parliament What could she do but permit its working? It was not that she had not tried tenderness—she had abolished many penalties, she had pardoned hundreds who had incurred death, she had done her best to please them, she had refused to believe evil against them; and time after time they had responded with treachery and assault. Even her own servants were against her Magdalene shrank from her—she knew that very well; Master Norris was indifferent, though loyal; Master Underhill, she did not doubt, hated her and her Faith, and had plotted against her person, though there was no legal evidence against him.

What could she do with her people? She could neither understand them nor explain herself to them Yet she assured herself that it was not for want of trying

Again, as regards heresy, what was to be done? She had begun by hoping that the Faith was not extinguished, and that by acting gradually, by restoring little by little the old worship, the light would be re-kindled. And her people had answered by attacking her priests, mocking her Religion, and weaving sedition and heresy so inextricably together that it was impossible to punish the one without glorifying the other If God had not brought her to the throne that she might re-establish the Faith of His Church, why had He brought her there at all? She felt stupid and bewildered from the torment of the morning's decision and her own sickness

Eighteen months ago she had been so happy. The Legate had come with a splendour that promised great things, England, she thought, had been restored to unity, her husband had been with her, the babe had leapt in her womb—the dear babe that was to take up the government when she laid it down. Now it seemed as if all were a ghastly delusion; the Legate indeed was still here, but how powerless 'The heart-shaking scene in Westminster Hall was no more than the rehearsal of a play that seemed postponed indefinitely, her husband had disappeared into silence, and the leap of the child was the thrill of a horrible disease.

Her head sank lower still on to her breast, and her tired eyes closed.

Half an hour later she opened them again and sat up a little Her head ached intolerably after the heavy doze

She must see Master Manton, he had been waiting so long There were none too many faithful servants left; and then she must write to Philip, again he had not written for three days.

She went painfully across to the door, called to one of her ladies and gave directions, then returned once more and saw down.

She had not long to wait, the door presently opened and Master Manton came across the floor, knelt and saluted her, and stood upright again as she gave the signal

What was it that she was to say to him? She had forgotten, What was it he had done? Ah, yes! She made an effort and sat upright

"I wished to thank you, sir, for your zeal——"

No; that was too cold. She must show more gratitude . the lack of it had been one of her mistakes

"I am very grateful, sir, for your courage and discretion. Master Norris tells me you put yourself in great peril I told you once before that I valued faithfulness above everything; I tell it you again now, more than ever."

She looked up a moment at the young man; but his face was in shadow; and he said nothing

She went on, twisting her rings round her shrunken fingers.

"The fellow is in the Tower, is he not?"

"Yes, madam"

"Yes; well, there will be more there soon I have seen the papers you took from him, and the names—you kept all private, of course? '

"Yes, madam."

"I must think what reward will be fitting. We will wait, perhaps, till His Highness comes here That will be soon now, please God."

Again there was silence. Mary could not think what else to say to this stern gentleman of hers. She was blind and stupid with headache.

"We must wait too," she went on presently, "until we have sifted the matter to the bottom. I am astonished that Master Kingston is in it. He was released from the Tower scarcely six months ago I thought him a foolish fellow, but no rascal Are you sure he is in it, Master Manton?"

"I know he came to see Master Ashton at Oxford, and his name is in the list. I know no more than that, your Grace.'

Mary considered a moment.

"Well, we shall know more soon when Master—Master

"Brownrigg, madam."

"When Master Brownrigg speaks"

There was a pause.

"Did you speak, sir?"

"No, madam"

She wished she could see his face; but it was impossible. He stood with his back to the window, and the light beyond his head dazzled and stung her tired eyes. There was certainly some emotion close to her; or was it merely her own weariness and nerves?

"It is a greater affair than I thought at first, Master Manton. We moved the money from the Tower, you know, sir, some while ago They were after that; but that is not all; and your prisoner proves it. It is strange there were no more papers on him? '

"Perhaps he feared treachery, madam," said the steady voice.

"There were no more? You searched him well?"

"I searched him well, madam."

"Ah! well—"

She could not bear any more talking Her head throbbed and burned with pain, and she mechanically put out her hand once more to be kissed.

She caught a glimpse of his face as he knelt and took it, and it seemed to her that it was older than she had thought; his lips, too, were hot, though they scarcely touched her hand.

"I tell you again, sir, I am grateful to you; and shall not forget it."

When he was gone she still sat a minute or two before going to her table, closing her eyes and leaning back in her chair.

She had done that at least—thanked this ungracious young man personally; and it was a good deal in these days when she refused audiences to almost all who applied for them She was weary of councillors; prosperity did not lie that way. Rather it was to be found in fearless action, and above all in finding the will of God by prayer and devotion She was doing what she could, she told herself, towards restoring those old roads to His Heart down which grace had passed for so many centuries; the Observant Friars were back in their old home where her mother had worshipped—herself a tertiary of the Order; the Black Friars were moving into St Bartholomew's The Carthusians would be back at Sheen before the end of the year, and there was a great scheme for the return of the black monks to Westminster Master Feckenham was coming to see her, she remembered, in a few days. Had she not, perhaps, been too anxious about many things; too faithless to the resolution which she had made before Stephen Gardiner—(Jesu rest him!)—to trust God and believe the best of man?

To believe the best of man! Well, she must write to Philip.

She rose and went to her table.

The broad paper was laid out and the pounce-box beside it. The pens were ready to her hand, and the ink-horn in front

But she could not begin She had begun so often; she had poured out her heart again and again—her heart restrained and guided by her cautious head—and it had been so useless. He was so unreasonable, too, the men that came from him at long intervals brought no letter of love, but they brought impossible demands instead—impossible to all who knew England as she did Was she hard on him? God knew she had given him all she could, and the love of her heart with it Perhaps he was too busy with his wars and with the control of his huge dominions to understand how difficult was this vehement little country which he had left his sick wife to rule

She must write once more, but the tears blinded her as she began

"Monseigneur…"

3

Greenwich was in a greater stir a few days later than had been seen there for many months The newly-made Archbishop was come from Bow Church, where he had that day received the Pall, to pay his respects to the Queen Outside, a fleet of barges and boats rocked at the steps, and a strip of scarlet carpet ran from the water's edge to the grand entrance, a crowd of priests, gentlemen and servants congregated here to see the prelate come out, and a steady buzz of talk went upon all sides in the sunny air

It was thought by some that a new era had begun. So long as Cranmer was alive there had been complications, for although he had been deposed and degraded, it had been thought better that the diocese should lie vacant until his fate had been decided; now, however, the last obstacle had been removed, and the Cardinal was in full and lawful possession of the See and all officers belonging to it. It was the party that took this view that talked the louder this morning on the palace-steps

There were others who were silent

Within Placentia itself there was not the same expression of opinion, except in groups here and there gathered in the parlours on the ground floor. The long corridors upstairs and down were lined with silent figures, that leaned forward and craned watching heads this way and that, as great personages swept up and down, or ushers scurried along from the direction of the little suite of rooms where the Queen and the Cardinal were closeted together.

In the first of these rooms there was one group of which the members knew perhaps more than anyone of the real state of affairs, and of the reasons for hope and fear, but they talked very little.

Old Father Peto, the Greenwich friar, in his grey habit, who had weathered many storms under Henry, and had been in peril of his life again and again, was saying his office in a chair drawn up to the hearth, his bare feet crossed before him

Monsignor Priuli, the Venetian, and the intimate friend of Reginald Pole for many years, who had refused the sacred purple that he might be near the Archbishop, was standing in the window-recess and looking out at the crowd of boats, the mob of sightseers and officials on either side of the scarlet cloth and the sunlit river beyond

Dr Feckenham, designated Abbot of Westminster, was beside him, dressed and shorn as a secular priest, was looking out too.

The Italian sighed softly once or twice, and turned round.

"When do you go to Westminster, sir?"

Dr. Feckenham told mm, in the autumn, he thought.

"I spoke with her Grace yesterday," he said.

He was a little man, stout and rosy, with quiet contented eyes and white teeth. It was very pleasant to him to contemplate the return to Westminster, and he beamed as he spoke of it.

"Her Grace is doing wonders," he went on. "The Religious are coming back everywhere" He indicated Father Peto with his head. "He is more fortunate. He is home again already.'

"Why, yes," said Monsignor shortly He paused, "And what of Master Cranmer?"

"What of him?" asked the monk.

The Italian raised his delicate black eyebrows and pursed his lips.

"A heretic all the while!" he said softly. "He has lost his soul But he has saved us?"

Dr. Feckenham looked puzzled.

"You mean his final recantation?"

"I mean that, I mean that what Master Latimer said is true. They have lit a candle between them And they all hate my lord of London like the devil, though he be a kindly man at heart"

The monk was silent a moment Then he came a step forward close beside the other

"Would my lord Cardinal not have burned him then?"

Monsignor Priuli looked over his shoulder, but the old friar's lips were moving, and he wore a heavy frown of attention as he said his office.

"Why, no; my lord would not. But her Grace would have it so. My lord said it was useless to speak"

He turned again to the window and began to drum on the glass softly, with his fingers. Then he went on again in a yet lower voice

"And now there is this new matter of the plot. They have Throgmorton, Peckham, Brownrigg, Daniel and Rosey in the Tower, with above thirty others. And God knows how many more will be in it soon"

"Master Ashton is in France, I hear," observed the monk presently.

"But he will not stay there," said the other priest bitterly, "I wish to God he would!"

They talked of the plot for a few minutes in undertones; and it was indeed enough to alarm the most sanguine optimist. Someone had blabbed within a day or two of Brownrigg's arrest. There had been strange parties going about the City, pointing to the comet that shone like a pale streamer of cloud in the blue sky, and telling folks that it portended great things, and the Council had acted swiftly and decisively Nearly forty persons were already in the Tower, some of them prominent men—Master Rosey, for example, was the keeper of the Star-Chamber; Master Uvedale, who was on his way to London under arrest had held no less a post than that of Captain of the Isle of Wight; John Daniel had been a confidential servant to Lord Northampton. The pretext for the plot was supposed to be King Henry's will by which he had attempted to leave the kingdom away from both Mary and Elizabeth if they married without the Council's consent, and King Edward's "device" for the succession of Lady Jane Grey, and the object of the plot was to depose and execute Mary, and set Elizabeth in her place. No man knew how far the conspiracy did not extend; the Earl of Westmoreland and Lord Williams were under suspicion, Sir Anthony Kingston was certainly attempting to raise men in Wales, and even the King of France was supposed to be privy to the whole affair. There was no doubt that Ashton and Horsey were at present at his Court and under his protection; but these had not yet been actually proclaimed as traitors.

"Master Jernmgham and Master Hastings were with the Council this morning, I hear," said Monsignor Priuli at last "It is they who are to examine the prisoners"

"And the Lady Elizabeth is at Bishop's Hatfield?" questioned the monk softly.

The Italian shrugged his shoulders eloquently once more.

"I shall not be surprised if she is sent for," he said.

Master Feckenham sighed, and his eyes looked melancholy in his rosy face He hated these affairs, and could not understand why folks were so troublesome There was not the shadow of a doubt in his mind as to which side would win; of course the old faith would come back, and he and his fellows would sing again in Westminster, and the old Catholic life begin to beat again in England's shrivelled veins And why would not others understand that, and leave rebellion alone, and learn to serve God and their prince loyally, as their fathers had done?

Well, it was not his business It was her Grace who had to deal with them; and if only her Grace would not be so cold

He broke off his meditations as the door from the direction of the Queen's inner rooms opened, and an usher came through.

"My Lord Cardinal will be coming out immediately," said the gentleman bowing, and disappeared back again.

Old Father Peto sprang to his feet, thrusting a finger into his breviary, and began to mutter a paternoster to mark the break

"Who was that" asked Monsignor Pnuh, turning to the monk "I have seen him at Lambeth"

Master Feckenham shook his head He had not noticed

"That man has something on his soul," whispered the Italian shortly "Did you not see his eyes?"

The monk turned astonished

"I know him now," went on Monsignor, as if talking to himself. "I remember"

"Who is it then?"

"That is Master Guy Manton."

The door fell back between bowing gentlemen and the stately bearded figure came through in rochet and scarlet cape smiling at the three friends who awaited him A couple of boys carried his tram

"To Lambeth," he said, "come with us, my lord Abbot."

Master Feckenham beamed, and followed

4

There were others besides Monsignor Priuli who noticed that there was something the matter with Master Manton. It seemed to Jack Norris that his friend was a very tiresome and incomprehensible fellow. A week had passed since Brownrigg's arrest, and he had not had a word with him. Guy had gone about his duties silent and sullen, his door had been locked twice when Jack had tried to open it, and there had been only the shortest answer when he tapped And yet the man had done a brilliant stroke; he had laid hands on an important unit in the plot before the officials had done much more than suspect that there was a plot at all He had been thanked personally by the Queen, and a reward was imminent What more did the fellow want? He had always complained of lack of work, and was now dissatisfied when he had got it.

There were two possible explanations to Jack's mind. One was that the paper which Guy had retained held something unforeseen which altered the state of affairs; the other that there was truth in what Brownrigg had said, and the two had indeed been friends at College The former of these two solutions appeared unlikely; but the latter was surely more unlikely still It was not credible that a man should show such zeal and skill in the capture of his friend

Jack determined to get the truth out of Tom; he was certain the boy knew it

On the evening of the day that the Cardinal had been to Greenwich Master Norris sent a message to the household at supper that he desired Master Bradshawe to come to the music parlour at seven o'clock and to bring his notes with him

There was a charming virginal there, once belonging to King Henry, that had somehow found its way to the pensioners' room; and this Jack Norris had caused to be set in a separate little chamber where a harp or two was also kept. He knew he would not be disturbed here this evening; and the music, too, was a pretext for sending for the boy

He was so absorbed in the delicate tinkle of the strings, and in his own ingenious harmonies, to the air on the paper propped before him that he did not notice Tom's entrance. The boy waited a moment, and then came across the room softly.

"Ah! you are come then," said Jack, without turning round "Listen to this."

He began to play the Miserere very softly and movingly, murmuring the words, and singing aloud between each verse the refrain, *"In diebus illis mulier guae erat in civitate peccatrix...."*

He sang half a dozen verses and stopped

"Do you know what that is, my lad?" he said, still without turning round.

"No, sir," said a melancholy voice.

"It is the Maundy music, which you will sing when her Grace washes feet next week."

He began to touch the notes again.

"What have you brought?" he said.

He heard the same desolate voice name a song or two, and perceived from the tone that he would have to put the boy at his ease before approaching the great subject; so he still did not turn or look at him, and began to play softly the prelude to one of Walter Mapes' Latin drinking-songs that young Mr. Byrde had lately set, with his eyes fixed steadily on the blaze of painting above the keys where the King's beasts, ramping within a gilt Garter, pawed the crest that held the Royal arms

But the performance, which should have been rollicking, was a very dreary affair Tom seemed strangely out of spirits, and Jack kept back his criticisms with considerable difficulty. He proposed another song, and that was sung too, and then the accompanist wheeled swiftly round and faced the singer "My lad," he said, "What is the matter with you?" He saw instantly the boy's face break into lines, and his eyes fill with tears. He leaned forward and took him by the arms, drawing him close up

"Tom, tell me, is it Master Brownrigg?" The boy struggled violently and the tears ran down his cheeks. But Jack held him

"Who is Master Brownrigg? Did you know him at College?"

"He—he gave me a gown once," sobbed the boy with a convulsed face Then he tore himself free, and in another moment was out of the room, leaving his music-sheets scattered on the floor

Jack sat a moment considering. Then he turned round again and began to play

He was so rapt m contemplation that he did not hear a step coming down the passage; but he heard the door violently thrust open and then shut to again; and turned round astonished to see Guy, his face white with passion and his mouth working, looking at him from the centre-of the floor.

"God damn you, sir! How dare you tamper with my servant?"

Jack made a motion as of whistling and set his hands on his knees surveying Master Manton from head to foot, insolently.

"Your servant can sing no better than a cat to-night," he said.

Guy's hands rose swiftly; and Jack rose with them, defiant through fear

"See here, Master Manton, I will not have this threatening. I am your officer, sir. How dare you speak to me like that?"

Guy's mouth opened to answer, but Jack was beforehand.

"It is my business to see that .there be no trickery. How do I know if you be not sheltering Master Brownrigg with that paper you hold back?"

The other's face closed like a trap; his lips snapped together and his brows came down

"You swore, sir" he said.

"I did swear," said Jack. "Then do not make me break my oath"

The two eyed one another a moment; but Guy's defence was weakening, and the other saw it.

"Why will you not tell me what is in it?" he said more quietly

Guy's lips worked a little. Then he broke out—

"Because I do not know myself. I swear I do not; it is in cypher"

"Pooh!" said Jack, "a hundred can read it."

"But I dare not show it"

"Well, then, let me see it."

Guy's face darkened again; and Jack smiled a little bitterly.

"Well, then—that priest who was here to-day—my lord Priuli, he is skilled in such things"

Guy shook his head.

"I will show it to no one," he said, "this is my affair."

"Pah! But the paper is not what is troubling you It is Master Brownrigg"

Once more Guy's face became hard, but there was something else in it too Jack could see he was only controlling himself with a great effort.

Then he spoke with a loud hard voice.

"It is not, sir; Master Brownrigg may save himself. He is a damned traitor."
He wheeled and went out of the room.

Jack stood looking after him a moment or two; then he sat down at the virginal again, and began to play little minor chords, sounding the fifth below in soft resonant taps.

Then again he paused with his fingers on the keys.

"The poor devil!" he said softly.

Nthtl difficile amanti puto
Cic. *Orat.*

CHAPTER V

MARY THE QUEEN DECIDES SOME MORE MATTERS

I

IT was not until the beginning of June that the Queen sent for her sister.

In the meantime many of the conspirators had been disposed of. Uvedale, who had promised to betray the Isle of Wight with Hurst Castle, and John Throgmorton suffered at the end of April, and William Stanton a little later. Sir Anthony Kingston had killed himself on his way up from Wales under arrest; M. de Noailles, the French ambassador, had taken his leave of the Queen a week before, after a very narrow escape from being proceeded against by the Council for his supposed share in the conspiracy against her. A large number of other prisoners were in safe keeping in the Tower Most of these under torture had given up details and names, communications were passing almost continually between the Tower and Greenwich as new facts came out, and letters came fast enough now from Philip at Brussels who feared for his power in England

The arrival of the Lady Elizabeth was carried out with such secrecy that few, even in the palace itself, suspected who it was that came down the park in a closed litter and was whisked through the private door at the back Orders had been given that most of the household should be gone on that day to prepare for Corpus Christi at Whitehall, and not more than half a dozen persons were aware of the Princess' coming The Queen had taken these steps lest additional cause should be given for the suspicions that were already active enough as to her sister's complicity in the plot.

Mary was waiting ill-at-ease upstairs in a little room opening out of her bed-chamber. She had had news two days before that made it very difficult for her to believe in her sister's innocence; Master Jerningham had himself come across from the Tower to tell her that there was no reasonable doubt but that the Princess' household was truly implicated, and that Mrs. Katharine Ashley, her governess, had certainly been privy to the whole affair, as well as Sir Henry Peckham, one of her officers. The only question before the queen was as to whether her sister herself had been cognisant of it, or had been merely the unwilling figure-head of the matter.

The memory of the Princess' past history did not encourage Mary in her desire to believe the best. And besides, in this present affair there had been a remarkable letter or two shown to the Queen, addressed to M. de Noailles from one of the conspirators in France which left very little doubt of Elizabeth's guilt.

"Et surtout," she had read, *"eviter que madame Elizabeth ne se remue en sorte du monde pour entreprendre ce que m'escrivez; car ce serait tout gaster, et perdre le fruict qu'ilz peulvent attendre de leurs desseings, qu'il est besoign traicter et mener d la longue."*

"Le fruict—" What was that?

Mary now sat with her back to the window, her arm on a little table between her and the fire, and her feet raised on a great carved stool. A chair had been set for the Princess a yard opposite, where her face could be plainly seen. The Queen was wondering what to say; she could not accuse her sister directly of conspiring her murder; she could hardly ask even indirect questions. She had determined merely to state the facts, and await Elizabeth's comments. She would not be emotional or appeal for pity; far less would she threaten; she would just be cold and dispassionate in the business, and affectionate as regards personal relations. So she resolved. But she felt miserably ill, and afraid; and her face showed it. Yet she knew she must be strong.

As she heard the footsteps in the passage she took her feet off the stool and drew herself more upright in her chair, gripping the lion-heads in her two hands to steady their trembling.

Then the door opened; there was a moment's pause, and the Princess came forward. The door closed softly behind her as the Queen stood up.

The girl stood there a moment in the full light, a picture of royal grace and dignity, and Mary recognised it with a pang at her own heart She had thrown back her hood and travelling cloak, and her pale oval face, crowned with auburn hair and a tight white head-dress, looked fearlessly out; one slender strong hand held together her cloak, and, beneath her peaked stomacher with points of light here and there from a few jewels ran down into the straight full folds of her brocade skirts. Her attitude was superb, the fingers of her other hand were lifted a little, one buckled red shoe was advanced, and her head was thrown slightly back. The expression in her narrow bright eyes, and the curve of her red lips, was a triumph. She might have served as a mirror for outraged innocence.

Then as the Queen came towards her she swept down to the ground in a great courtesy, rose and stood with downcast eyes, as her sister put her arms tremulously round her shoulders, and kissed her on both cheeks.

For a moment Mary could not speak. There was a jealousy to be dealt with—a jealousy of that youth and dignity, and of the long years that they seemed to promise In that instant she had understood as never before why it was that the country cried out joyously for the girl and was silent and resentful under the rule of a withered disappointed woman, old before her time. She made a violent effort, and led her sister to the chair, kissing her again from behind as she seated her. Then she went to her own chair, sat down painfully and drew a long breath.

"This has not troubled you, my sister," she said, "this coming?"

Elizabeth lifted her eyes and dropped them again.

"I would come further than from Hatfield, very gladly, to see your Grace."

She spoke in a perfectly quiet and deferential tone, with just the shadow of a reproach in her voice.

"It was necessary for me to see you, sweetheart," went on the Queen, almost apologetically, "and I could not come to you, though I shall hope to do so; but I am too ill."

The girl looked up again with a courteous sympathy in her eyes; and down again at her own white hand laid on her knee.

She sat perfectly still, forward and very upright, a little turned away from the Queen.

"There are a thousand troubles to vex me," went on Mary, watching the girl's face; "His Highness is not here to help me. He has his own troubles. And now there is this last matter, worse than all."

"The affair of Master Kingston and the rest?" said Elizabeth quietly, "I thank God who has preserved your Grace from their malice."

"Yes, sweetheart, the affair of Master Kingston. You have heard that he judged himself, no doubt?"

"Master Parry told me so."

"And we have judged others; and God will judge all."

There was nothing in her sister's face but a slight distressed interest as she nodded in answer Mary watched her for a moment longer and then went on.

"One of my greatest sorrows too is the thought that I have given you such officers."

Elizabeth turned her face and looked deliberately into the Queen's eyes

"What is that, your Grace."

"Such officers as Master Peckham," said Mary steadily.

"I do not understand, sister. He is not arraigned yet, surely"

"He is not arraigned yet, but the others have told enough We know that he is guilty."

"Under torture?"

"Why, yes," said Mary.

Elizabeth kept her bright eyes fixed on the Queen's an instant longer, and then looked pensively at her hand again, stretching her fingers a little as if to admire the rings.

"Under torture men will say anything, I think," she observed.

"They will say the truth, yes. Is there any other manner of getting it?"

"At least I do not know it," said the girl softly.

Mary saw her advantage; it was plain now from Elizabeth's slight air of embarrassment that she did not know how much the prisoners had confessed, or even whether they had implicated her The Queen determined to keep up the mystery, and, if possible, to make her sister put the question direct.

"At least they have spoken," she went on; "they are kept separate, and their tales agree." She paused a moment. "They have told us some strange things."

The Princess did not answer, she was curving and straightening her fingers as a cat her claws.

"And there is Mrs. Ashley too, sweetheart—"

A little thrill went over the slender figure in the chair; it was as if she had been touched unexpectedly Her fingers closed tightly for a moment, then uncurved and lay still. Mary watched every movement from tired, anxious eyes. She repeated the prick cautiously.

"Mrs. Ashley too—"

This time it went home. Elizabeth turned briskly in her chair and faced the Queen, with her head thrown back and her eyes proud and candid.

"Your Grace, am I to understand that I am under suspicion?"

Mary was taken completely aback. She had expected cringing or expostulation, or a burst of tears; but not this clear fierce challenge. In her last interview with her of this kind there had been wailing at the misjudgment, indignant crying upon God, but not this air of fearless innocence She hesitated a moment, uncrossed and crossed her feet again, licked her dry lips.

The Princess stood up, with an extraordinary dignity in her face and figure; and again came the challenge, a little louder and on a higher note with a ring of indignant hysteria in it.

"Your Grace thinks me privy to it?"

Mary made a violent effort to control herself, took her feet down from the stool and clutched her hands together in her lap. What would happen next? She had not an idea what to answer to the direct question, though she had provoked it deliberately. The next instant her hands were caught by the girl, who had thrown herself on her knees, and a torrential stream of lamentation began.

"Oh! Christ! and your Majesty can think that! And I the hottest of your lovers and defenders! And your Majesty always so cold and unkind to me! And it is I who have been plotted against and traduced and betrayed, and would believe no evil of your Grace, or that it was your will that kept me in prison, and set me about with spies! And when my chamber was set afire they told me it was your Grace who ordered it, and I cried out that it was not. And when the warrant was sent down I told them it was not your will And your Majesty can believe this of me in spite of all—and that I could give myself to their foul plots! And I have prayed so for your Grace and his High ness, and that God might send you a son, and I be relieved from the crown that lies so heavy—and all the while—your Grace—could think—"

Then sobs began, her whole body shook with them; and Mary felt the young ardent lips kissing, kissing her withered hands, and a flood of tears raining down on them.

"Sister, sister."

"And I have been so true and so patient—and—and—have never complained—or made moan—to any—but to your Majesty and God And— your Grace can think——"

It was intolerable. Mary was worn out with sickness and despair

"Sister, I did not believe——"

"Ah I but your Grace did believe it," cried the girl passion ately, lifting her flushed tear-stained face "Else why did your Grace press that about Mrs. Ashley? And I—all the while——"

Down went the face again upon the Queen's hands and rested, murmuring and sobbing there

There followed a silence

The Queen was horribly distressed. Her mind told her one thing, and her heart another. Her mind told her that the girl had overdone the sorrow, that it was too dramatic, too sudden and too vehement; further her mind told her that it was impossible for such plots to go on in the household at Hatfield, and the shrewd mistress of it all not know it. She remembered, too, that the girl had never cleared herself two years ago, except by her own fierce and tearful oaths

On the other side her whole heart went out to this poor child who could cry so bitterly at suspicion, who could kiss her hands so ardently, not as a courtier but as a lover; who could throw herself down so vehemently, body and soul at once, who could pour out such piteous eloquence, who could reproach so lovingly And this sour woman longed so much for love!

Even the simulation of it, if so fervent as this, was worth the having.

She waited a moment longer, driving down her own emotion. Then she drew out one of her hands from the languid weight that grew heavier as she did so, and laid it tenderly on the white nape of the neck that lay on her knees.

Even then she noticed the contrast between the firm warm flesh that she touched, with the auburn hair curling up under the linen, and her own dry, wrinkled fingers. She began to stroke and caress softly

Then she spoke in her hoarse man's voice

"Nay, nay, dear heart, lie still—I love to have you so "She gave a great sob of self-pity. "I do not believe a word of it. It was because I did not beleive it that I had you here secretly I would not have others believe it of my darling I know you would not You love me too well, is it not so? But you have had wicked folks round you, and it has been my fault You will forgive me that, sister——?"

The girl made a movement to lift her head, but the wrinkled hand, heavy with rings, held her gently down.

"They have said cruel things against you. I will listen to them no more And you, sweetheart——" the heavy voice choked a moment—" you, sweetheart, will not believe them against me? We will love one another better I cannot have you here, sister, you know that But you shall be very happy. I will send you other officers instead You shall be very happy until your time comes, it will not be long now, I think I am very old and ill, my dear, and it may be——"

Again the white-wrapped head strove to rise, and again the steady hand held it down. It was wonderful to feel that warm cheek so.

"That is as our Lord directs And meantime, dear heart, as I said, you will believe the best of me. Trust God and believe the best of man, that was what my lord said . Kiss me, sweetheart"

Masters Norris and Kearsley were in the secret of the Princess coming, and stood bareheaded in the dusk a couple of hours later as the slender figure swept out of the narrow doorway to the rear of the house and across the gravel to where the litter waited.

Neither saw her face as the hood was drawn forward, but they watched her go across the space and disappear into the darkness of the curtains. Then the little cavalcade was gone without a word up the path through the park that led to where the carriage waited in the shadows half a mile away.

They went back then in silence to the parlour. Jack stood by the window a moment whistling softly. Then he turned round.

"Fooled again, I suppose," he said

Master Kearsley lifted a venomous face and bared teeth in answer.

2

Lady Magdalene Dacre was riding back from Whitehall to St. James', whither the Court had removed, on the eve of Corpus Christi

The Queen, who was too ill to hope to take part in the procession had sent her with a Spanish lady and an escort of gentlemen to report on the preparations and to see that all was in readiness for the next day.

It had been a gorgeous sight. The great hall was furnished with an altar under the musicians' gallery; and four more altars were set up in the corners of the gravelled court outside. A way had been made here, too, along which the Sacrament would pass, lined with a hundred young oaks, and strewn with sand, passing round the walls and up the centre. In the chapel, the altars were decked in cloth-of-gold, and furnished with their plate; sheaves of gilded partizans, for the Queen's Guard to carry, rested by the door, and in the sacristry were laid ready the regals for the use of the singing-men in the procession, as well as the torches and candles which would be borne throughout its length

Magdalene was a little silent as she rode back with Donna Luisa beside her. She had been touched by what she had seen, and by the evidence that it offered of her mistress zeal in religion, every detail that she had looked upon was the work of Mary's wishes Yet there were evidences of her Grace's zeal in other directions that she found hard to reconcile with this tender and laborious care to do honour to the God of mercy

As they turned in from the open park beneath the trees towards the gateway of the palace, Lord Montague came up beside her, from the escort behind.

"Master Manton desires to have a word with her Grace, mistress. He asked me to ask you I do not know what is amiss with him."

He spoke in a very low voice, and she understood that she was to do the same.

"Tell Master Manton to come to me in the long gallery," she said.

He fell behind again, then, till they reached the dismounting block, and as he helped her to alight he spoke again.

"I will send him up, mistress."

Magdalene walked up and down the gallery for two or three minutes, wondering what the message meant She did not know if she could do what he wished, the Queen saw very few persons at this time. However, she would try, if he gave an adequate reason. She did not know very much of this gentleman; she understood that he was a scholar, that he had once been of service to the Queen at the time of her accession, that he had distinguished himself in the recent plot, and that he had a capable appearance and bore himself well in his official duties. He also had a boy for his servant who sang very exquisitely. That was really all that she knew of him She would certainly hear what he had to say.

He appeared presently, still in his riding dress, at the lower end of the gallery, and bowed as she came towards him,

"You wish to see her Grace, sir?" she said

"Yes, madam."

He spoke in rather a strained voice, she noticed, and kept his eyes on the ground.

"Can you give me any reason?" she asked. "Her grace sees very few now."

"It is for an act of mercy, madam; I fear I ought not to tell you more. You remember I did her Grace a little service a few months back Perhaps that may be my plea."

Magdalene considered.

"An act of mercy," she said doubtfully

"For Christ's sake, madam," hissed Guy suddenly. "I can bear no more waiting."

She glanced at him astonished and a little frightened at his vehemence. It was a very sudden change from his restrained air just now. He had come a step nearer, and was looking at her with an extraordinary fierceness in his eyes What curious fellows these gentlemen were!

"An act of mercy!" he said again

She turned, still hesitating

"Come with me, Master Manton I will see her Grace."

She left him in one of the little ante-chambers of the Queen's apartments, and went through herself into the room beyond

The Queen was in her chair as usual with a book on her knee, and candles beside her, and looked up as the girl came in

"Well, sweetheart, and what of Whitehall?"

"It is all ready, your Grace I will tell your Grace presently. But if I may speak first, there is a matter——"

Mary nodded.

"Is it of Master Norris?" she asked smiling.

Magdalene turned scarlet.

"No, madam. It is Master Guy Manton. He came to me just now. He desires very much to have a word with your Grace. It is an act of mercy, he says."

"Master Guy Manton?"

"Yes, your Grace He is very much troubled. I told him I would speak for him. I do not know what it is; he would not tell me."

"Is it aught to do with the plot? Did he speak of that?"

"He spoke of it, madam, but I do not know   "

"I will see him," said the Queen, laying her book aside. "Do you wait next door, sweetheart."

Master Manton was standing where she had left him three minutes before, with that same look of anxious misery on his face. It deepened rather than relaxed when she gave him the message, and she heard him draw his breath as if in pain as he went across the floor.

Then she sat down and waited. She was still indignant at her Grace's clumsy banter about Master Norris She had told the Queen already that she desired never to see his face again Why would not the stupid woman understand, and leave her alone?

It was a very long interview, she thought. The twilight darkened to night and she lighted the candles, and still there was no sign of his return. She could just hear the sound of talking now and again through the curtained door She supposed from what Master Manton had said that he had gone in to plead for one of the conspirators. Or perhaps he had some new information.

Mistress Dormer came in presently, and was passing through to the Queen's room when the girl stopped her

"Master Manton is with her Grace," she said.

"Master Manton!" exclaimed Jane "Why, what has he——?"

"I do not know," said Magdalene "He has been with her this half-hour."

As she spoke, there was a hand laid on the latch, and the door opened a little They could hear a man's voice with a strange tone of emotion in it

"I thank your Grace with all my heart"

The door opened wide, and Master Manton came out. The two women saw his face plainly as he bowed to them, but he could not speak, and went swiftly through and out at the other door

The Queen was sitting as Magdalen had left her just now, with her hands empty on her lap, and her head on her hand, smiling with a puzzled look She said nothing as they told her it was time to go to bed, but rose silently and went out into the bed-chamber, and they knew her too well to ask any questions

When the other women were come and gone, the Queen paused a moment before getting into bed.

"I have done a strange act of mercy to-night," she said. "I have promised a man that his friend shall be put on his trial for treason"

She got into bed, painfully and slowly, and Jane drew the coverlet to her chin

"But it is not so strange as it seems. He could not bear the thought of the rack"

She was silent again as Magdalene blew out the candles on the table

"I suppose men do fear pain more than death," said the rough voice behind the curtains meditatively

A month later Stephen Brownrigg was hanged at Tyburn with Sir Henry Peckham and Master Daniel.

3

In spite of the Queen's anxiety that the monks should go back to Westminster as soon as possible, there were difficulties in the way.

Up to King Henry's death three masses were said daily in the Abbey, but in Edward's reign the Communion had been substituted, and the vestments, the candlesticks, the angels and the lecterns disposed of by auction. After the flight of Dr. Cox, who had plotted for Lady Jane Grey, Hugh Weston had been appointed Dean, and one by one the prebendaries had conformed to the old Religion, and by the time that peace was restored, the Queen announced her intention of bringing back the monks and of making restitution of the estates that had been taken from them by her father But a position had to be found for the Dean, and the necessaries for divine worship properly provided; and it was not until Michaelmas that Dr Feckenham came from the Deanery of St. Paul's to make preparations for the return.

He was very happy as he went about the cloister and the dormitory and his own house, with a Glastonbury monk at his side, who took down his decisions as to the disposal of the rooms and furniture. There was a couple of months' work required before the buildings would be fit for occupation. A quantity of things would have to be moved out and sold, a great deal of cleaning and whitewashing, but the abbot loved to dwell on every detail. His eyes shone with pleasure as he looked about him.

This was the way by which his brethren had been used to come down from the dorter to the cloister; here was the abbot's own private door, and his pew looking out into the nave; this little room had been the private oratory.

"A stone altar here, my son," said the rosy little abbot, beaming with smiles, "and we will have a pair of angels on either side to give perpetual thanks to God for taking away the oyster-board. A piece of matting here; it is more cleanly than these rushes."

The two went into the church presently, and passed along towards the little obscure corner where the Confessor's body had been laid at King Henry's spoiling of the abbey. There was a figure in the Queen's livery kneeling there already, face in hands; but it rose as the two monks came up. Dr. Feckenham glanced, smiled and bowed as he recognised Master Manton.

"You are come for his intercession, sir?" he asked.

"Yes, my lord, and I ask your prayers also."

The abbot beamed and nodded; then the two monks fell on their knees.

"Sancte Edwarde," said the abbot after a minute's silence.

"Ora pro nobis," answered the Glastonbury monk with tight-shut eyes.

"We will have his saintly Majesty home again soon," went on Dr. Feckenham, standing up, "he shall have the homecoming that he deserves See to it that a good pall be provided; if her Grace does not send one."

Dr. Feckenham was almost dazed with delight two months later as for the first time again for fifteen years the monks went through the cloister, with the silver-wanded vergers leading them, in through the south door and up into the choir. How marvellous was God's goodness in bringing back the sons of St. Benedict to their own again! There were not very many of them as yet; only fifteen all told, with new-shaven crowns and fresh black cowls. One blind old monk from Glastonbury wore his old cowl, green with age and creased by disuse, in which he had sung before Abbot Whiting of glorious memory, who had died on the high Tor for the Faith that they both professed. Abbot Feckenham thought that perhaps that cracked voice was not the least sweet of all in God's ears, and St. Benedict's.

The Queen was hardly less happy as she watched from her pew to which she had come, hooded and cloaked, by a private way from the old palace as dusk began to fall.

Matters had gone better with her of late. Her health was improved by her stay in the country; the rupture between Philip and the Pope which had caused her great distress in the summer had been nearly healed, and, best of all, the King's pages and stable-establishment had returned to London, and she had had a letter from him saying that he would not be long after them.

Finally, here were her dear monks home again in the Royal foundation, to pray for her and her hopes, and set an example of good living to all her subjects.

Deus in adjutoriutn meum intende:
Domme ad adjuvandum me festina:
Gloria Patri et Filio et Spiritui Sancto:
Sicut erat in principio et nunc et simper: et in saecula saeculorum
Amen. Alleulia.

Then she sat down for the psalms, and Magdalene slipped a book into her hands from behind

How strange it was to sit here privately, high above the shrine, and to know that she had done all this!

Overhead the huge columns aspired into darkness, to right and left the transepts ran out, and before her the immense nave ran down, broken by the rood and the three figures which stood out faintly luminous in the light from the tapers beneath The wide choir was empty except for the double horse-shoe ring of stalls along its edges, and the eagle-lecterns for the cantors that stood in the centre A row of tapers burned round the western end, as well as on the lecterns, and threw radiance upon the seven or eight faces that she could see The lights looked like little bright haloed stars in the vast darkness. There were not very many stars yet, they were only as the precursors that come out while the sky is yet bright, one day they should be as the host of heaven, strung out from end to end of the choir, overflowing into the minor stalls beneath, with a praying singing monk behind each

The sound of praise, too, was not what it should be one day. The voices seemed very far away and little in the huge stone space, though she could see heads thrown back and mouths singing lustily, it was but as the crying of a child in an empty world: but that small noise, too, was the promise of something greater, of a pealing voice that should rise insistent to God, roar out His glory, and demand His grace upon a country that was dead and is alive again, that was lost and is found

"What are they at?" whispered Mary leaning back.

Magdalene leaned over her shoulder and put a white finger on the page.

"Vidi supra montem," read the Queen, "I saw upon the mount the Lamb standing, and from beneath his foot a living stream pours forth"

She ran her eyes down the antiphons

"From whose foot a living stream pours forth; the flow of the flood makes glad the City of God…All the peoples of the world have believed in Christ the Lord"

It was a glorious omen Could she have asked better?—than this prophetic tale of triumph, of a world divided in all else but united in faith, of nations that had snarled and torn, as England and Spam had done, but who crouched now side by side like thirsty tigers, drinking together from the same river of salvation, of a City into which all peoples and kings brought their honour and glory, whose builder and maker is God

She sat back, smiling and dreaming to the accompaniment of the tramping psalmody

At the *Magnificat* she stood up again with hands on the ledge before her, looking out between the two candles that burned there. Magdalene behind could hear her hoarse voice muttering the words as the monks sang them

"*Ecce enim ex hoc*—behold, from henceforth, all generations shall call me blessed For He that is mighty hath done to me great things, and His Name is Holy He hath showed strength with His arm, He hath scattered the proud in the imagination of their hearts . He hath filled the hungering with good things. He hath helped Israel His servant; He hath remembered His mercy…as He spake to our fathers,"

It was that that she had cried two years ago almost to the day——"*Magnificat anima mea Dominum*"

When all was done she still stood waiting, a stiff motionless figure, watching the monks go out. The two wand-bearers were bowing now before my lord abbot's stall, two by two the black figures were coming out, inclining together, and wheeling together round the corner that led to the cloister

She turned and looked to where her grandfather's chapel opened behind the shrine in a further gulf of darkness It was there that she would sleep one day. she could not but be conscious, as she lay there—as surely as these other old Catholic kings were conscious, even at this moment, smiling in their sleep—of the strange and familiar monkish air that once more breathed in this place

Ah! she would know it then, she imagined to herself. How quietly would she rest here when her life's work was done, and all the bitter striving over, when men's tongues would be silent out of honour to the dead, and the children of those who mocked her now would show her more justice than their fathers had shown, when England had learned to call this Mary blessed, too, to whom the Lord had done great things, and to whose humility He had had regard.

As the two stood presently below, it was too dark to see the ruined shrine plainly; the altar was gone, and the pillars and walls bore marks everywhere so far as they could see, from the axes and hammers that had hewn off the precious metal and jewels with which earlier kings had adorned it.

Mary knew the inventory well; she had been through it with the abbot, and she remembered some of the details now—the beryll cross, the maser-bell, the agate basin set with gold and pearls, the Islip altar-hangings worked with lions, heraldry and fieur-de-lys, the famous Saint Peter cope. All those had been "reserved for the King's use" It would be the business of this Queen to restore them to God's use.

"To-morrow," said the Queen, turning away; "and tonight after supper we will see to the jewels"

Magdalene went to bed that night irritated at her mistress* inconsistency. Here was a woman universally reprobated as stingy and avaricious; the fewness of the dishes set on her table was the wonder of the Court; the money spent on pageants would have been a disgrace to a country gentleman, and yet the list drawn up that night of what was to go to Westminster Abbey amazed this lady-in-waiting. It seemed that the altar of St Edward was to be restored, plated with precious metal and covered with jewels; that the shrine was to be rebuilt and adorned as the abbot directed; that a heap of vestments worn in the royal chapel on great days was all to be given to the monks' use—as well as numerous crosses, chalices and images that had lain for twenty years in the Royal treasury.

It was very beautiful no doubt, said Magdalene to herself, this desire to do God honour; but she wondered whether it would not have been more reasonable first to roll away the reproach of parsimony, and then to pay off more of the debts of Edward and Henry that had been for years such a dram upon the Queen's resources. Surely!

4

Since the marriage two years before her ladies had never seen the Queen so happy as she was during the anxious months immediately preceding Philip's return.

Yet the Council sat twelve hours a day for one dreadful week in November, couriers flew to and fro between England and the continent, and none knew the cause. There were fifty rumours; the truce between Mary and France was to be broken, it was said; the King was ill; the English fortresses were threatened; a huge subsidy was to be raised for the reinforcements of Philip's; another plot had been discovered. Tongues wagged, and the Lords of the Council were eyed and shouted after in the streets, and men wondered what new sacrifice was to be demanded of them for the sake of the hated young Spaniard.

Yet Mary was serene through it all. She was not able to be present in Westminster Abbey at the celebration of the anniversary of the kingdom's release from schism, which absence in another mood would have caused her distress; but she lay cheerfully in bed, and said her prayers alone.

A few days later she was able to receive the Princess Elizabeth, who had come to Somerset Place with a great retinue; and the meeting of the two in public was all that could be wished by those who loved unity.

So the winter days moved on, Christmas came and went, kept quietly at Greenwich, and every hour that passed brought the King nearer to his wife.

Mistress Dormer was passing along a corridor that looked on a court at the back of Placentia, towards the evening of a March day.

A link was burning below, and two or three of the Queen's guard were on duty beside it. She paused a moment to look at them as they stamped about in their great cloaks, for a keen wind was blowing through the open gate, and as she looked, a tired horse, with a rider on his back, stumbled through and drew up with hanging head. Half a dozen other mounted servants followed immediately, and one of them leapt off and ran to his master's stirrup.

They were too much directly below the window for Jane to see who was the leader; but she saw the guards straighten themselves and salute as the man climbed wearily off. Then she passed on to her room, not sufficiently interested to make inquiries; for personages arrived at all hours, and the matter might be important or trivial.

Half an hour later she was sent for in haste to the Queen.

"My Lord Robert Dudley is come," said the page excitedly.

"Her Grace desires——"

But Jane was out of the room and half-way down the passage.

She found the Queen nearly hysterical with joy.

"He is come," she cried in her deep broken voice. "His Highness is at Calais, *Laus Deo!*"

She caught Jane passionately and kissed her on both cheeks.

She had been a little depressed earlier in the afternoon; for three days had passed without a message from the King. Now the change was extraordinary. Her withered cheeks were flushed with crimson, and her dull eyes bright and excited. She moved up and down before the hearth, forgetting her dignity, describing the King's adventures, speaking of a storm of rain which had drenched him a week before, telling little tales that she had drawn out of Lord Robert.

"He will be here in three days," she cried again "He will cross the sea to-morrow Oh! Jane, pray for fair weather. Thank God for His mercies!"

It seemed as if she had wholly forgotten the perplexities that surrounded her husband's coming, the difficulties of the Cardinal as regarded meeting one who was still professedly at war with the Sovereign Pontiff, the anxieties of the French situation and the labyrinth of the yet unravelled conspiracy. She could only speak of how His Highness' rooms must be prepared at once—summoning a page to send him in haste to bring Master Rochester—of the progress that must be made through London so soon as the King was sufficiently rested: of how my Lord Cobham and the Lord High Admiral must bear the swords-of-State at mass on the morning after the return.

Jane watched her, listened, counselled, soothed; and wondered meanwhile whether her mistress had forgotten, too, the change in her own appearance, her fallen cheeks, her unhealthy pallor, the wrinkles round her short-sighted eyes, the clumsy weakness of her gait and figure Mary ambled to and fro, a piteous sight to her friend, and surely an unwelcome sight to her young husband!

The three days passed in an unwonted bustle, the whole aspect of the Court changed Within the palace men ran about with messages and bundles, the hall was filled with the tumult of hammers, and the courtyard with waggons laden with clean rushes, hangings, and furniture Grave men bent on stately business were run into by boys who flew about on errands; Lords of the Council were refused admittance—it was told them that her Grace was in the King's rooms and must not be disturbed It seemed more like the bridal preparations of a girl than a middle-aged woman's welcome of a disillusioned husband.

On the morning of the day itself she could settle nothing. Hour after hour she paced up and down the long gallery, watching the weather, with her ladies about her, causing the splashed couriers who arrived one after another to be brought to her immediately She laughed like a child at the tale that Philip had been forced to pay the student's fine for entering Canterbury Cathedral in his spurs She was delighted with the news of his reception at the coast and the firing of the salute, she enquired again and again as to how he had fared on the journey, whether he was tired, whether it had rained She dined alone upstairs, for the great hall was still under the upholsterers' hands, and left the table hastily to walk again in the gallery; she could keep neither still nor silent

"His Highness will be weary," she said; "he will sleep late to-morrow I will not hear mass till I hear it with him Tell a priest to be ready at ten o'olock We shall have music to-night after supper; but not too long Master Bradshawe must sing; but I spoke to yon of that, sweetheart, did I not? I fear I shall not be able to ride with his Majesty on Monday, see that the litter be ready for it To-morrow we will see no one; we shall have too much to tell one another, is it not so? There is a horse's hoofs Sweetheart, see if it be not another courier."

As it grew towards evening her mood changed a little. She appeared worn out by excitement, and went back to her private parlour with Jane, where she sat with twitching hands and tapping feet, bolt upright on the edge of her chair opposite the fire. She caused the curtains to be drawn and the candles lighted, and more than once rose and looked at herself in the mirror, smoothing out the heavy folds of cloth of silver that hung from her waist, patting her brilliant head-dress, staring into her own reflected eyes with pursed lips, while Jane watched her, dreading questions

Again she came back, sat down, threw an arm round Jane and drew her towards her.

"Talk to me, sweetheart."

"Madam, what can I say? Does not your own heart tell you more than I can?"

Mary kissed her.

"It tells me so much," she said, "that I cannot bear to hear it. Is all prepared? Tell me again, Jane, is all prepared?"

"Your Grace, there is everything The gentlemen are in their liveries; I have seen the hall myself; the hangings are in place The boy is to sing in the parlour"

"I shall receive His Highness in the Presence-Chamber," went on Mary for the twentieth time that day, "and shall bring him in here immediately. He will have so much to tell me. And we sup at seven. Tell me, Jane, there is nothing wanting to pleasure his Highness? I have forgotten nothing?"

"Your Grace has forgotten nothing '

"He is very late, is he not? Is it dark yet, sweetheart?"

"Why, no, madam, it will be half an hour yet to dark."

Far away a trumpet pealed, and there was a sound of running footsteps in the corridor outside Mary sprang to her feet, and her hands dropped to her sides

"Come, madam," said Jane, and led her out.

The Presence-Chamber was ablaze with lights as the Queen came through with her ladies behind her, and went up the step beneath the cloth-of-estate.

Wax candles burned in sconces along the tapestried wall and in tall standards on the floor. A double line of guards in green-and-white, holding gilt halberds formed a lane of glory for the King to come up, and behind them on either side crowded the gentlemen and pages of the household A great carpeted space was left at the higher end of the room at the foot of the two thrones, where the dignitaries would stand for the formal greeting; on the right side by the Queen's chair with their backs to the wall stood her Grace's ladies; among whom towered up the beautiful head of Lady Magdalene Dacre. The corresponding space on the other side was left vacant for the King's gentlemen.

Again the trumpets pealed nearer, and a crash of guns sounded from the river. Mary rose and stood upright in her gorgeous dress, staring down the long passage of soldiers towards the further door.

Again the guns sounded, and noise of distant cheering followed it; the company in the hall began to shift and murmur, as a confused tramping made itself heard from outside Mary came down the steps; the ladies formed behind her, and she stood rigid in the centre of the floor, with folded hands.

She made a little movement forward as the first figures began to appear; then recovered herself, stepped back, and stood swaying slightly.

As the ushers advanced up the carpet, there was a cheer raised by the door—one clear sonorous voice:

"God save the King and the Queen!"

In a moment the whole hall was one tumult of sound, one stormy forest of waving hands and tossing caps, while the guns still thundered outside. The candle flames flared and leaned this way and that; the arras stirred and flapped upon the wall.

The last ushers came up, bowed low and wheeled aside to their places, and Philip appeared walking alone, his cap on his head, his long face flushed with wind and exercise, his cloak thrown back, his riding cane still in his hand, and his legs splashed from ankle to knee.

He stopped dead as he saw the Queen, drew himself up, lifted his cap, and sank down in a deep reverence that answered to hers.

They both rose together, advanced; he took her hand, bowing over it, and kissed it; then in a moment the arms of each were round the other, and their lips met, while the room thundered ironic applause and congratulation.

BOOK III

Nunquam inutilis est opera civis boni.
Sen. *de tranq.*

CHAPTER I

MASTER MANTON SERVES THE QUEEN AGAIN

I

MONSIGNOR PRIULI was sitting over his books in his room in Cranmer's Tower, a day or two after the beginning of the New Year; but he was not attending to them

There were a hundred things to occupy his mind. First there was the news from abroad. The Cardinal had had a letter from Philip two days before, and the Queen had sent on the letter she had received from Lord Wentworth, deputy-governor of Calais, and both contained formidable tidings. Newhavenbridge had fallen, Ruysbank was on the verge of catastrophe; Calais and Guisnes were threatened. There was a grievous insufficiency of men; for the troops in England were being drawn off to resist the French invasion in Scotland, and the loss of prestige that would follow England's expulsion from France was not pleasant to contemplate. The Archbishop had ordered public prayers.

Neither were Monsignor Priuh's home-prospects any more pleasing. The Cardinal had been accused of heresy in Rome and summoned to answer it; he had been deprived of his powers as legate a *latere*; and his official deposition and the substitution of the amiable but feeble Friar Peto in his place had only been prevented from reaching him by Mary's prompt action in seizing the papal messenger at Dover and suppressing the letters he carried. For some months that state of affairs had continued; the Cardinal had ceased to exercise his supreme legatine power, and now acted only as *legatus natus* and Metropolitan of the realm, but any day the blow might fall; a messenger might get through from Rome, and there would be no choice but to throw up the management of the troubled kingdom, and obey the summons.

It was reported by humourists that Monsignor Priuli had said more than once the mass *ad postulandam gratiam bene moriendi* on behalf of the reigning Vicar of Christ

The one bright spot in the prospect was the rumour that the Queen was pregnant; if this were true, as the Cardinal believed it to be, all else sank into insignificance; if it were not true, the view was darker still It was certain that the Queen could not live many years longer; and her successor could be none other than the Princess Elizabeth. Of coursese this lady might be sincere in her profession of the Catholic Faith Monsignor judged no man or woman hardly; but he would not have staked his eternal salvation on that sincerity, and was not inclined to stake even his temporal welfare

The priest sighed, pushed away his Plato's *Republic*, rose and went to the little high window that looked out on to the river.

It was a clear winter day, sunny and keen The grey tower, where was the prison, was to his immediate left; and beyond and at his feet flowed the broad river, wrinkled and scrawled with currents On the further side lay the low marshy land; the roofs of the palace and abbey rose up misty and romantic against the pale sky. Something in the view recalled him; and he went almost immediately back to his table, sat down and took up a letter that lay there, and read it again.

"Monseigneur:

"I thank your lordship for your letter in answer to mine: and your kindness in allowing me to wait upon you It is a matter very private, and I was recommended to come to your lordship on it nearly two years ago, but I have had great sorrow, and the affair lay neglected. I pray God that the delay has done no harm. I shall be able to tell you, Monseigneur, of all this better when I come to you I will present myself on Tuesday at ten o'clock. Your lordship's most humble servant, Guy Manton, Lieutenant of the Queen's Guard at St. James' Palace."

The priest remembered Master Manton very well. He had spoken to him three or four years before at Lambeth, soon after the Cardinal's arrival in England, and had noticed him again particularly, once at Greenwich, besides seeing him at other times in an official way He did not know he had been made lieutenant, and supposed this must have been done when honours were distributed on the previous Christmas Day He wondered what this matter was on which Master Manton wished to see him; it would not be very important if it had been delayed so long.

It was now half-past nine. The priest had said mass in the presence of the Cardinal at seven o'clock, and had been at his books ever since. He would give himself a rest now, and walk about a little

Half an hour later he tapped upon the door of the page's closet, and sent the boy downstairs to Morton's gateway to see if the gentleman were come. After five minutes he heard footsteps on the stone stairs outside, and stood up to receive his visitor.

It seemed to him as he gave his hand to Master Manton that the young man was considerably changed since he had last noticed him. He was thinner in the face, there were little wrinkles at the corners of his eyes, and his whole expression had lost the look of slight arrogance and self-sufficiency that had been there before. His bearing, too, was very quiet and modest, and contrasted oddly with his gorgeous dress, the impression offered by the long sword gathered in his left hand, and the great rowelled spurs on his boots.

"I must congratulate you, sir," said the priest, smiling pleasantly out of his black eyes "I suppose it was on Christmas Day."

"Yes, Monseigneur. Master Rochester recommended me for it, when he was to be made Lord Chamberlain."

The voice, too, was quiet, and entirely without self-consciousness; and the priest had a distinct emotion of attraction towards this young man.

"Sit down, sir," he said. "It is an hour before dinner yet. You will dine with us?"

Guy shook his head.

"I am on duty at noon," he said. "I must not."

The priest nodded, settled himself in his chair and crossed his feet.

Then the other began.

"It is on the subject of a cypher, Monsignor, that I wish to consult you, Master Norris gave me to understand that you had studied such things."

"I have a little skill in it," said Monsignor.. "It has been my pastime."

"Well, sir, this is a letter in cypher that I took from one of the conspirators two years ago. I do not know whether you heard any tale of my adventure?"

Guy was perfectly self-possessed, but a little pale; and his eyes were keen and bright as he looked the priest straight in the tace.

Monsignor nodded gently.

"I heard a tale——" he began.

"This man had been my friend," went on the other without flinching. "I had warned him two or three times that now that I was in her Grace's service loyalty was before friendship. I forebore to follow him once when I might have laid hands on him. Then I caught him plotting again and gave him up.... I make no excuse, and ask none.... The paper that I took on him I kept to myself; I wished to make my way with it; to make some discovery that would bring me honour. I tried to read it; but could not. Then—then my—the fellow was put to the torture; I obtained from her Grace that he should be put upon his trial at once—he had been my friend, Monseigneur. He was tried and cast, and he was hanged a little after...."

The priest was looking discreetly into the fire now and was smiling gently. There was silence a moment,. then without lifting his eyes he slid in a word.

"And the paper, Master Manton?"

"The paper, Monseigneur, I put away among my things. I had not—I put it away, Monseigneur..."

"I understand, sir," murmured the priest softly. "And then no doubt—"

"Then I forgot it," said Guy, "or if I remembered it, it was only for a day or two. I found it again by chance last week, in one of my books that I had not opened for a long while—a Plautus, Monseigneur. I have begun to read the classics again lately I looked at it a little, but could make nothing out...Her Grace has made me a lieutenant now, I thought it my duty that it should be read—and if it is of no service to her Grace—and it is likely not to be—it can be destroyed and forgotten."

His voice, which had wavered once or twice, was steady again now, and the priest was not afraid to look up at him. He was even paler than he had been just now, but his closed lips were firm and his eyes downcast, as he drew out a Little folded paper and handed it across the table.

Monsignor took it without a word, unfolded it carefully and smoothed it out. It was about six inches square with rough edges, and was written without breaks with half a dozen lines of letters and signs. He studied it carefully a minute or two in silence, then laid it on the table and looked across at the young man again.

"You must leave this with me, sir," he said. "As you say, it is probably of no importance. It does not seem to be a formal document of any kind"

"I know nothing," said Guy briefly.

"Where did the—the man carry it?" said the priest avoiding his eyes again.

"It was with two other papers in a little leather pocket-book," answered the other without a tremor

"Very well, sir; I will do my best I will communicate with you. I may have to ask a question or two. And if after all it is of importance?"

"I shall follow your advice, Monseigneur. No one but your lordship and myself will know its contents—perhaps not even myself."

"Ah! but I shall tell you what I find. Forgive me, Master Manton; but even if you have no ambition left, you still have your duty."

There was a moment's dead silence. Then Guy's voice came hoarse and low, almost fierce.

"How did you know that, Monseigneur?"

The priest looked tranquilly at the fire as he answered.

"It is a priest's business, sir, to know such things, and to read hearts and faces so far as Almighty God permits. I knew you were in trouble when I saw you at Greenwich, in fact I said so to Friar Peto And it is further my business," he added smiling, "to read cyphers. You told me so yourself."

"And the ambition?"

"Ambition is a fever, Master Manton. You are in no fever

now, but a chill, or perhaps I should rather say"

Guy laughed very softly, but without a trace of bitterness.

"You are perfectly right, Monseigneur. I have lost the fever—recovered, I should say. I do not know in what state I am now, but it may very well be a chill. And again, Monseigneur, how did you know it?"

The priest smiled still more.

"It was not hard, sir. You had no interest in your own promotion when you spoke of it; and an ambitious gentleman does not take to his classics again when he has left them off. Besides you confessed you had once been ambitious. Is more wanted?"

Guy still looked at him with a curiously steady interest in his eyes.

"And do you understand why I did what I did?"

"Not yet, altogether, sir?"

"Will you hear my confession, Monseigneur?"

The priest bowed and made as if to stand up.

"One moment, Monseigneur, I would like to say a word first, so that I need not keep you so long I approached the sacraments last Easter, and again at Christmas? I am trying

to lead a good life—to be simple and tender—" Guy paused a moment——

" to be simple again I am weary of the other. I have been a hard devil, as—as I meant to be. But—but the priest did not understand, he told me I had been right in what I did—and again at Christmas——"

Monsignor bowed gently

"Yes," went on Guy with an effort. "I do not say he was wrong I do not know God knows! But—ah! you understand, do you not, father?"

"I think I understand"

"There were other matters beside what I did; he puffed them away; he told me they were venial. Perhaps they were so, but do you understand, father?"

"I understand that venial sins may torment a soul like hell," said the priest

Guy stood up abruptly His face had changed; he had no longer the appearance of careful self-control, he was smiling a little with parted lips and his brown eyes were wet and bright.

"Are you ready, father? Here?"

The priest pointed out a kneeling-stool against the wall, and stood up himself. Guy went across and knelt down by it; while Monsignor drew out of the drawer of his table a purple stole. He went across and sat down, and Guy, with his eyes fixed on the ivory crucifix, began his story .

2

Guy was in his room a week later with Master Kearsley talking over the terrible news that had come last night of the fall of Calais, and of the arrival too late of the five hundred men whom the Queen had sent off to its relief.

He had found himself oddly drawn towards this silent bitter man during the last year of his life at Court, Dick was no longer bitter towards him; he would come up to see him sometimes, and sit for an hour or two almost without a word, gnawing his fingers and staring at the hearth; but neither had yet given his confidence to the other. Dick was a mystery to him, though his story was not; he had entered Edward's household as a man of thirty, and had been promoted on Mary's accession, it was understood that he had always been a very fervent Catholic who had concealed his opinions in the previous reigns He appeared devoted in his sour way to Mary's cause, but met with no particular recognition from her

Guy had been describing the talk he had heard downstairs of the preparations to be made to re-take Calais; every ward of London was to supply a couple of hundred men; and a good force was to set out in not less than three days.

Dick grunted.

"There will be no pains spared," observed Guy.

"Pains!" snapped Dick "And of what good will they be? Without treachery it could not have been taken, and without treachery it will not be re-taken"

There was sense in this; Calais had been taken with suspicious suddenness and a yet more suspicious lack of mortality.

"Her Grace was out of her bed at six this morning," went on Guy, "and my lord Cardinal was with her again by seven."

Dick blew out his lips contemptuously and set his chin on his hands

"They say it will break her heart," added the other.

Dick did not move or answer.

Tom Bradshawe looked in presently to say that there was a servant from Lambeth below with a letter. Should he come up, or would Master Manton come down? The letter was to be delivered into his hands.

Guy went down, and telling the man to wait, took the letter into a parlour to read it. It was from Monsignor Priuli.

"Master Manton," it ran, "I can do nothing with your matter. It is a very difficult one, and therefore it seems to me likely to be important. I have tried the usual methods in vain. It appears to me to be an affair of a key-word. That of course we have not and without that it is desperate It must be a word, sufficiently long, where no letter is written twice over; that is if they have followed that method as is usually done. If you know of any such that Master Brownrigg carried about him, or a ring or a paper or such-like, send it to me He is likely to have carried it on him; if not, it will be an easily remembered word I have tried near a hundred already, and with no success. But I do not yet despair. There are not very many such words, I have a little book that I made of them a year ago; for, as I told you, it is my pastime I am thinking now that it may be Latin; that is usual when the writers are of various nations as in this case. I have tried all that I can think of, such as the names of those who had to do with the plot, but with no success."

The letter ended without signature.

Guy was astonished at the serenity and zeal of the writer, considering the circumstances in which England now found herself. It seemed to him that Monsignor Priuli's description of cypher-solving as his pastime was a very inadequate phrase.

As regarded the request Guy was bewildered at the impossibility of complying with it He never remembered having seen Stephen with a ring; there was not the faintest clue; and surely such key-words as Monsignor described must exist in endless numbers.

He wrote a line back, telling him that he had no evidence to offer; gave it to the servant and went upstairs again, to find Dick gone.

Ever since Guy's interview with Monsignor Priuli, he had been wondering at the acuteness of the man. His own character, only half-known to himself, had been laid before him in the little room in Cranmer's Tower with an astonishing and a convincing precision. He had told his own story obscurely and hesitatingly answering now and again questions that appeared to him strangely irrelevant; then the priest had been silent for a full minute; then in a perfectly quiet and dispassionate voice he had stated his diagnosis.

The penitent was told that he had sinned against light. God had endowed him with the jewel of sympathy, and he had mistaken its nature; or rather he had wilfully desired other virtues that were not within his reach, and for their sake had sacrificed what he already possessed. This, the priest told him, was one of the most subtle dangers that the Evil one presented to the soul of man. There were some men born hard, Unicorn-passionate, resolute, and self-centred. These were the souls that God set to be rulers. He was not one of them, and he had tried to be. Others were by nature piteous, perceptive, and courteous; of this class was the penitent; it was these whom God ordained to be servants and lovers. The effect of a man's attempt to change the one nature for the other meant the ruin of fine qualities; such an one, as in this case, became brutal and passionate. He had the fire of the lover's nature to inspire his actions, without the restraint of the ruler's continence.

As regarded the actual guilt involved in this instance Mon-signor had said very little. He had named restlessness, ambition, and a perverted chivalry as the motives for his action. He had pointed out that the sin before God lay, not in handing Stephen over to justice—that act, inspired by other motives, might have been a magnificent sacrifice, acceptable to God—the sin lay in the vindictiveness, the wounded pride, the fury of self-advancement that had accompanied the act

Then the priest had stopped dead a moment.

"Of the guilt now, I will say only this," he had gone on in his slight foreign accent, "that God's mercy is infinitely greater. That that mercy has fallen upon you is proved by your sorrow and change of mind. You have detested yourself—is it not so? That is good. Now you must love God instead Amendment for you, my son, lies in the way in which you have already begun to tread. Your ambition is slam by love; see that it has no resurrection. You must be tender now; tender towards your Saviour whom you have crucified; tender towards your neighbour whom you have offended; and tender towards yourself whom you have despised. Entreat for the gift of tears. If there be any towards whom you feel hardly, be zealous in the discerning of their virtues. And, as you yourself have said, you must be simple. You must take what God sends without deprecation; and do what He bids without fearfulness. You will take for your holy penance the Litany of the Holy Name of Jesus, which you will say upon your knees each day for one week."

By the time that Guy was seated in the wherry to take him home, he had capitulated to this shrewd priest who knew him better than he knew himself. There were points in what had been said to him that he did not yet fully understand, but he yielded now in these, too. This man knew better than he.

His sense of the priest's skill was with him still, as he contemplated the bewilderment of the cypher. It seemed a hopeless task, but was any unravelment too complicated for Monsignor Priuli?

In the larger world, as the days went on, it became apparent that there were complications there too, that needed shrewd heads and strong hands

The country was sullen and furious at the loss of Calais; and resented it against the Queen It was this cursed foreign marriage, they said, which they had always distrusted, that was at the root of the disgrace Philip had embroiled them with France, in spite of his promises, it was that that had led to the fury of the assault on the English forts, that and the persecution which he had stirred up, and which always re-awakened when he was in the country, combined to set London smouldering with indignation against the Queen, which was not dispelled either by the rumours of her pregnancy, nor by the efforts she had made to re-take the forts When Guisnes fell three weeks later the smoke nearly burst into flame

Dick Kearsley appeared in hall one night with a great piece of plaister across his forehead He scowled so furiously at all who looked at mm that he was asked no questions; but Guy found him following afterwards on the stairs up to his room.

They sat down together by the fire, and were silent. It was fully five minutes before Dick burst out

"It was a foul knave who cursed her Grace in the park. The damned hound! But he will curse no more for a while. I cracked his head for him Then his fellows came round and I scarce got through on my horse"

Guy had learnt that Dick liked sympathy best when it was unexpressed, and said nothing He was astonished a moment later.

"And her Grace has done all for them "Dick broke off abruptly, and spoke no more except by scowls and monosyllables

Two days later Guy had a greater surprise still

He was crossing the court on his way to hall for dinner when a figure came swiftly out of the archway on his right, stopped and turned towards him It was Monsignor himself, carrying a little leather bag

Guy went forward and saluted him, and the priest took him by the arm.

"Come with me, Master Manton, to some private place. I have news for you"

There was no word spoken on the way upstairs, and it was not until the door of Guy's own room was shut that the young man put his question:

"Yes," said Monsignor gravely.

He turned to the table, opened the bag and shook out the papers and a little leather-bound book He selected two or three of the sheets, pushed the rest aside and drew up a chair.

"Prudentia I—" he said, as he sat down. "I have run her to earth."

Guy looked at him in astonishment The priest's face beneath its thick white hair seemed sharper than ever, his eyes were alight with some emotion, and his nostrils worked like a hound's.

"And is it a matter of importance?" asked the young man, sitting down opposite him

Monsignor nodded.

"Wait," he said, "you shall have my adventures first"

He drew out one paper from the three before him, and pushed it to Guy

It was a copy of the original paper, but the rows of letters seemed slightly rearranged, and were marked here and there in red ink

"I attempted it in a score of ways," said the priest, "by Polybius his methods, by Trithemius, even by the scytale itself—"

"Monseigneur—" began Guy.

The-priest went on relentlessly.

"I was convinced then, as I wrote to you, that it was written on a key-word, by which method each letter of the message is rendered by various other letters.

You will observe presently, that the letter 'I 'is written first as 'X 'then 'Z,' then 'C '

"Monseigneur," cried the young man again.

"But to discover that we must have the key-word—the priest leaned back and put his fingers together. "Now I tried a hundred from my little book here, as I told you; and with no success. Then I tried all such words as I could think of which might have to do with the conspiracy—such names as Ashton, Horsey, and the like. I told you, you remember, that no letter should recur in the key-word. If so, it is easier to discover because——"

Guy sighed desperately It seemed to distract the priest, for he drew out a little square of paper and pushed it across. It contained, so far as Guy noticed, a solid block of letters of which the top line was the alphabet written in its proper order.

"There is the key," went on Monsignor. "I tried all such words; and no success Then I bethought me, as I wrote to you, that the word would likely be a Latin one; such as English and French and Scotch and Welsh would alike understand. It must be a simple word, such as they would remember, too. I went through my dictionary and wrote down all such; there were not a great number, by God's mercy, such as would fulfil all the conditions. I attempted the names of countries—such words too, as *libertas*—and at last I caught her among the gifts of the Holy Ghost; and by His guidance I doubt not."

He leaned across the table and pointed with a lean brown finger to the left-hand column of the key. Guy followed it down, below the letter A, and saw that it spelt the word *Prudentia.*

"Master Manton, there was God's finger in it. It is the hardest of all cryptographs; and very rarely used but in France. It was that that set me thinking"

"And the message—" cried Guy.

There was a footstep at the door, then a tap and a brisk voice calling out.

"It is Master Norris," said the young man hastily rising.

Before he could answer the door was open, and Jack stood there. Monsignor Priuli made a movement to seize the papers, saw it was hopeless and that he had betrayed himself by the action, and sat back again, smiling uneasily. Guy gave him a desperate look.

"Come in, Master Norris," said the priest. "You have caught us plotting. You are discreet, are you not?"

Jack's face changed. He looked embarrassed.

"I beg pardon, Monseigneur. Yes, I am discreet——"

"Come in, sir; you will understand presently how needful is discretion."

The Italian looked swiftly across at Guy, who understood the look It was better that Master Norris' mouth should be sealed at once. He went to the door, motioned Jack within, then pushed the bolt

"It is a matter of a cypher," he said as he came back. "I will tell you afterwards, Jack. Yes, Monseigneur?"

The priest looked quite serene again now, and more human then when he had come in five minutes before

"Well; the message," he said genially, taking up the third paper." I will read it to you It is a note or two for Master—for the fellow who bore it, I should suppose of some message The first three are dead fish, as I told you—they are too stale for our pan"

He lifted the paper nearer his eyes

Guy was conscious of an extraordinary excitement. It was as if a voice was to speak from the dead. He stared fixedly at the priest's brown face, his black bright eyes, his thatch of white hair.

"'Item,' read Monsignor with an intolerable deliberate-ness," 'Master Arnold is to go to Abingdon next month'

"'Item: The arms to remain in their place'

"'Item the King here waits for the truce end'—I should suppose the King of France," went on the priest lowering the paper a little, "but that does not concern us now"

"Yes, Monseigneur," said Guy's voice hoarsely.

"Ah! Master Manton," said the Italian, looking sharply across at him, with an authoritative air. "I had forgot one thing. You remember our talk last month?"

Guy bowed The priest glanced at Jack who was sitting, staring at both with open mouth.

"I understand that you will follow my counsel in this matter?"

"I will, Monseigneur"

"For if you will not, I had best keep the last item to myself."

"I promise."

"And from you, Master Norris, I ask silence."

"I will keep silence, Monseigneur," muttered Jack.

"Well, then—" he lifted his paper once more . "'Item: The Princess E——' —that is the Lady Elizabeth—' will not hold to any promise she may make as to Religion. She has sworn this to Mrs. Ashley twice She cannot have the crown else. She is of the new religion.'"

The priest laid the paper down, and looked across at the two young men.

In rebus aspens et tenuibus fortissima, quaeque consilia tutissima sunt. *Liv.*

CHAPTER II

MASTER MANTON FAILS TO SERVE THE QUEEN

I

A WEEK later Guy stepped out of his wherry at Lambeth water-gate, and passed up into the post-room where Monsignor was awaiting him to take him in to see the Cardinal.

It had not been possible to arrange it before; the pressure of business had been overwhelming; and the Cardinal who, in Philip's absence, bore most of the weight of the government, was occupied in affairs from morning to night. The Queen had to be visited every day; there were numerous meetings of the Council, and a flood of messengers and letters poured in continually from all parts of the country There was little doubt which way the tide was turning.

The rush of business was evident in miniature even in the post-room as the two went through towards the chapel. Men-at-arms, in pikes and breastplates, stood at the four doors and allowed none to pass without credentials Half a dozen benches were grouped round the central pillar and others along the walls, and all were crowded with persons awaiting their turn to go through to the palace. A couple of couriers, splashed from head to foot with hard riding, stood by the chapel-door talking to the sentry, and stepped aside for Monsignor and his companion to go through.

They passed through the chapel, making their reverence to the newly-restored altar beneath the five lights at the eastern end, and turned up to go through the lobby towards the private parlour beneath Monsignor's own room

In spite of Guy's promise to the priest, he had been hard to persuade Monsignor had insisted that the information gained through the cypher should be followed up; and that the man through whom it had been forthcoming" was the proper person to act Guy had argued that the paper was two years old, that nothing could be done now, that the matter was best forgotten but both the priest and Jack Norris had been loud in disagreement It was real evidence, they said, as to the Princess' dispositions, for the note had formed part of a memorandum held by one of the conspirators; the Queen had a right to see it, they declared, it might be of immense weight in any action she might make towards the bequest of her crown Guy had protested, entreated, and fallen silent; and as a solution at last Monsignor Priuli had persuaded him to see the Cardinal and abide by his judgment.

They had half an hour to wait before the Cardinal made his appearance, and it was passed in almost complete silence. Monsignor took his seat at once at one end of the three tables set in the dark-panelled parlour, and began work upon a pile of correspondence that waited there, tearing open letters, annotating, writing a line or two, and setting the broad sheets one by one spread wide for his master's inspection. Guy went across to the little sliding window that looked into the interior of the chapel, and stared out with unseeing eyes at the devout gloom, the low arched gallery on the other side of the sanctuary from which late-comers might hear mass, the splendid sombre altar to his left with its hanging pyx and flickering light.

He was very ill-at-ease He regretted having found the paper at all; he regretted still more the priest's astonishng skill and good fortune in deciphering it The whole matter was interwoven for him with shocking associations, there was a bruised spot in his soul that was now laid bare again to assault. The miseries of the past two years came crowding on him again, the memory of Stephen, and his own action towards him. And all the present flowed so inevitably out of that. If he had not been vindictive, if he had been less zealous, if he had been less ambitious and obstinate in keeping the paper to himself at first—all this would not have happened. He had sinned, as the priest had told him, and here was the penalty of it.

He bad begun to desire simplicity and peace more than anything in the world, and behold! his quest for that was leading him once more towards elaborate intrigue He would be interrogated, doubted, blamed; or worse—perhaps even commended.

He looked across at the busy priest bent over his letters in the dark corner below the single window by which the room was lighted; at his leisurely assured movements, his concentrated keen face standing out in the candle light, his delicate fingers poised with a paper between them, or deftly smoothing out the creases and laying it flat on the little growing heap. Why could not he himself be quiet and business-like too? But it must be easier here, he thought, in this peaceful and pious household, where there was a mighty head and a Christian temper to bear responsibilities, than in the feverish unsettled Court, whose ruler was a woman, and a sick one at that, where men gossiped and fooled and slandered and mocked, unrebuked; where it was so bitterly hard to steer a steady course

He knew there was no escape from the present difficulty; a stronger man than he had his hand on the affair, and must be obeyed. And even without that a little event had happened, which the young man had not yet dared to tell him, which put quiescence out of the field He would tell him in the presence of the Cardinal

The door suddenly opened: Monsignor sprang to his feet, and Guy closed the window and straightened himself as the stately Cardinal-Archbishop in his long robes came forward unattended into the room, and the heavy door swung to behind him.

He was very grey now, the young man saw—far more so than a year ago. His long forked beard was streaked with it thickly, and the silver hairs showed the more plainly across his scarlet cape and the jewelled cross on his breast. His curly hair, too, retired further back than ever under the square red cap, and showed snow-white above the temples; only above his large brown eyes the eyebrows were still dark and young

Then Guy was on his knee, kissing the oval sapphire ring on the slender fore-finger.

In a very few sentences Monsignor had sketched out the story, and as he talked the Cardinal looked across the candles once or twice at Master Manton in his chair on the opposite side of the table

"Master Manton has agreed to follow your Eminence's advice," the priest ended "He is unwilling to push himself forward in any way. I have told him that I think it a matter in which he must forget himself and his wishes. No man but he can vouch that the paper is genuine, and I believe your Eminence will think with me that it is an affair that must be placed before her Grace."

Monsignor laid the sheet before the Cardinal, bowed slightly to both the men, and sat down himself

The Cardinal lifted the paper, balanced it a moment irresolutely, as if to speak, then checked himself; held the paper before his eyes, read it slowly and laid it down on the oak table.

"If I understand Monseigneur aright, Master Manton," he began in his deep tender voice, "this paper came into your possession from the person of a spy. The date is two years ago."

Guy bowed. He felt a little reassured by that kindly tone and virile presence. What a pair were these friends, he thought, the one as keen as steel, the other as strong as iron. And what, could he, a poor wooden thing, do between them?

"Two years ago," went on the Archbishop, "at the time when the great plot was discovered The spy was secretary to Master Christopher Ashton, and therefore likely to have true information. These notes, I understand you to think, Mon seigneur, were parts of a verbal message that the secretary was to give to some man—we do not know whom"

"Yes, your Eminence; we suppose so The last point, about the Lady Elizabeth, would bear very greatly on the plot. It would encourage those of the conspirators who were attached to the new religion, and dismay the Catholics. Therefore, I should think, it would be told to these and not to those. It would be kept for example from the King of France"

"I understand, Monseigneur. Well, that does not concern us now; except so far as it was probably true then. What was the Lady Elizabeth's religious position at that time?"

"Her Highness had conformed more than two years before, and furnished her chapel then," answered the priest instantly, "but no man that I can find has ever believed in her conversion, except perhaps her Grace and a few of the common folk."

"And at the time of which we speak?"

Monsignor shrugged his shoulders.

"*Chi lo sa?* Her Highness had begun to hear mass. But your Eminence knows better than I."

The Cardinal smiled at the brisk tone of the other.

"I have never had any great faith——" he began. Then he turned to Guy.

"You understand, Master Manton, do you not? Now I will tell you this, which is a matter for your ear alone. You know that her Grace has power to leave the crown to whom she will—at least, 'tis supposed so. She is not greatly inclined to the Lady Elizabeth, even now. You understand that if the Lady Elizabeth is legitimate, then her Grace cannot be; for their mothers and their common father were alive together. But I think her Grace will overlook that, if she is satisfied that her sister is a good Catholic. Her Grace told me once that she will have a promise out of the Lady Elizabeth, before she leaves the crown to her—should God give no son to her Grace—that she believes and will maintain the Catholic Religion."

Guy bowed. He saw what was coming, and his heart sank.

"Well then, Master Manton, if the Queen's Majesty should hear that her sister thinks herself absolved from her promises in such circumstances—nay, if even she should suspect that it might be so; I doubt whether she would ask for such promises at all She would leave her crown to another—to her husband, maybe. There would be war, no doubt; but better war than Satan's peace. You understand me, sir?"

"I understand, your Eminence."

The Cardinal paused a moment, fingered the paper again, and glanced at Guy reassuringly. The young man felt more than ever now how hopeless was even the thought of resistance to that dominant will. Yet, at the same time, he felt more secure. There was a sense of protection in that scarlet presence, those tranquil eyes, and in the sound of the voice.

"I think then, with Monseigneur in this," went on the Archbishop. "The Queen's Majesty should certainly see this paper. It may be that she will pay it no attention. Also, I think, that you are the proper person, Master Manton, to show it to her. It will further your own prospects"

"Master Manton has no ambitions," put in the priest swiftly.

"Ah! so much the better. Master Manton then is free from very subtle enemies; and it is the more merit for him to approach her Grace so. But you must go, Master Manton; there is no choice. I will go with you, if you will, or Monseigneur here will. But there is no choice."

Something seemed to strike Monsignor suddenly, and he interposed with rather a doubtful air

"I had not thought of this, your Eminence. Supposing that her Grace pays the paper no attention, and the Lady Elizabeth should ever come to the throne, it will not be a happy day for Master Manton"

The Cardinal looked sharply from one to the other.

"It will not be a happy day for any of us, my friend, but] understood you to say that Master Manton had no ambitions."

"Indeed, your Eminence, I have no ambitions, save to be quiet now," burst in Guy, feeling himself slightly wronged. "I wish Monseigneur had not said that. I do not fear for myself There is another matter, too, my lord, that I have not yet spoken of; but it bears now upon the question. I have not even told Monseigneur."

The two looked up at him.

"I have been ashamed to tell it," went on Guy uneasily, "ashamed for a friend of mine, but the affair has got abroad through his indiscretion. He confessed to me last night that he had bragged of this matter in his cups"

"He——?" snapped Monsignor.

"The gentleman who was with us when you came to St. James', sir. I do not know how far it has spread; but two days ago I was questioned by one or two as to whether I had not something against the Lady Elizabeth"

Monsignor sprang up.

"Then that ends it, your Eminence. There is no longer the shadow of a question. Master Manton must go to her Grace at once. What was it that Master Norrins said, sir? I will never trust one of the Court sparks again!"

"I think that my friend said that I had something that might set them all at ease; that the heretic would never come to the throne."

"And who was present?"

"Half a dozen I should suppose. Master Wentworth, Master Bassett, and some others"

There was silence for fully a minute. Monsignor sat down again and looked at the Cardinal; Guy stared at the ground, and the Cardinal once more fingered the paper doubtfully.

Guy had not been quite prepared for the sensation that he had caused. He had thought it annoying that Jack Norris had blabbed; but very characteristic; and he was sorry to have to put him to shame before these two ecclesiastics. He feared that they would not understand Jack's harmlessness.

But he had not thought more of it than that, and he was considerably startled by the Cardinal's next little speech, which he uttered with a good deal of solemnity.

"Master Manton, I am very sorry for it. You must look to yourself sharply The Lady Elizabeth has friends who stick at nothing You had best leave the paper here with me; and tell any so who trouble you. They can do nothing without that. I will think over the matter for a day, and let you know when it will be best to go to her Grace I should say not until after Easter; there is too much on her Grace's mind; and she would not deal with it as she should. And look to yourself, Master Manton."

There had been two or three taps upon the door that Guy had just noticed; he had supposed that it was one of the household officials. Now the tap came again, sharp and insistent.

Monsignor noticed it, rose with an air of slight annoyance, and went to the door, and opened it Guy saw a page on the stone landing outside lean forward and whisper to the priest, and the next instant to his astonishment the door was pulled wide, and Tom Bradshawe stepped into the room in his page's dress, flushed and excited.

Monsignor closed the door, bolted it, and came forward past the boy, who made his obeisance, and then stood irresolute, looking eagerly from his master to the Cardinal and back again

"It is a message from the Court, your Eminence," said the priest; "this boy is sent for Master Manton." Guy stood up with beating heart. "Well, Tom?"

"If you please, sir, we are to ride to Bishop's Hatfield to-day."

There was a moment's breathless silence. Guy stared at the boy's flushed face and black eyes, scarcely understanding yet what the message implied.

"By whose orders?' asked the Cardinal quietly.

"By her Grace's, your Eminence."

"Why?"

"I am to sing before my Lady Elizabeth to-night," said the boy.

"And Master Manton?"

"Master Manton is to go with me, my Lord"

Then Guy spoke, and his voice sounded natural enough, in spite of the effort which he was making.

"Go down, Tom; wait for me in the post-room. I will be with you in five minutes."

Tom went out after a hasty salutation to the prelates, and the door closed.

2

There was silence in the dark room till the footfalls ceased. Then the Cardinal lifted his rochet a little, crossed his knees, looked straight at Guy, and spoke.

"Master Manton, you will want a cool head. Can you trust yourself? Or shall I go to her Grace?"

"Your Eminence can trust him," put in Monsignor breathlessly.

"It is far better that I should not go to her Grace. There are a hundred reasons. She is sick and cannot bear much more; she will not act strongly. I had determined already to bring nothing before her that was not necessary. And I do not think you need fear for your life, sir, if you take some strong friend, and let it be known whither you are going. Yet I should go armed, sir, for all that. It is after you have seen Her Highness that you will have most to fear."

"And the paper——" began the priest.

"The paper shall be in your keeping, Monseigneur. Master Manton can tell Her Highness so. He must not even have a copy with him. Do you understand, me, Master Manton?"

"I understand, Eminence."

The rush of excitement had subsided and left him passive. He scarcely yet foresaw all that threatened, he only understood that he was in the hands of those two men, and must go whither they directed.

"It may be that God is helping us," went on the Cardinal quietly. "We shall learn much from Her Highness' behaviour as to whether she fears the evidence or no. Of course one of her friends has told her what the talk was. I suspect she has a bad conscience, or she would not have sent for Master Manton."

"Your Eminence will give Master Manton some instructions?" suggested Monsignor.

"I see no need for them," said the Archbishop, "We cannot instruct in what we do not know. All that this gentleman has to do is to be wary, to tell nothing, and to remember all that is said."

He was silent again Then he stood up, stepped forward and lifted his hand as Guy sank down on his knees.

"*Benedicat te Omnipotens Deus,*" *came the deep voice.* "*Pater...et Filius...et Spiritus Sanctus.*"

"*Amen,*" said Monsignor Priuli.

On the way home Tom gave him details. The order had come through the new Comptroller of the Household, Sir Thomas Cornwallis, that Master Bradshawe was to sing before the Lady Elizabeth that night; that his master was to go with him, and take three or four servants for escort. Master Manton still held his position among the pensioners, and in that capacity was subject to Master Cornwallis' orders; his post of lieutenant in the Queen's Guard was little more than an honourable sinecure.

There was no possibility of appeal even if Guy had wished for it. He must first obey

He said nothing to Tom then beyond bidding him to go upstairs and begin to pack, telling him he would be with him presently, and himself went straight off to Master Kearsley's room.

Dick was just preparing to go down to dinner. Guy shut the door when he had entered, and stood with his back to it.

"Dick," he said. "I have a favour to ask of you. I am sent for to Bishop's Hatfield You have heard talk of something I have against Her Highness It is true that I have, but I have given an undertaking not to speak of it till the proper time. I think I may be in some danger at my lady's hands. Will you ride with me?"

Dick looked at him with his head a little on one side and his eyes all alert.

"At what time do you ride?"

"At three o'clock."

Dick nodded.

"I will come with you," he said shortly.

"And you will come armed?"

The other laughed bitterly.

"I would not go to my Lady Elizabeth other than armed

Guy saw that he sufficiently understood the situation, and left him.

There were not very many preparations to be made. Guy gave directions as to the horses, and ordered three of his men to ride with him, then he went back to his room

"Tom," he said, "we dine here together I do not wish to be questioned, nor you either And I have a great deal to tell you. Go and tell the cooks to send dinner up here Stay; you had better bring it And do not gossip."

It was an extraordinary pleasure to Tom to dine with his master, and still a greater pleasure to be a person of such importance. He had never before been sent for to sing before Her Highness; his voice was on the very point of breaking, for he was already sixteen, and it seemed to him a special grace of Providence that had sent him this honour just in time. It was a small matter to sing with others in a Cathedral or the Queen's chapel, where good music was a matter of course; it was quite another thing to be sent for to Bishop's Hatfield.

"Her Highness sings herself, sir, does she not?" he said, as he brought the pewter dishes in and set them down.

"I daresay," said Guy "Shut the door. Say grace. Sit down Now listen to me '

He put half a pigeon on the boy's plate, and the other hall on his own.

"Now Tom, listen to every word You must repeat it all to me afterwards. You remember Master Stephen Brownrigg?"

Tom's fork sank again with the meat still on it.

"Yes, boy. Master Stephen Brownrigg. You need not look at me like that. Well—*Defunctus adhuc loquitur* You understand that?"

Guy was determined that there should be no emotion. He had had a difficult task two years before, when the tragedy had happened to keep the boy from lamentation in public over the death of the man who had once given him an old gown. He put a violent constraint on himself now. He desired Tom to become accustomed again to that name that had not been spoken between them since the July day when the bearer of it had ceased to claim it. There might be need of self-restraint at Hatfield.

"You understand that?" he said again. "Do not be a fool. 'He, though dead, still speaketh.' Well, you remember the little paper that I took from him. It was in cypher, I told you; and I could not read it. Another has read it now, and it holds news of my Lady Elizabeth So far, you follow?"

"Yes, sir," said the boy in a subdued voice.

"You must not pull long faces. When you feel so, pray for his soul instead. That will do him good, instead of. Well, my Lady Elizabeth has heard of that little paper; she desires that the Queen's Majesty should not see it…. Yes; another pot of ale…. So she has sent for you and me, to—to—I do not know what—but at least to ask us questions. Those questions must not be answered. If she asks——"

"Does my lady then not wish to hear me sing?" asked Tom, more dismayed than ever.

"Yes, foolish boy; or she would not have sent for you at all But there are some questions, too. Now, if she asks you questions, I will tell you what to say. Listen carefully. You are to say that you knew Master Brownrigg at College, that he was not a good Catholic; that you and I were at the taking of him for conspiracy, you did not understand it all, but that I forced you to do it, because you were my servant, that you have never seen the paper; that you do not know where it is; that you do not know what is in it. Now tell me, what is it you may say to my Lady Elizabeth?"

Tom repeated his instructions tolerably, with a little prompting, and before the pigeon was done had his lesson learnt.

"If my lady presses you over much or asks you about Master Ashton and the rest," ended Guy, "look foolish, and make as if you do not understand. There will be no difficulty in that, I know."

Then Guy led off on to music, questioned him about his songs, bade him sing well, and had him reassured again by the time that dinner was done.

He felt ashamed of his sharpness of manner when the boy had left him at last, but he knew that it was the only way. Tom's sentimental nature was already ardent enough to make him dangerous; if the Princess playedupon that, as she well knew how, and broke down his defences, Tom could tell her a good deal that Guy did not wish her to know, perhaps she suspected the information he had sprang out of that old plot; but she could not be certain of it, and he did not propose to tell her. It was his part to draw her on to commit herself in some way, and to keep his knowledge to himself. Probably she did suspect the origin of his information, or she would scarcely have asked that Tom Bradshawe might come to Hatfield too—unless indeed his singing was merely a device to get his master at the same time. At least it was plain that a good deal of adroitness would be needed, and he did not want his cards to be shown by any indiscretion on Tom's part.

It was after sunset before the party of six came up by the inn and saw the roofs of Bishop's Hatfield against the sky.

The two gentlemen had ridden fifty yards in front of the servants all the way, and Guy had found Dick a soothing companion. He had told him a little more of the errand on which they were come, mentioning Master Brownrigg as being the source of the information, as well as the fact that Monsignor Priuli had the written paper in his keeping, but he did not inform him as to the nature of the statement; nor did Dick ask: it was enough for him that it was a weapon against the Princess Elizabeth.

Guy had never before recognised how deeply his friend hated and distrusted that lady. He had learnt to like Dick lately, but he did not know why; his character when looked into seemed neither lovable nor loving; his chief passions appeared to be those of scorn and hatred and mistrust, directed against most persons with whom he was brought into contact and against a good many whom he scarcely knew more than by sight. However, Guy liked him and trusted him, and was pleased that he had made him his confidant.

They were apparently looked for with some impatience at Hatfield, for the arched doors flew wide swiftly when the porter understood who they were, and a servant walked beside them with a link, from under the gate across the graveled space to the west front of the house itself. It was a great buttressed brick building gabled at this end and that, and Guy looked with some excitement at the double row of mullioned windows, bright below and dark above, wondering in which of them his ordeal would take place.

There was a clatter of dishes as they dismounted within the central tower.

"My lady is at supper, sir," said the man. "You are to be served upstairs."

The three were taken on—for Tom in honour of his invitation was to sup and sleep with the gentlemen—through the inner court and up a staircase on the left, along a corridor or two, up and down a couple of small flights, and were shown at last into what seemed an upstairs parlour with a further room opening beyond.

"The bed-chamber, sir," said the man to Guy, setting down the trunk; then he appeared suddenly thoughtful. "But there are only two beds, sir; I was not told"

"There must be three then," said Guy tersely.

The servant hesitated.

"If you are in any doubt," added Guy sharply, "you may send word to Master Pope. He knows me."

The man went out without speaking.

"We will have nononsense," said Guy. "My Lady Elizabeth is not mistress here after all"

They set to work to dress at once, for there was no knowing how soon after supper they might not be summoned, and were ready before the man came in to tell them that supper was laid in the outer room, and that there would be no difficulty about the beds.

Dick had not troubled to bring his best suit; he had not been invited after all; and in any case he had no great wish to do this woman especial honour, but the other two were a superb sight.

They were alike dressed in the Queen's colours—green and white: Guy was in white ribbed silk throughout, his sleeves and trunks slashed with green velvet, and green leather belt about his waist with a long sword hanging from it, and a dagger on the other side. Tom was in white satin, slashed with green satin again, with white shoes; his cap and ruff each bore a little emerald brooch that his master had lent him. It was only the second time that he had worn the dress, and he regarded himself with some satisfaction. The two gentlemen also were not displeased with him, as he stood on tiptoe craning his head to see as much of his figure in the mirror as possible, with his pale cheeks flushed faintly with excitement, and his eyes, bright with the air and exercise, burning like black jewels in his face

"Enough mincing," said Guy abruptly. "Sit down, Tom. Her Highness does not wish to see you, but to hear you."

They did not talk much at supper, there was too much excitement in the air From below they heard the crash of the band in the court as the Princess came out of hall, the tramp of feet and the buzz of voices Then all was still again Once or twice a footstep passed down the corridor outside, and five minutes after they had finished supper the servant came in to take away the dishes.

Guy was a little anxious that Tom should not forget his lesson, so he took him through into the bedroom under pretence of looking over his music, and shut the door behind him

"You remember?" he said "No folly now! Tell me what you have to say."

Tom repeated his lesson with roaming eyes.

"And no word of Master Ashton, or Oxford," added his master.

"No, sir, I will remember."

Guy looked at him doubtfully, and as he looked heard the outer door open, and a voice speaking

"The music, boy! quick!" he hissed; and the two came out together with the candle to find a page standing at the further door.

"Master Bradshawe is to come down," said the boy superciliously, running his eyes up and down Tom's figure.

"You damned puppy!" snapped Dick explosively. "Is that the way my lady sends messages to the Queen's gentlemen?"

The page winced and turned scarlet.

"I beg your pardon, sir. Her Highness desires to see Master Bradshawe in the parlour"

"Go, Tom," said Guy, looking at him steadily.

Tom opened his mouth, drew a long breath, eyed the page with an overwhelming contempt, looked at his master, sighed, took up his music and went out.

Guy could not have believed that an hour in a pleasant room furnished with hangings on the wall, a little shelf of books, a bright fire and the company of one of his friends, could have passed so slowly. Half a dozen times he went to the door and listened, once he opened it, and heard from far down the corridors a glorious boy's voice singing below. Once he drew aside the curtains and looked out at the night, at the row of lighted windows like pale streaked eyes between the buttresses of the hall on his right, the central tower and the pair of slender chimneys against the stars

Each time he came back and sat down again in silence Dick did not speak, but sat with his chin on his hands staring into the fire Once he yawned, twice he sighed; once he took a book and turned its pages, but laid it down again and fell to staring once more.

In spite of his yawning Guy could see that he was on the alert. He longed to tell him the whole story, but hesitated after what Monsignor had said But he found a certain strength in looking at that thin grim mouth, lined with middle-age from nostrils to chin, at the square Jaw, and the tangled bushy eyebrows beginning to turn a little grey

He wonderedwhat Kearsley was thinking—how much he had guessed Then he thought of the Cardinal again and his advice; of Monsignor Priuli and his shrewdness, and back his thoughts leapt to the present What was happening downstairs? Had Tom been discreet?

It was a real relief in spite of the ordeal that was to follow, when the page appeared again, and with a good deal more courtesy than he had shown before, said that the Lady Elizabeth desired to see Master Manton in the parlour.

Guy looked once at Dick, but the other had moved his eyes without changing the position of his head, and was looking up now like a dog that has awakened from sleep but is too idle to stir. Then Guy followed the boy

They went along the corridors up which he had come on his first arrival, down the grand staircase, and turned to the right along another passage or two The page opened the door of a room on the left, and motioned Guy in; and then himself passed through the little chamber, and out at a further door leaving him standing there.

A whiff of hot air came through the door, and a burst of laughter from a woman's voice. Then the door closed.

There was a profound silence for a minute. Then the page returned, and with him again the hot whiff of scent. He seemed amused at something

"Her Highness is ready," he said, with an apparent effort not to laugh; and threw the door wide."

3

It was a low parlour, ceiled, walled and floored with oak. A spider-candlestick of brass hung from the centre, ablaze with lights, and others burned round the room There was a fire burning on a wide hearth immediately opposite the door by which Guy had entered; over this hung a piece of arras embroidered with arms, and two pair of curtains hid the windows on the right hand side In the left and further corner stood a virginal, and before it a chair was wheeled round with two figures in it, a woman in a white dress and a boy in white satin and green A tall girl stood by smiling; three or four sheets of music lay on the floor by the chair as if suddenly dropped.

Guy saw these things in the swift look he threw round the room as he came in. Then as, the girl who held Tom on her knees lifted a laughing face and looked over the boy's shoulder, Guy fell on his knees, but he still stared, amazed.

Tom was sitting astride of the girl's knee, his white-shod feet dangling, his head on her shoulder, and leaning back, as if he had been suddenly caught and pulled there; one hand had seized the girl's bare arm that held him there as if to keep his balance. Then as Guy watched he saw the Princess lift herself a little, bend her head, and kiss him again twice, once on the neck so close to her own, and once full on the lips.

"You darling," she said, "and what a blessed mouth to sing so! There, enough."

Tom struggled forwards, recovered himself, slipped to his feet and stood up, flushed and embarrassed, with tumbled black hair. He threw a piteous look of shame towards his master and sidled away towards the fire

Elizabeth smoothed her skirt

"There," she said. "Ah' Master Manton, you have caught me making love to your boy But who could help it?"

She stood up, went to the fire and turned round again.

"There, Anne; take him away and put him to bed.'

She held out her hand to Tom, who after one more miserable look at his master, dropped on his knee and kissed her fingers.

"Good-night, sweetheart," cried Elizabeth smiling, as he went across towards the door. "I would kiss you again if I dared."

The door closed behind the two, and the Princess held out her hand once more.

"Now, Master Manton"

Guy rose with a sense of outrage in his heart that he scarcely understood, came across to her, knelt, kissed the gemmed fingers, and stood up once more

Elizabeth sat down, and pointed to a chair beside her.

"Sit down, sir; you and I must have some talk. What a boy that is of yours, and what a divine voice!"

"I am happy that he pleases your Highness," said Guy icily.

"He has pleased me very much, by his singing and by his talk," said Elizabeth sedately.

Guy glanced at her, a little uneasily The Princess was sitting quietly enough now, her white hands in her lap, her narrow eyes downcast and her small red, upturned mouth smiling as if with some secret pleasure He noticed that her clear pallor was a little flushed on her cheeks Her auburn hair, drawn up tightly under her white gemmed head-dress, and the muslin about her breast was tumbled as if with a struggle It seemed to Guy that Tom could not have yielded too readily to her wooing.

"Now, Master Manton," said Elizabeth again, "you and I must have some talk together—but your boy fought so that I am all out of breath. He is modest enough, by God's Son!"

"I am pleased that your Highness thinks him so."

The little red mouth smiled again.

"Well, then, for our business What have you got against me, Master Manton of her Grace's household?"

Guy was dazed by the sudden attack, and it was the more effective in that the girl did not look at him as she spoke, or change the tone of her voice. It was as if she had asked him whether he had supped well.

"Against your Highness?" he stammered

Elizabeth looked at him a moment, still smiling They were almost facing one another, with the fire between; either could look at the other without much movement of the head.

"Oh! do not make as if you did not understand. Indeed, I am no fool, and I know quite enough. What is it that you have against me?"

Guy was silent.

"You do not believe that I know anything, then?" went on the girl. "Well, then, must I tell you of Master Ashton and Abingdon, and Master Brownrigg, and the little house at Lambeth?"

He felt those narrow bright eyes on him now, but he was aware that the mouth still smiled.

"Ah!—" he cried, and stopped.

"Why, of course, sir, your boy has told me everything. Did you think he would not? Did you think that a maiden does not know how to woo? There is nothing I cannot get from a lad like that."

Mingled with his fury there was a touch of relief. First, there was less for him to conceal, and secondly, Elizabeth was plainly pretending to know more than she did; Tom could not tell her "everything," because he did not know it. Presumably then she was alarmed. He registered that guess, and then answered quietly.

"Your Highness will tell me what you please"

"Very well then, listen"

Elizabeth threw one knee over the other, and clasped her hands round it.

"Master Brownrigg was a friend of yours at Gonville College, Cambridge; you entered my sister's service a little more than a year after she came to the crown. Master Brownrigg came to London a little afterwards You saw no more of him then, though you heard of him from your boy, until you were at Oxford for the burnings of the heretics, you followed after him then, and caught him at last in an inn at Lambeth. You took two or three papers I say two or three, for I do not know whether there were three or two—two or three papers from him You gave two papers to Master Norris, and I think, though I do not know, that you kept one for yourself Master Brownrigg was racked, and then hanged with other traitors to the Queen's Majesty—and very justly, I say, though I say so to his friend

"she glanced at him swiftly and down again——" Then nearly two years went by

"Now, listen, Master Manton, very closely to this It will show you that I know more than you think for A week or two ago you went to Monsignor Priuli, my lord Cardinal's friend, and showed him a paper which you said—which you said you had taken from Master Brownrigg This paper holds somewhat against me; I will not tell you what that is, for you already know; I daresay you have it on you at this moment"—she paused again. "Monsignor Priuli read the paper; it was in cypher, and you said—you said that you could not read it yourself. And now you mean to go to the Queen's Majesty with that paper, to tell her the same tale, and do me an injury. There is the text, Master Manton. I shall be happy to hear the gloss upon it."

Elizabeth unclasped her hands, clasped them again behind her head, leaned back and looked at him.

Guy had listened intently to every word. Then he licked his dry lips, and parried carefully

"I have no gloss, your Highness"

"You cannot contradict it, then?"

"I do not contradict it, madam."

Elizabeth laughed pleasantly.

"That is very adroit," she said, "but I knew you were adroit. Then shall I supply the gloss as well as the text?"

"If your Highness pleases."

"Very well then. First, I love loyalty, I do not know which I love most, loyalty to a friend or loyalty to a mistress. You have the advantage to possess both. You showed loyalty to your friend when you let him go the first time, and loyalty to your mistress when you took him."

Guy was tempted by this.

"Or disloyalty to my mistress when I let him go, madam; and disloyalty to my friend when I took him."

Elizabeth laughed again delightedly.

"You are a treasure, sir Add that to your virtues But I prefer to think the other, it is a matter of choice after all; and I wish to think the best of my friends; and I am sure you will be that, sir, before I have done"

"Well, madam?"

"You showed loyalty again to your mistress when you went to Monsignor Priuli with the paper; but scarce loyalty to me who, please God, will be your mistress some day; but may He long avert that day 'That disloyalty to me is the one defect in you; but you can cure it, and I can forgive it"

"I can cure it, madam?"

"Why, yes; do you not know how?"

"Monsignor Priuli has the paper, your Highness; I have it no longer."

She did not wince at that, for he watched her

"Do you not know how, Master Manton?" she repeated.

"I do not, madam."

"Oh! that is too adroit! But I will tell you presently. Let me speak of another matter first."

Again she unclasped her hands, leaned forward a little, and re-clasped them round her knee. Guy noticed the white slender roundness of the arm nearest him, as it emerged from the deep satin sleeve, and the faint line of rippling muscle below the elbow. She was quite aware of her seductiveness, he knew; and he was beginning to be aware of it In dramatic contrast there flashed on him the memory of the Queen, of the fallen face, the hard tired peering eyes, the sour lips, the wasted distorted body. Elizabeth's next words drove the contrast further home.

"Master Manton, you are in Her Majesty's household, and you and I know what others do not Her Grace will have no child. We know that, you and I, and others know it, if they would but speak"

She paused a moment, her voice was tender, as if with pity for the delusion.

"And her Grace is sick. She has been sick for years, and I think she is broken-hearted with the coldness of her people, and—and of the Prince of Spain. Master Manton, you see that I speak plainly; I have nothing that I keep back from you. Well, when folks are like that, I think that God has pity on them "—her voice quivered a little—" pity on them, and takes them home."

It seemed to Guy, watching her closely, that her lips shook too; as if with compassion and sorrow He was astonished at the change.

"God knows!" cried the girl passionately "Christ is my witness that I do not desire her death, though wicked folks have said so. I pray every day that she may have a long life, and bear a son to His glory, and that I may be spared from the burden of ruling this heretic country But, Master Manton, I do not think that

God has heard those prayers. He has His own purposes for me and England, and as He sees us now, I tell you that I do not doubt that I shall come to it soon Not all that my enemies—and I have many of them—not all that they can work against me will hinder His will. They failed when my house was set afire, and I near burned with it; they failed again when the warrant was sent down for my death, and when they slandered me to her Grace. Not even the paper that Monsignor holds in his strong box in my lord Cardinal's house can keep me from what my Maker wills for me."

She wheeled round and faced him with blazing eyes and passionate face.

He was almost convinced Her sincerity seemed overwhelming For a moment he doubted the evidence of the past five years, the tale after tale that ran about the Court, the confessions drawn from her friends on the rack, even the little paper of which she had spoken. It seemed brutal to suspect this loyal hot girl who spoke with such a fire of love and compassion and resolution. He made a violent effort and set his teeth.

"Yes, madam?" She sprang up.

"'Yes, madam,' "she sneered. "And do you not understand me now, sir?"

Again she sat down, and he could see her trembling. For a moment she could not speak, she drew a sobbing breath or two, clasped and unclasped her hands, and sat quiet in her old position.

"Well, Master Manton, you are not so clever as I thought, or else more clever yet. This is what I mean. No man can hinder me from being Queen. They have tried often enough, God knows! You cannot hinder me. Well, then, why will you try? Do you wish to be my enemy always? Have you thought of that?"

She had dropped her voice almost to a whisper, and was looking at him.

Still he did not understand what she asked of him. Surely he had made it plain that the matter had passed out of his hands.

"Madam; I do not understand. I have told your Highness that the paper is in Monsignor's Priuli's hands." She sighed, almost ostentatiously, he thought. "Well, you will say that I insult you, I know; but I cannot help that, and—and one who has done as you have done has no right to protest. Well, then—do you think that I do not know that you wrote the paper yourself?"

The shock was so sudden that his hands rose convulsively; he knew that the colour had left his face, that his mouth was open and his eyes staring. Yet he could not control himself, or look other than guilty; and he knew it.

"Ah I Master Manton; I do not wish you to be my enemy nor to be yours myself. I desire to have such a man as you as my friend and servant. I can forgive the treachery and cure it, and I can use your wits for truer ends. Will you not do what I ask?"

"What is it that you ask, madam?"

His voice sounded hollow in his own ears. It was as if another spoke for him.

"I ask this only," said Elizabeth softly. "I ask you to spare my dear sister the sorrow and anxiety that this tale will cause her. I know she will not believe it when I see her and tell her all, but she will suffer so much, and she suffers already. I ask you to be brave and tender; to write your confession and leave it with me. I swear by God that I will not show it till you be out of the country. If you need money, I will provide it, until the day that you come back to be my servant and my friend."

There fell a dead silence in the little room. The fire had sunk to a red core; there was not even the leap or crackle of the smallest tongue of flame to break the stillness. The heavy folds of the girl's dress had sunk down and were quiet, and she herself sat, an image of hopeful patience, waiting for the word that would make this young man hers. Outside all was still; the hall was closed and dark; the last servant had long left the corridor, and was gone upstairs. Within and without the room it seemed that all waited in expectant quiet for the decision to be made. It was a full minute before the silence was broken.

"Oh! by God!"

The Queen's gentleman had sprung to his feet, his hands clenched, and his white face glaring at the woman who had tempted him.

She rose, too, and went to the fire, turned round and faced him.

"Then you will not do me this kindness?"

"I will not do this damned treachery."

She looked at him for a full quarter-minute through half-closed contemptuous eyes. Then she spoke:

"Very well, Master Manton. I have no more to ask. I shall command next time."

She put out her hand to be kissed.

He looked at her a moment longer, almost dominated by her personality; then he wheeled to go across the floor.

"Master Manton!"

He turned, breathing heavily.

"There was no need to bring Master Kearsley. I do not stab my enemies in the dark I shall have other weapons some day."

Her voice rose a little, with an odd ring in it.

"I shall remember that you showed me neither kindness nor courtesy on a day when I could not command it."

He turned again, and as he reached the door, the voice cried after him.

"God keep you, Master Manton! and sweetheart Tom!"

He went very slowly upstairs.

Two pairs of eyes were fixed on the door as he came in; and the boy ran across, still in his court-suit, seized him by the arm and lifted a tear-stained face.

"Oh! Master Manton, Master Kearsley has said such things to me! I could not help it. She was so clever, she seemed to know all already. And I did not kiss her, she kissed me"

Guy patted him mechanically on the shoulder.

"Yes, yes, dear lad I know she is clever. Go to bed now. I must talk to Master Kearsley. My God! how clever! Dick, do you hear? She does not even now know what is in the paper!"

4

The three left again on the following morning about nine o'clock.

They saw nothing more of the Princess. Tom came upstairs an hour before they started with the news that she had gone to mass as usual. It seemed that she heard two masses each day, for the living and the dead They rode out through the archway with their servants, and the salutes of the porter, and were out immediately on the Queen's highway—not Elizabeth's.

Guy had told Dick everything the night before, under the strictest confidence, and had received his counsel such as it was. Master Kearsley approved heartily of all that his friend has said and done, and especially of his leaving the room without paying his homage.

"That was well done," he said; "it will do the minx a world of good"

He had recommended also an immediate visit to the Cardinal, and the placing of the paper in her Grace's hands at the earliest opportunity.

"If you do not, my lady will get at her first. Oh! she will manage it, whether she is sent for or no."

There was one fact that Guy had not revealed, he was too much ashamed of it, and that was the very real struggle he had gone through during the silent minute after the girl had made her proposal.

He was rather silent during the ride to London, in consequence, reviewing what had taken place in his soul, for he was beginning to take pains again with that part of his being. He could hardly believe that he could have hesitated. But the struggle had been made possible for him, he saw now, by the girl's extreme skill in conversation Ah! how skilful she had been; and he? he had hesitated!

He made another discovery about himself later in the day that he could not understand.

They arrived home in St. James' as the ladies were going across the court to dinner, and dismounted and uncovered as they went past The Queen of course was not there; she was dining in private; but young Mistress Dormer detached herself from the group, and came towards him.

"So you are back, sir," she said pleasantly. "You are early. Her Grace told me to ask you how you had sped, and whether my Lady Elizabeth was pleased with Master Bradshawe's singing."

Guy walked across the court to the hall door with her, telling her the superficial part of the news. Tom had sung excellently, he believed, but it was the swan-song of his voice, he feared. Master Tallis had said a month ago that it was a miracle it had not gone already. Her Highness had honoured himself, too, with a few minutes' conversation; she had looked very well and happy and had asked after Her Majesty's health. Her Highness had heard mass that morning They had left at nine o'clock; the roads were in good order He begged Mistress Dormer to convey his duty and thanks to her Grace.

It was then that he made the discovery, and he pondered it all the way up to his own rooms. It was that his feelings towards her Grace had undergone a certain change There seemed a kind of link between her and him that had been wanting before; the wall of ice seemed thinner. He found himself interested in the thought that she would hear his adventures; he even experienced a faint envy of Mistress Dormer who would tell her them. The feeling perplexed him a little; he was not a good enough psychologist to understand it

He dined downstairs, came up an hour later, and found Monsignor Priuli waiting for him.

"I was obliged to come," said the priest smiling, and taking his hand. "I could not rest till I knew. I have been anxious."

Guy gave him a seat, and closed the door Then he sat down himself.

"Monsignor," he said, "you need not have been anxious on my behalf. Her Highness is too clever"

"Too clever?"

"Too clever to do me an injury. She told me that I need not have troubled to bring Master Kearsley, and that she did not stab in the dark."

"The whole story, my dear friend I "cried the priest eagerly, rubbing his hands softly together between his knees

He sat very quiet and attentive as Guy told him, nodding from time to time, putting a question once or twice, and nodding again vigorously at the answers he received

"But I am a knave at heart, Monsignor," he ended desperately. "I tell your lordship that I hesitated; that for a while I did. not know what I should do"

The priest's face grew grave and tender.

"Forgive me, my son, but you speak as a fool. When will souls learn that there is no sin in temptation, and that there can be no temptation without a lively image being presented to the mind? Have you not heard an hundred times that sin lies in the will, and not in the imagination?"

"But I hesitated," said the young man persistently.

"Of course you hesitated It was there that temptation lay. Satan presented the picture through Her Highness' words you regarded that picture, and said No, like a good Christian and a true man Put that clean away, Master Manton: I tell you that you are not guilty before God Rather you have acquired merit. So Her Highness feigned that you had written the paper yourself, and begged you to be honest for once "'

"She feigned so," said Guy, "but, by God, she knew the truth."

"Why, yes, she knew it, but we cannot prove that. She has said nothing that we can use"

"Even had she done so," went on Guy bitterly. "it would have been of no avail She would have sworn that she had not."

"Yes, but we could have sworn that she had And now we cannot. We shall be forced to tell her Grace that the Princess protested her innocence from the beginning"

He was silent a moment

"I shall see my lord Cardinal to-night," he said presently; "my lord asked if there were any news this morning, and I told him No, there could not be. I will tell him all to-night, and we will hear his advice as to going to her Grace. We cannot forestall the Lady Elizabeth She can have written even by now if she intends it at all. I think we had best do nothing until Easter is over"

There was little more to be said, and a few minutes later Monsignor took his leave

He held Guy's hand a moment in his slender brown fingers.

"You have come very well out of it, sir. Her Grace has at least one faithful servant in her house. God bless you, my son."

A letter was put into Guy's hands as he came out from supper that night. It was from the priest, written in Latin, and told him that the Cardinal still held to the former plan, and that the Queen should not be approached till Easter was over The Archbishop wished his congratulations and blessing to be conveyed to a man who had acted well and faithfully in a difficult affair, and he desired to see him within a few days

Guy went to his room that night very content. He had been relieved by the priest's interpretation of what he himself had considered a moral failure. Perhaps he was not such a knave after all.

He said his prayers with devotion, and found himself praying for the Queen with a fervour which he had never experienced before. He wondered that he had not hitherto realised her loneliness; that he had not understood that emotionalism was out of place in a ruler—Monsignor Priuli's words to him on the subject a month or so before came back to him now, and he questioned himself as to whether they had not been intentional; certainly he had confessed to a cold devotion to his sovereign. Then his thoughts leapt to the Queen again He sat back on his heels and considered her. No, she was not lovable in the ordinary sense, but was she not admirable, and pitiable too? He remembered her disappointments, the mockery of her mortal disease, the failure that walked with her from cradle to crown, and seemed likely to go further and take her to the grave itself.

Had he been fair to her? Had he made the allowances that he desired others to make for him? Surely compassion, and not contempt, was the proper emotion. She was so old now, and with an age more piteous than that of years!—so zealous; so well controlled, and yet so passionate and simple when she thought it right to let her heart go out to the man whom she called her husband, and who gave her a courteous hatred in return

As he knelt upright now at his bedside with his hands clasped, the image of the two sisters came before him once more—Elizabeth, flushed with youth, narrow-eyed, red-lipped, supple, indomitable; Mary, withered, peevish, pathetically dignified, heart-broken There the two stood, as they had stood this time last night. Each invited allegiance. The one with years and honour before her, with rewards in her hands, the hope of a restless people fixed on her, and their hearts and bodies at her service, with a religion that made but little claim on faith or life, and a policy that flattered an island's pride And the other sinking down to the grave, hated by those who knew her and distrusted by those who did not, powerless to help or to reward except with thanks, and sparing of those, with a faith so keen that it could not abide unfaith, and a plan of rule that would make England one with the nations instead of setting her aloof in a fierce and capable insularity. The one had offered him honour; the other had neglected him.

These were the two that asked for his homage, and this time he did not hesitate.

He knelt staring before him a minute longer, then he beat on his breast, and threw his face forward on to the bed. His eyes were bright with tears.

"God be merciful to me a sinner!"

5

The Court went down to Greenwich to keep Easter, and returned to Richmond soon after Low Sunday. A piece of news was made public during this time that caused some astonishment; it was to the effect that the Count de Feria had proposed for the hand of Mistress Dormer, and had been accepted, though she had previously refused such great persons as the Duke of Norfolk and Lord Devon; but what gave greater surprise was that although it was said that the Queen had consented, yet no announcement was made as to when the wedding would take place Men asked one another why there need be delay; her Grace could not expect to keep her friend always at her side. It was supposed that the Queen was depressed and could make up her mind to nothing. Everything was going wrong; the attempt to re-take the French forts had failed wretchedly. As Master Kearsley had remarked, they had fallen by treachery, and they could not be regained without it, and French treachery was not so easy to win as English The result of the failure was to increase still further the Queen's unpopularity, and she seldom set foot outside her palace.

Her domestic affairs, too, were in a miserable state. Her ladies whispered that she spent hours in writing to Philip, and that the arrival of his letters in answer always meant tears and unhappiness. It was supposed that the subject of dissension between them was the proposed marriage between Elizabeth and Prince Philibert of Savoy, which the King urged and the Queen refused to sanction The arrival of Princess Christina, of Denmark, did not improve matters. It was said that Philip was in love with her; at any rate it was obvious that Mary was jealous of her. She would hardly ever see her alone; she took every opportunity to avoid her, and the Princess went again after a few days without having accomplished anything with regard to the King's desire on the subject of the Savoy marriage.

It was towards the end of April that the Cardinal arrived at Richmond, and sent the same evening for Guy Manton.

Guy went to him, and found him in his rooms that looked out over the park It was already dark, and the shutters were drawn across the windows. When he had kissed hands and sat down the Cardinal began at once

"I have seen her Grace," he said, "but I had no time to speak of our affair. But I am to see her to-morrow at ten o'clock, and will tell her then. You had best be in the anteroom, and I will send for you at the proper time. I will tell her Grace first all the story, and of the Lady Elizabeth's words to you; then she will no doubt wish to ask you questions herself."

Guy assented.

"Keep nothing back, Master Manton, and add nothing. I mean, do not make the case stronger than it is. The burden of it is not upon us, but upon her Grace, though I would we could lighten it."

"What do you think her Grace will do, your Eminence?"

The Cardinal raised his dark eyebrows and smiled.

"How can we know, sir' If she already doubts, it may make her doubt a certainty If she is already convinced of the Princess' innocence, it may make her doubt it In the first case, I think she will bequeath the crown to another; in the second case it may cause her to look with more favour upon this foreign marriage. Have you spoken with her Grace at all, Master Manton?"

"No, your Eminence."

"She seemed to me very sick. She hardly spoke to me, except what was necessary. She has been a burning and a shining light in this dark country; one little lamp in a wilderness, blown upon by every wind, and preserved only by her own innocence. But the oil is low, Master Manton, unless God replenish it."

He spoke very softly and serenely. Guy wondered what he thought as to his own prospects should the Queen die. The last Cardinal in England who had raised his voice in an heretical Court had lost his life for doing it; his own mother had died on the scaffold for the same cause. What would be this man's fate should Elizabeth come to her throne and find him still on his?

Guy served the *lavabo* at the Cardinal's mass next morning kneeling on the footpace of the temporary altar, and was vividly conscious as he did so of the Queen's shrunken presence in the great chair in the background, and of her ladies behind her. She did not know yet what part he was to play in an hour or two. He wondered what she would think and say, and what form her thanks would take.

At ten o'clock he was in the second ante-room, and knelt as the Cardinal presently swept through in his scarlet. Then he sat down again and waited

There were half a dozen others there, waiting to see her Grace, or to catch the Cardinal as he came out. Guy wished that Monsignor Priuli had been able to come, but he had been told last night that it had been found impossible for the secretary to leave Lambeth at the same time as his master. It would have been pleasant to have had his kindly strong presence

He scarcely knew whether the time seemed to pass fast or slow. At one instant he dreaded the interview so intolerably that it seemed hardly a moment since he had come in, at another he hated the waiting so much that he thought it must have lasted an hour already. It was not a pleasing task, this of accusing one sister to another of the most sordid kind of deceit; he would have to accuse himself, too, of misdemeanours—of holding back an information for nearly two years, of having shown unwillingness even then to do justice. Yet he did not doubt that she would be grateful at her heart for what he had done. He recalled his last emotional interview with the Queen, when he had gone in to beg that Stephen's agony might cease. She had been so slow to understand, so searching in her questions, so cold when she consented Would she freeze him again now before thawing? It would be harder to bear this time too. He did not relish the prospect of even a temporary injustice from this woman.

"Master Guy Manton to go in to her Grace "The shrill voice startled him; he had not seen the page open the door. He passed through the first ante-room with a painful throbbing at the base of his throat, and went through the further door that the boy pushed open for him.

The Queen was in her upright arm-chair with her back to the light, and did not turn her head as he came in. On the other side of the hearth sat the Cardinal, his scarlet robe lying out across the rushes, and his little cap a vivid vermilion spot against the oak mantel-piece. One of his hands rested along the arm of his chair, and the other held the fatal paper. His eyes threw a kindly momentary look at the young man on his knees by the door, and then moved back to the Queen's face.

There was silence for a moment. Then the Cardinal broke it.

"I have told her Grace, Master Manton, about this paper that I hold, and how it came into your possession; and I have held myself responsible for having troubled her Grace with it now. I have related, too, the whole story of how you went to Bishop Hatfield, and of what the Lady Elizabeth said to you there. Her Grace now wishes you to answer a few questions in her presence."

The Cardinal paused, lifted the paper and looked at it. There seemed to be a few notes written upon it.

"First Master Manton, why did you not give up the paper sooner?"

Guy moved his eyes from the Cardinal to the Queen and back again. Then he drew a breath, and still kneeling began to answer.

"Because, your Eminence, I was ambitious. I kept the paper back at first because I wished to distinguish myself. After Master Brownrigg's death I laid it aside—I could not bear to look at it. Then I mislaid it, and thought no more of it."

"As soon as you found it then, you gave it up?"

"As soon as I found it I brought it to Lambeth, to Monseigneur Priuli."

Guy glanced again at the Queen. She had not moved a muscle. Her face was in shadow, and he could not see her expression Her thin hands were gripped on the arms of her chair.

"Good, Master Manton," said the Cardinal, looking at the paper again.

"What did you tell Monseigneur Priuli when you saw him?"

"My lord, I told him that I understood he was skilful in cyphers, and that I could not read the paper myself. I told him that, if his lordship could read it, I would do what he bade"

"How long a time passed before you saw Monseigneur again?"

"Monseigneur wrote to me once and asked me if I knew any words—he called them key-words, my lord'—that Master Brownrigg had engraved on any rings or such like. I told him I knew of none. That would be about a week later. I saw him again, when he came to St. James' to tell me he had read the cypher. I should say after a fortnight or three weeks more ""Have you any skill in cyphers yourself?" "None, your Eminence."

"Could you explain to her Grace the cypher of which we are speaking?"

"No, your Eminence"

"Then you cannot swear that Monseigneur has read it rightly?"

"No, your Eminence; except so far as I could swear to Monseigneur Priuli's good faith"

The Cardinal smiled faintly, but did not lift his eyes. "When you saw the Lady Elizabeth at Bishop's Hatfield she told you that you had written the paper yourself?" "Yes, my lord."

"Did Her Highness know what was in the paper?" "I think not, my lord." "Why do you think not, Master Manton?" "Because Her Highness told me a great number of other things that she had discovered, but said no word of that, except that she feared it would trouble the Queen's Majesty to hear of it." "How did Her Highness speak of the Queen's Majesty?" Guy hesitated

"She spoke of her Grace with an appearance of great love and pity."

A deep rough voice jarred suddenly from the Queen's chair. "Why do you say 'appearance,' sir?" Guy was horribly startled. He hesitated again a moment. "I think it was only an appearance of it, your Grace." "Did you think so at the time, or afterwards?" said the harsh voice again.

"I was not sure at the time, your Grace." Again there was silence. The Queen had not stirred while she spoke. The Cardinal looked up questioningly, then lifted the paper once more and went on

"Her Highness asked you to leave the country, and to give her a confession that you had written the paper yourself?"

"Yes, my lord. She offered also to supply me with money while I needed it, until——"

"Well, Master Manton?"

"Until Her Highness came to the throne."

Guy's voice shook as he spoke. It was as if he were driving swords into the heart of the woman who sat there. And the worst was that she did not flinch.

The Cardinal went on, with a touch of haste.

"How did Her Highness discover that you had such a paper at all?"

"A friend of mine blabbed of it, and   "

"Stay, sir. What did he say? Do you know?"

"He said that I had something against Her Highness that would hinder her ever coming to the throne, and that Catholics need be in no fear."

"Well, Master Manton?"

"My lord, I can only suppose that one who heard it told Her Highness that. Then she sent for me, through Master Cornwallis"

"Did any go with you?"

"My servant, Tom Bradshawe, one of her Grace's choir, was sent for also by Her Highness; and I took Master Kearsley as well, with three servants."

"Why did you take Master Kearsley?"

Again Guy paused. But he knew he must not incriminate the Cardinal.

"I took him, my lord, because I feared Her Highness."

"Did any tell you to take a friend?"

"Yes, my lord!"

"Who was it?"

"Yourself, my lord," said Guy with an effort But he was grateful for the friendliness

The Cardinal paused just long enough to let the answer sink home, and then went on without any sign of discomposure.

"What else did Her Highness say to you, sir?"

"She threatened me, my lord."

"Threatened?"

"Yes, my lord. Her Highness said that I need not have brought Master Kearsley, for that she did not stab her enemies in the back, but that she would use other weapons some day."

"What did you understand by that?"

"I understood that she would use the law against me my lord, when—when she was able."

"The law, Master Manton? But you had done no wrong?"

"No, my lord."

The Cardinal looked at the paper again.

"Why was Master Bradshawe sent for to Bishop's Hatfield?"

"Her Highness said that she wished to hear him sing"

"And what do you think of it, Master Manton?"

"My lord, I think it was that she might discover if he knew aught of the paper."

"And did Her Highness discover aught?"

"She discovered how the paper came into my hands."

"How did she prevail on Master Bradshawe to tell her that?"

Guy eyed first the Archbishop, then the Queen. Then he looked down.

"My lord, I found the boy on Her Highness' knees. She was kissing him."

He saw the Queen's scarlet-clad foot tap two or three times 'and cease.

"I have just finished, Master Manton," said the Cardinal. "But tell me this. Will you swear before God and the Court of Heaven that you have spoken the truth, that you had no hand in the making of the cypher, and what the paper says is true?"

"My lord, I swear before God and the Court of Heaven that I have spoken the truth, that I have had no hand in the making of the cypher I cannot swear that what the paper says is true, because I do not know. But I swear that I believe it to be true."

The Cardinal laid the paper on his knee, and looked at the Queen.

Then the woman turned in her chair, and Guy, waiting for her thanks, saw her pinched agonised face, her hard wild eyes, and her drawn mouth. Then her harsh voice began:

"Master Manton, I do not believe it I am amazed that you should believe such things of Her Highness. Her Highness is a good Catholic—a good Catholic, my lord Cardinal, I tell you. I am astonished, Master Manton, I say, at your giving credit to a scrap of paper two years old, and written by an enemy of myself and Her Highness. There be slanderers enough, God knows, without seeking for them in mine own household I forbid you to speak of the matter again, except to deny it to any who speak of it to you. You are no just judge or witness, Master Manton, in such a cause You have believed the worst without sufficient reason. You had best pray our Lord to purify your heart of such thoughts. You have been wild and indiscreet. The only reason that I do not turn you from my household is that I think you have been honest, and have told the truth as you believe it. But I am disappointed in you, Master Manton. You have my leave to go."

A moment or two later Guy followed the Cardinal out of the room, stumbled after him through the staring ante-rooms, down the corridor, and into the Archbishop's own chamber, and stood there shaking.

The Cardinal put his hand on the young man's silken shoulder.

"There, there, Master Manton; you must not grieve. Her Grace is near mad with suspicion and sorrow; and Her Highness has written to her. But she believes it, sir; she believes it, in spite of what she said There, there, Master Manton!"

Plures amicos re secunda compara:
Paucos amicos rebus adversis proba.

Pittac *apud Auson.*

CHAPTER III

MARY THE QUEEN PREPARES FOR A JOURNEY

I

IT was on the evening of a hot August day that the Queen came home once more to St. James'.

Mistress Dormer had been unwell at Hampton Court, and had been sent up to London a week or two previously in the Royal litter, as the Queen thought that the journey by water would be harmful to her health, and she met Mary now at the foot of the stairs to welcome her back. The Queen asked her how she did. "I am reasonably well, I thank your Grace ""So am not I," said Mary, and went wearily upstairs.

It had been heavy weather both in town and country. Day had followed day, parched and breathless; the rain that fell from time to time had no freshness in it; the hot ground had drunk it and craved for more; the river that flowed past Hampton Court had reflected the trees on the other side as in an oily mirror; the foliage in the park had hung motionless day after day, and seemed to exhaust rather than enliven the starved air. Again and again by night there had been seen strange fires, pale and blue, that gathered, stirred, hovered and dispersed, and caused the supernaturally minded to whisper of stakes and faggots, and the physically-minded to fear fever.

It had told terribly upon Mary. The face that Jane had seen at the foot of the stairs had been drawn with exhaustion, her eyes unnaturally bright under heavy lids, and she held painfully to the balustrade as she went up, stopping to pant at each landing.

Mistress Dormer was not well herself; she had had a touch of fever at Hampton Court, and her convalescence had left her weak and tired out; but it did not prevent her, after she had seen the Queen to bed, from going into Magdalene's room to hear the details of the past fortnight.

"It is no more than before," said the girl wearily, leaning back in her chair in her loose wrapper, with her hair on her shoulders. "We are all tired out together. Oh! Jane, it has been terrible."

"Terrible?"

"The whole spring together; all is amiss. God knows how it will end! His Highness will not write; he is angry at something, and she writes and no answer comes And the folks are all against her, and crying out for her sister. And there was the matter of the child again, as you know, when she made her will, and all has ended in nothing."

"Has she spoken of it again?" asked Jane quickly.

"Not since April; she speaks very little now. She has not given me a word good or bad for a week, except what was necessary"

"Has aught been heard of His Highness' return?"

"Not a word. He will not come. She gave the word for the ships to disperse, and has not spoken of him again."

"Does she sleep?"

"A little towards morning, and sometimes after dinner in her chair"

"Does she complain?"

The girl shook her heavy head.

"She says nothing now."

Jane stared at the floor without speaking She hated the thought of this lethargy; she distrusted the doctors, especially the Italian who prescribed for the Queen; she furiously resented the King's absence; it was this, she thought, that caused more than half the mischief—that and his persistent efforts earlier in the year to make his wife grant what she would not. The Queen was suffering from despair of soul rather than an actual sickness of body; it was that that sapped her strength and allowed her infirmity to gain ground. There was but one thing for which Jane was thankful, and that was that her mistress had come home, and that she could tend her herself. She would have no more nonsense with drugs and bleeding; it was not that that was required

"You look ill yourself, sweetheart," she said to the girl.

Magdalene opened her eyes slowly

"I am just weary of it all," she said. "I would we had stayed in the country, or better still that I might go by myself.

"And leave her Grace?"

"I cannot help it, Jane. I cannot love her. She knows it now; she would sooner I were not with her."

Jane's lips worked a moment, but she said nothing.

Magdalene went on sleepily.

"I have tried, my dear, but she is so cold. I think she cares nothing——"

"That is enough, my dear."

"Why Jane!"

Mistress Dormer got up.

"I tell you that is enough. You have a pretty face, sweetheart, but I think you have no heart at all I must go to her Grace."

Magdalene lay still a minute longer, wondering drowsily at her foolish friend. It was absurd to pretend to love such a mistress; it was insincere, she thought— a little unreal. Of course it was all sad enough, but there was a plenty of sad things in this sad world She must go to bed; the cool sheets would be better than this tapestry chair.

So Magdalene went to bed.

Jane passed along the corridor and turned into the little parlour that adjoined the Queen's bedroom, nodding good-night as she went by the sleepy page; who blinked at her and smiled back.

She was not in the least angry with Magdalene; she was only a little contemptuous. It was astonishing, she thought, that a woman of ordinary intuitions, who had had brains enough to refuse Master Norris, and who had such opportunities of observing her mistress, should call that mistress cold! Cold! Why it was a fever that burned in that infirm body—a fever of passion for a man who hated her; a fever of hope for a country that despised her; and a fever of love for God who had made her and redeemed her, and now seemed— Jane paused; then she finished her thought defiantly—a God who now seemed to have forgotten her altogether.

The little parlour was empty now except for one old woman who sat over her sewing at the further door that led through to the bedroom, with a candle on the table beside her. Jane signed to her to sit still, and came noiselessly across the floor towards her, raising her eyebrows in a question.

The old woman shook her head.

"She is awake yet, mistress," she whispered. "She called to me five minutes ago."

"She did not ask for me?"

"No, mistress—she asked for water"

"Has she been praying?"

"She was praying from her book when I went in."

"Is all ready for mass to-morrow?"

"Yes, mistress."

Jane drew back the curtain softly, and pushed at the half-open door within The great dark room was lighted by one candle outside the curtains of the bed. The single flame seemed to have no penetrating power in the huge gloom; it showed only the sombre wreaths embroidered on the hanging beside it, and half a dozen fleur-de-lis on the arras against the wall. Beneath the candle lay a book open. The rest of the room was in deep shadow, and Jane moved hesitatingly across it, afraid of stumbling or knocking against a piece of furniture The book was a hopeful sign; perhaps the Queen had laid it down when she felt sleep coming on.

She came across, scarcely daring to breathe, and looked down at the book; it was open at the old place—the prayer for the unity of Christendom. The petition for the woman in childbirth had not been used for three months now; that cause was lost, and left the other more imperative.

There was no sound from within the curtains, as Jane stood there listening. Perhaps, indeed, the Queen was asleep. The exhaustion of the journey might have done what drugs could not do.

She stooped and drew off her shoes, and then, still without a sound, moved round the bed in the dusk to which her eyes were getting accustomed, closed a cupboard door, set the jewelled pins straight on the table beside the silver-framed standing mirror, looked at the altar set opposite the end of the bed, where mass" would be said next morning and saw that the two candles had been put in the holders, and the three cloths laid in order over the stone slab. The cruets and the silver canister and the rest had been set there just now to prevent any confusion in the morning. At last she passed round to the further side of the bed, drew the curtain gently, and looked.

At first she thought that the Queen was asleep. Mary was lying on her back, with her hands as usual clasped across her breast, and her hair gathered up in a white linen cap, scarcely whiter than her face. Jane could make out the thin profile, the pursed lips, the sharp chin and wasted throat.

Then the eyes disclosed themselves wide, turned to Jane, and closed again.

"It is late, sweetheart," said the harsh passionless voice. "Go to bed."

2

Downstairs in the guard-room there was plenty of talk about her Grace.

Master Wentworth, the cofferer, straddling across the hearth in his velvet and gold chain, was laying down the law about poisons to the group that was gathered about the back-gammon board at the end of the long table.

"There be some," he said, "that leave no trace. Folks just waste away under them There be some that give pain, and others that have a stench; but cunning fellows use not these. And of all men the Italians are the cleverest in such things."

"Who can tell?" said an officer who had just come off guard, and was still in his green-and-white. "Fever or poison are the same. Your shrewdest physician cannot tell. And I like the Italian man no more than you"

"He may be a blessing in disguise," remarked a humorous stout man in black, with a pen behind his ear, looking up from the board; "—a blessing to us all and to the poor lady herself. In God's hands be the issues!" He rolled his eyes piously.

"It may be there is another child toward," went on the officer chuckling. "And then what of my Lady Elizabeth?"

"My Lady Elizabeth has weathered more storms than this. In six months she will be no more at Hatfield."

"Please God I shall be there before that," said the secretary. "If I can make my way through the crowds that will run there. She is a jolly lady. And you, Master Wentworth?"

"I shall run when the rest do," he said, "with Master Norris here, if he can leave his lady-love."

Jack looked up smiling from his back-gammon, and took up his pot of hypocras.

"My lady love may do as she wills. I shall neither run nor stay with her. I think I shall give myself to devotion."

There was a murmur of laughter, which silenced suddenly as a face looked in from the darkness outside Jack glanced up, saw Guy, and dropped his eyes instantly

Then the face vanished again without a word

Jack went on with an effort.

"At least, Her Highness is no Catholic like this one," he said.

"Not like this one, thank God," said the officer. "I have never been so out of conceit with the Religion as now. Her Grace's blessing would turn sweet wine sour, I think"

He yawned and stood up

"We shall run together, I tell you," repeated the man in black, "and so will Master Norris when the time comes, with young Bradshawe here"

Tom grinned uneasily across at Jack, from his corner.

"That will be when the King comes home," put in Master Bassett of the privy-chamber.

"He is all for my lady now, since De Feria went to her in June"

"He will marry her yet," said the officer, "and then we shall have children enough"

A page looked in through the open door

"Good evening, gentlemen; we shall have rain to-morrow. The clouds are coming up."

"Come in, Roger," cried the soldier "Give us the news."

"There is no news, sir," said the boy, "save that I am sleepy and that Master Kearsley is in the inner court."

"What is he doing there?"

"He is a-walking, sir, and a-cursing all who speak to him," said the page as he disappeared

"The fellow is always a-walking," remarked the officer. "He was up and down in the privy-garden last night at Hampton Court. And Master Manton is another like him. God knows there is enough mourning without that."

"And a man cannot speak to Master Kearsley nowadays without being cursed at," complained the secretary. "He is more like a bear than a man Good-night, gentlemen, I am for bed."

The game ended as he spoke, and there was a clatter of the benches as the rest rose.

When the others had gone, two still lingered a minute. Then Jack took up his light cloak, and stood swaying a little

"Come, Tom," he said, "it is time for us, too. Roger will be back presently."

As they went across the floor together, the man took the boy's arm and sighed. He was a little drunk.

"It is a hard world, Tom; she has refused me again; and Master Manton will scarce speak to me"

Tom sighed sympathetically

"But we shall all run," went on the other softly, "when the time comes, but we need not brag of it before. Now Master Manton will neither brag nor run."

"No, Master Norris"

"You are well rid of him. Now I am a wiser master, and a kinder, am I not?"

Jack's eyes filled with tears of self-appreciation

The guard-room lights were out presently, and the palace lay asleep in the heavy dark.

3

The night-sleeplessness of the Queen did not amend.

Throughout this hot noon of the year Jane watched her each day, drowsy after dinner when she would doze heavily in her chair, rousing herself for necessary interviews, and gradually awakening as night came on with its evening-fever; until by nine o'clock she sat bolt upright with bright eyes, a spot of hot colour in each cheek, and dry hands that clung and twisted and expanded their fingers over the cool carved bosses of her chair-arms.

There was a fierce irritability in her manner, but none in her words. The spasms of nervous anger that seized on her at contradictions of circumstance or sudden noises, exploded silently within her, and no more than the smoke of them was visible in her face.

She spoke very little, and she did not seem to welcome much conversation. Jane would have thought that she was indifferent as to whether she were alone or not, if it had not been for the little words and movements by which she would express herself, when Jane was thinking of leaving the room

And still there came no letter from Philip.

Jane particularly disliked the doctors, and wished to exclude them, but the Queen would not hear of it, and followed their prescriptions with the greatest care She drenched herself with drugs, the windows were kept carefully closed to keep out what was believed to be the poison of the miasmatic air, and at night the curtains of the bed were always drawn tightly to secure that result yet further.

As September passed on there was certainly a slight improvement, in spite of the horrible shock of the Emperor's death. The Queen was less irritable, a little more inclined to hear conversation, she fell asleep two or three times even before midnight, and her face lost the look of an unnatural mask set with fixed, shining eyes.

The two had a long talk one evening shortly before the news of Charles' death arrived.

Jane came up from supper about six o'clock and found that the curtains were already drawn and the candles lighted in the Queen's parlour. Mary herself had sat up on her couch behind the screen, and had a piece of the old embroidery between her fingers on which she had worked so much at Hampton Court.

"I am better, sweetheart," she said. "I shall sleep better to-night, I think."

"Will your Grace not go to bed then?"

"Not yet," said the Queen, "an hour yet. Talk to me, Jane."

Mistress Dormer sat down at the end of the Queen's couch nearest the hearth with her hands in her lap.

"My lord Cardinal is better too," she said. "Master Manton told me to-night."

Mary said nothing, and Jane watched her careful fingers, trembling a little with weakness, pushing the long steel needle strung with gold thread through the sheath of the stiff pomegranate that lay on her knee.

"Your Grace has near finished the piece," she said.

"I shall finish it," said Mary shortly "I am pleased that my lord is better. The ague is all abroad just now."

"Your Grace must be careful——"

"I do not need it," said the Queen smiling; "my old guest is enough.'"

"Madam——"

"There, there," said Mary, "that is enough."

They talked a long time that night, or rather Jane talked, and the Queen listened, patting her embroidery softly at intervals, smoothing it out, holding it up to look at it—of small events about the Court—Master Norris' new mare, and Magdalene's third refusal of him; the great happenings were not for that room. It seemed to Mistress Dormer that the Queen had not been so much herself for months past, and yet that self was more tranquil, too. The girl did not fear hysteria as she had once feared its; the flame she watched was steadier and less liable to flare; but it was a little lower also.

They spoke at last of Croydon where they had stayed together more than once. The Queen laid down her embroidery and leaned back as if tired out. Jane sprang up and lifted the small silken feet on to the couch

"There, there," said Mary, "that is enough. Do you remember the poor man there who had lost his cart?"

Jane remembered him perfectly. While the two ladies were out visiting the cottages they had discovered a man whose cart had been pressed for the Queen's service.

"Master Rochester had never paid him," said the Queen softly, "I have often thought of that; he took all and gave him nothing."

"Madam——"

"Yes, sweetheart. I have been tempted to think that my God has used me like that"

Jane looked at her astonished; it was the first word of that kind that she had ever heard from her. She had complained of a lack of human sympathy sometimes, but never of Divine Love.

"It is a temptation, Madam," she answered bravely.

"Have I not said so?"

Then a sudden thought came to the girl

"But your Grace remembers the end?"

"The end?"

"Your Grace paid him in full The supreme Majesty was not unjust."

Mary sighed.

"Well, well…. The Little Office, my dear. I know I must give what I can."

Old Mrs. Clarentia came in before they had done, and waited by the door while the two voices, one harsh and the other soft, finished the stately prayers, and the two books were laid one upon the other on the table Then she came forward.

"It is time for bed, Madam"

"Well, well, help me up, dear heart."

Once in the night the Queen called softly Mistress Dormer
was at her side in a moment

"There is nothing in the room, Jane?" asked the Queen, sitting up and
looking about her at the heavy curtains, with bright weary eyes

"In the room your Grace?"

"I thought I heard somewhat—a running of footsteps. Look, Jane."

The girl went obediently round the room with her candle, lifting the
tapestry, stooping to peer beneath the bed, opening the great presses beside the
hearth. She even went to the door, pulled aside the curtain and looked out The
woman in the outer room was sleeping heavily in her bed drawn across the door.
Jane shook her softly by the shoulder.

"There has none been walking?" she whispered sharply, looking down at the
bewildered face.

The maid shook her head; she was stupid with sleep. Jane pulled to the door
and went back,

The Queen was still sitting up in bed, her hand clasped round her knees. Her
face was a little flushed and her lips parted

"There is no one, your Grace. Perhaps it was a dream"

Mary shook her head. It seemed to Jane that she did not look so well again
Her eyes had the glassy look in them that had been there during the fever. The
girl put out her hand and laid it on the Queen's.

"You are sure it was no dream, your Grace?"

Again Mary shook her head, sighed, and lay down.

Jane lay awake an hour or more. The touch of those lean, hot hands had not
been reassuring. Besides, she never remembered, during all the times that she
had slept in the Queen's room, being deliberately awakened before She had
often gone to her, uncalled, as she heard her moaning in her sleep, or tossing to
and fro with wakefulness, but the Queen had never called to her

There had not been fear in her eyes just now, no more than a little
apprehensiveness—that, and something like expectation or hope.

But it was all quiet enough again now, there was just the sound of even
breathing from behind the curtains, with a deep breath like a sigh drawn now
and then; and then the even breathing once more.

She was at the bedside again as the birds began to chirp outside two hours
after, and the sounds of the awakening palace came up from the courtyard Mary
stirred in her sleep, and turned over, opening her eyes.

"Is the priest come?" she asked.

"Not, yet, your Grace—it will be an hour yet. Will your Grace take
something?"

Mary shook her head as it lay on the pillow.

"Go and dress, Jane, and make all ready."

When Jane came back she went softly about the chamber, first drawing back
the curtains to let the light in, and then clearing away all signs of the night; a

woman came in to take the truckle bed into the next room, and in ten minutes all was prepared; the candles lighted on the altar, and the cruets placed close to the hand on a little table.

She went to the bedside again with the wrapper which the Queen wore while the priest was in the room, and drew back the hangings at the side.

"Madam——"

Mary sat up without a word, put her arm through the loose sleeve, turned round and adjusted the other, and then sank down again.

"The curtains——" she said.

Jane drew back, too, those at the end of the bed, so that a view was disclosed of the altar against the wall; returned and pulled forward those at the side, so that the occupant of the bed could see without being seen, then opened them again for a moment to give Mary her mass-book.

The Queen beckoned to her with her head.

"Jane, is the priest come?"

"He is ready if your Grace is ready."

"There is no one in the room?" whispered the other hoarsely.

"No, Madam"

"Nearer, sweetheart…. Do you know what I heard last night?"

"No, Madam."

"Nearer, sweetheart."

Jane knelt forward on to the bed, and Mary passed her arm over her neck so as to draw the head down to her mouth.

"Listen," whispered the Queen "I heard it twice. I was lying awake It was the running of a child; I heard his footsteps come across the floor; I thought he would look in at the curtains, but he did not."

She released the arm, and sank back on her pillows, smiling painfully at the bewildered eyes that stared at her.

The priest that said mass that morning—a pleasant rosy man—declared, as he broke his fast afterwards on beer and bread in the parlour downstairs, that her Grace was better, that she had made all the responses as loud as a clerk, and that they would soon have her about again

But his talk was silenced as the doctor looked in half an hour later

"Her Grace is not so well again," he announced to the expectant room "Mistress Dormer sent for me just now."

There was a chorus of questions.

"No, no," he said, "but just a little fever. Her Grace did not sleep well, and was disturbed in the night."

4

It was not until October was well advanced that the Queen knew that she was dying She was silent for a long time after Mass one morning, and at last sent Jane Dormer on a message.

There was intense excitement in the palace when it became known that Commissioners had started for Bishop's Hatfield; it was widely guessed on what errand they had gone, and a little crowd gathered that evening after sunset at the entrance to the palace to see them return But the great personages rode by in the dusk with their guards about them, and paid no attention to the salutes of the mob outside or the courtiers and grooms and servants within the gate. They were seen to dismount at the door of the inner court, and disappeared within

Magdalene Dacre was sitting alone in her private parlour an hour later when her servant came in to announce that Master Kearsley wished to have a few words with her ladyship, if he might be allowed

He came in immediately, and she was astonished at his appearance; his hair was disordered, his sallow face was flushed as if with running, and his mouth worked. He was in riding-dress, and carried his hat and cane in his hand.

"For God's sake, mistress Is her Grace dying?"

"Dying, sir? Why, no"

"I am but just come from Richmond—they told me her Grace was dying. I could find no one who knew What of these Commissioners, mistress?"

"They are returned from Bishop's Hatfield, sir.'

"On what errand?" barked Kearsley

"I do not know sir; it is said——"

"Well, mistress?"

He came a step nearer in his anxiety; and she could see those fierce overhung eyes full of a kind of angry entreaty. She drew back in her chair

"It is said, sir,—but I do not know with what truth—that her Grace sent them to ask the Lady Elizabeth of her religion again"

A sound between a sob and a snarl burst from the man, and he wheeled towards the door, but turned again.

"And you do not know what answer they brought, mistress?"

"I do not," said Magdalene.

As he reached the door it opened, and Jane came in. She stopped abruptly as Kearsley made a swift movement towards her.

"For God's sake, mistress, are you come from her Grace? My lady here knows nothing Why did her Grace send to Bishop's Hatfield?"

Jane looked at him steadily.

"That is her Grace's affair, Master Kearsley."

He was gone in a moment, and the two girls heard his step cross the outer room and pass through the door.

Jane said something to herself softly that Magdalene could not hear.

She looked worn and distressed as she came across the room after closing the door, and sank down on a chair. Magdalene eyed her questioningly.

"Her Grace is silent again" she said in answer. "I cannot bear it: she will not talk or move"

"And the answer?" said Magdalene.

"Oh! Her Highness swore she was a good Catholic; she desired the ground to swallow her up quick if she were not; she swore to defend the Faith with her life."

"And her Grace believes it?"

"I think so There are some jewels to be sent to-morrow. I have looked them out."

"Who is with her now?"

"Mistress Clarentia sits and sews by the bed"

The two sat silent awhile. Magdalene went on deliberately with her embroidery; she had not an idea what to say, she knew well enough that the Queen would not have sent to her sister if she had not lost hope of life; but she could not pretend to be broken-hearted So far as she allowed herself to wish, she wished with all her power that this were all over. The slow process of dying on the part of a woman whom she knew and disliked was an unpleasant strain on the girl. A decorous grief was necessary, but she found it hard to present an appearance of it

"Magdalene, I am tired to death," said Jane suddenly. "I must sleep, and I cannot sleep there"

Magdalene looked up with startled eyes

"No, no, it is not that I know she will not die yet; but I cannot sleep there Will you sleep in her Grace's room to-night?"

"I cannot," wailed the girl. "I dare not."

"Sweetheart, I am so tired."

Magdalene threw herself on her knees and took Jane's hands in hers

"My dearest, ask me anything but that You must not ask me that. Oh, Jane!"

Jane closed her eyes again and nodded quietly, leaning her head back.

Magdalene felt intolerably selfish as she sat down, but she knew she was incapable of consenting to what the other had asked She began to make excuses to herself. If she had cared for the Queen, if she had ever been really sorry for her, it would not have been hard, but it was an unbearable thought to pass the night in that great sombre room, alone with the sick woman. Who knew what might happen? what demand might not be made upon her? If a cry came from behind those curtams—if that dreadful sleep-talking began that she had heard once or twice'—what would she do? If yet worse things happened—if some of the associations that hung round Mary Tudor—the thin presences that surely moved with her—manifested themselves in any way—if the candles flared into tall lances, or the curtains rustled with no hand to move them; if the pale eyes in the hanging seemed to move or the lips to speak—she had heard such stones before now; and the Smithfield fires had been seenphantom-wisem London—if some thing came what could she do but go mad with fear—dear God 'what could she do?

She was willing to do a great deal for Jane Dormer, but not this.

"Jane," she said uneasily, "is there aught else that I can do? Or cannot Mrs. Rise sleep there?"

The other opened her heavy eyes again for a moment.

"No, sweetheart"

Magdalene began to wonder presently about Master Kearsley, as she stitched on in silence. That had surely been remarkable behaviour for a gentleman of the privy-chamber! She did not like Master Kearsley, he was too silent and too sour-looking for her taste; he rather resembled her Grace in that. But she disliked his sudden burst of questions still more. What had the fellow meant by it?

Master Manton had lately become a little like him, she thought. Master Norris had told her so, too; he had said that he could not understand Master Manton, that he never talked now, that he seldom came to the gentlemen's parlour, and as for Tom Bradshawe, the singing boy, he had transferred his allegiance months ago now to a gayer patron.

All this was very unusual, and Lady Magdalene Dacre did not like the unusual. Then she sighed again, as the heavy pressure of memory came back. When would this dreadful situation be over, and she released from a position for which she felt so hopelessly inadequate? Court life was not what she had once hoped that it would be; she had thought it to be a comedy, and she was disappointed

Jane stirred herself in her chair, and sat up. Then she rose to her feet.

"I must go, sweetheart. Good-night."

Magdalene threw her arms round her.

"Jane, you are not vexed?"

"Not vexed, my dear."

"You are vexed," cried the girl, looking into the bright tired eyes. "It is a shame, my dearest. Cannot Mistress Clarentia sleep there to-night?"

Jane shook her head, still looking steadily into Magdalene's face

Magdalene kissed her and released her. She did not like to be looked at like that.

"My dear," said the elder girl steadily, "you understand nothing. If you knew one-tenth of what Master Kearsley knows"

"Master Kearsley?"

"Yes, that old bear as you call him—but he is better than poor Jack Norris. Good night"

Jane went to her room for supper. She was silent until she had nearly finished, then she rang the hand bell for her woman.

"See if Master Manton can be found," she said. "I wish to speak with him"

She was standing by the hearth when he came m five minutes later His gorgeous dress was in curious contrast with his face, as he stood, pale and grave, beyond the candles.

"Master Manton," she said quietly, "Master Kearsley was with me just now. I could not answer him before my lady Magdalene . and—and I cannot bear a scene. Will you tell him this, sir, if you please—that I do not think her Grace will live very long, but that I do not think she will die yet. She sent to Her Highness to-day, as you know, and Her Highness swore that she was a good Catholic, and would preserve the Faith…. That is all, sir."

He did not move, and, as she glanced at him, she saw that his steady eyes were on her still She turned away.

"That is all, sir," she said again.

But there was no movement or sound With a great effort she forced back her rising tears, there must be no scene, she told herself; she needed all her self-control Her voice was quite steady as she spoke again

"Yes, Master Manton, I understand You shall know all that is to be known. And you shall be with her at the end, if that is possible. She spoke of you to-day, sir"

She turned to look at him again, and the sight of his face, pale and piteous, filled her own eyes with sudden, blinding tears. "Oh! Oh! for Christ's sake, Master Manton!" She leaned against the mantel-piece, trying to wipe away the tears. Then she heard his voice at once, broken and strong. "Thank you, madam; that was what I wished." "I must go to her Grace," she said tremulously. As she passed out of the door she paused. "Your boy, Master Manton? What of him?" "He has left me, madam," said Guy, very upright, holding the door for her.

As she came into the lobby, through the door twenty yards away, she saw the lean overhung face of Master Kearsley watching beneath a lamp. Ah! well, there were some true hearts left after all; she was not the only friend who understood and cared.

As she came through into the Queen's room, Mistress Clarentia stood up from her seat by the curtained bed with her finger on her lips. Jane went back immediately into the ante-chamber, and the old woman followed her, closing the door behind her.

"I think she is asleep," said Mistress Clarentia softly. "She has not spoken since you went. I looked at her once, and she had her eyes closed. We must wake her presently for her draught, my dear."

The old lady was perfectly controlled and capable now that the crisis was so near; the only sign of anxiety was in her wide-open eyes that peered into the girl's face.

"She has not talked to herself?"

"She cried out 'Calais! 'once, my dear, but that was all. And what of my lady?"

"My lady will not come," said Jane briefly. "I must watch again."

"You will not let me be with you?"

Jane took the old woman's wrinkled hand a moment, and held it.

"No, no; you are too tired, my dear."

"But you will call for me if you need me? I shall be in the next room to-night."

"I promise," said Jane.

They stood so an instant, looking at one another. Then together they turned and went into the Queen's room.

Ex vita ita discedo, tamquam ex hospitio, non tamquam ex domo.

Cic *Cat mai.*

CHAPTER IV

VIARY THE QUEEN DECIDES HER LAST MATTERS AND TAKES HER LEAVE

I

THE Queen awoke one morning a fortnight later to find her pain almost gone, and with the withdrawal of it reality came back

These past weeks had been very strange to her, it appeared that reality went no further than the four corners of her bed: the lion on the coverlet over her knees had been far more of a personality to her than the people whom her intellect or senses informed her still existed; these seemed like persons whom she had known long ago, like dwellers in a far country, or like shadows In this: they had their lives and their business, but these lay so apart that they had been scarcely worth consideration. Even the faces that looked in on her through the curtains, the brown-bearded head of the Italian doctor, the eyes of Jane Dormer and the wrinkled cheeks of Mistress Clarentia—all these were no more than the masks or the symbols of persons whom she had once known. They slid into her world for a moment, set food before her, murmured together, held glasses to her lips, and then disappeared again into the shadows The world had contracted itself into the little rectangular space bounded by green hangings, the wreaths and the lions had been the important facts of life; there were times when it shrank even smaller into the formlessness of her own pain; there were yet other moments immediately before or after sleep, when even that was left alone, and her soul sank down, self-conscious and self-absorbed, as through depths of glimmering water into an unknown world where nothing was strange or unexpected, where she walked and talked with those who were long dead, and did not wonder to meet them there.

Yet she had been clear enough when she had sent two lords of the Council to Elizabeth. She had awakened that morning with a distinct knowledge of what lay before her, and of what she must leave behind. She had known that death was not far off, and she had not feared it even for an instant; but she knew that England must be left behind, and for that she had feared a little. She knew that Elizabeth was true, that she intended what was right, and yet she desired her to say so once more and to enter into a solemn contract with her.

Nearly all day she had been clear-headed; she had talked a little to Jane; she had noticed that one of the candles opposite her had guttered in a draught; that must be removed; it was not seemly.

The Commissioners had come back at nightfall; they had knelt, with the curtains drawn back, and told her expressly that the Lady Elizabeth had promised to keep and promote the Catholic Religion and pay her Grace's debts. Very well, then her Grace said; the crown should be hers. It had not pleases God hitherto to send a prince to England; therefore it was His will that a princess should rule again. The lords had kissed her hand and gone, and with the effort she had made, the kindly unreality had come back.

Now this morning the veil had lifted again. She still felt a little heavy and weak, but facts had a solidity of their own, and her head was clearer than it had been for weeks.

There were a few arrangements to be made, and she must be brisk.

"Sweetheart," she called out.

There was a rustle, the curtains parted on the right side, and Jane's face was there

"Pen and ink," said Mary.

The face vanished again

She certainly felt much stronger this morning. Was it possible that God should yet raise her up? Probably not; at any rate she must make her arrangements. What a long time Jane was; she was surely very slow!

Again the curtain were drawn back.

"What time is it?"

"It is seven o'clock, Madam"

"Very well. There will be time Are you ready? Write—

"'Mary the Queen. This Codicil made by me, Mary—by the Grace of God Queen of England, France, Naples,—no, no! set down et cetera after England—' and lawful wife—to the most noble and virtuous Prince Philip—by the Grace of God '"—she paused a moment—" 'by the same Grace of God King of the said realms and dominions—of England'—et cetera—' What day is it, Jane?"

"The twenty-eighth, Madam"

"Set that down, then; and the year Set the year of His Highness' reign before mine"

The pen scratched over the paper.

"Jane"

"Yes, Madam"

"I cannot do it like this—I do not know the terms. Bid a lawyer write it out fair, and do you take down what I wish."

She felt suddenly very tired again. She raised herself a little in bed, knowing that she must not give in.

"Do you hear me, Jane?"

"Yes, Madam."

"Set down that if God gives me no fruit of my body, I require that my heir shall pay my bequests."

"…Yes, Madam."

"To the House of Religion and the rest."

"Yes, Madam."

"Set down that I beg His Majesty to be a father to this realm, and aid my successor."

"…Yes, Madam"

"I can do no more, Jane, now Bid a lawyer write it out fair and bring it to me this evening"

"Yes, Madam."

When the curtains were drawn again, she felt comforted. At least that was done, or it would be this evening It was foolish to have put it off so long. There were other matters, too; she would think of them presently Meanwhile she had not said her prayers. That was shocking!

"Jane."

The curtains rustled and opened.

"Sit by me on the other side and read my prayers to me. Is the priest come yet?"

"He will be here in half-an-hour, your Grace."

"Very well, then"

Then the voice began, but she could not attend very well, and the words did not mean very much; they were uttered and gone again, like wrinkles on a river. She joined in the *Paternoster* and the *Ave*, and said the *Amens* in her hoarse voice; that was all that she could do. She would be better after mass; that always uplifted her, for it did not matter so much as that whether she could follow or no, for God was merciful, and wrought for her in the Sacrifice what she could not do for herself. At least He could not be displeased with her; she was trying to honour Him as she had always done.

She was thinking all day about the Codicil; it appeared to her of vast importance that it should be sealed and signed; so much might depend upon it. She felt a little annoyed with Jane for not showing more excitement. In the afternoon it was brought to her room, and she raised herself to listen while the formal voice read it out of sight She added a few sentences here and there, and waited till the pen finished its scratching at the end of each, then the paper was taken away again for a fair copy to be made.

"Let four gentlemen be brought to witness it when the fellow comes back," she said. "Master Wentworth had best be one"

"Master Wentworth, Madam?"

"Why, yes," said Mary peevishly, "the cofferer."

"I told your Grace last week "began Jane, looking at her anxiously

"I beg pardon, sweetheart I had forgotten."

It was astonishing, Mary thought, how she could have forgotten that Master Wentworth had died last week. It had been one of those pieces of news that had come like a shadow and gone again She remembered perfectly now that she had prayed for his soul

"And my lord Cardinal?" asked the Queen presently.

"My lord Cardinal has sent his loving regard again, Madam."

"How is he?"

My lord is not so well. Monsignor Priuli was here just now."

Mary said nothing for a few minutes; she was watching the lion on the coverlet over her knees; his tail seemed to move, she thought. She roused herself again

"Beg my lord to remember me in his prayers. I must see Master Manton one day, Jane. Not to-day." "Yes, Madam."

After supper the lawyer came back

Mary heard several footsteps in the room, and lay waiting for the usual withdrawal of the curtains. It came, and with it a paper and Jane's face and a writing board She raised herself in bed, and for a moment her head swam

Then it cleared again.

She looked through the pages carefully, and addressed herself to write. She was scarcely aware that the room was open now on the left, and of the four faces that watched The pen would not write well; it seemed instinct with perversity, and to fight cruelly with her lean fingers; but the letters were formed at last.

"Marye the Queue."

"There!" said Mary the Queen

When she had done that, she thought it a pity not to do more, so she turned the stiff sheets over, made a cross and wrote with great care beneath it—

"This is the laste wyll and testament of me Marye the Quene"

"Take it, Jane."

She sank down again, drew up the coverlet to her chin, and lay still, panting a little.

There was a smell of wax in the air, the murmur of a voice, the scratching of a pen. The curtains were closed again now. Then footsteps sounded, and silence.

"Sweetheart."

"Yes, Madam"

"Is any here?"

"No, Madam, they are gone."

"I am going to sleep, I think."

It was very strange a while later to find herself able to see the whole room; but she was very much tired, her head ached intolerably; and she could not trouble to ask why the curtains were all drawn back now

But the room was plain enough, and it seemed very large, she could see the rugs laid across the rushes to deaden sound, the altar against the opposite wall, but the candles were alight. Why was that?…

It was still more curious to see children all about the room—little figures in green-and-white, moving noiselessly to and fro. It was very pleasant to see them, but how had Jane come to let them in?

Some of them had virginals, one or two, regals, it seemed that a concert must have been arranged. What a beautiful thought of Jane's that was! How kind of her to know what she would like, and to do it without telling her.

There was a lovely boy now at the foot of her bed, leaning on it with his elbows and smiling at her so boldly; that could not be little Lord Darnley?…he was in Scotland, was he not? Besides he was older than this child, and not near so beautiful. This child wore a little crown, too—a tiny circlet of fleur-de-lis set with blue jewels. . Why he was surely her own boy, to whom she had given birth at Hampton Court...she remembered it all so distinctly, and how he was brought to her in his cradle How quickly he had grown....

He was gone again now—melted into that gliding throng of children who went up and down in the brilliant light, each pausing to bow and smile at the foot of the bed. These dear children.! Who were they all? And how came it that there was a lawn under their feet?...

Ah! they were going to sing. they were standing in rows now, like her own choir. The strings were beginning to ripple. She would close her eyes and listen.

How sweet it was! But what music was that that they sang? It must be Master Byrde's—a new piece that he had written for her, but it was very strange that no one had told her.

She would soon be well if this went on. How clever of Jane to think of it! The pain had ceased The lights were going low now, she must give one more look, and thank the children, and tell them

What was this? They were gone again The curtains were in their place, enclosing her once more It was all dark....

"Sweetheart, sweetheart," cried the harsh voice.

"Yes, Madam."

"Who were those children?"

"I do not understand, Madam?"

"The children that were playing and singing all about the room."

The curtains were parted, and a face was looking at her.

What was the matter with Jane? Why did she look like that?" Sweetheart, I am much better. What time is it?" "It is eleven o'clock, Madam?" "Why are you crying, Jane?"

2

As the days went by, Mary's mind lay nearly as passive as her body. Through both coursed sensations, that distressed or comforted her according to their nature, and that appeared equally uncontrolled by her conscious volition

Occasionally she made efforts; she raised herself a little in bed and drank her medicine, she gave small directions and answered the Cardinal's frequent messages, and the questions that came to her from the mouths of persons, whom she seemed to herself to have once known, who knelt like figures in a show, at the foot of her bed, framed in the green folds of the hangings.

She understood for the first time how weak she was, when a letter came from her husband

There was a murmur of voices one evening, one was Jane's, and the other was one less familiar but which she thought she knew. Then the folds lifted, and De Feria knelt there with a letter in his hand.

He said something, but she could not understand it. She was only thinking that this man was to marry her dear Jane. It was something about Brussels...as swift as possible . .. His Highness detained....

Then there was a voice at her ear; that was Jane's again, and she understood. She lifted her thin hand slowly.

"Give it to me," she said deliberately. "I cannot read it now; I will read it later. No, none must open it but myself"

Her fingers closed on the thin package, and sank down again on to the coverlet still holding it

What did they want now 'There was surely nothing more! They might leave her in her happiness for a little; it was so good to hold a letter of his in her hands again, there was his dear love in it, and she wanted no more than that.

Ah! she understood now what they wished.

She laid down the letter and drew out her other hand.

There were two rings on her third finger, one of black enamel that he had given her, and one gold ring of her own. Her hands shook with weakness as she drew off the second, and held it up. Some warm fingers took it from her.

"Yes," she said, "to my dear husband, with my dearest love"

She was alone again now in the green gloom, the curtains had fallen noiselessly, then the door closed softly She lifted the letter again between her fingers and put it to her lips. Then it sank down and rested on her breast

The days moved on, marked for her only by the stirring sounds outside the palace; for the windows were always shuttered now and the candles burned day and night

She still made her efforts now and again, roused herself to answer the necessary questions that seemed more urgent and frequent than ever, to attend to the silent priest who went about his wonderful and beloved work at the foot of her bed morning by morning, even to sign her name once or twice to papers that were held before her. But for the most part she lay quiescent with closed eyes, watching the little scenes that her memory brought up

It was hard for her to distinguish sometimes between the work of her senses and of her imagination. The faces and voices of her servants and those of long-dead had equally the same quiet unreality Two or three times she awoke out of her daze, believing that she had talked with her mother and Stephen Gardiner and Philip, and it was not until she moved her head on the pillow, stared at the painted canopy overhead, and touched the palms of the her hands with her in-turned fingers, that she remembered that her mother slept in Peterborough, the Bishop in. Winchester, and that her husband was far away.

Her confessor came to her two or three times, and before his visits she would do what she could to remember her sins. But they were not very many, she had given way to secret pride sometimes, she had been irritable with her servants; she had not felt or shown sufficient gratitude to them, she feared she had been unjust to one of them For the sins of her past life—they were the same, for the most part She had not always believed the best of those who had seemed to injure her; she had broken a resolution she had once made about that; she had given way to passion sometimes; especially once, when she had slashed with her knife a portrait of her husband—that was when she had thought him unfaithful. She had allowed resentment in her heart against the heretics; but she had not been unjust to them; she had given them every opportunity to clear themselves, and had only enforced the laws of the realm Worst of all, she had once signed a paper, when she was a girl, denying the prerogative of the Vicar of Christ. She had tried to make amends for that by zeal; but she had only done a very little. Yes, she had made amends to her sister. Yes, she was a pure maiden but for her husband.

One night she awoke—she supposed it was night by the silence round her; but there was one sitting by her bed, with a purple stole across his shoulders. Ah! her confessor again. She must have sent for him then.

She turned slowly in her bed and put her hands together.

"*Confiteor Deo, beatae Mariae....* Who are you, father? Ah! yes—Confiteor Deo...I cannot say it, father...These are my sins. I have twice struck——No, no, of course, those were dreams; I cannot remember. I have shown anger once by my face. I...I have doubted God's love three times. No, I do not doubt it now. I have forgotten His Presence wilfully.... Father, I cannot remember...*Precor Sanctum Mariam, omnes sanctos Dei, et te pater*...Father, I have not made amends in one matter—I will do so; and I have not paid my debts; but I could not—*te pater, or are pro me*"

Then body and soul lay quiet again to listen to the mercy which she desired.

Presently she awoke and called.

"Jane."

"Yes, Madam."

"Master Manton, I wish to see him."

"Madam, my lord is coming with the holy oils and Viaticum," came the crisp trembling voice at her ear

"Master Manton first—I must make amends." There was a long silence.

When she opened her eyes once or twice she could see the glimmer of candles through the curtains at the foot of her bed. That was right then; my lord was there with all that was necessary. She tried to pray.

She opened her eyes again at a rustling sound, and Master Manton's face was there, with the altar beyond. She noticed his crumpled ruff and disordered hair, and his eyes fixed on her. Why what ailed the man?...Was there not an old arrow-wound?....

She made a great effort.

"Master Manton, I am sorry I spoke as I did...in the matter of Her Highness. It was not just."

His lips were moving, but she could not hear what he said.

"It was not just. Master Manton, what will you do now?"

Again his lips moved, and she heard a murmur of sound.

"Jane, I cannot hear, tell me what he says."

The crisp young voice spoke in her ear a few sentences. Ah! yes, she understood now. He was going abroad with Monsignor Priuli and Master Kearsley; that was best. It might be that Elizabeth——. No, she would not think that; but it was best that he should go.

"Jane."

"Yes, Madam."

"See there be some provision for them. I have not done my duty."

"Yes, Madam"

"And for Master Bradshawe."

Again there was a talking that she could not hear.

"What is that, sweetheart?"

"Master Bradshawe is gone, Madam," came the penetrating voice

"Gone? Whither?"

It was a moment or two before she could understand; it was so unexpected.

"Who is gone with him?" she asked presently.

"Master Norris, Madam."

"I cannot hear, Jane."

"——And—and others, Madam," faltered the voice.

Mary made another effort.

"You say they be all gone to Bishop's Hatfield. What, all?"

"Very many, Madam."

"Is that why the house is so quiet?"

"It is evening also, Madam," came the trembling, compassionate voice once more

Mary lay perfectly still, trying to understand.

They were all gone then, except these few. That was why she had seen so few. How strange that they could not wait a little longer. And was Master Kearsley gone?

She asked that aloud, and the face at the end of the bed lifted itself and cried something that rang confusedly through her head.

"What does he say, sweetheart?"

"Master Kearsley is not gone, Madam. And he will not."

Well, that was better. There were one or two left then. But she did not quite understand yet

"With Monsignor Priuli, does he say?"

"Yes, Madam"

"But what of my lord Cardinal?"

"My lord is dying, Madam."

Why, of course she knew that. How foolish to forget! She had asked for his blessing scarcely an hour before, and he had sent it her. She had known it would be his last, until they met again presently.

"Sweetheart."

"Yes, Madam."

"Master Manton understands—I am sorry—and ask his pardon. But he was wrong you see—about Her Highness."

"Master Manton understands, Madam."

"Yes—well—Jane I cannot hear you. Why is Master Manton weeping? I am not angry now. I have asked his pardon have I not?"

"Yes, yes, Madam"

Then the curtains sank noiselessly once more, the heavy darkness closed in swiftly, whirling across her tired eyes, and droning stupor into her ears

She did not know how long it was before she heard a voice again, but she came up from depths of blackness through twilight, and saw a hand before her face, with a great ring on it, and something white between the fingers There was a man's voice talking, too, but she could not understand what was said

The hand advanced swiftly and poised itself, and on the white disc she saw a cross in relief.

Her lips opened, and her eyes closed Then her lips closed, too, and she lay there, feeling something melt on her tongue, and striving to realise what it was that had come to her.

She was conscious of her body again now, her wasted limbs, her shrunken breast; and through every fibre of it stole a sweetness. It was to that hideous and distorted thing that the rent Body of her Lord had come; it was that piteous soul that had so toiled with troubles, and striven with desire and fierce passion, perplexed, buffeted, despised, that the stainless and tormented Soul, the awful Divinity of the God whom she had tried so ineffectually to serve, had deigned to visit

"Jesu! Jesu!" she whispered, *"esto mihi Jesus!* I have failed, dear Jesus, but Thou hast not "

The twilight faded again to mellow gloom, and the gloom to blackness.

Then someone was touching her, she was conscious that a hand had passed across her face, pressing her eyelids and lips, and a voice that murmured from an infinite distance said words that she could not hear.

Her feet grew cold, and she half drew them up before she understood. Then she stretched them again towards the anointed hand.

By the time that the voice had ceased, she knew everything. All that could be done was over. She had only to wait now, passive and expectant, for the call that could not be long in coming

She felt perfectly content and unafraid What was there to fear? She had failed, she knew very well, in everything to which she had set her hand But that was not her affair now, for it was not of her will that she had failed. There was but one thing asked of her now, to still without sinning in thought or word. She must go to her judge in innocence

"O Lord Jesu 'which art the health of all men living, and the everlasting life of them which die in faith, I, wretched sinner, give and submit myself wholly unto Thy most blessed will....

What was that voice reading? Why, she knew very well; it was Jane, and it was the prayer that she had told her to read when the end came.

"…willingly now I leave this frail and wicked flesh, in hope of the resurrection, which in better wise shall restore it to me again…. I see and knowledge that there is in myself no hope of salvation, but all my confidence, hope and trust is in Thy most merciful goodness I have no merits nor good works which I may allege before Thee.

That was true enough, God knew, she had nothing but failure to allege—Philip, England, Elizabeth, Calais; she had failed even in that in which the most desperate sinner succeeds—she had failed even to win love and confidence from those who knew her best—Magdalene, Mistress Rise, Philip, Elizabeth, Master Norris and the rest—not one loved her. There were one or two others perhaps who did—the old woman who was crying now on the other side of the bed, the girl whose voice shook into sobs as she read; even perhaps those two strange gentlemen, whom she had never been able to understand, Master Kearsley and Master Manton But could she plead that before her God?

"…Now, most merciful Saviour, let all these things profit me which Thou has freely given me, that hast given Thyself for me—"

That was true, too Even He had seemed to fail…There stood by the Cross of Jesus His mother, and Mary, the wife of Philip;—no, not Philip; how did it run? But there were not more than three or four; the rest had forsaken Him and fled

"…When death hath taken away the use of my tongue and speech, yet that my heart may cry and say unto thee, *In manus tuas Domine*"

The deadly heaviness was coming again, droning and roaring. She could not hear or understand. Was this, then, how death came? The faint green glimmer was fading; a horrible sickness stole up her body, the sweat poured off her face and hands

Ah! but that was a relief. She would sleep again now. She would just repeat those last words to herself It was not death, yet, after all

"Domine Jesu—accifie sptiritum meum Amen"

That was better She would sleep a little.

3

She awoke finally, and a huge peace enfolded her.

It seemed to her that she was lying somewhere in the sun, alive again after death. The heaviness had lifted and the pain had gone. Her head felt perfectly clear, and she knew all.

Behind her lay the storm and the tossing and the deadly sickness, and she was come to port.

She had not thought that death would be so quiet at the end; she had expected an agony, an onslaught of demons, a wild struggle in the dark, a sense of battle and pressure; but it seemed that all that was behind now She knew that there would be no more fighting; there was just one silent change and all would be done with. Well' God was kind, then, after all.

She tried to move her head, but could not; her fingers twitched a little on her breast as if with their own motion, but they seemed not to be her own That then was the beginning, she told herself. Were her eyes and voice, too, passed out of her control? No, she could move her eyes at least; she could see the hangings on this side and that, and the crack of light at the foot of the bed. Someone was watching her from there.

She closed her eyes again

She began to consider what hour it was; but she thought she could not make the effort to ask It was probably morning; it felt like the morning. It was like the peace of a summer garden before the dawn, when the earth is breathing noiselessly, drinking the dew, stirring slightly with expectation, full of fragrance and mellow coolness after the hot night. It surely must be morning.

The sunrising would be her summons. It would not be the material sun, but another that would rise upon her with healing, and draw her up from this sweet lawn, and that which she would leave behind was so mean and ugly and wrinkled; why should she mind the parting? She feared it would be troublesome; but it would be as little troublesome as possible; it was to be dressed in the brown habit, with the cross and the beads; and it was to be put away soon without any crown or show. Oh! if the world only knew how great and sweet was death; how little and sour and useless was all else—if only she could tell them all, explain to them all that she knew now! She would like to explain. .

"Yes, Madam."

That was Jane's voice. How clear it was, like bells after ram; but it seemed far away. No, she would not explain now; perhaps she might later on. And that was Jane's face looking at her.

She closed her eyes again; she did not wish to be interrupted in her thinking about death, and its ease and its pleasantness.

And what of those she left behind?

Well, they would be provided for. Jane was to go for the present to her grandmother in the Savoy: Mrs. Clarentia had a competence. Master Kearsley and Master Manton were to go abroard with the Venetian, Lord Montague and his wife would look after Magdalene if she needed it. But how foolish of the child to refuse good Master Norris who was so fond of her!

And for the others who had left her? Had she any resentment? She searched her heart and found none. It was only natural. She was sorry for Philip, and she would have liked to see him; but he was busy and could not come; it was not his fault; it never had been his fault

How stupid and passionate she had been about his picture! But she was sorry for that, and had been forgiven by God

She would have liked to see him, however, and explain to him that empires and wealth were not worth very much; they lasted so short a while; and God always did what He pleased with them in the end. Even England did not trouble her; if Elizabeth did not keep her word, it did not matter very much; God would keep His word And so with all the rest, she had done what she could, she had failed, and all was perfectly right and safe in His hands.

Meanwhile here she lay, and the morning was coming up the sky.

What of purgatory? She scarcely knew; a little, clear spiritual flame; it would not be more than she could bear. God knew how little she could bear. But it did not greatly matter; it would be what was needed, when the time came, and. she would be helped and speeded from the altars she had built and the holy houses she had founded; and meantime she lay here in the morning peace with the light broadening.

There were others in the garden now; she could hear them stirring behind the green hedges on either side; perhaps the children were there again; she would like to see them and hear them sing again; and especially that dear boy of hers who had nodded and smiled from the foot of her bed. Perhaps they would be in presently.

There must be several in the room; she heard a metallic sound as if a string had been twanged; how delightful it would be to be sung into death, to rise up from the lawn and go with the music growing faint behind her.

She must open her eyes, if she could, and see the children....

Ah! how foolish of her; it was no garden after all; but her own bedroom. They were curtains, were they not?—not green hedges; and there is something better than even the children. There is the altar decked, and the priest in his holy dress coming in with the vessels. It was indeed morning, and the sun was near at hand.

She moved her eyes round the room and saw faces here and there; some watched her and some the priest. Master Manton was there and Master Kearsley beside him; she could just see them, past the bed-post and the carved emblems of the Passion. My lord of Winchester was somewhere; she had caught sight of his clean young face just now, but it was gone again. There was Mrs. Clarentia; how strange she looked! And Jane—why, Jane was beside her, close on the left with her book in her hand There were others, too, she could hear them behind the curtains. Had they been here all night?

The priest had come down now in his yellow vestments, and faced about. That was the sign. She must join with him if she could.

"Sed libera nos amalo"

Whose voice was it which said that?

It sounded very hoarse and deep. It could not be her own surely But she felt the muscles vibrate in her throat, it was indeed her own voice How wonderful that she could speak; she had not been sure whether she could.

Her voice moved on, and she stared steadily at the sulphur-coloured vestment and the huge red cross, and the rich collar above. How homely and sweet it was to hear mass again, to see the holy things about her, and how good was God to allow it

"Confiteor Deo, Beatae Manae, omnibus sanctis, et tibi pater quia peccavi ntmis, cogitatione, verbo et opere—mea culpa...."

It seemed that her hands would not move to beat on her breast; but it did not matter. God understood.

She finished—*"te pater or are pro me"*

She could not hear what the priest said, but her lips formed the words, it was pardon again of which he was speaking, and she desired that.

She could not hear the introit; but it was a yellow vestment, and therefore the feast was of a confessor, of one who had suffered and witnessed, though not unto blood. She must listen for the collect and catch his name if she could; she wished to have his prayers, and she did not like to ask Jane.

Kyrie eleison…. Christe eleison…. Christe eleison…Kyrie eleison.

That was what she desired—mercy and pardon.

How swiftly he went!

Amen…. Et cum spiritu tuo.

Now he had turned; she would hear the name.

"Deus qui beatum Hugonem…"

Ah! it was an English saint, blessed Hugh himself! Blessed Hugh intercede for this poor English daughter of yours who desires your prayers!

There was another collect; it was very long, perhaps there were two, but she did not care about them; of course she desired all blessed saints to pray for her, but Hugh was enough to think about—Hugh who had lived with kings as their friend and counsellor. If she had had him with her perhaps she would not have made so many mistakes.

The Epistle was done, and she had not attended. What was the gradual?

"Thou hast set upon his head a crown of precious stone…he asked life of thee and thou gavest it him, even length of days for ever and ever. Alleluia!"

It was good to hear that; she had not done with crowns then, if God was merciful. And it would not be a crown of thorns this time! Neither had she done with life; there was another *in saeculum saecuh*. O blessed Hugh, pray for me that I may have that life '

She lost the Gospel, all but the last words. "Lest when He come He find you sleeping, what I say unto you, I say unto all, Watch."

He was at the offertory now, lifting the golden vessels; now he was bowed over them; no w he was washing his hands, and she could see his lips in profile moving against the silk tapestry; but there was a candle-flame just behind that bewildered her, and she closed her eyes.

How still the room was, and with all those people in it

Yet there were not very many after all; the rest were run to Elizabeth, were they not? She thought someone had told her so Well! God help her to rule well and keep her word.

It seemed a little darker when she opened her eyes and answered once more——

"Et cum spintu tuo."

Why! he had finished the secret prayers. How swift he had been.

"Habemus ad dominum....
"Dignum et justum est."

There was the voice murmuring again, but it was further off than ever; it talked on like a voice heard in a dream. There was a murmuring in her ears, too, that drowned it. Surely these persons were not talking!

No, no! it was a sound within her own head; the tinkle of the bell dispelled it, and all was perfectly still again.

She was back in the garden now, lying on her back in deep-grass, and looking up into the sky that deepened clear and luminous above her. The hedges were about her again, like those at Richmond, fragrant and dim, with red flowers at the foot and cherry-blossoms above. The birds were silent, but she could hear the rush and gurgle of a stream not far off. There were footsteps swishing softly through long grass on all sides, under the cherry-trees, as if there were a company of children, holding their breath, coming up to surprise her; once she thought she heard a little tender laughter stifled at once…It was rapturous to lie here, with the pain gone, and the heaviness lifted, in this sweet dark air that waited for the coming of light…. She would lie still a little longer, then she would look….

She started slightly at the sound of a bell. That was the signal for the sunrise, was it not? She had been told so as a child—that silver bells rang among the flowers just before the dawn, that they might be awake to meet their Master—*ne cum venerit repente, inveniat vos dormientes.* She must awake, too; for she, above all others, must not be found sleeping.

How difficult it was to open her eyes! It was like a dream when one cannot wake. The bells were ringing everywhere now, a ripple of sound with pauses, and she struggled a little, hearing her own breath panting in her throat

Ah! it was no use; her eyes were too heavy; once she lifted them for a moment, and caught a glimpse of a yellow glory, not the sun himself, but his light upon eastern hills, then they closed again. It was not her fault; she could not be blamed; she was so tired.

The bells had ceased now, and she was conscious of a light upon her eyelids, fresh and healthful.

How little a thing was this passing from night to day!—marked only by the tinkle of bells, and then the miracle was done. Nothing had moved about her; there had been no cry of trumpets as when a king came; He was only heralded by a breeze among flowers, and in a mystery all was changed. The colours had sprung broad awake, the scents poured out at His coming, and the music of a thousand birds welcomed Him. It was like death itself, which she had thought to be cold and heavy and dark, but of which she had now learned the secret that it was sweet and warm.

How quiet it was again; there was only the rush and gurgle of water, and the footsteps coming through the grass, nearer every moment…

She must open her eyes and see….

Why! there was a greater mystery than sunrise in a garden I A vast figure stood before her, vast and far away; he seemed to fill the heavens from side to side, translucent with yellow light, and down and across from east and west, from sky to earth, burned a gigantic sign.

This man hid the sun, for he held it at his breast; but the glory streamed through him and about him on every side. There were two spear-shaped pinnacles to right and left that caught the light and threw it back, and huge clouds of splendour overhead.

From an infinite distance, through the rush of the pouring water, came tremendous words that shook her heart, and set her throat vibrating

Agnus Dei, she heard, and answered, *Miserere nobis*, not knowing that she spoke.

Agnus Dei . . Miserere noibs.

Agnus Dei.... Dona nobis pacem.

The pause seemed interminable, but through it ran a sense, that the whole universe was gathering up itself in sound, colour and shape to meet some ineffable event; all things hung for a moment on a brink;—then, like the slow movement of a mountain the dim, huge figure bowed itself; the light poured out in floods of colour and glory—there was something tearing at her heart that would not be silenced; it must speak and cry out His beauty.

She cried out—and lay still.

THE END

PRINTED BY THE ANCHOR PRESS, LTD, TIPTREE, ESSEX, ENGLAND

Lightning Source UK Ltd.
Milton Keynes UK
10 November 2010

162635UK00001B/58/P